Justine Lewis writes uplifting, heartwarming contemporary romances. She lives in Australia with her hero husband, two teenagers, and an outgoing puppy. When she isn't writing she loves to walk her dog in the bush near her house, attempt to keep her garden alive, and search for the perfect frock. She loves hearing from readers; you can visit her at justinelewis.com.

Michele Renae is the pseudonym of award-winning author Michele Hauf. She has published over ninety novels in historical, paranormal and contemporary romance and fantasy, as well as writing action/adventure as Alex Archer. Instead of writing 'what she knows' she prefers to write 'what she would love to know and do.' And, yes, that includes being a jewel thief and/or a brain surgeon! You can email Michele at toastfaery@gmail.com, and find her on Instagram, @MicheleHauf, and Pinterest, @toastfaery.

Also by Justine Lewis

Swipe Right for Mr Perfect
Italian Tycoon to Remember

Princesses' Night Out collection

How To Win Back a Royal

Summer Escapes collection

Dating Game with Her Enemy

Also by Michele Renae

Reunion with Her Highland Rival

Art of Being a Billionaire miniseries

Faking It with the Boss
Billion-Dollar Nights in the Castle
Jet-Set Nights with Her Enemy

Fairy Tales in Maine collection

Cinderella's One-Night Surprise

Discover more at millsandboon.co.uk.

FROM SPAIN WITH LOVE

JUSTINE LEWIS

MICHELE RENAE

MILLS & BOON

All rights reserved including the right of reproduction in whole or in part in any form. This edition is published by arrangement with Harlequin Enterprises ULC.

This is a work of fiction. Names, characters, places, locations and incidents are purely fictional and bear no relationship to any real life individuals, living or dead, or to any actual places, business establishments, locations, events or incidents. Any resemblance is entirely coincidental.

Without limiting the exclusive rights of any author, contributor or the publisher of this publication, any unauthorised use of this publication to train generative artificial intelligence (AI) technologies is expressly prohibited. HarperCollins also exercise their rights under Article 4(3) of the Digital Single Market Directive 2019/790 and expressly reserve this publication from the text and data mining exception.

® and TM are trademarks owned and used by the trademark owner and/or its licensee. Trademarks marked with ® are registered with the United Kingdom Patent Office and/or the Office for Harmonisation in the Internal Market and in other countries.

First published in Great Britain 2026
by Mills & Boon, an imprint of HarperCollins*Publishers* Ltd,
1 London Bridge Street, London, SE1 9GF

www.harpercollins.co.uk

HarperCollins*Publishers*, Macken House, 39/40 Mayor Street Upper, Dublin 1, D01 C9W8, Ireland

From Spain with Love © 2026 Harlequin Enterprises ULC

CEO's Spanish Fling © 2026 Justine Lewis

Match Made in Seville © 2026 Michele Hauf

ISBN: 978-0-263-41939-9

04/26

Printed and Bound in the UK using 100% Renewable Electricity at CPI Group (UK) Ltd, Croydon, CR0 4YY

CEO'S SPANISH FLING

JUSTINE LEWIS

MILLS & BOON

To my amazing, clever and beautiful sister Rebecca, who had her appendix out just as I was finishing this book. May your life be filled with handsome Spanish CEOs. xx

CHAPTER ONE

Seville had not changed at all in the ten years Cara had been gone. Not the smells, the scent of oranges and jasmine drifting on the breeze like a subtle perfume. The sounds were the same, the distinctively soft Andalusian accent and the guitar playing somewhere in the distance. But most of all, there was the sun. Hot, bright and ever present, warming her pale skin like a welcome fire. It was just as she remembered. The Moorish palaces, lush gardens, labyrinthine streets and shaded courtyards all remained impervious to centuries of invading empires and hordes of tourists. It was too much to hope that the past decade had changed anything about this city at all.

The last time she had been in Seville the events had been traumatic and life altering, but the group of people affected by them had been small. The city had not even been bruised, though Cara still suffered the aftershocks. A trace of the tragedy that had upended her life must be somewhere to be seen. She looked in vain for some trace of the man she had fallen in love with, but there was none.

It was just as well. If she was going to get through the next two weeks, then rule number one had to be Don't Think About Him. If she couldn't manage that, then rules two, three and four were mandatory: Don't speak his name. Don't go to his old neighbourhood. Don't seek out anyone who knew him.

If she could do all that—and, in a city of seven hundred thousand people, it seemed possible—she would be fine.

Only a job as lucrative as this one would have been incentive enough to make her return. She had resisted the contract at first, but her reluctance had been interpreted as driving a hard bargain and the client Richard Westwood had offered her twice her usual rate. When she refused, he'd doubled it again. Cara had been horrified until she realised that this money would be the last few thousand dollars she needed to engage the lawyers to take on her case against Liam.

She'd sent the email accepting the job with a shaking hand and now she was here.

Standing near the Puente de San Telmo, the bridge crossing the Guadalquivir River near the ancient Torre del Oro. The bright light and vibrant blue sky were such a contrast from the home she'd grown up in on Cape Cod, with its cool greys and soft whites. She shielded her eyes from the sun and rubbed the side of her waist. She had strained something a few days ago and was waiting for the pain to pass, but annoyingly it seemed to be getting worse. Over the river, a short stroll away was the university and her old neighbourhood around the heaving historic centre of Seville.

She would not be going there.

No. She was far better off staying on the other side of the river, in this part of the city. A district she had hardly visited with Pablo, but the pull across the river was strong. The memories were bubbling close to the surface. And try as she might, she was powerless to stop them.

Seville. And Pablo.

Every smell reminded her of him.

The charming, bright and artistic man she'd met while on exchange at the University of Seville. She had lived here for six months intense language study as part of her college degree.

Pablo was ostensibly studying but much of his time was spent creating characters and storylines for the computer games he and his friends dreamt of building. He was like no one else she'd ever met. Raised in a small town on Cape Cod, her trip to Seville was her first big adventure overseas. Pablo was compassionately curious. Charmingly quick. Devastatingly handsome. Heartbreakingly…

Well, in the end, simply heartbreaking.

Standing by the river she gave in to the feelings and let herself remember him. The magical night of their first meeting when they had talked all night about their lives and dreams. Being inseparable from that first meeting. The late nights and lazy mornings. She'd neglected her studies but had learnt a whole different type of Spanish not covered by the curriculum. Another language of passion and joy, longing and desire. The only language she saw herself wanting to speak ever again. Her concern for her studies faded as she realised that Pablo had changed the course of her life. The life she'd planned as a diplomatic interpreter was forgotten, her life would now be with Pablo. In Seville.

So when the unthinkable happened…

No. She had to stop. It had taken her years to pull herself back together and this short visit to Seville was not going to set her back.

She looked up at the monuments, at the bridges that had allowed armies to cross. Seville didn't care about her heartbreak, her memories or the tragedy that had befallen Pablo. The locals and tourists walking past her didn't care either. Each time she dodged someone she felt the pain in her side. An annoying pain that had been building over the past couple of days. Ebbing and flowing. Now it was accompanied by nausea and not letting up at all. Food poisoning.

Just what she needed. She could hardly cancel this job, not when she was being paid so much to do it. Not when she'd already told the lawyers to start preparing the case against her half-brother, Liam. All that she needed now was the last fraction of their retainer. But she didn't want to think about Liam and his betrayal because that caused a whole different type of pain, and right now the one in the side of her abdomen was all she could deal with. If she could just sit down for a moment. Rest. Get out of the heat.

There were still a few hours to wait before she could access the room in her hotel. She looked for a café nearby. There was a four-lane road buzzing with cars and bikes she needed to cross in order to get to the row of restaurants and cafés that promised a seat and a cold glass of something. Maybe even air conditioning.

It was early May, one of the loveliest times of year in Seville. The weather warm, but not oppressive. The jacaranda and jasmine were in full bloom, filling her lungs with their scent and decorating the colourful historical streets. It was no wonder this was the only city in the world she had ever contemplated settling in.

What had happened to Seville since she and Pablo had both left? What about his family? His friends? Cara had been in occasional contact with Pablo's mother, but that had fallen away over the years, as Cara sensed it just brought them both pain.

She should call Pablo's mother while she was here, though the idea of doing that weighed heavily on her.

You'll be gone in two weeks. If you don't call her, she'll never know.

As Cara waited to cross the road, the pain in her side intensified. She needed to keep her mind off it and if that meant recalling things about Pablo, so be it.

She thought of Pablo's minuscule apartment, the one he shared with his funny friends. Chaotically brilliant Valentino. What had become of him? Was he doing something amazing, like they had always thought he might? What about Pablo's other friend? Stern, disapproving Mateo? Cara didn't actually care what had become of him. He'd never liked her much and the feeling had been mutual. They'd tolerated one another for Pablo's sake, but that was as far as it went. He was forever steering Pablo away from her and back to the projects they were all working on. Cara had never wanted to distract Pablo from his work or his studies, but the way Mateo carried on anyone would have thought Cara was trying to kidnap him and drag him off to the underworld. Teo had made his mind up about Cara without even bothering to get to know her. He'd barely even spoken to her in the five months she'd been with Pablo, with one significant exception.

As she crossed the road the pain took her breath away. She walked slowly to the other curb, finally grasping a light pole when she reached it. Maybe she should forget the café and find a doctor's surgery.

'Are you alright?' a voice asked. Cara couldn't even focus on the face that addressed her.

Then everything went black.

Teo put his phone down on his desk. His office was in the tallest building in Seville, the windows overlooked the river and his view went right out to the outskirts of the city and the horizon beyond. His desk was wide and neat. The view was blue and vast. The floor solid beneath his feet.

But for a moment it was as though he was back in his old student digs, its minuscule living room crammed with the computers they were using to build their first game.

Both calls were unexpected, though this call was as confusing as the first had been upsetting.

'This is the San Sebastian Hospital. We have Cara McCartney admitted as a patient. We're trying to reach Valentino Vasquez but he's unavailable and his assistant suggested we speak with you.'

Dread gathered heavy in his stomach.

'Is she alright?' He didn't recognise the sound of his own voice.

There was no love lost between him and Cara, but he didn't wish her pain.

'Her condition is serious and we're about to operate. We are looking for someone to contact. A next of kin.'

'I don't know. I'm sorry.'

'Do you know Señora McCartney?'

The question was more difficult than it should have been. He settled on a reluctant 'Yes.'

It felt like a trick. Like he'd slipped through some portal and back in time ten years.

Except he wasn't in his old room near the university with the peeling paint and the faint smell of frying food from the café below. He was on the thirtieth floor of a new office building and all he could smell was the espresso on his desk and clean carpet. And he wasn't a struggling student, he was one of the joint CEOs of Verdadero, a billion-dollar company that designed and built virtual reality games.

'Appendicitis, but we believe it has ruptured and the infection has spread. She's been rushed into emergency surgery. Can I confirm that you will come?'

He took a few deep breaths but the dread was no less acute.
This isn't like that other call. This isn't like Pablo.
Pablo had not been involved.

Because Pablo was dead.

Teo's gut clenched further, not with fear but memory.

His oldest friend. The man to whom he owed almost everything. His business, his reputation. His life.

Not in a literal sense, though it might as well have been.

When Teo had first arrived at high school he wasn't just

short, spotty and uncoordinated—crimes that at the large sporty boys' school he attended would have been bad enough. Worse than that, Teo was an outcast. Untouchable. Unbefriendable. Even his teachers viewed him with suspicion.

Teo's life had changed the day his father had been arrested for defrauding hundreds of people out of millions of euros. A white-collar crime Teo hadn't fully understood as a fourteen-year-old, except that it meant that his family, his mother and three younger siblings, had to move immediately from their large house to a small apartment. And it meant that no one, not even his old friends, wanted to speak to him.

At a new school, with a newly jailed father, he had clung to the shadows. If he could just be invisible then he might just get through the seventh circle of hell that was his high school.

He watched life from the sidelines, until he noticed Pablo doing the same thing. But the difference between him and Pablo was that Pablo was an artistic genius. He saw the world like no other person Teo had known before or since. Pablo also stayed at the edges of their classes, not to hide, but to draw and sketch and write stories to go with his pictures. Pablo wasn't interested in maths or science but excelled at Spanish and history. And of course, art. In breaks Pablo kept himself busy with his pad and his pencils and didn't mind Teo silently sitting next to him, watching.

He didn't mind that Teo was shunned by everyone else. Pablo didn't care that Teo's father was undergoing a high-profile trial that was on the news every night. He didn't blink when Teo couldn't participate in after-school sport or hang out on weekends because he had to help at home with his brother and sisters. And when Teo's father was sentenced to thirty years in prison, Pablo had put his arm around Teo and told him that he must take after his mother. The only person in the world ever to do so.

Teo and Pablo hadn't sought out Val, so much as become

shackled to him when Valentino Vasquez was told to help them both with their maths work. But after helping them pass their maths exam, Val stuck around. He also didn't care about Teo's father, or Pablo's obsession with drawing and stories. Val had his own idiosyncrasies going on; perpetual tardiness, distractedness and most of all brilliance.

Teo didn't have Val's genius for numbers, nor did he have Pablo's artistic ability, but somehow the three of them worked as a unit. Val the maths whiz, Pablo the creative wonder. Teo just making sure that both of them got to class.

It wasn't until later, much, much later, that Teo realised what he brought to the threesome. Organisation. The other two were utterly brilliant but would get preoccupied when they were deep in a project. Teo didn't have the gift—or burden—of being outstanding at anything, but he was a hard worker. And he was methodical. And whereas neither Pablo nor Val could be depended upon to arrive somewhere on time—Teo could. He'd had to care for his brother and sisters while his mother worked, holding the family unit together throughout his father's trial and conviction. And everything that came later. Teo was good at getting things done. Teo was good at *being good*.

It was Teo who had suggested that Pablo's designs and stories could be a video game. Teo who had suggested Val try and develop the code for it. Not that either of them needed much encouragement, they were both ambitious, but they needed him to point them in the right direction. They needed him to stand up in front of the private equity investors to sell the concept. They needed him to make the deals. They needed him to rent the offices, employ the staff and pay the salaries.

Teo was a doer, rather than a creative mind. He thanked his luck every single day that Val and Pablo had put their faith and their creations into his hands.

He owed Val and Pablo an unrepayable debt.

Especially Pablo.

Pablo, who hadn't lived to see the success his designs and stories had become.

Pablo who... Teo's throat tightened and closed over.

Teo had spent his whole life making it up to Pablo, doing the best he could with Pablo's creations but this phone call brought everything back.

Cara McCartney was in Seville. That was surprising enough; he doubted she'd ever want to return after what had happened. He hadn't heard from her since the day of Pablo's funeral, a state of affairs that he suspected suited her as much as it did him.

Teo and Cara had never been friends. She had eyed him with the same suspicion many people did when they found out who his father was. And Teo viewed Cara with similar mistrust. Pablo had fallen for her deeply and eternally. Pablo would have followed Cara to the ends of the earth. Which was what worried Teo the most. He didn't want to begrudge his friend his happiness, but couldn't he have found that happiness with an equally lovely Andalusian woman, not an American with ambitions to travel the world?

As he hung up the phone, memories of that other phone call came flooding back. Things he hadn't allowed himself to remember in years. The nonsensical nature of what they told him still took his breath away.

'There's been an accident. A car mounted the pavement. Pablo didn't make it.'

Pablo had died.

Teo had gone to Cara's small apartment and found her dressed for an evening out, in a short black shirt and heels. She'd looked relieved when she'd first opened the door, but her smile had fallen when she'd realised it was Teo at the door and not the man she had been expecting.

Always the responsible one, Teo knew he had to be the one

to tell her and suggested she sit on the nearby sofa. He'd tried to think of the right words but in the end, it hadn't taken more than a look from him. She'd turned from him and curled in upon herself. Even so, he still needed to tell her. She hadn't looked at him as he'd told her about the accident and Pablo's near instantaneous death.

'Cara, I want you to know how very sorry—'

'Spare us both your sympathies.'

'I'm truly sorry, if there's anything—'

'I don't need anything from you. You never liked me, so don't pretend to now. Just leave.'

'Cara, please,' he'd tried but her cry echoed across the room.

'I said get out. Go! Get away! I hate you! I never want to speak to you again!'

Teo had been torn, he wanted to stay to convince her to accept his help, but knew she'd never take anything from him. They were nothing to one another and now that Pablo was gone, they were even less than that.

So now, when a voice on the other end of the phone told him he had to come to the San Sebastian Hospital he wished, more than he'd ever wished, that neither he nor Pablo had ever met Cara McCartney.

CHAPTER TWO

CARA'S STOMACH STILL HURT, but it was a different kind of pain. It only sliced through her if she moved. So she didn't. She lay still and tried to make sense of what was happening around her. She was in a hospital. If not, she was in trouble, because there was a drip in her arm, her fingers rested on stiff sheets and a constant beeping was coming from somewhere nearby. She was being looked after, but where? And when?

The last few hours were a confusing blur. The pain had been intense and she'd fallen in and out of consciousness several times. Finally, the pain had ceased but she remembered nothing after that. Until now.

'Good morning, sleepy-head!' The bubbly nurse spoke in Spanish, with a strong Andalusian accent.

Because you're in Spain. Seville.

She'd known it was a bad idea to come back here and she was right.

'What happened?' Her mouth was completely dry and tasted strange. It was still morning. The last thing she remembered was going to get some lunch. Waiting for her hotel room.

'Your appendix burst!' The nurse spoke as if she were announcing a party. 'It made quite a mess. You've had surgery and are now on a huge dose of antibiotics to clean it all up.'

Cara moved and felt the drip in her arm again.

'How are your pain levels?' the nurse asked.

'I'm not sure.' It was manageable if she didn't move, but when she did… 'Seven out of ten?'

The nurse went to the drip and pressed some buttons.

There was a lot to take in. Appendix? That would explain the pain she'd thought was just an upset stomach.

'Have I had surgery? I don't remember.'

'You were quite out of it, apparently. Which isn't surprising. The doctor said it's one of the worst cases she's seen in a long time.'

Cara didn't do things by halves when it came to Seville apparently. First Pablo's accident. Now this.

'The doctor will be around shortly on her rounds. In the meantime, we need to get you moving a little. Can I help you sit up?'

'I can manage,' Cara said, with more confidence than was warranted. As soon as she flexed her stomach muscles the pain gripped her and she cried out.

'Steady on. Let me help you.'

With the nurse's help Cara got into a sitting position. Just doing that was exhausting. Once she was upright, she could see the room properly. It was a private room, neat, clean. Reasonably quiet. She was glad about all of this yet had no idea what her health insurance was likely to cover. Or what she might be expected to pay. A different kind of pain clenched her gut this time.

'Try eating some ice to start with and then we'll try a little breakfast.'

'Breakfast? What day is it?'

'Wednesday.'

'So the next morning?'

'Yes. They operated yesterday afternoon and you've been asleep ever since. I don't blame you. You were quite sick. You still are.'

Cara popped a cube of ice into her mouth. It was refreshing on her parched lips and tongue. Everything tasted strange. The room smelt strange. No more jasmine. Just disinfectant.

'Dr Magdalena will be here soon, but in the meantime, you have a visitor.'

A visitor? Maybe Mr Westwood? But that made no sense. How would he know she was here? She had to let him know she might be late to the job. If she could even still do it. She had no idea how long it would take her to recover. Right now, her brain was a fog of pain and exhaustion and she wasn't even sure when she'd be able to stand up. Let alone when she'd be able to work.

'Who is it?'

The nurse grinned and wriggled an eyebrow.

'You can come in now, sir.'

Maybe it was the infection. The anaesthesia. Or simply the pain. But Cara was definitely hallucinating. Or maybe she was still asleep and dreaming, because there was no other reason Mateo Ortiz would be in her hospital room.

The nurse winked and left the room.

Definitely dreaming.

'Cara, how are you feeling?' He spoke matter-of-factly, as though they spoke every day. As though the last time they'd spoken, she hadn't told him to get out of her life and stay there.

'Sore.' Confused.

Deeply, deeply confused.

'What are you doing here?' she asked.

His face gave nothing away. That wasn't unusual for Mateo. Feelings weren't something he did. His facial expressions only covered the spectrum of annoyance to disapproval. This current look skewed more to annoyance.

It was a shame because when Teo smiled his entire face changed. Almost like he became a different person. She'd occasionally notice how he looked at other people, people he actually liked, and how different his face was to when he looked at her. Why wouldn't he ever just smile at her? She'd never understood what his problem was with her.

He definitely didn't smile now. His mouth was tight and his forehead creased downwards in a frown as he said, 'The hospital called me. You gave them Val's name but he's on his way back from business meetings in Japan.'

She shook her head. She had no recollection of giving anyone Val's name, but then she'd been in agony. Who knew what she might have said. But that didn't explain why Teo was here. She hadn't seen him in over ten years. Not since the funeral. And she'd never expected to ever hear from him again.

'I don't understand.'

'Val and I work together. When they couldn't reach Val, they were put through to me.'

'Work together?'

'Verdadero. The business we started with…'

Teo didn't finish his sentence. But he didn't have to. Cara understood his missing words and understood why he didn't want to say them. Why he couldn't even bring himself to say Pablo's name.

'Yes, yes. I understand.' For once they agreed on something. He didn't want to say Pablo's name and she didn't want to hear it.

Pablo isn't here. Because Pablo is dead.

Something began to rise up inside her. At first, she thought it was tears, but at the last moment she realised it was something else. She covered her mouth and looked around for something to catch what was about to come out of it.

A plastic container materialised in front of her and she vomited. Liquid only.

She felt awful. Dizzy. Sore.

Great. She'd just vomited in front of Mateo Ortiz.

But as bad as she felt just now, it was nothing compared with how she'd felt the last time she'd spoken with Mateo.

Her current physical pain could not compare with the emotional anguish she'd felt when Teo had arrived at her door to tell her that Pablo was gone.

A woman in a white coat entered as Cara was wiping her mouth, saving her from having to look Teo in his dark and disapproving eyes.

'Oh dear, what's happening here?' the woman asked. She was in her thirties, with a telltale white coat. 'You're a bit unwell, anaesthetic can do that. I'm Dr Magdalena.'

'Cara McCartney,' she said.

'So I hear.' The doctor's gaze flicked to Teo. 'I'm glad we tracked someone down. You were all alone when you came in.'

'Mateo Ortiz. I'm an old friend.'

A different part of Cara hitched at the sound of his smooth, deep voice calling her a friend. It was a generous description of their relationship.

'Well, Cara McCartney, apart from just now, how are you feeling?'

'Nauseous, sore. A little confused.' That was just a soundbite of her symptoms. She was worried about her work, concerned what this hospital stay would mean for her client. And she was tired. Even though she'd done nothing but sleep for the last eighteen hours she could easily sleep another eighteen more. To top it all off, Teo was standing at the end of her bed looking at her with an expression even she, a person who spoke six languages, couldn't interpret.

'How much do you remember? You were quite unwell yesterday.'

'It's all a blur. I remember passing out, I think on the street, and some people helped me.'

'Yes, paramedics attended to you and gave you some pain relief.'

'I think that's the last thing I remember.'

'I'm not surprised. By the time you arrived here you could barely tell us your name. You had a ruptured appendix and we had to operate as a matter of urgency to stop peritonitis. We managed to remove the appendix and clear the infection using four incisions.'

Cara's gut clenched, causing more pain.

'At one point, we considered open abdominal surgery, but fortunately it didn't come to that and we were able to remove all the damage using just keyhole incisions. This will hopefully decrease your recovery time considerably.'

Good news. Bad news.

'What is my recovery time? I'm here for work. I'm meant to start the day after tomorrow.'

It already was Wednesday. No, she was due to meet Mr. Westwood first thing *tomorrow* morning.

'I'm afraid you're not going to be able to work for at least a week, and I would recommend allowing yourself considerably more than that. Two, if possible, until you return for your review.'

'Review?'

'Yes, we need to see you in two to three weeks to check the wound is healing and to make sure the infection is subsiding. You're not from Seville, are you?'

Cara shook her head.

'Where do you live?'

She shrugged. 'I move around for work.' Usually this was something she said with pride but for the first time in a long time her lifestyle was working against her.

She expected further questions, further judgement, but the doctor simply said, 'Then I recommend you stay in the vicinity for at least two weeks.'

'How long will I have to stay in hospital?'

'We'd usually let patients go home the day after surgery, but yours is a particularly serious case and we recommend you stay another night. You're staying with Mr. Ortiz?'

It was more a statement than a question to which they both said 'No' in unison.

'Well, make sure that wherever you go, you have someone to keep an eye on you.'

Would a hotel concierge count? Probably not.

'You have to rest for the next week or so, though I suspect you won't feel like doing very much. No heavy lifting. And no stairs.'

'I'll be fine,' she said.

Both Teo and the doctor narrowed their eyes at her, but neither said anything more.

'Dr Magdalena, do you know why this happened?'

'Appendicitis? We don't really know. It can run in families, though we don't know why. Has anyone in your family had it?'

Cara simply didn't know. Her mother had passed away when Cara was ten and her father seven years later. She didn't speak to her only living relative, her half-brother, Liam.

'Not that I know of.'

'It can be triggered by all sorts of things. It's reasonably common in people your age in fact. I'll check on you again but you can assume you'll be able to go home tomorrow, all being well.'

Dr Magdalena moved on to the next room, leaving Cara and Teo staring awkwardly at one another. The vomit she'd had minutes earlier far from a distant memory and still in the bowl in her lap. The sooner Teo left, the better.

'Thank you for coming, but you really didn't have to,' she said. *Take a hint and leave already!*

'They needed someone to sign your papers, agree to the surgery and agree to meet your out-of-pocket costs.'

'I have insurance. I can take care of whatever isn't covered.' She spoke with a confidence she most certainly did not have. Dr Magdalena had just told her she'd miss the next week of work, and very possibly the one after that. She'd lost her big pay cheque from Mr Westwood. She'd have to call her lawyers and tell them she wouldn't be commencing the action to recover her house anytime soon. She needed that money, she was running out of time.

'I'm sure you do. We can sort that out later. The hospital didn't have any details for you, no other contacts. Not even your passport.'

She nodded. She'd left most of her belongings locked in the hotel safe.

'Well, thank you again.'

If seeing Teo wasn't strange enough, this perfunctory conversation was at least on-brand for the two of them. They had never been close. Despite Pablo wishing otherwise.

Teo and I don't need to be best buddies, she'd said to Pablo. They had been polite, civil, but that was only ever as far as it went. They didn't get one another, but they didn't have to. Pablo was the only thing they'd ever had in common and now that Pablo was gone…

Teo was still not budging other than shifting his weight from foot to foot. Couldn't he get the hint and leave? A memory from last time came back to her. She'd yelled at him. She'd somehow forgotten that entirely. A completely understandable reaction to the grief she'd been suffering, but the memory still filled her with shame.

'Just let me know what I need to sign. My details are all in my phone,' she said and then gasped.

Her phone! *Please tell me I haven't lost my phone.*

Teo looked to the chair at the end of her bed and pointed to it with a nod. Her handbag was sitting on it.

'My bag. Thank goodness.' She moved towards it but fell back to her pillow with a wince.

'Let me,' he said.

Teo walked to the chair, and while his back faced her, she took the opportunity to study him. The gangly man she remembered had filled out, ever so slightly. But everything else was as she remembered, his muscles held his posture straight and proper. Guarded. Even from behind, his body language screamed, *Don't get too close.*

She couldn't help comparing him to Pablo, just as she still compared most men to Pablo. Teo was as tall as Pablo but that was where the similarities ended. Teo's face was closed, whereas Pablo's had been open. Teo's eyes were shuttered and dark but Pablo's were always looking for the light. For his next inspiration.

Pablo was open to the world's possibilities, Teo was always looking for the problems.

Just like now.

He handed her the phone and asked, 'Why didn't you see your doctor about your pain earlier?'

'I don't have a doctor.'

'Why don't you have a doctor?'

'I don't need one.'

'Clearly you do.' He looked around the hospital room with a glare.

Since leaving Seville a decade ago, Cara had been everywhere. She was an in-demand freelance interpreter. She spoke English, French, Spanish and Portuguese to the level required to interpret high-level business and diplomatic meetings. She could also get by conversationally in Cantonese and Japanese. Her German and Russian were rusty, but she knew enough to tell any presumptuous Russian exactly where he could stick his wandering hands.

The longest she'd stayed anywhere lately had been an entire month in London, working on a protracted merger involving two multinational companies. Once she'd been offered a one-year contract in Belgium at the EU headquarters. Cara had felt her skin crawl and her knees twitch. Staying in the one place? No. Never. She needed to be on the move. When you stayed too long in one place bad things always happened.

So what if she didn't have a regular doctor? Or a regular dentist. She was young. She looked after herself. Besides, moving around suited her. She didn't have anyone to come home to. She liked to live lightly, without deep connections. She'd already lost enough for several lifetimes.

'Can you just get off my case? What business is my health to you anyway?'

He gritted his jaw so tightly she expected to hear a crack.

'As I said, I was the only name the hospital had.'

'Yes, and thank you for coming. But I'm awake now, I can sign my own forms.'

He didn't answer. He didn't nod.

He didn't even budge.

'I can take it from here,' she said. All that was left to say was *Get out of my room*.

'Where are you based these days?' he asked.

Oh, that question again! What was everyone's obsession with her having an address?

'The world,' she said, and he rolled his eyes.

'Where do you *live*?'

'For the next week, here in Seville.'

'Okay, try this. Where does your mail get delivered to?'

She held up her phone.

'Your physical mail.'

'Not that I get any, but if I ever need to give a postal address it's in Ridgewood, New Jersey.'

'That wasn't so hard now, was it?' he said, and she thought she saw him try not to smile.

'And I've been there exactly two times in my life. My mail gets delivered to my friend Hannah's house and she lets me know if there's anything I need to know about.'

He shook his head.

'Just because my life's different to yours it doesn't make it wrong. There's more than one way to live.'

'I—' he began but if he wasn't going to leave her room he would listen to what she had to say.

'I'm not a fool, you know, I've been doing this for the past decade. It suits me fine. It's not as though I have a family.'

'None at all?' Everyone has a family, his tone implied.

'My mother passed away when I was ten, my father seven years later. Things you might have learnt about me if you'd ever bothered to speak to me.'

The skin around Teo's eyes tightened. His jaw, which had already been taut, was seconds away from shattering. It was kind of Teo to come to the hospital but he'd fulfilled whatever duty he felt he had and it was now time for him to leave.

Cara was so tired of being asked where she was from. As if it were important information. As though an address would define her. She had an amazing life, she'd travelled to almost every continent of the world, met so many amazing people and had got to glimpse into so many different cultures.

And the downsides of a nomadic life? Not many she was aware of. A mailing address wasn't the big deal some people tried to tell her it was. She never felt anxious moving around. Quite the contrary, she felt uneasy if she stayed in one place too long.

Home wasn't just an address, it was people. And Cara

didn't have many people. She had friends, her best friend and college roommate, Hannah, was a case in point.

The one time she'd considered putting down roots had been ten years ago. In this very city. But the accident and Pablo's death had shown her what a bad idea settling down in one place was. It was better to keep moving. Besides, there was a whole wide world out there and Cara still had more of it to see.

A few years ago, after completing a job in Canberra, Australia, Cara had travelled to North Queensland where she'd gotten a small tattoo on the top of her foot. A turtle. She was that turtle, with her home literally on her back. She always used backpacks, rather than wheelie suitcases. Wheelie suitcases were a pain to drag over cobblestoned streets and getting up and down stairs. Most places in the world were not as accessible as some would think. Backpacks were the way to go.

So when Teo kept asking about her life, her hackles were well and truly raised. Teo, who had never bothered to learn anything about her in her life yet still felt it was his right to disapprove of her.

'Please leave.'

'I have to make sure you're okay.'

'Why?' *When you can barely disguise your hatred of me?*

'Because I signed the forms.'

Oh. Now she understood.

The nausea rose up in her again. It wasn't bad enough she'd have to tell the lawyers to stop work on her case, now Teo wanted his pound of flesh. 'You want money?'

'Of course not. Besides, we have an excellent public health system here in Spain.'

'Then what?'

Teo shifted again, back and forth on his long legs. He was tall. Or was it because she was sitting down, but he seemed to loom over her like a tall tree.

'I can't just leave you.'

'You can, it's easy, you turn and keep putting one foot in front of the other until you're out the door.'

Teo shook his head.

'Why not?'

He let out a deep, loud sigh 'You wouldn't understand.'

'Because I'm an idiot? A child? What?'

'Because it's about loyalty.'

Ouch.

'What? Who do you owe a loyalty to? Because you certainly don't owe it to me.'

He glared at her.

No, not her.

But to Pablo.

He owed it to his dead friend, her dead lover, to make sure she was alright.

And because she had loved Pablo and because she'd never forget him, she fell back against her pillows.

'I understand loyalty,' she said.

'That's why you don't stay in one place long enough to have a doctor? Get your health checked out. Your teeth?'

Cara's face burnt. The nerve of this man! 'What's wrong with my teeth?'

He shook his head. 'Nothing. That's not what I meant.' Pink bloomed across his cheeks. *Good.*

'Then get off my case. You've come, you've seen me. You've satisfied yourself that I'm okay, now you can leave. Thank you for signing all the forms, email me my bill.'

'Fine,' he said through his teeth. 'Where are you staying? In case I need to contact you about anything else.'

She gave him the name of her hotel and hoped that would finally be it.

He nodded and then slid a card onto the table in front of her.

Mateo Ortiz
Verdadero
CEO

Blast.

Teo stepped outside Cara's hospital room and dragged deep breaths into his lungs. Being here brought it all back. The smell of the ward, the squeak of the linoleum under his shoes. Everything about this place transported him back a decade. To this very building.

To Pablo. It was so nonsensical, so strange. Hit by a driver who had suffered a medical episode, lost consciousness and control of his car before mounting the curb. Not premeditated, just a horrible, senseless accident. If he had been walking a second faster or a second slower Pablo would not have died.

Teo had been the one to formally identify Pablo so that his parents didn't have to. That memory unhelpfully resurfaced now so he did what he always had when it happened. He thought of the mark on the wall, just above the body, that he had focused on after glancing at his poor dead friend. The mark on the wall inert, inoffensive. Far better than what lay on the bed.

So seeing Cara, strangely unchanged after all this time, lying still, vulnerable, small in her hospital bed. Still looking at him as though she wanted to burn a hole right through him. It brought it all back.

At least she didn't scream at you this time.

He'd never done anything to upset her, he was sure of that, yet he'd never done anything warm to her either. There were reasons for that, maybe not noble ones, but reasons, nonetheless.

As hard as identifying Pablo's body had been, the visit to Cara's apartment had been worse. She'd looked at him and, somehow, she'd known; Teo arriving unannounced at her apartment must have signalled that something was very wrong. She'd glared at him with her big amber eyes, as though it was all his fault. And at that moment he'd almost believed it was.

I said, get out. Go. Go! Get away! I hate you! Can't you see I never want to speak to you again!

And there it was. What she really thought of him. He couldn't argue with her; he'd simply staggered from her apartment and steadied himself against the corridor wall. Just as he was doing now.

Pablo had been Teo's best and oldest friend. And Pablo had loved Cara in the same way he'd done with everything he'd cared about in his short life: completely, passionately, without abandon or reservation.

He'd signed the papers, seen Cara. Assured himself she was okay. Job done. Now to go back to the office. The deal they were working on was progressing. Verdadero, their VR gaming company had done many big deals over the years, each seemingly bigger than the last, but this one carried an additional emotional significance. A studio in California was interested in adapting their first game, the one Pablo had created, into a film. The deal was undoubtedly lucrative, would bring them more exposure than they had ever had in the past, but more than any of those things, it would also honour Pablo.

Pablo would've loved this.

The thought had sustained Teo over the past few weeks, ever since they'd first been approached by the producers, Jerry and Doug. Verdadero had received interest from film producers in the past but negotiations had never reached this stage. Val had flown in from Japan this morning and they needed to update one another on all the recent developments. Teo had to look over the specifications for their newest game. Attend a budget meeting. He had things to do.

Yet, three hours later he was back in Cara's hospital room

carrying the backpack he'd collected from her hotel. It hadn't been a simple thing to get it, but after he'd paid the bill for the rest of her stay as well as an additional and generous amount to ensure they kept her room vacant should she wish to return to it before the end of her booking they were more than happy to let him take her belongings.

Cara, however, was less than happy to see them.

'What?' was all she had to say but the anger in her eyes was sadly familiar.

'I thought you might need something.'

That took the wind out of her sails, the anger from her words.

'I was managing,' she muttered.

'I have no doubt you were, but I thought you might appreciate a change of clothes, your own toiletries.'

'They just let you take it?'

'I left them all my details, they know where to find me if I did something I shouldn't have.'

She took some deep breaths but needed to calm herself.

'Thank you,' she said finally.

'It's not a problem. Is this everything you have? Not another suitcase?'

'No, that would defeat the purpose. This is everything I own.'

'Wait, this is everything you have in the world?'

'Essentially.' She shrugged.

'Essentially? This is all your clothes. All your *things*?'

His sister took this much stuff for an overnight stay. Her beauty products alone would fill half of it.

'I keep a few things in my friend's attic. Some winter coats, that sort of thing. But yes, this is everything I have. And all I need.'

His face must have said it all. Wow. He thought he was a light traveller, and yet…

'I'm an interpreter. I need to blend into the background, I'm not supposed to stand out. Black suits are my work uniform. Those, and a couple of casual outfits is all I need. I sometimes buy new clothes for the change of season and donate the things I don't need.'

He recoiled.

'Oh, come on. I expect this kind of response from women, but I rarely get it from men.'

'What response is that?'

'Shock. You're slightly horrified, aren't you? Rest assured I wash and dry clean everything regularly. My backpack is the size of a standard suitcase. It's remarkable what you can fit inside it.'

'What about books? Mementos?' he challenged.

'Books are easy. As soon as I finish reading something I donate it to the next little library I see in a street. Or a hotel. There's no shortage of places to leave behind books.'

'And mementos. Trinkets?' Teo was intrigued, disbelieving and also slightly concerned, for reasons he couldn't even name. He too liked to travel light, but he had a place to call home.

She laughed. 'I'm not particularly sentimental. Life's much easier that way. Besides, I think most people have too much stuff, especially people in Western countries.'

He nodded, not entirely convinced but not prepared to argue the point any longer. A bigger argument lay ahead and Teo had learnt early in life to choose his battles.

'Well, thank you very much again. I appreciate it.'

Teo shifted from foot to foot, but didn't make a move to leave. He had to be careful how he approached this. How he approached her.

She hated him.

'How are you feeling?' he asked.

'Slightly better than I was a few hours ago. Still tired and sore.'

He nodded.

'Thanks again.' She rolled one hand in a forward motion to indicate he should say what he'd come to say or leave.

'I've come to ask if you will come to my place to convalesce.'

'Oh.' Her face fell. Not the reaction he was hoping for but better than the one he expected.

'Thank you for the offer, but I'll be okay at my hotel.'

'We both know that being on your own in a hotel was not what Dr Magdalena had in mind when she said you need someone to watch you.'

'How much trouble can I get up to in a hotel room?'

'That's not the point. The doctor said you should have someone to keep an eye on you. Not that I'll be watching you 24-7. But I have a housekeeper. She can check on you. There will be someone to call if you need anything.'

She narrowed her eyes, didn't dismiss the idea right away. Mostly, he was glad she didn't yell at him to leave.

'I'm not going to force you to do anything. But I understand you don't know anyone else in Seville. I know it isn't ideal for you to stay at the hotel you have booked and that you would be safer and more comfortable staying with me.'

She looked at her backpack and him, though her gaze didn't cross his face, but rather rested on some unspecified point in the middle of his chest. He resisted the urge to put his hand on his heart, which was suddenly beating faster than it should be.

'I know you haven't always warmed to me,' he said.

She scoffed. 'The feeling's mutual, you don't need to pretend otherwise.'

He didn't hate Cara, not in the way she seemed to hate him. But she was right, he'd always been uneasy around her, though he didn't want to dwell too long on the reasons why. It took Teo a long time to trust anyone. With Cara it might have been more than that. Something he didn't want to analyse further. The way his skin felt warmer when she was around. The way his body seemed to notice her presence even before his eyes.

'I don't want to impose,' she said.

'You wouldn't be. We wouldn't even need to see one another. Alba is happy to do anything you need. In fact, she'll be very annoyed with me if I don't get you to agree to stay.'

The corners of her pretty eyes twitched. She was thinking about it.

'My house has two storeys, there is a guest bedroom on the ground floor, with its own bathroom. My rooms are upstairs, you won't need to climb the stairs, or even see me.'

He couldn't have offered her a more ideal proposal, yet Cara shook her head.

Maybe it was time to bring out the one thing he didn't want to mention. He didn't want to do that. But if she left him no choice…

'Rightly, or perhaps wrongly, misplaced or otherwise, I feel a sense of loyalty and obligation towards you.'

Hopefully those words would be enough. He really didn't want to spell out why he felt these obligations to her. And nor did she.

He simply said, 'You know what he'd want you to do.'

Cara looked down at her lap. Her long, slender fingers played with her bedsheet absentmindedly.

'I'll pay you back,' she said finally.

'There's absolutely no need.'

He had no idea how much a freelance interpreter earned. He suspected she was good at her job, the Spanish she was speaking while ill in the hospital was pitch-perfect. If she could speak a language that was not her first under those circumstances, then she was probably an excellent interpreter. Though that didn't mean she had total financial security.

Fancy not having a fixed address! Flitting from place to place all over the world!

It sounded romantic to be sure but the reality was likely anything but. When did she relax? How could she when she wasn't around anything familiar? But most importantly, where were her friends? Her support network? Her *family*?

He remembered with a pang that Cara's parents had both died before she'd last been in Seville. He should have been more sensitive to the fact, particularly as he knew what it was to lose a parent himself. But what about other family? Teo's own mother still lived on the outskirts of Seville. He knew she and his siblings were close by if he needed them. His mother was an active and healthy sixty-year-old and his family were all there for one another, his mother, brother and his sisters. He couldn't imagine not having them in his life.

No doubt Cara had friends all over the world, but it wasn't the same as having someone close by when you were in trouble. Or sick.

As she was now.

What if this had happened somewhere else? Somewhere she didn't know anyone. Somewhere he wasn't there to help her?

He shivered at the thought.

'Just a night or two,' she said.

'Two weeks,' he said. 'Until your check-up.'

'One week,' she countered.

He wasn't going to stop her leaving his house but hoped she'd feel comfortable enough to stay as long as she needed. He nodded.

'I'll let Alba know we're expecting you tomorrow.'

She bit her lip and nodded as well.

'Thank you, Mateo. Truly. I'm sure it won't be for long.'

'Yes, I'm sure too,' he said, silently vowing that she would stay until she was one hundred percent recovered.

Pablo would never forgive him if he didn't do this. Even though he was gone, Pablo still played a significant role in Teo's life. He'd come up with the idea for their first game, his drawings and stories had allowed the three of them to begin their business. Teo lived with Pablo's creations every day of his life. To say nothing of his legacy and the charity they had established in Pablo's memory. The Pablo Pascal Foundation funded various programs and projects to promote education, particularly for children who had suffered disadvantages. Children from low economic areas, children displaced by war or famine, and children with learning difficulties. Its portfolio was varied and they funded initiatives across the globe.

Cara would stay with him for as long as she needed to. Teo would just have to handle the unusual fluttering in his heart, and surely she could put aside her dislike of him for a week or two. They both owed it to Pablo and his memory.

I hate you!

Her words had shocked him. He knew he'd never been friendly with her, but *hate*? What had he done to her? Maybe it was the emotion of the moment, she was grieving too. But her remark had hurt, even the memory of it still stung now, years later.

Having Cara stay would be awkward, but it would only be for a short time. Then she could take her backpack and go wherever she wanted to flit to next.

He'd be polite, welcoming. They didn't have to become best friends. She didn't like him, but she was wrong about him not liking her. Cara was smart, intriguing. Sassy. Good company. Very pretty.

More than pretty. Stunningly beautiful. Pablo always had had a good eye. But that was beside the point.

Cara was and always would be Pablo's girlfriend so whatever Teo thought about Cara was beside the point.

CHAPTER THREE

CARA LOOKED FROM her passenger seat to Teo, who was driving his small sports car through the oldest streets of Seville.

Earlier that morning the hospital had discharged her with antibiotics, painkillers and a promise to return for a review in two weeks' time. Cara had also called her hotel to cancel her reservation only to be told her bill had already been fully paid. It could only have been Teo.

But why? Letting her stay with him was already above and beyond, but to pay her account as well? She was undecided about whether she would say anything and this also rattled her. Usually, she spoke her mind without thinking twice, but something about this situation with Teo made her hesitate.

She shifted uncomfortably in her seat. Partly due to the pain in her abdomen, but mostly because of the uneasiness in her chest. She really was beholden to him, now that he'd taken it upon himself to pay her hotel bill. All out of some misplaced loyalty towards her because of Pablo.

Loyalty. And obligation.

That's what he'd said.

And it hit her. He missed Pablo. It was different to the way Cara missed Pablo, but he'd loved Pablo all the same. Pablo had been Teo's best friend, business partner. Like a brother to him. And Teo still hurt.

You should cut him some slack.

Or should she? Teo had never liked her, never bothered to get to know her. He'd barely spoken to her.

Yes. She remembered now. The feeling of confusion. Wondering why he didn't like her. What she'd done to earn his contempt.

Teo's dark hair was combed back smoothly from his face. *Never a hair out of place.* Literally. That was Teo. He'd always been like this. Unlike Pablo, whose hair had been long, wild, unkempt. Pablo who only ever wore T-shirts because the buttons of a shirt were too much hassle. Pablo who often forgot to wash his clothes and resorted to buying new underwear, a luxury he could hardly afford.

Not only did Teo almost exclusively wear button-up shirts, today he had paired his with a jacket. It was loose, on the casual side of business, but it was spring in Seville and he was only collecting her from the hospital.

Loyalty or not, she wished he hadn't asked her to stay. Paying for her hotel should have been enough to cover any loyalty he might have felt. If this car trip was anything to go by, her stay was going to be as painful as her stomach.

She couldn't give him the satisfaction of telling him she had little choice. She'd had to cancel the job with Westwood and on top of losing all that money it was also possible she wouldn't make it to Paris for the work she had scheduled the week after next. That was four weeks of missed work, missed savings, and missed opportunity to begin the case she needed to bring against her half-brother to recover her parents' house. *Her* house.

Liam. Her older, estranged half-brother who had managed to take most of her father's estate when he passed away. A confluence of a badly drafted will, an unscrupulous brother, and loopholes to do with her age and him being the executor and her guardian meant that Liam had managed to take most of the property himself, including her parents' house. Cara had been given some money that Liam held in trust until her twenty-fifth birthday. But by the time she turned twenty-five, Liam had managed to spend most of that money, claiming expenses as her guardian to take care of her, which he hadn't at all. Cara had worked her way through college and by her twenty-fifth birthday there wasn't even enough money left in the trust for her to instruct lawyers to challenge the situation. Which had probably been Liam's intention all along.

Liam and his wife lived without a mortgage and carefree in her parents' house. Her lawyers were helpful but given the low prospects of succeeding in her case, they needed money upfront to start the proceedings.

And now? Now the chances of getting that money looked increasingly small.

Teo pulled up on a cobbled street in a square in the old district of Santa Cruz. He opened her car door for her but when Cara lifted her right foot out, she winced. Twisting her torso was particularly painful.

'Careful.' Teo bent down to her level and his voice was soft. 'Take it easy. There's no rush.' He offered her his hand.

Climbing out of the low seat of a sports car was not easy for someone two days' post-surgery so she gave him her hand, completely unprepared for the sensation of warmth that slipped around her when she did. Comforting, strengthening. Soothing. All at once. She lifted herself up and with Teo's assistance the transition from sitting to standing was almost painless. Thankfully he pulled his own hand away immediately once she was upright.

When she saw where they were she gasped again.

'Are you okay? Have you strained something?' He leant in towards her again.

She rubbed her side and nodded. Let him think that, but her wound felt fine. It was the house that had made her gasp. *This* house?

A free-standing two-storey villa in the traditional Spanish style. The windows were shaped like arches and the rooms on the first floor had small balconies overlooking the quiet square.

Most of all it was painted a gorgeous pale pink with orange accents that shouldn't go together but somehow did.

'You live here? *Here?*'

'What's the matter?'

'Nothing,' she whispered. Only everything. It was too strange. She *knew* this house. She'd never been inside, but she'd walked past many times with Pablo and secretly, as she held his hand, imagined what it might be like to live somewhere like that with Pablo.

That was in the brief period where she'd contemplated being that sort of person. The type of person with a house. With a job in the same place every day. A person who owned their own cutlery. And their own sheets. A person who slept in their own bed every night. Even the sort of person who had potted plants.

If she was ever going to do any of those things, she had thought it would be somewhere like this.

Teo lifted her bag from the boot of his car and walked to the large front door. Wooden, painted a shiny white with two big gold knockers. Gorgeous.

'Have you always lived here?'

'No. Why?'

Of course he hadn't. She'd have known if he'd lived in her dream house, wouldn't she? Besides, Teo had shared a small apartment with Pablo and Val, not far from the university. Not far from her student digs.

She'd never told anyone how much she loved this house. Not even Pablo. Because why would she? Ten years ago, it was beyond the realms of all imagining that either of them would be able to afford a place like this. Besides, she and Pablo were going to travel the world together. What use would a beautiful house in the heart of Old Seville have been to them.

And yet…

Teo pushed open the door and called out, 'We're home.'

She followed him inside to where the cool marble floors and darkness provided a welcome reprieve from the heat. When her eyes adjusted, she noticed the high ceilings, the floor-to-ceiling windows and white curtains that fluttered in the welcome early evening breeze.

A giant staircase loomed above her. Down a corridor, past the staircase, she glimpsed a courtyard and heard the tinkling of a fountain.

The house was even more lovely inside than she'd imagined.

Even before seeing her room she knew Teo was annoyingly right. This place was far nicer than her hotel. Though it remained to be seen whether her host's mood would lose his villa several stars from its rating.

'I'll show you to your room,' he said.

'What if I want to look around first?'

The way his eyebrows shot up let her know he hadn't anticipated this level of sass.

'Unless you need a moment to tidy up down here? Pick up your underwear, dirty clothes and the like.'

His lips were tight but she wasn't sure if it was a grimace or a suppressed grin.

He coughed. 'I have some help. As I said, Alba is my housekeeper. She and her husband live in the garden house and take care of everything. The cleaning, cooking, washing, garden.'

Cara didn't take in much after 'garden house.' It implied not just a garden, which was a luxury in itself, but a whole other building. As though this one were not enough.

Did he live here on his own? She'd just assumed as much

because, after all Teo was vastly unpleasant, but he was also, it seemed, quite well off. Someone must think he was a catch.

Not her though. He was grumpy, uptight. Reserved. And not even his sharp jaw and definitive cheekbones could compensate for that. Nor could his height or his broad chest, which she conceded, wasn't nothing. Teo Ortiz was, she had to admit, handsome. Objectively. If you didn't know him and didn't have to take his brittle personality into account.

'Do they know I'll be staying a few days?'

'They know you'll be staying as long as it takes you to recuperate.' Teo stepped towards her, but Cara wasn't sure which direction he was going in and if she was meant to follow. Somehow, they ended up with only a foot of air between them, facing one another. Somehow, her heart was in her throat.

'I'm very grateful for you letting me stay, but how long I stay isn't up to you. I assume you don't propose to lock me up?'

'Of course not. But I do plan on making your stay so comfortable that you'll never want to leave.'

A laugh bubbled up through her, responding to his joke, but when her gaze caught his, her laugh froze. His eyes were dark, but focused on her. He hadn't been joking.

He almost looked serious. The air crackled between them.

'Never? That's quite the challenge you're setting for yourself.' Her voice was rough, but that was surely still the effects of the operation. She wasn't herself.

His voice, on the other hand, was soft and certain as he said, 'I always rise to a challenge. You should know that about me.'

She was certainly getting to.

She knew she should step back; they'd been standing too close to one another for far too long. She could see the weave in his silk tie. The strain in his jaw. But her body was tender and quick movements painful, so she remained where she was.

The sound of a throat being cleared made Teo turn his head. In the second it took Cara to follow she thought she glimpsed a hint of a pink flush climb up Teo's neck.

'Alba, this is Cara. Cara, this is Alba, my housekeeper and general lifesaver.'

'Cara, it's lovely to meet you, I'm sorry it's not under better circumstances. How are you feeling?' Alba asked.

'Thank you. I'm doing fine, all things considered.'

'I've made up your room. It's on this floor as I understand you mustn't climb stairs?'

Had Teo told her that? Or did she just know? Either way Cara's body felt a sense of relief. Walking was an effort. Stairs would take everything out of her.

'You'll also find some new clothes as well, nothing fancy, but I hope you find them comfortable as you convalesce.'

'Oh, you didn't have to. I would've made do.'

As if on cue, Alba glanced at her backpack, still being held effortlessly in Teo's hand.

'That's all you have?' the older woman asked.

'That's all I need.'

Cara braced herself to explain yet again about her lifestyle but Alba simply said, 'Please leave out anything you'd like for me to wash.'

'There's no need...'

Alba's face fell and Teo shot her a look that said, *Do what this woman says.*

'Thank you, I will,' Cara said.

'I'll show you your room,' Teo said.

Cara followed him down a second corridor, away from the inviting courtyard, and towards the back of the house. She'd only turned two corners yet already felt lost. He opened a door to a large room that was dark and cool. Dark was good. A lie-down would be better.

'I imagine you want to rest.'

'Yes, thank you. I do.'

'You have an en suite. And if you need Alba, just pick up the intercom and call for her.'

'I couldn't—'

'You can and you must. Not only is it what I pay her for but she claims she's hopelessly underemployed looking after just me and is delighted to have someone else to fuss over.'

So he did live alone. It made sense. Not even a face as handsome as his could make up for his cool attitude.

'I won't need anything.'

'Presumably you'll need to eat?'

Yes. But she'd figure that out later. Food was the last thing on her mind. For now, she just wanted to have a reprieve from Teo, his dark eyes and contradictory smiles. And once she'd slept she wouldn't feel so rattled by the way his hand felt wrapped around hers.

He placed her backpack on a sofa, lying it the right way up.

'Do you need help opening it?' he asked.

Why was he being so damned helpful? It was too much. Too strange. Couldn't he see she was in a vulnerable place?

Her backpack contained most of her belongings. Travel light, travel with ease. She shopped at thrift shops, bought clothes made locally in places she visited, though she found she really only needed a handful of good quality outfits. She was acutely aware of her flight miles, but offset those by consuming and purchasing no more than she absolutely needed. One exception she made was earrings. They were light, compact and could transform any outfit into something memorable. Together with a few shades of bright lipstick was all she needed to make her feel special and inject a bit of style into her day. Besides, interpreters were not meant to stand out, her job was to blend in.

'I can manage, really.'

Teo backed towards the door, but didn't leave right away.

'Are you waiting for a tip?' she joked.

His face fell and she felt smaller than she ever had. He might have been rude to her in the past but he was making an effort now. Maybe he was trying to make amends.

'I'm sorry, that was uncalled for. I'm not at my best.'

'It's fine, I understand,' he replied, but he still looked crestfallen as he closed the door behind him.

But why? He didn't like her. He never had, so why was he being so different and helpful and downright contradictory?

It's because of Pablo. He doesn't know how to treat you and having you here might be bringing back sad memories for him as well.

Cara sat on the bed and sighed. She toed off her shoes. On the bed next to her were a pair of long silky pyjamas. Soft under her fingertips. She sighed again and decided it would be worth the effort to feel those against her skin instead of the rough cotton dress she was wearing.

She winced as she unbuttoned her dress, slipped it off and dressed slowly again. She could take more painkillers but needed to eat something when she did and didn't have the energy to deal with Alba, let alone Teo for the moment, but on a table near the window she spied several bottles of water, some sparkling, some still, and a bowl of fruit. Apples, bananas, strawberries. She peeled a banana, opened a bottle of painkillers and obediently took her tablets.

Then she did something she hadn't done before. Looked up Verdadero, the company Teo had established with Pablo and Val. The start-up she had known ten years ago was now a massive company, with so many games and parts of the business she didn't bother to count. Teo and Val weren't simply successful, they were the best in the world and had made Pablo's game into a success so many times over. She closed her eyes and lay on the bed. It was too much to take in: happiness, grief, regret, pride. Tears leaked from her eyes. She'd get under the covers in a bit.

But she fell asleep before she did.

Teo sat under the wisteria, which was in full purple bloom, and swiped through the morning's news on his tablet. He glanced over occasionally at the shutters to the guest room. They remained defiantly shut. He expected nothing else.

His house was clearly the last place on earth Cara wanted to be. It was written all over the smooth skin of her cheek bones, in the wariness in her golden-brown eyes and in the way she held her pink lips tight. *Why would she want to stay here when you've always been cold to her?* Cara really despised him and the passage of time had done nothing to dull that feeling.

Why would it? He had good reason for remaining aloof with her, as much now as then. He had to.

He needed to maintain the distance between them yet he didn't want her to be miserable. He contemplated explaining to her that he had good reasons for maintaining his distance, but that would prompt further questions. Questions he didn't trust her enough to answer. The same old conundrum.

So he stood and moved to the chair on the opposite side of the table, with his back to her room. There. Now maybe he could focus on the stock market and not the door to Cara's room or what the woman behind it was doing.

He poured himself a coffee from the pot Alba had brewed for him. Black. Long. All his stomach could handle for the time being.

Cara's presence in his house was more distracting than he'd anticipated. She brought memories and pain into his life and a sense of uneasiness he couldn't pin down. Distraction was the last thing he needed at the moment, not with the film producers due to arrive in Seville tomorrow.

His house guest wouldn't stay for long and once she left, he'd feel like himself again. While he knew Cara would keep to herself, having anyone he didn't know very well stay under his roof made him uneasy. You just never knew what they were up to or what they would say about him once they left.

People—ex girlfriends mainly—had told him he had a trust problem. Teo didn't see his reluctance to trust people as a problem, more of a solution: If you were cautious about who you let into your life, you had less to worry about. Most people in the world were just far too trusting. And that was where their problems began.

Pablo sprung to mind.

Pablo had fallen hard and fast for Cara. Too hard and way too fast if you asked Teo. And Teo had told Pablo as much. Told him to step back, take a breath. He didn't want to see his best friend hurt. Cara hadn't been the one to hurt Pablo, but that wasn't the point. Falling in love was reckless.

Teo hadn't thought of Cara in years. Not really. Occasionally something would bring her to mind and he'd wonder where she was, what she was doing, whether she had settled down. Not that he *cared*, but he was curious. For Pablo's sake. That was all.

A noise behind him made him swing his head. His body a hair-trigger. He stood.

There she was. Standing on the other side of the courtyard, in loose white pyjamas, her golden hair cascading around her face like a halo. Looking mortified.

'Sorry to interrupt. I didn't realise you were here.'

'Please don't apologise. Think of this house as yours while you're here.'

She raised an eyebrow. He had to get better at sounding sincere.

'Have a seat. Have some coffee. I'm about to leave.' Teo pulled out the chair opposite his.

She looked down. 'You have a full cup. Please just stay,' she said as she sat.

Before he could even ask if Cara was hungry, Alba appeared with a plate of freshly cut fruit and *bollos*, sweet rolls served with jam and butter, as though she'd been spying on him.

You know Alba and you know she definitely was.

His housekeeper had been delighted when Teo had told her they were going to have a house guest. She fussed over Cara, asking how she was feeling, how she had slept. Teo listened in, trying to keep his expression as neutral as possible when Cara said that she had slept well and was feeling much better than the day before.

Alba smiled broadly at Cara and winked at Teo before leaving.

Alba wasn't just a spy but also a meddler.

'This is a beautiful house. How long have you lived here?'

'I bought it about six years ago, but took some time to renovate and repair it. I moved in about five years ago.'

'I'm sorry I was so shocked yesterday. I...' She pressed her lips together. 'I remember this house, that's all.'

'You do?'

'Yes, it's beautiful. Not to mention pink!'

'What's wrong with pink?'

'Nothing. I'm trying to tell you I love it. I remember it from when we were at university.'

He let his shoulders relax a little. He'd always loved this house, its stately air, its location in the corner of the quiet square. The orange trees out the front. He'd loved it since he'd first moved to the centre of Seville as a university student.

'I was lucky it came on the market about the same time I was looking for something.'

It was only half a lie. He'd been looking for something sensible, an apartment suitable for a bachelor. Something low-maintenance. A lock up and leave.

Then he'd seen the realtor sign at the front of this house and he'd known.

He was rarely anything but conservative with his money; his childhood had shaken any recklessness out of him. He almost hadn't bought the house but when he'd taken his mother with him to help him choose a place, they had visited two sensible apartments and here. His mother had told him he'd regret not buying it.

She was right.

Six years later he owned half a dozen of those sensible apartments as sensible investments, but this was his home.

'I used to walk through this square on the way home from classes.'

'Me too. The walk down the avenue was quicker...'

'But not as nice.' She finished his thought.

Their gazes snagged and he smiled before he could stop himself.

'Yes,' he said softly.

They shouldn't think about those days because those memories only led in one tragic direction. So as much as he wanted to keep looking at Cara, trying to decide if her eyes were brown or gold, he looked down and cleared his throat.

'Do you need anything?' he asked.

'Wi-Fi password? I have a little bit of work to do.'

'Work? Aren't you meant to be resting?' He didn't want to tell her what to do but she needed to look after herself.

'I will but I told my client I'd help him find someone to take over my work for the next two weeks.'

'Will that be difficult?' He had no idea what being a freelance interpreter involved, but was always interested how others managed their businesses.

'Yes, interpreters are in high demand. The good ones especially. But I know some people and who to ask.'

'You should charge a finder's fee.'

'Charge my clients for replacing me? When I left them in the lurch?'

He shrugged. 'Yes, a commission.'

'But I'm the one cancelling the work.'

'Will the other interpreters charge as much as you?'

She shook her head.

'Then there you go.'

'No, you don't get it. I can't upset these people, they're my clients. I depend on them for work.'

'And they need you as much as you need them. Think about it. Are you going to freelance forever?'

She opened her mouth as if to say *Yes*, but the word didn't come out.

Interesting.

'What happens if you get sick again? Or can't travel for some reason? How will you earn a living then?'

Her mouth tightened. 'I'll figure out a way.'

'But you don't have a plan.'

Cara put her palms on the table and pushed herself up to standing with a slight groan. He'd gone too far. He was only trying to help but should have seen this was not the brand of assistance Cara would appreciate at all.

'Don't leave, please. I'm sorry if I was out of line. I only want—'

'To criticise my way of life?'

He shook his head. 'No, I'm only trying to help. I'm in awe of your life. It's something I could never do. I don't fully understand it, but I admire it.'

'You've done nothing but berate me since you arrived at the hospital.'

'For that I'm sorry. I feel a kind of responsibility towards you. I know it's misplaced, I know it isn't my right to feel that way, I am sorry for the way I spoke to you at the hospital.'

Cara gripped the wrought iron frame of the chair, but didn't sit.

Let her go. Things will be far easier that way. The tightness in his chest would dissipate for starters.

But he couldn't let her go. He wanted her close. He felt more at ease when he could actually see her. Which was strange. 'Please sit, eat something to get your strength back. I know you are more than capable of organising your affairs, but if there's anything I can do to help you with changing your arrangements, please let me know.'

She pressed her lips together in thought, but then sat again. He exhaled.

Cara rested one of her manicured fingers on the handle of her coffee cup, but didn't lift it. Her fingers were long and elegant. Unadorned by any jewellery.

'What's on *your* agenda for today?' she countered.

'Work.'

'I figured as much. What are you working on?'

He inhaled deeply through his nose. 'Much like every day.'

'Which is?'

He looked at her, but didn't speak. As a rule, Teo didn't speak much about his work to anyone who wasn't involved in it. You never knew what a person's motives were.

You think Cara's a spy?

Obviously not...

Probably not...

'So it's okay for you to offer me unsolicited advice about how to run my business but you won't even tell me what you do?'

'It's not very interesting.'

She scoffed. 'No, I'm sure being the CEO of a hugely successful tech company is deathly dull. Yes. I looked you up. Verdadero has come a long way since...'

Pablo.

She didn't say it.

Pablo.

'Since you were starting out.'

They had come a long way. Further than any of them could have imagined. A decade ago, their ambition was simply to design and build a game and find someone willing to buy it. They'd done more than that. Several hundred million people had been willing to buy it along with their subsequent games, making Verdadero's the most popular VR games in the world. Not only that, when they realised the existing engines would not be suitable for the games they wanted to create, Val and his team had developed a whole new one. Gaming architecture that they then licensed to thousands of other developers, meaning Verdadero was one of the most influential and powerful gaming companies in the world.

'You looked us up?'

'You gave me a card? Was I not meant to?'

'No. Of course, I mean...' What did he mean? The sight of Cara, sitting across from him in her practically diaphanous pyjamas was far more disconcerting than it should have been. He struggled to take his eyes off her, and when he studied her soft skin and sparkling eyes, he felt himself losing his grip on his surroundings.

'I'm staying in your house, of course I looked you up.'

And what else had she found out? Had she read about his father? About the scandal that had engulfed his family when he was a child?

As a child, Teo hadn't understood the significance of investment fraud, but as an adult he made sure he knew what it involved and, more importantly, how to avoid it. Along with all the other white-collar and corporate crimes it was possible to commit. No one would ever throw his father's crimes back in his face. And simply the idea that Cara might judge him for them made his shoulders tense.

'You know me,' he said.

She laughed. 'Hardly.'

And he knew she was right.

'Is it some big deal you can't talk about? What you're working on?'

Teo flinched.

'No. I mean, obviously I couldn't tell you if I was.'

'Don't you trust me?' The pain in her voice landed heavily in his chest.

'I don't trust anyone. It isn't personal.'

'I get not trusting others, believe me, but I just asked what you're doing today. I expected you'd say something along the lines of, "I'm going into the office," or "I have a few meetings." I'm not asking for all your passwords.'

He closed his eyes and grounded himself with some deep breaths. She was right. He should just be able to give a casual answer to a casual question. And yet...

'When it comes to business deals, I'm very cautious. I have to be. It's how we made the company into the success it is.'

She snorted. 'I'm hardly going to—'

'I don't for a moment think you would—'

'But?'

'People talk. It can happen unintentionally.'

'Okay, so you're working on a secret deal. Got it.'

As he finished speaking Alba returned to the courtyard.

Thank you, Alba for your impeccable timing. Remind me to give you a raise.

'Will Cara be joining you for dinner tomorrow evening?' Alba asked.

Teo dismissed any thought of giving Alba a raise.

Cara's eyes widened and her gaze flashed from Alba, back to him.

Damn. He still hadn't figured out what to do about the meal he was hosting with the film producers. He'd half contemplated moving the meeting to a nearby restaurant, but it was not his preference to do that as he wanted to discuss business. Val couldn't organise a business dinner to save the company.

Teo didn't want to disturb Cara either.

'I'm hosting a business dinner tomorrow evening. Just a small thing, there'll be four of us.'

'Five, counting Cara,' Alba added.

He really did need to have a word to his overeager housekeeper about minding her own business.

'You don't have to join us,' he said. 'I know you're recuperating.'

'You want me to hide in my room?'

Cara isn't a stranger.

'No. Of course not. I don't want you to feel pressure to join us, if you're tired, or if you simply don't want to.'

'Who'll be coming?'

Alba smiled to herself as she stepped away.

'Val. And two business associates.'

'Val? Oh! How is he?' Cara pressed her hand to her chest. 'I'd love to see him.'

Of course she would. There was no getting out of her coming to dinner now.

'What's the dinner for?'

'To discuss the project we're working on.'

'Ah, the secret project. No wonder you don't want me there.'

'It isn't that I don't want you there, but yes, it is a sensitive and confidential project.'

'It's okay, I don't have to come. But I can keep secrets. I'm an interpreter. If I told you half the deals I've worked on, I'd have to kill you. In fact, I'd wager I've been privy to far more top secret negotiations than you have.'

Shame welled up in him. Not only was Cara not a stranger, she was also a professional. Val would never forgive him if he made Cara stay in her room.

'I'll double-check with Val, but I'm sure it will be okay if you join us for dinner.' He stood. 'Please rest, your main priority is getting better. There's no need to decide now about tomorrow night.'

'I'd like to see Val very much. But I promise I'll leave you to your secret business dealings.'

Teo walked away with a heaviness coming down on him. Cara was a professional, she'd been at business and political meetings more important than this one, his head knew he could trust her.

Yet his heart? His heart wanted her to leave as soon as possible. Cara only brought trouble. And trouble was difficult to ignore when it sat in your courtyard wearing thin, soft pyjamas.

CHAPTER FOUR

CARA WATCHED TEO stride back into his house, tall, taut and annoyed about so many things.

He really didn't like her. And he really didn't want her there. And yet something about both those things sparked a challenge in her. *Why* didn't he like her? What had she ever done to him? Apart from loving his best friend, which as far as she was aware was not a capital offence, she hadn't done anything.

Whether it was logical or not she owed it to Pablo to make things right between her and Pablo's oldest friend. He'd hate the idea that the two of them were not getting along. The sounds and smells of Seville brought back so many memories of Pablo, of his big eyes, open demeanour, curiosity about the world and everything in it. Pablo adored Teo, so Teo couldn't be that bad, could he?

Back in her room, Cara turned to her backpack, still lying on the sofa where Teo had left it the day before. She might as well unpack and make herself comfortable. He wanted her to stay as long as she needed and maybe she'd been too rash to try to limit her stay. Especially now she knew what a beautiful house Teo lived in. And now she knew that his housekeeper was the lovely Alba. She felt she could relax here. She may be able to stay a while longer. The fact that she'd be annoying Teo was reason enough.

She unzipped her bag fully and placed her clothes neatly

in a pile on the sofa beside it. Her suits, her jeans, T-shirts and then the few dresses she owned. She settled on one of her black jersey dresses, the one that came to just above the knee. She wore it to professional functions and it would be just the thing for tomorrow night, which was a business dinner first and foremost.

Even if for her it was a reunion of sorts.

Val.

She placed her hand on her heart. That was why she'd agreed. Curiosity to see Val again. Val, at least, had always liked her. If only the hospital had been put through to Val in the first place.

Fate had a dark sense of humour. One she'd been on the wrong end of many times. Losing the only man she'd ever loved, watching both her parents slip away. Her half-brother's betrayal. She still grieved them, but at least now she knew her fate. She'd already lost everyone it was possible to lose and had no intention of ever letting someone into her heart again.

Yes, fate's sense of humour was very dark indeed.

And now it had sent her to Teo. Grumpy, disapproving, uptight Teo.

What happens if you get sick again? Or can't travel for some reason? How will you earn a living then?

If someone had asked her that even a week ago, she would have told them to mind their own business but the events of the last few days had made her feel exposed for the first time in years. The fact that she had little choice but to stay here with Teo in her current predicament only increased her feelings of vulnerability.

There was a knock at her door. Teo?

She opened the door with her heart in her throat. But it wasn't Teo. It was Alba.

'I've come to see if you would like me to do some washing for you.'

'I...' Her first instinct was to say no. She took care of herself, she always did, but her body ached and Alba seemed so eager. 'Thank you, that would be lovely.'

Cara walked to the sofa where her things lay spread out, but Alba waved her away. It usually felt odd to trust someone with her things and yet with Alba it didn't.

How could it be that she already trusted this woman and yet still struggled with Alba's boss, who she had known for much longer?

'How long have you worked for Teo?' Cara asked.

'Oh, about five years, since he moved into this house.'

Alba pointed to the black dress on the top of the pile. 'Are you wearing this tomorrow night?'

'Yes,' Cara said with a smile.

Alba draped the dress over her arm. 'I'll press it for you.'

'Thank you. And he's a good boss?'

'He's a wonderful boss. Yes.'

Of course an employee would say that. The place was probably bugged.

'Is he still here?'

'No, he's gone to his office. He probably won't be back until this evening. He works too hard. I can't remember the last time he stopped for a siesta.'

Cara shrugged. 'It's hard these days to take that time, I guess.' She was partial to a nap in the afternoon but modern work patterns made that next to impossible.

'Does he host many dinners here?'

'Sometimes, yes. Especially important ones.'

'And tomorrow night is important?'

'Oh yes, very.'

'Why?' Cara was aware she was pushing Alba too much but Teo had been so secretive about it all. It would help everyone if she had some clue what the meeting was about, if only so she didn't put her foot in it.

But Alba wasn't falling for it and somehow it made Cara only like her even more. 'I wish he had a hostess to help him with these things. He'd be so much happier if he had someone by his side.'

Cara doubted if anything or anyone could make Teo happy.

'Oh, Teo and I aren't...we're just...' *Friends* wasn't right. They were forced to be together due to a loyalty they owed to a long dead friend. They were friends once removed. 'Acquaintances.'

'You were friends with Pablo. Good friends,' Alba said. It wasn't a question.

'Yes.' Cara sat on the edge of the bed, the air knocked out of her as it was every time someone said his name. 'Did you know him?'

'Oh no. I didn't know Teo at all before I came to work for him, but I've heard all about Pablo.'

Cara hesitated before asking her next question. She longed to talk about Pablo. After leaving Seville she hadn't been in contact with anyone who knew him. At first that had been good, what she needed for healing. But as the years went by, she wasn't sure. She contemplated getting in touch with Pablo's parents, but she'd left it so many years since she'd last spoken to them that it didn't feel right. So, instead, Pablo was just a memory, something she kept locked away in her heart. Like her memories of her parents. No photos, no mementos. Nothing physical to carry around and weigh her down. Life was easier that way. Lighter.

But being back in Seville, the temptation to think about Pablo was too much.

'What have they told you?'

'Oh dear, you knew him, not I. I know he was remarkable. A gifted artist. And storyteller. I know his friends loved him dearly.'

Cara nodded.

That was all true. And it was enough.

Pablo also made her laugh, made her feel safe. He made her world whole. He made her see the world in a whole new, brighter light. She felt safe with him, loved. She hadn't felt that way since.

Cara cleared her throat. 'I don't know Teo as well. We haven't actually spoken since…well. You know. He lives here all alone?'

Alba smiled knowingly. Cara didn't care; she suspected that her knowledge of Teo's love life was the one confidence Alba might be willing to break.

'Yes, apart from Geraldo, my husband, and I.'

'No girlfriends?'

'Not to my knowledge and I know him pretty well.'

Alba washed his sheets, did his laundry. If anyone knew about Teo's love life, she would.

'Why not, do you think?'

Alba laughed now. 'Careful, you might cause me to breach my housekeeper privilege.'

'I'm sorry, I'm just… I'm curious. I don't understand him at all. The only thing I know is that he doesn't like me very much.'

It was a relief to say that out loud. It somehow lost some of its power.

Alba's brow furrowed. 'He'd hardly ask you to stay if he didn't like you.'

'He feels as though he owes it to Pablo. That's all.'

'Pish. That's not it at all. He could have just paid someone to look after you elsewhere if he didn't want you to stay. He's a very wealthy man.'

It was a good point. If Teo didn't like her, if he couldn't stand the sight of her, there were other options. He'd opened his home to her.

You don't need to understand him; you just need to accept his hospitality.

'You look tired, you should lie down. When you're hungry, let me know.'

Yes, rest was a good thing. Her body only seemed to have a few hours of energy to spare before she needed to be horizontal again. Alba closed the shutters and left Cara to rest. It was nice, she decided, letting someone take care of her for a change. It was nice being looked after. She was glad she had agreed to come.

Even though she'd never admit that to Teo. Not in a million years.

It was hours later when she woke. Alba had washed and ironed the entire contents of her backpack and everything was now hanging straight and pressed in the clean-smelling wardrobe. Even her backpack, her trusty, reliable friend, looked and smelt as though it had had a clean as well.

She mustn't let herself get used to this.

In a week or two she'd be back on the road doing her own laundry.

As though she had a camera in her room, Alba knocked on the bedroom door and came in with a tray of food, which she placed on the small table.

'How are you feeling?'

'Still tired, but maybe a little better.'

'Have some lunch. It's a bean soup I make for Geraldo when he's not well. There's more in the fridge anytime you want to help yourself. Along with some other things.'

Cara didn't think she'd ever have the opportunity to help herself to anything, given Alba's attentiveness.

She went through her emails as she ate and was relieved to see a message from a fellow interpreter, Leanne, agreeing to take on not only the job for Mr Westwood, but the work Cara had scheduled in Paris for the week after next.

Relieved, but still disappointed. Almost four weeks' worth

of work lost just like that. Teo's suggestion that she charge her client a finder's fee wasn't a totally foolish idea. Many people did do that. Agencies did that. But she wasn't an agency. She was a freelancer.

Yet, you found Leanne, you are vouching for her. Leanne is happy, the clients are happy. Cara had many years' experience. She had contacts all over the world in business, politics and law. And she knew many interpreters. She'd be ideally placed to set up her own agency.

No. Just the idea of what all that might involve overwhelmed her. She knew nothing about starting up a business. She closed her laptop and set it down on the bed next to her. Exhausted, she lay down. Even though it would only be for a short time, it was nice being looked after for a change. To feel safe. She was soon asleep again.

The following evening, Teo showered and changed into a fresh outfit. Trousers, white shirt and a jacket. No tie—he wanted to appear casual. He hadn't seen Cara since the morning prior, as she'd kept to her room, but Alba had informed him that Cara was feeling fine but resting. Alba had passed on the message from Teo that Val would love to see her at this evening's dinner.

He went downstairs, even though it was only eight thirty and the guests would not arrive until nine. Alba had set everything out and there was nothing left to do, which was a shame because if he had something to do with his hands, he was sure he'd feel much better. He had nothing to do but pace the living room.

He didn't usually feel like this before a business dinner. He'd done big deals before. Arguably bigger deals. And if this fell through there would be others.

It isn't the deal. You know it isn't.

It was the woman who had been staying in his guest room for the past few days.

And there she was, as though he had conjured her, standing in the doorway, barefoot, wearing a black dress that clung to her curves like a lover and showed off her hourglass figure to perfection.

'Good evening,' he said and realised his mouth had turned suddenly and unexpectedly dry.

'I'm sorry, I was looking for Alba.'

'She's preparing dinner. Can I help you with anything?'

'Um. I…'

'What is it?'

'It's my dress. There are buttons at the back I can't reach because I can't lift my arms.'

'Oh.' His heart leapt. That would be a better job for Alba but he said, 'I can help,' before he could think better of it.

'Are you sure?'

'Of course, it's not a problem.'

Of course it wasn't a problem. Why would standing right behind her and placing his hands next to the soft skin of Cara's neck and back be a problem?

Because somehow any activity that involved him being within a breath of Cara seemed to be a problem. Dry mouth. Trembling fingers. Completely irrational reactions.

She hates you, remember? She's Pablo's girlfriend, remember?

He walked slowly towards her, each step heavier than the next. She turned her back to him, tried to lift her hand to move her thick mane of hair out of the way but winced.

'I'm sorry but it hurts to lift my arms.'

'May I?'

She nodded and Teo braced himself before using one hand to push her hair to one side, thick, heavy and so much softer than seemed possible. He wanted to slide his fingers into it, feel the silkiness down the length of his fingers, but he shook the impulse away. He had to concentrate on the buttons, but looking down he was perplexed by the puzzle facing him. The dress was wide open, exposing all the creamy skin of Cara's back. A large lump formed in his stomach as his gaze travelled up and down her spine. This was far more than he'd anticipated.

It took him an age to actually locate the buttons hidden in the folds of the fabric. When he pulled the two halves of the back of the dress together, he saw that once the buttons were fastened they would create a large circle in the back of the dress. No. Not a circle. But a love heart against the smooth skin of her back. He gulped.

His fingers did not feel like his own and he struggled to grasp the delicate buttons without brushing his own fingers against the soft skin of Cara's neck. Her shoulders stiffened and she stood straighter, causing him to lose his grip on the small pearl-like buttons entirely. He began the Herculean task again, but the sight of her creamy skin was too distracting, the wisps of hair that kept falling back over his hands ticklish, the small divot behind her ear hypnotising. Not to mention her perfume, swirling around him like a spell. Three tiny buttons, three even smaller holes. He'd never been this close to her before, never touched her, but it shouldn't be this difficult. His fingers shouldn't feel so numb and useless. As he finally got the last button through, he sighed with relief.

They were the longest three buttons of his life.

It's just Cara, Pablo's out-of-reach girlfriend.

Ex-girlfriend? Was that the term? She wasn't a widow either.

Either way, it was a ridiculous reaction to be having. He didn't react like this to women as a rule. He usually managed to keep the distance he knew he had to, physically and emotionally. He never let himself get too close until he could be absolutely sure that he could trust them.

'How are you feeling?' he asked, praying she didn't ask the same question of him.

'I'm okay. I slept most of the day again.'

'Good.' She was on the mend and it was a relief.

Cara stepped back. Her feet were bare and he noticed a small tattoo on one of them that looked like a green sea-turtle. Apart from her feet, she was dressed and made up for an evening out. She was exquisite. His throat tightened. He swallowed but felt no relief. Tonight was happening, whether he was ready for it or not. He had to trust her. He at least had to let her in.

'I should probably explain what tonight is about,' he said.

'Only if you want to. I am very discreet. I am also happy to sign an NDA.'

'You are?'

'Of course, it's standard practice in my line of work.'

Teo felt the skin on his cheeks burn. He was being ridiculous. Cara was a professional, even though she was not here in a professional capacity, she still had a reputation to protect. One she could destroy if she leaked any details of tonight's meeting.

'That won't be necessary. I trust you.' The words felt strange on his tongue. Unfamiliar.

'Maybe you could start by telling me who your other guests this evening will be?'

'Val, of course. And two men interested in developing a project with us.'

'Another game?'

'No. Something different. A movie. They're from a Hollywood studio.'

Cara's eyes opened wider than he'd ever seen them. Gold. Definitely gold with hints of brown.

'Wow, that's huge.'

'It is.'

'Which game?'

'*Matador*.' Again his tongue was too big for his mouth. Would she recognise that as Pablo's game? Their first game?

She nodded but didn't speak. He had his answer.

'I didn't mean to be rude about you attending tonight. It is a business meeting first and foremost.'

She shook her head. 'It's okay.'

'It's a big deal for us. Not just financially, but because we want to make sure that the people we choose to make this movie with are the right people. That they'll respect the intent of the game, its essence.'

'Yes, of course. You want to make sure they do it right.'

Because of Pablo, he thought, though neither of them said that.

'I'd better finish getting ready,' she said.

'You already look beautiful.'

He was as shocked by his remark as she looked. He hadn't meant to think it, let alone say it. For the longest second, they both stood, frozen, staring at one another.

Her golden eyes were wide open and her jaw slack. Apparently, she couldn't believe what he'd said either. A giggle burst out of her. She almost sounded nervous. 'Shoes would be good though. I don't want them to think I'm a complete heathen.' She spun and left before he could respond. His heart still in his throat.

What had just happened?

He knew what. He knew that his main mission for this evening had changed. He should be focused on the deal, on the producers, but instead his main aim would be to keep his thoughts away from Cara. On the way her hair felt in his fingers. On the colour of her eyes. Gold? Brown? Amber? If he could manage to do that, the evening might not be a failure.

His last glimpse of Cara leaving the room, her long strawberry-blonde hair swishing against her back, hiding the large love heart in the back of her dress that he now knew was there. That no one else would know about but that he wouldn't be able to keep his thoughts away from.

That and the tattoo on her foot. The little turtle.

A turtle? Why would she mark her body permanently with a turtle?

For the first time since seeing her in the hospital Teo decided it wouldn't be such a bad thing if Cara cut her stay with him short.

You're going to push her out onto the street if she's not better?

Pablo wouldn't want that.

Yeah, but Pablo also wouldn't want Teo getting all tingly over a few buttons. Pablo wouldn't want Teo's mouth drying up at the sight of the skin on Cara's back and neck. Pablo, who had trusted him with his games and his legacy.

Pablo would probably tell Teo to put Cara up in a hotel if he knew about the unwanted and unbidden thoughts that were managing to creep their way into Teo's head. No one must know about those thoughts. Teo must only acknowledge them long enough to push them far, far away. Under lock and key.

CHAPTER FIVE

CARA'S NECK CONTINUED to tingle at the memory of Teo's fingertips brushing the sensitive skin on the nape of her neck. Rough against smooth, cool yet scorching. Light and feathery and discombobulating. Even after her recent abdominal surgery, she'd trembled with awareness when Teo had touched the small spot on the back of her neck. The warmth had fanned out down her spine.

He was anxious about this evening and the deal, that was all. She was looking forward to seeing Val again. No wonder the air around them was charged.

Back in her room, she slipped on a pair of black sandals and applied her signature red lipstick. Then she sat and waited until it was closer to nine and the time for the arrival of the guests. Enough time for doubt to creep in. Why had she agreed to this? Teo was right, she was better off staying in her room. She wasn't well, as shown by the fact her heart was racing at a simple touch from Teo. But she'd wanted to prove Teo wrong. To find out his secret. She'd wanted to get the better of him.

And now she knew his secret—and it was a good one. A movie deal! That was huge. For Teo and for Verdadero.

Matador.

That had been Pablo's game. And now it might become a movie. The emotions that rocked her were complex: pride that something Pablo had created had been so successful, sadness that he would never see it. Gratitude to Teo and Val for making it such a success. For honouring Pablo in such a way. Teo might have been unfriendly to her but he was still a good friend.

Mateo Ortiz, confusing as always.

When she returned to the living room, Teo was standing with a familiar-looking figure. His hair was shorter than the last time she'd seen him but she would know him anywhere.

Val.

'Cara! Cara! It's been too long. How are you? Can I hug you or are you too sore?'

She laughed. 'Gently, and yes.'

Val stepped towards her and she anticipated the sensation of his body touching hers. Would it scorch her like Teo's had? Val wrapped his arms around her and she fell easily into them. It was nice, comforting, but her heart rate remained steady.

Interesting.

'It's so lovely to see you,' she said, stepping back to look at him. 'You haven't changed one bit.'

'But you have. You are even more beautiful.'

They both laughed at his compliment. Things with Val had always been easy, even brotherly. No sparks. Confusion. No annoyance, only smiles. No dark looks like the one Teo was giving them now.

The two producers arrived not long after. One American, one British. Both older than Teo and Val, who were in their early thirties, but not significantly. They greeted Cara with a puzzled look but their faces brightened when she greeted them in English with her American accent. The Spaniards spoke good English, but speaking other languages was Cara's job, as was mediating between people so smoothly that no one even noticed her presence.

Teo introduced Cara as an old friend of his and Val's who was staying with him for a while. He didn't mention her operation, for which she was grateful. She was easily welcomed as part of their party.

While Teo got the two men drinks, Val took her aside and picked up her hand.

'I'm so sorry you're here under such circumstances, but it really is lovely to see you.'

'You too, Val, it's been too long. And that's been on me.'

'Nonsense, it's on all of us. We've been busy.'

'It was just easier…' She faltered and he squeezed her hand.

'I understand and I suppose you've been reminiscing about Pablo with Teo. I don't want to bring it all up again.'

She shook her head. 'No. We haven't talked about him much. Or, actually, at all.' Now she came to think about it, she'd been doing a lot of thinking about Pablo, but she'd never spoken his name and nor had Teo.

'He hasn't mentioned him. What? Not at all?'

Cara shook her head. 'No. Not directly.' Though his presence hung heavily over both of them.

Val pulled a face and then looked over to Teo, who was passing one man a beer and the other a wine. 'Interesting,' he said.

Though Cara didn't find it the least bit interesting. It was part of Teo being aloof and distant with her. They didn't share personal feelings with one another. That was how it was with them.

The evening went more smoothly than she'd anticipated, and she wondered what Teo had been concerned about. Teo and Val spoke some English and the American man knew some Spanish. If Cara hadn't been there the four of them would have managed, but she naturally fell into the role of a semi-formal interpreter and filled in all the gaps in the conversation. They spoke less about business than she had anticipated, but more about general topics, their lives, families and hobbies. It wasn't exactly like working, but not unlike it either.

Alba brought them their food, a large spread of tapas dishes that she laid out on the table in front of them, including garlicky shrimp, empanadas, pork belly *pintxos* and chorizo croquettes. Cara ate more than she had in days.

Alba whispered to Cara, 'I will be leaving now for the evening, Teo knows this, so don't even think about clearing this away, I will do it in the morning.' Then she placed her hand on Cara's shoulder and whispered, 'It's good to see you looking so well.'

Cara's heart warmed, Alba had been such a support. When she turned back to the table, she caught Teo looking at her and for once he wasn't frowning. His face was relaxed, almost wistful. The frown lines had vanished and his eyes were bright.

Cara's throat turned dry and she reached for the carafe that held the water but at the same instant Teo did as well. Their fingers brushed as they both pulled their hands sharply away. The spark she felt brought back the memory of the buttons and the heat zipping up and down her back. Judging by the way Teo blinked and flinched he felt it too.

'Sorry,' he said and smiled, before taking the carafe and filling her glass.

It was so lovely when he smiled. Which he hardly ever did at her.

When he smiled his whole demeanour brightened and she found it difficult to pull her eyes away from him.

He doesn't like you, he never has. You don't care how handsome he might be.

It might have been the mood or the glass of wine she allowed herself but Cara began to relax. She had made the right decision to join the men; it was a nice evening.

She had a long talk with the American man, Jerry, about

his family and then a chat with Val about all the things they had both been doing since they last saw one another. Val gave her the potted history of how they had built their business, from launching their first game, then deciding to develop their own gaming engine and branching out into VR hardware.

After Pablo's passing, they had used many of his story ideas but brought in others to help develop them. Val's technical brain and Teo's drive had made the company grow larger and larger. Cara could see from Teo's house that they were doing well, but she hadn't really turned her mind to how well they must have been doing until she heard Jerry describe Verdadero as 'The most impressive gaming software company in the world.'

She was so pleased for them. These men were only boys when she first met them, just starting out and fumbling around.

And then it came, the sadness that hit her in the chest and then radiated out into the rest of her.

Pablo should have been here too.

She was in the middle of a conversation with Jerry, so she couldn't just stand up and leave, but that was what she wanted to do. Get up and run back to her room and sob and sob.

She was no stranger to this feeling, it hit her at all sorts of inconvenient times and places, and it was not just about Pablo, but something would often bring her parents to mind and she would have to let the feelings sit where they were, breathe deeply and wait until they subsided, as she did now.

She'd become practised at letting the feelings not overwhelm her. As she did now.

She was barely thirty but had already dealt with a lifetime of grief. She refused to let it stop her; her parents and Pablo would have wanted her to live her life. So she got on with things, to honour them, but that didn't mean that sometimes it all didn't catch up with her. She could only be so strong. And she knew she'd never be strong enough to let anyone into her heart again. It was the only way she knew to cope.

Teo leant in her direction and whispered, 'How are you feeling?'

She looked at her watch rather than meet his eyes. He placed his hand over hers and her breath caught. It was so natural to touch him, it felt so right. And yet her thoughts still swirled with Pablo and she took her hand away.

'It's getting late,' he said. 'You should leave if you wish.'

Even though Teo had been subtle, the other men also looked at their watches and the evening began to wind down, with promises to finalise their dealings the next day.

It had been a success and she was glad to have helped. Whatever else Teo was, he was a good host and taking very good care of her.

As Val bid her good evening he asked, 'Will you stay for the ball?'

'What ball?' Cara looked from Val to Teo and back again.

'The tenth anniversary ball,' Val said as though it was obvious.

It was not the tenth anniversary of the business. She knew that. Or of Pablo's death. Besides that was hardly something to be celebrated.

'Of the Pablo Pascal Foundation,' Val said.

What? She'd never heard of a charity named after Pablo.

That's because you've been actively avoiding anything to do with Pablo or Seville. Because when she did it lead to the very feeling she was having now, tightness in her chest and pressure behind her eyes.

Going to such a ball felt like too much so she simply shook her head.

'That's a shame. It would have been so fitting to have you there.'

She caught the look that passed between Teo and Val: a sharp warning from Teo and a puzzled frown from Val.

What didn't she know?

Once everyone left the house and he had closed the door behind them, Teo turned to Cara and his breath caught. Again.

Hopefully this new reaction to her presence was just a temporary thing. *It'll disappear after a proper night's sleep. It's just the stress of the dinner and the deal. The strangeness of having someone else sleep under your roof.*

'I'm sorry it's so late and we kept you up.'

Cara smiled and his breath caught again. She looked bright and she was smiling at him.

It was as though something had unhooked in his shoulders. He'd trusted her, he'd let her in and not only had the sky not fallen but the evening had been a resounding success. It hardly made sense to him.

'It's fine. I've been sleeping so much the past few days. It was good to be around people.'

'Thank you for tonight you were…' Wonderful. Heavenly. Cara's presence had meant that the evening had gone even better than he'd hoped. It had been more of a relaxed social event than tense business deal. They had all got to know and understand one another a little more and that always made doing business so much easier. 'Great, really great. It was really good to have you join us.'

An understatement. He and Val would have plodded on with their adequate English, but Cara brought an easiness, a fluency to the whole evening that none of the men on their own could have managed. And she connected with the producers on a level that was far more personal than he and Val ever would have on their own.

He expected her to turn and leave for the night but instead she said, 'Tell me about the foundation.'

'It's a charity. Val and I set up after…' Under most circumstances he loved talking about the Pablo Pascal Foundation. But this was Cara. And this was a conversation topic that would lead to Pablo. The one thing he didn't want to speak about with her. Talking to Cara was tricky enough, but talking with her about Pablo? That just seemed too much. They both missed him so deeply, and yet their relationships with him had been so different, even contrary at times.

Cara and Pablo had loved one another, pure and simple. Teo's relationship with Pablo wasn't as simple, Pablo had been the first person outside Teo's family to welcome Teo after his father's disgrace. More than that, without Pablo's creations, Teo could not have built Verdadero. Without Pablo, Teo wouldn't be a success.

'That's wonderful. Is it a fundraising ball?'

'Not exactly. We don't tend to fundraise. It's an event we give to thank our patrons and the people who work with us.'

'How do you raise the money for the charity if you don't fundraise?' she asked.

'One-third of all the profits of the business go to the charity.'

She gasped. 'One-third? You donate one-third of your business to charity? But that must be…'

Billions of euros, yes.

His spine straightened. 'Yes, we do. Do you have a problem with that?'

'No! I'm just shocked. You give away a *third* of your earnings?'

He'd heard this before many times, especially when they were first starting out. Not long after Pablo's passing. Investors, banks, all thought they were mad to be doing that from the outset. *You're giving away a third of your money when you could be reinvesting it? Don't you realise how foolish that is?*

'I wouldn't put it like that. I've never considered that money to be mine.'

'Why not?'

He shook his head, but didn't have to speak.

She answered her own question. 'Because it's Pablo's. One-third is Pablo's share. Is that it?'

Teo looked down. He was so proud of the foundation. And he was tired of people doubting their decision to divert Pablo's share of the profits into the charity. He thought Cara, of all people, would agree with it. Bracing himself, he looked her in the eye. 'We have permission from Pablo's family. They're happy for us to be doing this.'

Cara clenched her fists together, as though she were angry about something.

And then he realised.

'If you think that you might be entitled to some of that money, then by all means, we can discuss the matter.'

'What on earth are you talking about?' She spoke slowly and his heart fell. She was furious.

'That's what you're getting at, isn't it? That it's Pablo's money and you're wondering if you're entitled to any of it?'

'You think I'm after the money?' she spat.

Okay, that was *not* what she meant.

Cara's face was white and he was torn between resolving this misunderstanding and getting her to sit down, lest she fell.

'How could you even think such a thing?' Cara's eyes were wide.

'You seemed angry.'

'I certainly am now!'

'Are you okay? Should you sit down?'

'Don't tell me to sit. How dare you! How dare you even think that I'd want Pablo's money.'

'I…ah…that's not… I mean…'

Be quiet, Teo. You're only making things worse. He wasn't usually lost for words but when it came to Cara the ground beneath him often felt unsteady.

'I'd only been seeing him for a little while.'

Cara clenched her fists even tighter.

She's not angry, she's just upset. Really upset.

'I didn't love him because of his money! I loved him because he was him.'

And finally, Teo understood.

He was the fool.

'I cannot believe you, Teo. After everything. After what you've seen of me in the past few days, do you honestly think I'm trying to get my hands on part of this business? Do you honestly think I'm trying to take a cent away from the charity? I was simply amazed that you would be so generous.'

Ah. That was it.

'You seemed so upset.'

'The only thing I'm upset about is that you seem to think I'm some sort of stealthy gold-digger. Does anything you've learned about me suggest the money means anything to me? Or possessions? I don't need anything I can't earn myself. And I certainly don't need money destined for a charity.' She blinked back tears. 'I think it's best if I find a hotel. It's too late now, but I'll leave first thing in the morning.'

No. She mustn't leave.

'Cara, you don't have to.'

'Clearly, I do. You've got some weird misconception in your head about who and what I am, yet the stupid thing, Teo, is that you don't know the first thing about me. You've never even tried to get to know me. You made your mind up about me from the start. I told myself I didn't care what you thought of me, that it didn't matter, but just now you were so far out of line I don't think I can stand to spend even one more night under the same roof as you.'

Cara turned and left the room. He knew he should stop her but he was rooted to the spot. Besides, if he spoke he was only bound to make things worse than they already were. Why couldn't he just speak to her like a normal person? Why did he always have to think the worst of other people? Especially Cara.

Teo lifted a cushion from the sofa, pressed it to his face and screamed.

He was a normal person, wasn't he? A normal, functioning human who had never had such difficulty with any other person. Why couldn't he just get his act together around Cara? She had never been the enemy.

He hated himself at that moment. Even for thinking she was after Pablo's share of the business, much less saying it out loud.

Because the crazy thing was, he didn't think that at all about her. Not for a second. Oh, how he wanted something to dislike about her, because then everything about this situation would be so much simpler. But the harder he looked for something to dislike about Cara, the more he liked her. And the worse he felt. He couldn't like her. He couldn't be attracted to her. He couldn't feel sparks when he touched her. He just couldn't.

The sound of a throat being cleared forced him to remove the pillow from his face.

Just when he thought the evening couldn't get any worse, it just had.

'Are you okay?' she asked, but there was an edge to her voice.

'I'm fine.'

'That's why you were screaming into a cushion.'

'I always do that when I'm happy.'

And the strangest thing happened. She laughed. Not just a scoff, but a loud, deep laugh, straight from her belly. Which she then clutched with her arms. 'Ouch, don't make me laugh. It still hurts.'

'I'm sorry,' he said.

'Teo, you're messed-up. You know that don't you?'

It wasn't a joke, she was serious. And so was he when he replied, 'I assure you I do. I am so sorry. There was no excuse for what I implied before. None at all. I apologise profusely. If you want to leave my house, I wouldn't blame you but please don't, I will leave myself. Alba can look after you for as long as you need and I'll go to a hotel. Please don't leave because I was unspeakably rude.'

She stood still and calm, staring at him, contemplating her next move.

'I just don't understand you,' she said.

'*I* don't understand me.'

'That's not an excuse, Teo. You're a grown man and clearly competent. Tonight, you were negotiating a multimillion-dollar movie deal. You're not a fool.'

But when it came to her it seemed as though he was.

'I don't know how to behave around you,' he admitted.

There it was honest. And maybe too revealing.

'Why on earth not?'

'Because of Pablo.'

There. He'd said it. Said his name. And surprisingly the earth hadn't opened up. 'Because Pablo is still such an important part of my life and you loved Pablo and because I loved Pablo and I...'

That was a sentence he couldn't finish because it would prove once and for all that he was as petty and mean as he was afraid he was. And she'd yell at him again.

Because Pablo was my friend and I shouldn't have these thoughts about you. I shouldn't be imagining what it is like to touch you. To kiss you...

No. His emotions were on him. He needed to deal with his feelings and it wasn't her fault.

She just nodded. 'Yes, I see. I miss him too. I always will.' She pressed her palm to her heart. 'But instead of being all weird around me, can't you just relax? I'm not going to fall apart when I speak about him, I promise. It was a long time ago.'

She was right; she had spoken to Val about Pablo several times this evening. He'd even heard her laughing when she did.

'You don't miss him?'

'Of course I do, but I deal with it. Yes, it's hard being back here, in Seville, but I'm honestly alright. We can talk about him, you know.'

She was more generous than she needed to be and he nodded.

'And besides, can you imagine what Pablo would say to you right now? "What on earth do you think you're doing, amigo?"'

Teo's lips twitched. Yes, that is exactly what Pablo would have said.

'And he'd probably have hit me on the back of the head.'

Cara laughed again and it vibrated in his chest. He wanted to hear the sound again, like his new favourite song.

'Yes, he would've. He'd be horrified to know that we aren't getting along. And sad.'

Teo's gut clenched. Pablo would be upset. Devastated.

He'd be more devastated if he knew that you are wondering what it would be like to step up to Cara now and slide your hand into her hair and tilt her lips towards yours.

'I promise to do better. I find it hard to talk about him. And having you here, it's…' He didn't finish the sentence. He couldn't, because by that point Cara was next to him, placing her hand on his forearm and his entire body froze. Waiting. For what might happen next.

'It's okay, we don't have to talk about him if you don't want to. But I'm not going to fall apart. I'm okay,' she said.

Needing to breathe, Teo stepped back and her hand fell.

'I thought you'd gone to bed.'

'I did, then I remembered the buttons.'

The blasted buttons. She turned her back and he steeled himself before he got close to her again. He placed his hand against the shock of her golden hair and moved it aside as slowly as he dared, letting the silky waves wash over his knuckles. His fingers shook as he slipped one button through the loop and then the next. He wasn't faking difficulty, he was trying as hard as he could not to make contact with her skin. He didn't need that kind of confusing torture. Not now. Not after everything that had just happened. Yet the buttons were so small, the loops they had to go through even smaller. Even with the best of intentions, his knuckles still scraped across the tender skin of her neck. He still felt the silkiness against his own skin, every pore on high alert.

As soon as he released the last button he said, 'I'm truly sorry about before. I miss him. And sometimes I don't know what to do. And seeing you again…it's brought a whole lot of things back up.' That wasn't a lie. It was perhaps the most honest thing he'd said to her since she'd arrived.

Cara turned and before he could step away, she lifted herself on her toes and brushed her lips against his cheek. The room spun and his skin burnt.

By the time he'd pulled himself together she was out of the room and he had to resist picking up the cushion a second time.

He didn't want Cara to leave in the morning, that wouldn't be right. He hardly knew Cara, and yet here she was staying in his house, learning all about his most secret business deals. He never trusted anyone this quickly.

If she was going to remain, then they had to establish some firmer ground rules for her stay. To protect him from saying—or doing—something he'd regret.

If only he knew what those rules could be.

CHAPTER SIX

THE AIR WAS already warm by the time Cara woke the next morning. Late nights were common in Spain, but even after going to bed she'd ruminated for ages over the argument with Teo.

The sight of Teo screaming into the cushion had done something to her. It had been so unexpected, so revealing and so utterly unlike the Teo she knew. He was exposed, vulnerable. Losing his carefully constructed control. She didn't know whether to laugh or hug him.

It was possible…just a little possible that she hadn't handled the conversation about Pablo well. Teo's assumption that she wanted Pablo's money had been incredibly rude and each time she thought about it she became angry all over again. But he had apologised profusely. And said some very strange and personal things.

I don't know how to behave around you.

She understood that he was still sad about Pablo, but that still didn't explain why he was so strange around her. Did he think she was made of glass and would crack at the slightest touch? It was ridiculous. Yes, being back in Seville had brought back memories of Pablo, but not all of them were sad. She'd had a wonderful time reminiscing with Val about happy times last night and he didn't think the subject of Pablo was as fraught as Teo seemed to.

She missed Pablo, she still felt his loss in her bones. But

she'd lived a third of her life since then. Now the loss of Pablo was wrapped up in her mind with the loss of her parents. Coming only three years after the death of her father, the two losses linked to her young adulthood. That made her the person she was.

People died. People left you. She wouldn't make the mistake of putting all her happiness on one person again, but that didn't mean she couldn't stand to say Pablo's name.

Despite Teo's promise that he would leave and stay in a hotel, she wondered if it might be best if she simply left to save them both another argument. She and Teo did not get along—she didn't much like him and for some reason or another he'd never liked her. It was clear to her now that they could never be friends.

Except…

There had been moments last night when they had been talking with his guests and looks had passed between them, small flashes of understanding. She knew what he was trying to say before he'd even said it. There had been times when the light had caught his eyes and they had warmed from black to a beautiful brown. When he'd smiled at her and her insides had turned inside out. Teo never smiled at her, yet he had at dinner.

And then there had been the buttons. Damn buttons. If she ever met the person who invented buttons that small she'd give them a piece of her mind. Teo had fumbled, and with each slip his fingers would brush against her bare neck, sending heat zipping down her spine.

What was that about? It was as though the air crackled around him. Like he produced his own electricity and she was a lightning rod.

Ridiculous. She was not attracted to Teo. Sure, he was good-looking, she could see that as well as anyone. And maybe she did find him attractive. But it wasn't the sort of feeling she could act on. That was simply out of the question. Besides, it wasn't as though he was interested in her. Far from it. So it wasn't attraction, but maybe appreciation. Entirely objective, of course.

Cara splashed water on her face, then ran her fingers through her hair. Movement was easier this morning somehow. Each day she felt noticeably better than the last. She'd only need to stay another day or so.

If she could handle being under the same roof as him, then Teo should be able to as well.

Cara opened the shutters and door but the courtyard was empty. The shutters on the other side were still closed as well. She walked back through her room and out to the entrance hall. Also quiet. Alba would no doubt be in the kitchen. She hoped Teo hadn't actually carried out his threat and left the house. His behaviour hadn't been perfect, but he didn't need to leave.

Yet there was no denying Teo was quite messed-up.

It's Pablo. *He loved Pablo, he misses him and having you here is more than he bargained for. Pablo is still a big part of Teo's life. More even than yours.*

Teo was brilliant, perhaps a little flawed, but who wasn't? Last night he had been charming, intelligent, great company. Everyone in the room had hung on every word he'd spoken. Val was engaging as well, but Teo was the one who held the room together.

There was noise in the kitchen. Alba would know if Teo had left, but it wasn't Alba standing at the coffee machine and swearing at it, it was Teo.

'Hey,' she said.

He spun. Teo looked stressed. For the first time since her arrival his hair wasn't brushed, but wild and sticking up in all directions. It suited him. If she had her way, he'd mess it up even more. She pressed her lips together and held back a smile.

A film of perspiration lay on his high forehead.

'What's up?'

'I can't get the coffee machine to work.'

'Where's Alba?'

He groaned. 'She's had to go away for a few days. Her daughter's unwell and she needs to help with her grandchildren.'

'Oh.'

'Geraldo's gone with her, so we're on our own.'

'Oh, well. If we needed a further sign that I should move to a hotel, this is it.'

He shook his head. 'No. I can manage.'

She raised an eyebrow. He did not look like a man who was managing.

'We're two grown-ups, surely we can look after ourselves for a day or two?' he said.

'Yet, you don't know how to make coffee.'

'I know how to make coffee. I just don't know how to work *this* machine. It's like you need a special degree for it.'

'Then use a pot.'

She opened a few cupboards and found a regular metal coffee-pot for brewing coffee on the stove. He stared at it.

'Do you know how to use this?' she asked.

'Of course.'

Then she laughed. 'Good, because I don't. I am utterly useless in a kitchen. I'm not sure I can even make toast.'

He stared at her. 'What?'

'I never learnt, I was never allowed to. Dad was determined that I wouldn't step into the role of housewife after my mother passed away, so he did the housework and cooking himself. Then I lived in halls at college and I've been on the road ever since.'

'But...'

'Look, can we just make a temporary truce? You won't criticise my way of life and I won't pick on you?'

'I wasn't going to criticise. Honestly. I'm the one who can't figure out his own coffee machine. I think since having Alba I've de-skilled somewhat.'

She could sympathise, not having developed many of the basic skills in the first place.

'Where do you keep your coffee grounds?'

He shrugged and she laughed again.

'Okay, this'll be fun.'

She went to the fridge, he went to the pantry. He produced an unopened pack of coffee, she produced an open one.

He took it from her with a smile.

'You should sit, I can do this,' he said.

'I'm fine.'

'Sit, please. Are you hungry?'

'If I say yes, will it be a problem?'

'Not at all, I can get us something.'

'Don't you have meetings today?'

'Not until later.'

Cara sat, partly because she was tired of arguing but mostly to see how Teo would manage getting her breakfast. He opened one cupboard after the next without finding what he was looking for. He wasn't even dressed, but wearing long pyjama pants and a white T-shirt. It took her one second to realise he wasn't wearing underwear under the pants, the thin fabric of which suggested a well-toned bottom. Her face warmed but she didn't look away.

Interesting.

Not simply the fact that Teo's butt was very watchable but also the fact that she wanted to watch. He was off guard and unguarded, with an especially firm bottom. She shouldn't think about what else was under that thin fabric, but she couldn't help herself.

Maybe what she felt was more than appreciation but a very unwelcome and awkward attraction. The realisation landed uncomfortably in her stomach.

No. She was hungry, that was all.

'I've never cooked in this kitchen. Alba made it her own.'

'I understand,' she said, getting a perverse pleasure in seeing Teo out of his depth. He always seemed together to the point of being uptight. Last night's argument the exception. She liked seeing Teo bemused. Flustered. Shaken.

She really was perverse.

Eventually Teo laid out a pot of fresh coffee, figs, peaches and strawberries, along with some bread and cheese on the large kitchen table, then sat with her. Cara sipped her coffee. It wasn't bad. Not as good as Alba's but she'd suffered through far worse.

'No wonder you couldn't find anything, this kitchen is enormous.'

Teo looked around as well as though he were also seeing it for the first time. The room had high ceilings like the rest of the house, marble bench tops, a big kitchen island. Like the rest of the house it had been renovated, though, she was glad to see, restored in a traditional style and not modernised into an impersonal default neutral. The walls were painted in pale blues and yellows and felt happy and calm all at once.

Teo could have ordered in some food, but he'd taken the time to make the breakfast himself and she was touched.

After he'd finished eating, Teo cleared his throat and said, with his serious face, 'I've been thinking. About your work. I know you've had to cancel your job here, and possibly others.'

She looked at her plate. 'Yes, I was due to be in Paris for a two-week job after this and I've had to find someone to take on that as well since I can't leave until after my check-up.'

'I understand.'

'I'm going to try to see if I can pick up some online work.'

He nodded. 'I also have an idea.'

Teo looked her straight in the eyes. His were not angry, but held a certain openness. Maybe even a spark of friendliness.

'It would be better for your health to stay in Seville for a few more weeks, until you're sure you've recovered.'

'What are you saying? That my business model is risky? My lifestyle unsustainable?'

'No, Cara, I wasn't going to say anything of the sort.'

'Though you think it.'

'I already told you, I don't think that at all. I don't have a problem with your way of life.'

No, but you have a problem with me. 'That's what you said, but…'

His brow creased with confusion. 'I really don't have an ulterior motive. You need a job for the next little while, but you need to stay in the vicinity of Seville. I'm suggesting you work for me.'

'Oh.'

'You can say no, but you were amazing last night. Doug and Jerry really liked you and you've established a rapport with them. If you could be available to help Val and I while we complete this deal, I would be grateful. You would be doing me a favour. And Val as well.'

She sat with the idea for a moment. Three days ago, she would have dismissed the idea outright, but since starting to see another side of Teo, she wasn't as hasty. The idea did have some merit.

'They leave today, but will be back in about a week. If you're well enough by then—'

'I'll be well enough.'

'Then you'll do it?'

She'd walked into that one. She hoped to be well enough;

the doctor had told her that after a week she might be fine to do light work if she felt up to it.

'Can I think about it?'

'Of course, and if you agree, I'll put you in touch with our contracts department. They will handle your pay and conditions and all those details. I won't need to be involved. While I would be happy to pay you anything you ask, I get the feeling you'd be more comfortable with the arrangement being made at arm's length from me.' His dark lips lifted into a soft smile. 'And, if you agree to stay, you will stay here. I owe it to Pablo to make sure you're okay.'

Far from being insensitive, if anything Teo was overly sensitive to everything surrounding her.

I don't know how to behave around you.

'Thank you, that's considerate. I will think about it.'

Teo stood. 'I'll be back at lunchtime to fix you something to eat.'

She laughed again. 'Teo, please, stay at the office. I'm not going to starve. Besides, Alba told me she'd left some soup in the fridge.'

His eye twitched. 'She did?'

He closed his eyes, breathed deeply and then exhaled, as though he was trying to calm himself.

But as though she could read his mind, she sensed what was wrong.

'Do you think Alba knew she wasn't going to be here?'

'I'm starting to think it might be a possibility.'

Though Cara couldn't think why Alba wouldn't tell them she may have to leave, by the way Teo was muttering under his breath he seemed to.

'Then I'll be back to prepare it for you.'

'You're working on a big deal, please just go.'

'And you won't leave?'

'Is that what you're worried about? That I'll sneak out?'

He didn't answer.

'I promise I won't leave.'

She couldn't leave now. Apart from anything, someone needed to look after him. Teo was nearly as hopeless in a kitchen as she was, which was saying something. Besides, watching him fumble around, trying to make her breakfast when he clearly didn't know what he was doing was...sweet. Yes, strangely sweet.

Teo was not the impenetrable force she'd always thought. Something about his vulnerability made her heart warm a little more to him.

He was offering her a way through her financial problems. This way there was a chance she might be able to gather enough money to engage the lawyers to fight for her house after all. She closed her eyes and drew in a deep breath. Her parents' house, with its wind-battered shingles and the flowering dogwood in the front yard.

But it wasn't just that.

Besides, Pablo had loved Teo.

She could at least try to like him as well.

Alba. She'd get a piece of his mind when she returned.

Are you going to demand evidence of her daughter's health? If Alba needed some time off, she just could have asked. Granted, it wasn't ideal timing given Cara was staying but he wouldn't have refused.

Now he came to think of it, there was a larger number of prepared meals in the fridge than usual. Alba had planned to leave, Teo was certain. Though he was less certain if Alba's reasons for leaving were as noble as she claimed.

Misguided matchmaking.

He ground his teeth together as he showered and dressed. Alba was barking up the wrong tree, so to speak. She'd put two and two together and ended up with ten. Pick your favourite idiom, Alba was wrong. He and Cara could barely have a conversation without arguing. They'd never be anything more than acquaintances, and now, temporary colleagues. Alba had been so excited by the idea of a woman coming to stay with them she'd jumped to all the wrong conclusions.

He should have predicted it. Of late her hints that it was time for him to find a girlfriend had gone from subtle to outright blatant. He forgave her because he knew she meant well, but this time?

This time he wasn't sure what he'd say to her. Cara wasn't just any other woman, and what he felt about her was far too complicated to be able to humour Alba and her machinations.

Teo went into the office, attended the meetings he had to in person and in the middle of the day came home, via the *panadería*, with some bread and cake.

The house was quiet when he returned, the shutters to Cara's room closed. He left the bread and a spread of food from the fridge out on the bench in the kitchen and went to his study.

The deal with the producers was in its early stages. Doug and Jerry were interested but there were so many other things to consider than just money. Things like who would write the script, what their vision for the film was. How much of a say Teo and Val would have in the production. How they intended to represent Pablo's game.

There was a knock at his open office door and he turned. Even though he knew it would be Cara, he was still not prepared. Not for the sight of her, certainly not for the way she walked confidently in, hips swinging and her riotous hair falling down around her shoulders. She was wearing the same thin pyjamas but now looked brighter somehow. There was more colour in her cheeks each time he saw her. A lump moved from his throat, swallowed into his chest and down into his gut. He couldn't even find the breath to say *Hello*.

'I've been thinking about your offer.'

And? Offering her work had seemed like the decent thing to do since he'd messed up the night before and wanted to make it up to her. And he hadn't lied when he'd told her that she would be an asset to him and Val; the producers had warmed to her and even though he and Val spoke conversational English, when it came to negotiating the terms of a detailed contract, it was far easier with an interpreter assisting.

He wasn't sure how he was going to feel about her answer either way.

'And I'd like to accept.'

'Great, I'm glad,' he said, but his body had grown tight.

It was the right thing to do, and yet, he didn't feel like himself when Cara was around and he wasn't sure how he was going to manage that over the next few weeks. Along with everything else. His body seemed to react to Cara's presence before his brain had a chance to engage, requiring him to constantly remind himself who she was and why these feelings were wrong. It was the last thing he needed right now.

'I'll let our contracts department know and they can get something drawn up for you.'

She nodded, stepped away from his desk, and he could see the moment she first focused on her surroundings. His office.

Her eyes first travelled behind him to the floor-to-ceiling glass doors that opened down onto the courtyard, then to her left into the wall of bookcases, holding books, awards, photographs. Then they moved across his desk to the many computer monitors and finally to the wall with a display of framed prints. She walked over to them, and he kicked himself for not showing her out once their business had concluded.

'These are...' Cara lifted an index finger to one, but didn't touch the print. She walked to the next and stared at it even closer. There was no point fibbing. It was immediately apparent to anyone who knew him. These were the sketches upon which their first game, *Matador*, had been based.

'Yes, they're Pablo's,' he said. His tongue suddenly too big for his mouth. She turned to him, eyes wide and glassy but he could see the thoughts ticking over.

'Of course,' she whispered and kept staring.

'They remind me of him,' he said, for no reason at all. Teo's voice cracked on 'him.'

She nodded. 'I know he was important to you.'

'Very. Without Pablo I wouldn't be here today. I owe him a great debt. I owe him everything.'

Cara continued to slowly study the prints, moving from one to the next. After a while, once his gut was well and truly tangled in tight knots, she turned. 'He's still at the centre of your world, isn't he?'

'I don't… I mean, maybe. Yes.' He didn't know what she was getting at.

'Isn't that hard? Don't you feel that it's holding you back?'

'I don't know what you mean, and no, of course it isn't hard. It's an honour to be able to develop and sell Pablo's creations.'

Cara studied him through narrowed, focused eyes, looking at him so closely she could probably see that his heart was pounding to get out of his ribcage.

'Why don't you like me? What did I do?' she asked.

He shook his head.

'I'm serious, don't dismiss me. If I'm going to work for you then I need to know what I'm doing that has offended you so much.'

'I've told you, nothing.'

'Then why did you never speak to me?'

Pablo had been so happy, so in love. Teo envied his ability to fall for someone—anyone—so early, so naturally. Teo had never been able to. He found it hard enough to open up to anyone, let alone take a plunge like falling in love. In love.

He wasn't even sure what that felt like. He couldn't imagine trusting someone to take that kind of plunge. It would be like diving into a pool with no idea how deep it was. Far too dangerous.

'Because I'm me.'

'Is that supposed to be a reason?' She didn't laugh, for which he was grateful, but she stood, steadfast, waiting for him to say more. Him feeling like she was taking a knife to his chest and peeling his skin away. Just by looking at him.

'I have a hard time talking to new people.' He didn't trust people easily, and he couldn't trust Cara.

No. You can't trust yourself.

He'd known that since the first day they had met, when Pablo had introduced them and she'd smiled and his first and only thought had been—*Damn.*

Because he could see so well, so clearly how Pablo could fall head over heels for this woman. Teo had stopped himself doing the very same thing just in time.

Cara and Pablo were together.

He and Cara could never be.

'Spare me the Mr Darcy line.'

'It's not a line.'

Truly. Teo had always been a happy child, but everything that had happened with his father had taught him a valuable lesson: *Don't trust anyone. Nothing is as it seems.*

'Can I make you dinner this evening? As a kind of apology?'

'You think cooking for me is a good way to apologise? Sounds like you want to hurt me even more.'

It took him a beat to realise she was kidding. Her face opened into a smile and he let his follow.

Cara sat and made a point of watching him as he fumbled around the kitchen. He wasn't sure where everything was and opened each cupboard more than once to locate things.

He was serving bread, cheese and some of the leftovers from the night before. It shouldn't have been this hard. But it was. And having Cara sit at the bench and watch him was not helping one bit.

'If you're looking for the plates, they're in that cupboard on the left.' She pointed.

He had been looking for the plates and she was right. He'd opened this cupboard not two minutes ago when he was trying to find the glasses.

It wasn't as though he didn't know his own kitchen at all, but having an audience, and an audience who was watching him as intently as Cara, was off-putting.

He should've felt better now she'd agreed to stay and work with him. Except now she was asking questions about why he didn't like her, why he'd always been so distant around her. His answers were pathetic—at best. He was a grown-up, a successful businessman, he should know how to behave around a woman. Even a woman he found as beguiling as Cara.

Maybe it was a good thing he didn't feel like himself when she was around. He felt uncertain, but also full of anticipation. He felt untethered, but also a sense of lightness.

'Did it not occur to you that you could've ordered something in?' she asked.

He closed his eyes as he remembered that restaurants and delivery people existed.

'This is much better for you,' he said.

'Perhaps. The pre-show is pretty entertaining.'

He ignored the insult. Their truce was too fresh.

'I'm trying to look after you and I promised you a housekeeper.'

'Things have changed. You don't have to do everything yourself.'

'I do though.'

'Why?'

'It's the way I am.' There was food here, healthy food, they didn't need to go out. Besides, he'd given her his word that he'd look after her. He wouldn't go back on that.

'But why?' she asked.

'Because it's the right thing to do. You understand that, don't you?'

She shook her head. 'I like to do things properly, I take care to get things right, but I forgive myself for not getting everything right. I'm human. And so are you.'

He shook his head again. It was so easy for some people. Other people. People whose father had not swindled others out of millions of euros. People who didn't have to constantly prove to the world that they were worthy of trust.

Other people.

Not him.

After they ate—a meal not as good as one of Alba's but not a bad effort—Cara tried to help him clean up but he was adamant she sit.

'I've been sitting all day. And lying down. I need to move around.'

'I'm sure packing a dishwasher is not what Dr Magdalena had in mind.'

'I'd love to go for a walk.'

He drew a breath but she waved him down. 'Not a long one. Just around the block. It's allowed,' she said.

'I'll come with you.'

'You don't have to.'

'And if I want to?'

He wasn't going to force his company on her but he'd feel much better if someone was with her. She looked brighter and seemed well but only five days ago she'd been on an operating table. Cara nodded and he exhaled.

Outside, the sun was just setting and the streetlights were coming on. The city wouldn't really start to come alive again until it was dark, when the streets, the cafés and bars would be buzzing with conversation, laughter and music. Right now, though, the air was humid but cooling. Cara walked slowly and he kept pace beside her.

'Where do your family live?' she asked.

'My family?'

'Yes, you know all about mine, I'm curious about yours. If we're going to be friends.'

Friends? Colleagues and acquaintances was fine. But friends? Friends was something different. But any more resistance would only lead to more questioning.

Besides, he didn't know all about Cara's family, only the outline. Only that she had no family or no family able or willing to come to her hospital bed in Seville. But not knowing things about Cara made everything else easier. Because the more he found out about her, the more he thought about her, and the more he thought about her...well...the more he wanted to know and the cycle began again.

'I have three younger siblings. They all live around here.'

'Santa Cruz?'

'No, but in Seville.'

'And your parents?'

She was circling the topic like a shark. She wasn't going to swim away until he gave her something. Her motives were not malicious; she was genuinely curious. For most people the question 'Tell me about your parents?' was benign.

But not for Teo.

This is Cara, you can trust her. Pablo did.

Hadn't Pablo told her about his father? No, he doubted it. Pablo knew how fiercely Teo protected his privacy. Pablo would've known that this was Teo's business and no one else's. And if Cara did know about his father, then she probably wouldn't be asking these questions. Teo looked out over the square and took a deep breath.

'When I was twelve, my father was charged with multiple counts of investment fraud. His case went to trial and it was very big news at the time because he cheated so many people out of so much money. He was eventually convicted and sent to prison. He died there six years ago now.'

Cara sucked in a deep breath. He didn't look at her, it was easier that way.

'I'm so sorry, I had no idea.'

'I don't talk about it and those close to me know that. I'm not surprised Pablo didn't tell you.'

Although part of him *was* surprised because he somehow assumed that Pablo had told Cara everything, though he wasn't sure why.

'I thought we had money, but it turns out everything we owned belonged to other people. We moved out of the house I grew up in and my mother moved me, my brother and my sisters into a rented apartment. She went back to work and supported us.'

'That's awful. Did she…'

'Did she know what he'd been doing?'

Cara nodded.

'No, she trusted my father and believed his business was legitimate, but then so many people did.'

He let her sit with that information for a while and waited for her to step further away from him, half expected her to make an excuse and leave his house. He wasn't anticipating her next words. 'There's nothing worse than trusting someone and having them let you down, is there?'

He shook his head. He couldn't think of anything at all.

'Thank you for telling me, Teo. I understand a little better now.'

She meant that as a good thing, but Teo only felt more

exposed. Cara placed her hand on his upper arm, her hand small, her touch light, yet his entire body was entirely under her control. He wanted to pull her to him, to hold her, fall into her touch. But that was impossible. Yet stepping back from her touch was too. The corners of her gorgeous pink mouth lifted into a smile and her eyes looked at him as if anticipating an answer.

He wanted to return her smile, answer the question she was asking, but he was too shaken by the intensity of the situation, of everything he'd just told her. He'd already revealed too much of himself to her and he had to stop there. Cara dropped her hand and stepped away.

When Teo finally focused back on his surroundings he saw they were back at his front door.

'I'm exhausted, I'm going to turn in, if that's okay,' she said.

He couldn't argue. They had only walked a single lap of the small square and he felt as though he'd run a marathon.

CHAPTER SEVEN

THEY FOLLOWED A similar pattern for the next few days. At breakfast, Cara would point to the cupboards, direct him where things belonged, while Teo prepared the meal and cleaned up again.

Together they found a nearby grocery store, and decided what to order and organised delivery. Teo would go to the office, returning in the afternoon to work at home. Cara rested, read when she had the energy, watched television when she didn't.

They would eat dinner together and then go for a walk around the square. Each evening, as she regained her strength, their walks became longer. Slow walks encouraged slow, thoughtful conversations. As the walks became longer, they fell into the habit of finding a bench partway through and watching the world go by. The people going to bars, those coming home again.

Cara told him about her home in Woods Hole, her childhood, idyllic, until her mother died. She didn't dwell on the loss of her parents at the ages of ten and seventeen, instead talked more about the last decade of her life, her life on the road. One evening, as they were sitting on the bench she had come to think of as theirs, Teo surprised her by saying, 'Despite what you might think I do envy you the freedom of your lifestyle.'

Where had that come from? Even after nearly a week of

living under the same roof, the workings of Teo's mind were still a mystery to her.

'Freedom?' she asked.

'You're not tied down anywhere. You go where you choose and when you choose. It must be kind of nice.'

'It's not all freedom. I can't do anything I want. I have to make a living. And it's not always easy. Sometimes I have a lot of work, sometimes I don't have enough.' And sometimes she got sick and couldn't work.

But she did feel a certain lightness, there was comfort in knowing that she'd never become so attached to something or someone that she could be hurt again. That was the true freedom. Yet, the pull Seville had over her was strange. Leaving this beautiful pink house would be hard.

'I know about your parents but what about siblings? Grandparents?' he asked.

'My grandparents are all gone, my father was older than my mother and I never knew his parents. My mother didn't have a great relationship with hers but they're gone now as well.'

'No siblings?'

Teo had told her all about his brother and sisters, four kids in one family was such a foreign concept to Cara, who may as well have been an only child.

'I have a half-brother, my father's son from a previous relationship, but we're not close.'

'Why not?'

'That's a long story, maybe one for another time.'

'You don't have time now?'

He was going to get the answer out of her eventually so she might as well tell him.

'His name is Liam. He's ten years older than I am. Even though he stayed with my dad, our father, pretty regularly, it was always better when he wasn't there.'

'Any particular reason?'

She shrugged. 'I think he resented my mother. And maybe me. I don't really know.'

When she was younger it had bothered her that Liam didn't like her, she'd craved the attention and affection of her older sibling but had never received it. She'd spent more time than she cared to admit wondering what she had done until she'd realised that whatever the reason was it was his business and his problem.

'When Dad died, it was awful. Liam was executor of his estate.'

'I have a horrible feeling where this is going.'

'Yeah, well, my father had a will, and it made Liam not just the executor but my guardian. As executor, Liam managed to get the house transferred into his name, with some money put in trust for me until I turned twenty-five.'

'And?'

'When I turned twenty-five, I found out the account was mostly empty. He argued that he'd used the money to support me, which wasn't true at all. My college tuition was paid out of the money, but otherwise I had to work to support myself. What was left was not even enough to engage lawyers to fight it.'

'Oh, Cara, I'm so sorry.' Teo bunched his fists. He was struggling to contain something inside him.

'I've been trying to get lawyers to fight it ever since. But given the complexities of the case they want a down payment before they take it on. Even if I did get a judgement in my favour, we don't know what he did with the money.'

'He gave you nothing?' Teo's face was red in the evening sun.

'Just my tuition, as I said. And anytime I asked for more he'd tell me how generous he'd been. How I needed to be more careful with money.'

Teo bit his lip.

He's angry.

Cara had been angry too. Once upon a time. Until she realised it wasn't helping her get on with her life.

'Your parents' house? Did you fight for it?'

'I'm going to try. But it's in his name, he lives there with his wife and children. The lawyers have told me not to get my hopes up.'

'That's outrageous.'

She was touched by Teo's anger, but at the same time, it was an anger that she had to try hard to keep under control herself. It was complicated.

'Yes and no. I don't like the idea of kicking my niece and nephew out of their home.'

'But it was your home too.'

She sighed. It was all she could do. There was no happy ending for everyone in this story.

'You deserve something.'

Again, she sighed. She wanted Liam to suffer, but she didn't want to hurt anyone else. She simply wanted her rightful share. A nest egg. Something to fall back on when she could no longer travel the world.

'One thing I want is my mother's jewellery. A few gold necklaces. A pearl ring. Some antique brooches.'

'And he won't give you those?'

She shook her head.

'But it isn't his property.'

She laughed. 'Try telling that to him and his wife. She had the nerve to wear the ring the last time I saw them.'

'When was that?'

'A few years ago, now. When I was still trying to maintain a relationship with his children.'

But no longer. It was too painful, too complicated.

'I see now,' Teo said.

'What?'

'Why you don't stay in one place.'

'I don't know where I would stay. I don't feel at home anywhere, or rather, I don't feel any special connection to any one place.' *Apart from my old home.* 'I wouldn't know where to choose.' She gave a nervous laugh. She'd just admitted something deeply personal to someone she wasn't even sure she could trust.

'Since we're sharing, I have a few questions for you. Why do you work so hard? What's it all for? You don't seem to have a partner. A family of your own. You work ridiculous hours, but for what? As far as I can tell, the thing that you care about the most is Pablo's charity.'

'That's not true,' he said.

She looked at him but didn't have to speak. Her raised eyebrow said everything she wanted to.

'The charity is important, I can't see how you could possibly find fault with that.'

She softened. 'Not a fault. I'm just wondering when you get a turn.'

'A turn at what?'

She laughed. 'Exactly, you're too busy putting everyone and everything else first you don't even realise you're a person too.'

'I do,' he said but confusion creased his face.

His father. He would have cast a dark shadow over Teo's childhood.

She didn't hate Teo. And she was beginning to wonder if he didn't really hate her.

Teo stood. It had become dark while they had been sitting on their bench. Cara braced herself to stand, still tender from the surgery, but before she stood Teo offered her his hand. She took it and she felt weightless as she rose. Her head spun.

'Thank you.' Her voice was far softer than she meant it

to be. She didn't drop his hand immediately and nor did he. Teo looked down at her, a shadow of a smile on his lips, his eyes no longer shuttered, but open and welcoming. She felt herself falling closer to him, wanting to feel more than just his hand, but his arms, his chest. All of him.

He let go of her and she had to stop herself from grabbing his hand again. She wanted the warmth, the sense of safety. She wanted to feel that hand on her arm, on her shoulder, on her back. Everywhere.

No. No. She mustn't confuse this new friendship with anything else. She was glad she and Teo had become friends, but these absurd longings she was having about Teo had to stop.

Two weeks after Cara's surgery, Alba was still away, looking after her daughter, whose illness seemed to be dragging on for quite a long time. Anytime Cara ventured to ask about Alba, Teo got annoyed, so she left the topic alone.

Far from being a prison sentence, her stay with Teo had flown by. It helped that Teo was starting to get her involved in the work as well; she'd sat in on a few video conferences with the producers and investors and before she knew it, she was due for her check-up with Dr Magdalena.

Teo offered to drive her but she knew he was due at the office at that time.

'I can catch a cab.'

'I'll get you a driver.'

She laughed, 'I am well.'

Teo sighed and disappeared into his office.

He returned moments later and held out his hand to her. 'Here.'

It was a key. Cara opened her hand and he dropped the silver key into her palm.

'What's this?'

'A key to the house. You'll need it to get back in when I'm

at work. I'm sorry, I should have thought about giving you one earlier.'

She shook her head and turned the key over and over in her hand. A key to the pink house. She couldn't remember the last time she'd held a key to something that wasn't a hotel room or short-term apartment.

No. She could.

The key to her house in Woods Hole. She'd tried to use it the last time she visited Liam, only to find that it no longer fit. Liam and Avril had changed the locks. She winced at the memory, then pushed it aside.

The doctor was happy with Cara's progress but told her to listen to her body. 'You can do anything. I mean, I wouldn't lift anything too heavy, but working, driving, stairs, exercise are all okay.'

'What sort of exercise?' She didn't want to have to stop her evening walks with Teo. They were one of the highlights of her day.

'Walking, running. Sex.'

'That wasn't what I meant... I haven't...' Cara gulped and Dr Magdalena smiled.

You haven't thought about that? Of course you've been thinking about it. You've been imagining Teo and what it would be like to make love to him. It's some sort of perverse want-what-you-can't-have thing because there's no way he'd want to sleep with you.

Although, her relationship with Teo *was* changing. They were getting closer, in a two-steps-forward, one-step-back dance. She'd catch him looking at her and he'd be smiling, but as soon as he realised he'd been caught, the shutters would go up again.

Or they'd be easily talking away about anything and everything under the sun and then he'd clam up. Make an excuse to leave.

Teo had been wrong, he did know how to behave around her, only not all of the time.

As she made her way back from the doctor's to the pink house, she wondered if that was really what she wanted. She would miss him when she left. She'd become used to being under the same roof with someone, comfortable living with him, happy spending time with him. Someone who knew how she liked her coffee in the morning.

Yet. It was all temporary.

Live in the moment.

It was advice she often had to give herself. *Live in the moment. You can't revisit the past and the future isn't yet written.*

After she was cleared by Dr Magdalena, Cara joined Teo with the work in earnest. She sat in on the negotiations with the producers, Val and Teo, and otherwise stayed not far from Teo's side, reminding him what had been said, mulling over ideas. Much of her usual work consisted of interpreting in detailed business negotiations, so it wasn't just Spanish and English she was proficient at. She often surprised herself how much legal and business knowledge she actually had. For the first few days everything went well, but negotiations became tense when they began discussing the prospect of sequels. Doug and Jerry had some ideas that did not match Val and Teo's wishes.

There was a lot of goodwill between the parties, but Teo must have sensed that they were in danger of the deal breaking down.

One afternoon in Teo's office at home, he said, 'I think we need another circuit breaker. Another social occasion, something informal,' he said.

'Another dinner? With me as well?' Cara asked.

'Of course, if you're amenable.'

'Why wouldn't I be?' This was her job now, he was paying her.

'Val thinks we should take them for a flamenco evening.' He sounded hesitant.

'I love flamenco. I've always wanted to learn.'

'Well, it could just be your lucky day.'

Cara was familiar with the sort of thing they had in mind, an evening of drinks and tapas, while they watched a performance, followed by a lesson and then more dancing with everyone. A quintessential Sevillian experience.

'You can think of something better?' she asked.

'No, that's the thing.' He frowned and she laughed.

'It's a great idea. Why the long face? You think it's too touristy? Too cliché?'

'No.'

'Then what?'

Teo looked at her, deeply. So intently she felt exposed.

'Me?' Teo the grump strikes again. Did he not want to go dancing with her?

He shrugged. 'In case you're not well enough.'

His concern was strange. And unnecessary.

'I'll be fine. And I'll take it easy, I promise.'

Teo frowned again. Would she ever figure him out?

Teo's assistant arranged it all. A night of flamenco, tapas and music.

Teo went into his office to do some other work. After reading her emails, referring some work to other interpreters, she was at a loose end.

In preparation for the evening, Cara flicked through her clothes, which were now hung neatly in her wardrobe. She didn't have anything that was exactly right for a flamenco lesson. Her dresses were either too businesslike or too casual.

It was another beautiful day, bright, but not too warm, with a gentle breeze. She liked that she was able to get out and about and move again. Apart from the occasional twinge she felt as good as she had a month ago. She caught a cab to Calle

Sierpes, a pedestrianised street in the heart of Seville. She wandered along the bustling street and associated laneways.

She'd been here only once before, with Pablo, but hadn't lingered long at the fashion stores. He'd been impatient to show her some nearby art galleries and she'd never come back.

Even though she didn't collect many things, Cara still loved wandering around the shopping districts and markets of each town she visited, seeing what was unique and what seemed to stay the same no matter what country she was in. She loved watching the people going busily about their days and the ones sitting at cafés, meeting people. All the activities of everyday life. She also loved clothes. Even though she didn't own many, she liked to choose each piece with care and with longevity in mind. Today was no different. Even though she knew she may not have much use for this dress beyond her stay in Seville, she enjoyed wandering from store to store looking at the clothes. In a boutique in a laneway off the main street she tried on several dresses, each lovelier than the last.

In the end it came down to two dresses: a dark green one that felt safe and conservative, and a bright red one that would ensure she stood out. The red dress had a full skirt, not as decadent or frilly as a traditional flamenco dress, but it would be something that would swish around her legs, in the way she'd always admired. It was beautiful, but what if she wasn't in the mood to stand out?

'The second one is half price. You should get both,' the sales assistant said, and at that moment Cara had no good argument against it. So she did.

Cara met the men, who had come directly from the office, at the restaurant. Four pairs of eyes turned to her when she entered and the air cracked with tension, but they smiled as one when they saw her. All except Teo, whose smile almost immediately turned down into a frown when their eyes met.

Cara's heart dropped and her eyes cast down at her outfit. She'd worked up the courage to wear the red dress and didn't know what was wrong. She thought she looked good, but Teo's reaction suggested otherwise.

Val slid up to her. 'Wow, you look beautiful.'

Cara's gaze flicked past Val to Teo, whose eyes now looked thunderous.

'Don't worry about him, it's been a tense afternoon. We're counting on you to save this deal,' Val said.

'Me?' she spluttered.

Val laughed, 'I'm kidding, but we do need a break from money talk. If the deal falls through it will be because Doug is too tight and Teo is too stubborn. You know how he is when it comes to Pablo.'

'Touchy? Illogical?'

'And then some.'

'Why is he like that?' she asked.

'You tell me.' Val shrugged.

'I don't know, I hardly know him. You're his best friend.'

'He thinks he owes Pablo a huge debt. One he can never possibly repay. Most of it is in his head.'

This was as much as Cara herself had surmised over the past few weeks, Teo thought that he owed most of his success to Pablo and the game he created. As brilliant as Pablo had been and as much as she'd loved him, Cara knew that Verdadero's success was as much due to the grit and energy Teo had invested in the business as Pablo's contribution.

'But why? You and Teo have been responsible for Verdadero over the past ten years.'

'It isn't just the business. Pablo was his friend when no one else was. And now, well, I think he feels conflicted.'

'Conflicted? Why? Because of the movie deal?'

Val shook his head. 'No. Not that.'

She couldn't ask Val to explain because the sound of clapping hands signalled the beginning of the evening.

Their instructors were Santiago and Luiza and they began the evening by performing the flamenco with one another. Drinks were served, and the small crowd began to relax before Luiza said, 'Okay, now it's time for you all to try.'

Doug caught Cara's eye but then he looked behind her and slipped away.

Cara turned her head. Teo was on his feet, holding his hand out to her.

'Wonderful! You make a lovely couple. And there are plenty of women here for you, gentleman,' Luiza said.

Luiza lead Doug away to find another partner and Cara and Teo faced one another.

'Will you be okay?' Teo asked, his face no longer stormy but soft with concern.

'I'm fine, Teo, really.' She slipped her hand into his and there was that familiar electricity again. Why did his body feel different to other people's? Her body would recognise his touch blindfolded. The heat alone would give him away.

The couples were directed to drop hands and stand two feet from one another. Fortunately, the dance involved very few instances when the couples had to touch, but consisted mostly of complicated steps and hand movements, so there was little opportunity for further sparks to crackle between them.

Teo, as a native Sevillian, was naturally familiar with the movements. Val, who had at one point considered being a professional dancer, was proficient. Cara had to listen carefully to the instructions.

'You will learn the Sevillanas, Seville's own flamenco. It is about passion, sadness. Fire, darkness.' Santiago spoke forcefully. 'But also, elegance, strength. Intensity.'

Cara wasn't sure how she could possibly be all those things at once. While remembering all the steps.

Santiago explained the footwork, stomps, heel strikes, pointing of the toes. Luiza then followed by demonstrating the *braceo* and the *floreo*—the circular movement of the torso and the way to move the hands, wrists and fingers in circular motions.

They went through the steps so quickly Cara couldn't keep up.

'Can you repeat that please?' Cara asked but Santiago shook his head.

'Don't worry so much about the steps. You must use your body to show your emotions.'

'But I don't know what to do,' she said.

'Show your emotions! Show your passion!'

Cara sighed. If only it were that easy. If only passion was something she could share with the people in this room. With her dance partner, Teo.

Teo stepped towards her and whispered, 'The flamenco is as much about improvisation as the steps. Don't worry. Let the music and the beat inspire you.'

Cara closed her eyes, focused on the guitar and the doleful singing of the *cantor* and did as she was told, relaxed into the music. Her body found the beat.

She lifted her arms as she had seen Luiza do, stood tall, trying to appear more confident than she felt, and turned her body from the hips as Luiza was doing.

Teo stomped his feet, Cara followed his lead, though not his movements, the movements for men and women were subtly different. Once they were both moving, she tried to worry less about whether the movements were technically correct. No one else was watching her, they were all too focused on their own dance. The only person watching her was Teo.

She followed Teo, but also made things up, rolled her hands in the *floreo* movement, mixed the steps she remembered from Santiago and Luiza's quick lesson together.

But she didn't relax. She and Teo reflected one another's moves. They didn't touch one another, but the sustained eye contact they were required to hold with one another was enough to make her heart pound. Teo's expression was no longer annoyed, but unfamiliar. His lids slightly lowered, he looked almost drowsy, yet his body was anything but. Lithe, flexible. Strong. Cara was almost too breathless to move and slowed her pace to almost a standstill. But once she did, Teo began to move around her in a circle, stomping his feet, and she had to watch him up close. The line of perspiration across his forehead, the concentration on his face. The flash of light in his eyes when he looked down at her. She could feel his steps through the floorboards and they made her knees weak.

'Relax, *señora*,' Luiza said as she passed. 'Don't worry about the steps, just surrender to the passion.'

Teo was getting closer and closer to her. The air around her shifted with his movements, his attention entirely focused on her. Single-minded. She felt as if she might melt. Would he get so close that he touched her, and where would he touch her if he did? Her hand? Her arm? Her cheek? Or would he press his hip against hers? Which did she want more? These were the thoughts filling Cara's mind when she should have been learning where to put her arms and when to stomp her feet. She had to start moving too, she couldn't just stand there. She lifted her leg and brought her shoe down hard. She expected to feel floorboards but instead felt something solid. Warm. And alive. Teo. He winced but said nothing.

'Oh, Teo, I'm sorry, I…'

'It's fine. I'm wearing boots.'

'We don't have to do this, you know?'

'I know, but you want to learn, don't you?'

She did. She'd always imagined doing this dance. And he knew it. Since she'd stupidly announced her ambition earlier that day.

'Then we'll learn. Let's focus.' He dragged his index finger along her jaw-line, dictating the direction her gaze should take, directly to his eyes. He might as well have scorched her. The sparks travelled from his fingertip, over her skin, down her neck and straight to her core. Like two magnets, they held each other's eyes for a long moment, heavy, caught. *Frozen* wasn't the right word, since it felt as though steam was coming off both their bodies.

'Perfect,' murmured a voice. Santiago's. 'Now, use your hands.'

This was their cue to lift their hands to the sides of one another's faces. Not touching, just framing each other and not losing eye contact.

Her stomach, insides, everything had flipped over so many times she wasn't sure she'd ever be able to gather it all up and walk away. When Dr Magdalena had given clearance for physical activity, she doubted she'd had this in mind. Being totally and utterly consumed doing the flamenco with a very handsome man. Not to mention hot, hard and literally smouldering. A walk around the square was one thing. Heck, even sex with most of the men she'd been with hadn't left her this breathless. The air was warm and the smell of her perfume and Teo's aftershave wrapped around them both.

She could hardly breathe. Teo, she now saw, was holding his breath as well.

That's why he's so tense. He feels the same awkwardness as you.

His brown eyes appeared black in the half-light, and half hidden by his lids. He was a ridiculously handsome man. She'd known this, in theory. But this dance, this position they were now in was no longer theoretical. His arm was around her. He was holding her body closely, protectively against the side of his, looking down at her, his hand hovered next to her face and his eyes watching her. Not just watching her but *seeing* her.

Oh my.

No wonder this dance was so famous. It wasn't the clapping or guitar or the castanets. It was this. This look. Holding one another's gazes in an unbroken grip. It was intimate, vulnerable. You couldn't do this dance properly without getting a glimpse into your partner's soul.

And that's what she glimpsed now. Even as she sensed him moving her, leading her gently for the next few steps, she was unaware of her feet, practically floating. All she was aware of was his heartbeat. Thumping in time with hers. Forget the stomping or the clapping, as loud as it was, all she felt was his heart.

He, in turn, was showing her his soul. She'd never seen this look in his eyes before, so exposed, so vulnerable. Like she could read his emotions. It was like Santiago had said—passion. Fire. And most of all, intensity.

How could he act like he disliked her and yet look at her like this? She felt herself melting, clinging to him to stay upright. But the harder she held on to him, the stronger he held her.

He's not going to let you fall. He's not going to let you down.

Yet what was his deal? Obviously, he had a saviour complex, he was determined to help those in need. And did that include her? Was she just one of his projects? He was looking after her to repay the debt he thought he owed to Pablo. Maybe, maybe that was it.

From somewhere she heard Luiza's voice. 'Remember the Sevillanas is special. You may improvise. You are telling each other a story.'

'A story?' Cara whispered.

'We all tell ourselves stories. Some of them are true, and some of them are just in our head,' Teo replied.

He was right. She told herself all kinds of stories. How her parents had really loved her, how they would be horrified to know what Liam had done. How what had happened to Pablo wasn't her fault. She didn't always believe these stories.

'What stories do you tell yourself?' she whispered.

He was silent for so long she thought he was ignoring her question but then he said, 'That I must do everything right, that I'm being judged. I owe my success to Pablo and I don't know how I can ever repay him.'

He'd never been so honest with her and her heart went out to him. *No*, she wanted to say, *it isn't. You don't owe Pablo anything. People care for you, no matter what*, but her mouth was too dry. Teo was standing close to her, his scent wrapping its way through her body and her thoughts. It was too much and she closed her eyes.

She realised with surprise that she already knew Teo's story, that he had to fix everything and everyone. That his worst nightmare would be doing something wrong. Being like his father. Her heart cracked a little for the boy finding out that his father was not the person he thought he was, for the man now holding her in his arms who was too scared to live his authentic life in case he made some sort of mistake. She wanted to slide her hand up his arm, to cradle his face in her palm and tell him that everything would be okay, that he was not his father. That he had proven himself to be a good man many times over.

'What story do you tell yourself?' he asked.

Without opening her eyes she whispered, 'That everyone I love leaves, that the only person I can depend on is myself.'

Oh. The honesty of those words made her eyes pop open. She'd never admitted that to herself, much less to anyone else. The only thing she saw were Teo's brown eyes, looking back at her. The rest of the cantina had disappeared.

Brown and unguarded for once, they reflected her own

back at her. His eyes were wide with a question, but a question she couldn't identify, much less answer.

The click of fingers near her face brought them both back to the present.

'*Señora*, I can see you are keen to get to the part where you declare your love, but first you have to learn the steps. It is not just love, but struggle and intensity and first must come darkness.'

Cara's face burnt at the suggestion she might declare her love to anyone, let alone Teo.

Love! That was ridiculous. What she felt for Teo was attraction and confusion. Love had nothing to do with it.

From the moment Cara arrived at the cantina things started going wrong. Or right. Teo wasn't sure. She wore a dress of flaming flamenco red, with a long full skirt and a neckline that scooped down low to the swell of her breasts. Breasts he'd been trying to believe were not as beautiful as he'd imagined but now could no longer deny. Her hair was half up, fastened with a clip and showing her face and smile but also flowing around her shoulders. His decision to offer to dance with Cara had been instinctual, rather than fully thought out, for which he'd suffered the consequences.

There had been moments, though, as they had danced, when he'd forgotten that he wasn't meant to be enjoying himself and had surrendered himself to it. Surrendered himself to the music. And to Cara.

And nothing bad had happened. Neither of them had exploded or cracked, even though there had been times when he'd felt he might self-combust.

It was the most erotic moment in his life and they had both been fully clothed. Only their gazes were connecting. Holding one another's. Not letting go.

Cara was Pablo's girlfriend and off-limits. And it wasn't

just that. Cara was a free spirit; she made the entire world her home. Even if she did settle anywhere, what was to say she would choose Seville? No. Letting himself get close to her would only bring trouble that he couldn't afford.

After the dance lesson was over, they sat together at their small table, finishing their drinks. Val was regaling Doug and Jerry with stories of his time as a dancer, and from the point of view of rebuilding their business relationships, the evening had been a success.

But with Cara? With Cara his chest felt hot and tight. And wrong.

And when she stifled a yawn, he felt even worse. She was exhausted, still recovering from her surgery and she should get home. He stood.

Cara looked up at him and understood. She nodded.

They wished everyone a good evening and Teo ordered a car.

Neither of them spoke on the drive home. Was she also thinking of the dance? Of their conversation? Of the stories they told other people. Of the stories they told themselves, or could they leave all of that on the dance floor? He hoped so.

Once he'd let her into the house he looked at the staircase that led to his room, then turned back to Cara to wish her good-night.

'I think they all had a good time,' she said.

But did you? he wanted to ask.

What stories do you tell yourself?

That she had to keep moving. But she was so wrong. If only she could see that her grief was holding her back from all the happiness that she deserved.

'You don't have to keep running, you know,' he said. So much for leaving their conversation in the cantina where it belonged.

'What?' Confusion blinked over her face before she said, 'Oh, about before. I'm not.'

'You move around so much, it's almost like you're a fugitive.'

She laughed. 'Fugitives don't dress like this,' she said, and pointed to her red dress.

His mouth turned dry and he had to swallow hard. She was right. Everyone in the bar had noticed Cara and her dress.

'I've told you, I'm running towards the world. To new opportunities. Besides, you're one to talk.'

'What on earth do you mean?'

'Your games.'

He didn't play games. Especially not with women. He was always transparent about his intentions. Overly so. 'What games? I don't play games.'

'The games you *make*. And you do play them, you told me. It is literally your work.'

'It's hardly all my work. My work is the business to sell the games.'

'So, you sell games to allow people to slip into another world.'

'And why is that wrong? Books, movies, they all do the same thing.'

'You've just accused me of running away from something and yet I don't think you're living your best or fullest life either.'

'My life is great.' It was. His business was a success; his reputation was solid. He was a strong, contributing member of society. What was she talking about?

She shook her head. '*I can't get anything wrong. I can't make a mistake.* Sound familiar? That you will never repay Pablo. Teo, you don't owe Pablo anything.'

Stupid dance, stupid telling each other a story! What had

possessed him? Either of them to open up to one another like that.

She stamped her foot, as she'd been taught earlier that evening, and he warmed at the memory of her stomping on his foot.

Cara let out an exasperated groan.

'What's the matter?' he asked.

'You. You're the matter, Teo.'

He shook his head. 'What about me?'

'I can't figure you out.'

'Cara, I'm an open book.' Especially after tonight. She'd practically seen into his soul.

She pulled back. 'No, you see, you're not at all. Not one little bit. I don't understand you at all.'

'I'm so simple, really.' It wasn't a lie. Not totally. Most of the time he was honest.

Except when it comes to Cara you're not. You're not even honest with yourself about how you feel. Because if you were honest you'd step up to her and take her in your arms.

His gut twisted. He wanted desperately to tell her the truth, but he could never be honest with her about that.

'You work so hard, yet you rarely enjoy it,' she said.

'That's not true.'

'Yes, it is true. And don't even get me started on the charity.'

'What is wrong with the charity?' His exasperation made him breathless.

Or maybe that was just Cara, now standing so close to him he could see the freckles covering her nose.

'Nothing, nothing at all. It's wonderful. That's the point.'

'What? How is that the point?' he wondered.

'Because it's too generous.'

'How can something be too generous?'

'When you look after everyone else, but not yourself. And

I don't understand why you asked me to stay, especially when you never liked me.'

'Now, that's not true at all. We talked about that.' They had dealt with this. As best as he could anyway. And besides, he did like her. Didn't she see that?

'Isn't it? You're hot and cold with me and it's confusing and not nice.'

He looked down, away from her eyes. Shame washed through him. She was right. Each time he let himself relax around her, he'd remember all the reasons he shouldn't and would pull away again.

You aren't honest with her.

If there was a button to press to make him feel about an inch tall, she'd found it. And pushed it. He had been distant with her, even stern. But he'd never wanted to be dishonest.

'Cara—' his voice cracked '—I don't mean to be.'

'Then why? Why are you like this?'

'You're going to make me say it?'

'Yes, because I don't understand.'

He couldn't say the words. Not even to himself. Instead, he stepped up to her, slid his hand into hers and squeezed. Would that small gesture be enough for her to understand?

She entwined her fingers in his but still looked up at him helplessly. How couldn't she understand? Surely it was written across his face. Surely everything about this evening had told her how he felt? The dance, the embrace? The breathless conversation they had shared in the middle of the dance floor. Surely she saw it in everything he said, everything he did.

No.

You've kept it so well hidden, most of all from yourself.

Cara moved closer. She squeezed his hand back and pressed her body softly again his. Her perfume swirled in the air around him like a spell drawing them together.

She tilted her face upwards, eyes wide open and pleading. 'Teo.' That was all she said. Not a question demanding an answer. Just his name. Her fingers squeezed his. His heart stopped.

Something shifted inside him.

You have to tell her the truth. How much you really want her.

He leant down in increments; she didn't pull away. She waited, watched him, until he could stand it no more, and closed his eyes and touched his mouth to hers. Her lips were warm and tasted sweet, floral, fragrant, just like her. The relief he felt when she opened her mouth and kissed him back was incendiary.

Cara lifted her hands to the back of his neck and grasped the hair at the nape. He slid his own hand into her hair, as he'd imagined doing more times than he cared to admit, and tilted her head so their mouths fit perfectly together. He'd longed to do this for an eternity, to take her, touch her, bury himself in her embrace. To have her do the same. To hear her sighs, to taste her mouth. To feel her heartbeat against his.

Her lips parted, her mouth and arms wide open and he fell into them, explored, tasted, wondered and lost himself completely. It was like coming home, desire fired up inside him.

More. He wanted more. He wanted all of it.

He wanted to scoop her up, carry her to his bed and kiss every inch of her. To feel her on him, to hear the sounds of her pleasure. To give himself to her. To lose himself completely.

'Teo, don't stop. Don't.' She tugged at his shirt and her fingers were like ice as they touched the burning flesh of his stomach.

No.

This is wrong.

He pulled back, gasped for breath.

Cara was also panting, but the look on her face was more than he could bare to see. She'd just accused him of being hot and cold, and in an effort to prove her wrong he'd proven her right.

'Cara, that was...too much.'

'Too much?'

'And that's why we can't go any further. I'm sorry.'

'You're sorry for kissing me or sorry we can't go any further?'

Cara knew words. She believed in using them correctly. There was no hiding his thought behind imprecise language.

'Maybe both. You and I...it would be too messy.'

Cara blinked. Reconfiguring. Processing. But was she relieved or upset? He couldn't tell. At that moment he barely knew his name.

She sniffed, nodded. 'You think we should forget that ever happened?'

He exhaled. 'I think that would be best.'

'Well, let me know how you go with that.' She raised an eyebrow, grasped his gaze in her golden eyes and held it captive in a long, challenging look.

His heart fell and he struggled for a retort. He struggled simply for breath.

'Good night.' Cara shrugged, turned and went down the corridor to her room.

Teo watched her go. Head held high, her hips swaying confidently.

He closed his eyes and rubbed them hard with the palms of his hands, but his head still swirled with memories of that kiss. Heck, he could still taste her, his arms still tingled with the sensation of holding her.

She was right. Him forget that kiss?

Never.

CHAPTER EIGHT

IT WAS MORNING and Cara's body was on fire. And not because during the time she'd been in Seville the spring had become summer, but because her core temperature had not dropped since last night. At some point she'd tossed off the bedsheets which were now just a tangled heap at the foot of her bed. Dancing with Teo had been hard enough, but the kiss.

That kiss! That kiss had ignited something inside her that was still burning out of control hours later. Teo had stepped up to her, waited almost long enough for her to beg and then pulled her into his arms. She wasn't sure exactly how or why, detail was lost to her, gone the way of her inhibitions and common sense, leaving only desire in its place. Desire that was still pulsating through her veins the next morning.

Desire mixed with a decent amount of resentment. How could he have lit that fire, fanned the flames and then stepped away with barely a shrug? Telling her that more was impossible. Leaving her flailing around unsatisfied. Scorched.

She was proud of her parting shot to Teo. Surprised she'd had it in her, when her bones felt like liquid and she wasn't sure which way was up.

More is impossible.

The one thing she wasn't, though, was confused. Last night explained Teo's strange behaviour. He was definitely attracted to her. No one with lukewarm feelings kissed like that. But

Teo, hopelessly uptight Teo, he was the one who was confused. Not Cara.

A shower. She needed a shower. To start with.

But the cold water didn't tame the heat that still smouldered inside her.

A holiday fling was probably exactly what she needed. In fact, hadn't Dr Magdalena hinted as much when she'd told Cara to relax and enjoy Seville? When she'd told her that *all* activities were safe?

She had doctor's orders. Maybe she should tell Teo that? He was overly concerned with her well-being after all.

Cara smirked to herself and slipped a dress over her head.

She might not have had many relationships, but she did have a few friends with benefits scattered around the globe. People who she knew and had built up trust with, but who were only after the same thing she was: safe sex with a trusted person who didn't want anything more. Someone who shared her desire to remain unattached.

And Teo, surprisingly, seemed to fit this bill. In the past few weeks she had come to trust him, she was attracted to him and, like her, he was a loner. He wasn't looking for a relationship any more than she was. Cara looked at herself in the mirror. Yes, a fling was exactly what she needed. Let's face it. It was probably exactly what Teo needed as well.

Now the idea had occurred to her, it consumed her. She loved a challenge. And Teo was a challenge like no other. She smiled even more. This was going to be fun.

It was never because I didn't like you.

Teo did like her, but at some point, he must have determined that she was off-limits.

Because of Pablo? That had to be it. He was overly preoccupied with Pablo and with doing the right thing by him. Not to mention his almost pathological need to never make mistakes.

And yet, what she wanted from Teo was nothing like what she'd had with Pablo. She and Pablo had both been so young, so full of optimism and romance and hope.

But she and Teo were two flawed souls who were very physically compatible and in the same city for a while. Teo didn't need to worry that she would want anything more. That wasn't what she was after and not what she was offering.

Looking at her reflection, Cara changed her mind and took off her dress and bra. She wrapped her robe around herself, pulled it tight, then loosened the tie so it hung just a little too loose. This was her game and she could make up the rules.

'Good morning,' she announced brightly, entering the kitchen. Teo looked up and smiled, but the tightness around his lips indicated it was forced. Seeing him struggle only made her smile more.

Teo might pride himself on not playing games but she was happy to. She had set him a challenge to forget the kiss and what fun was a challenge if it was easy? She was going to make sure that while she was around, he never forgot that he'd been the one to wrap her in his arms and take her mouth.

'Did you sleep well?' she asked.

Teo had already made a pot of coffee and laid the table with bread, cheeses and fruit. She picked up a strawberry, opened her mouth for a beat too long before slowly placing the strawberry in it. Teo's jaw tensed, just for an instant, and he looked away.

She sat next to him at the large kitchen table, not across from him as she'd been accustomed to. He acknowledged her new position but shifted his chair slightly in the opposite direction. She held back a laugh.

'What's on today?' she asked.

'Nothing with the producers, they have meetings with their studio, so you can have a day off.'

That was good and bad. Days off were great, but a day away from Teo stewing about last night?

'Great!' she said cheerfully. 'I might have an explore, revisit some old haunts.'

At that comment, Teo's face darkened. They both knew what old haunts entailed. Rule one of the game must be 'Don't mention Pablo.'

'Good idea.' Teo's voice was gruff.

'But I think both of us have exhausted our cooking abilities. Why don't I let you take me out for dinner?'

She saw the expressions change on Teo's face, from aloofness to mild amusement, to something resembling relief? Or dread? Like a man who knew his fate.

'I know just the place.' Teo stood and pushed in his chair.

'I'm looking forward to it.' She smiled as sweetly as she could, though her intentions were anything but.

Let me know how you go with forgetting that kiss.

'Don't work too hard,' she yelled after him as he left the kitchen.

Yes. The dance was on. And this time she would take the lead.

Cara caught a cab back to the shopping district. She spent the morning going from shop to shop to find just the right dress, and after a few stores she found it. A deep, luscious pink. The colour of her lips.

It had a halter neckline, and dipped low into her chest. It showed exactly the right amount of skin, but the straps wouldn't cover any bra she owned, so she'd need new lingerie. The shop assistant pointed her in the direction of a lingerie boutique where she couldn't decide which bra looked best so she bought both and matching underwear. And her black sandals wouldn't do the dress justice so she needed shoes as well and the shop assistant in the lingerie shop sent her in the direction of a shoe shop.

Shopping was fun, dressing up was too. She couldn't take all these clothes with her, but maybe she could ship some back to Hannah's place in New Jersey.

Because what if the lawyers had good news for her? What if she *could* get her house back? Then she'd have a whole wardrobe to store these dresses.

One day.

Maybe one day.

Oh no.

Cara stood at the bottom of the staircase waiting for him. She clutched a small bag and he tried to focus his attention on that, or on her fingers, because looking anywhere else made his heart thump in his throat and his brain short-circuit.

She was wearing a dress he hadn't seen on her before.

Pink. Dark, dusty pink. A colour that suggested all kinds of other places. It's shape too, every one of her curves were hinted at, all the places he shouldn't want to kiss.

Let me know how you go with that.

He focused on her shoes, strappy sandals with a small heel. An even darker pink.

Heaven help him.

He'd chosen a bar not far from the house. It was a small neighbourhood place that he didn't visit often enough. Only when they arrived did he curse his choice. It was small, intimate, bathed in the glow of candles and small lamps that made the light in the room a warm, cosy red.

He had to stop it. So she was wearing pink? So what if she looked gorgeous? He'd seen beautiful women in pink before and hadn't reacted like this. He had to pull himself together, he was stronger than this.

She deferred to him to order, 'You know what's good,' and

she passed him her menu but their hands brushed in the process, sending the usual sparks skipping up his arm.

They ordered spicy potatoes, mushroom rice, and chickpea and chorizo stew. Half a carafe of wine only. They didn't need to linger over this meal. Not when she seemed determined to break him.

The bar had velvet bench seats, red and as seductive as the lighting. He foolishly chose one in the corner, thinking it would give them more space, but when a couple arrived at a neighbouring table Cara smiled at them before scooting along on the bench seat until she was a breath away, their thighs close enough to bump with each movement.

She's playing with you. That's what she's doing. The casual touches, her tongue lingering on her lips. All of it.

Let me know how you go with that.

She was challenging him, but why? She had loved Pablo, surely any sort of physical relationship with Teo should be off-limits to her as much as it was to him.

'Do you still think about Pablo?' he asked. It was one of those questions that sounded better in his head.

Cara sucked in a quick breath. They had spoken occasionally about Pablo, his name was no longer taboo, yet he realised too late that his question sounded like an accusation and he hadn't meant it as that. He'd only meant to remind her of the person who stood between them and the flirtatious game she was playing.

'I'm sorry,' he added quickly. 'That came out completely wrong. What I meant was...'

She shook her head. 'It's okay, I get it. You're wondering how I'm feeling about him, how I feel about being in Seville. If I miss him.'

Teo nodded, grateful for her generous interpretation of his question.

'We've hardly talked about him,' she continued. 'And that's

partly my fault. I can see he's still such a big part of your life, with the business, the charity. It's like he lives alongside you. That's been hard.'

'I didn't mean to suggest that you don't think about him.'

'But that's the thing, sometimes I don't. And it's not because I don't love him, or because I don't miss him, but because I couldn't function if I thought about him every day. The same goes for my parents.'

His chest, which had been tight with tension, now cracked. Oh, Cara. To have suffered so much loss by the time she was barely in her twenties. No one deserved that, least of all someone as lovely as she. And now he'd inconsiderately brought it all up.

'I love them, I miss them every day, but I can't let it bury me. I have to let it sit with me, walk alongside me. I'm sorry if that sounds heartless, but it's how I cope.'

He shook his head. 'It's not heartless. It's practical.'

She snorted. 'It's necessary. Circumstance has left me on my own, with only myself to rely on, so I have to get on with it. I don't have the luxury of letting it consume me, so instead I live with it. None of them would want me to spend my whole life mourning them.'

'You've never met anyone else?' Teo anticipated the answer to this question but asked it, nonetheless.

With a single shake of her head she said, 'That's another thing entirely. Being able to manage my grief is one thing, but setting myself up for more is entirely another.'

So their loss still affected her, just not in the ways he'd assumed.

He had managed his grief differently, pouring himself into Verdadero, and then the foundation. His grief for Pablo impacted his life every day, but it wasn't a problem.

Isn't it? Isn't it holding you back? Stopping you from ac-

knowledging your needs? Your desires? The beautiful woman sitting in front of you now?

With a single shake of his head he said, 'Grief is very personal, individual. I'm sorry again if I suggested yours was nothing.'

'It's okay, really. You loved Pablo too, you've dedicated your life to his memory. It's admirable, it really is. I don't know how you did it, living with him every day, with his ideas, his characters.'

The food and wine arrived like a saviour and he mulled over her words. She wasn't looking for a relationship. At least not to fall in love. That confession made him relax somewhat. She was only flirting with him, having fun. He didn't need to be so suspicious or jumpy. They compared notes as they ate, and for a moment all mention of Pablo was forgotten. As they finished eating, he reached for the carafe to pour them another glass of wine just as Cara happened to reach for it as well. She held up her hands to surrender the drink to him and he poured them both a glass.

'Thank you,' she said with a smile. As if to push the point home, she placed her hand on his thigh. Any moment now and he'd be a goner.

'You loved Pablo, didn't you?'

'Of course. I don't see what that's got to do with anything.'

Teo looked down at her hand on his knee.

She continued. 'I did love him. I was very young when we met, and it was a long time ago. Do you understand what I'm saying?'

Teo shook his head.

'I haven't been a nun.'

Oh.

His mouth went dry. His throat as well. The painful tightness spread through his entire body.

'Are you shocked? Upset?' she asked.

'No, of course not,' he spluttered.

'You look shocked.'

'I'm only shocked that you are *telling* me. Your private life is truly none of my business.'

She shrugged so subtly he doubted anyone else would've noticed.

'I feel you should know.'

But why? He'd never ask a woman about her sex life. Why was it any of his business? Because he'd be upset on Pablo's behalf?

He thought carefully about his next words, and even whether her statement needed a response. He eventually settled on 'I'm sure Pablo would've wanted you to move on.'

'Precisely,' she said.

Yet that still didn't explain why she was telling him.

'But you still look disapproving.'

'I don't disapprove at all. I'm happy for you,' he said, but the way he clenched his jaw and swallowed with an audible gulp suggested otherwise. How could he possibly tell her that it wasn't anything to do with Pablo, but the thought of her being with other men made every cell in his body freeze and sicken.

She laughed. 'You're a terrible actor.'

'I know,' he said. 'Anything artistic or creative, you can forget it.' He didn't have Pablo's talents or his family's. He was boring, traditional.

Cara narrowed her eyes and grinned.

'I haven't fallen in love with anyone else. It's not as though I've settled down with anyone. It's just sex,' she said.

'I'm not judging. I'm happy for you. Truly.' He pushed his empty wine glass away.

'I'm not going to break, Teo,' she whispered.

'I know, you're recovered. The doctor said.'

'Not my body. Teo, I'm talking about my heart. You aren't going to hurt me.'

And he understood. Cara was proposing something physical, not emotional. Her heart wasn't on the line. Their hearts, their feelings would be safe.

And as the warmth of her palm spread into his leg and worked its inevitable way up into his body, he believed her.

They could do this. They could give in to their attraction and it wouldn't be wrong.

That's what she was saying. He looked back at her and caught the sparkle in her eyes.

'Are you sure?'

She smiled. 'Yes, I'm sure. I like you, Teo, but as you said last night, you and I would be too messy. But I'm not talking about a romance, I'm talking about a fling. Between two consenting adults. While I'm in Seville.'

The smile that spread across her face showed her she knew what his answer was going to be before he'd even admitted it to himself.

How could he refuse her anything? Her heart wasn't in danger and so nor would his be. With that certainty, he did something he'd been longing to for days. He picked up her hand and rested it on his. Then he stoked her fingers with his thumb, looked at her pink nails, studied the softness of her skin. He turned her hand over and did the same with her palm, getting to know every crease, every pore, her hand slack in his, as she watched him study her, let him take his time. Then his quest went higher, up her arm, its silky-smooth skin, and to the bare skin of her shoulder that had been driving him to distraction all night. Her shoulder, the fading tan line, the single freckle proving she was real and not a flawless icon. Cara sighed, softly, silently but he saw her shoulders fall and felt her sweet breath mingle with his.

He pressed his lips to her shoulder, then worked a trail of kisses up over her collarbone and her neck until he tasted the spot behind her ear. Cara moaned and he was inspired. Teo pressed his lips against hers, carefully, thoughtfully, measuring each caress, like he was putting the final touches to a piece of art. Suddenly, she lifted her hand to the side of his head, turned his mouth to hers and took him completely. The force of her desire knocked the air from his lungs and the hesitation from his mind.

When he lost sensation in his knees and pulled her tighter, Cara, sensibly, pulled her mouth half an inch from his and sighed. 'I think we should move somewhere more comfortable, don't you?'

Teo went to the bar and paid and Cara followed, not moving more than a foot from his side.

CHAPTER NINE

CARA'S BODY WAS aflame by the time they got back to Teo's, pressed flush to the front door of the pink house. He fumbled with the key, but she couldn't keep her hands off him, ran them over his shoulders down his arms, which only caused him to fumble the key even more. Even once the key was in the lock, his shaking hand still struggled to turn it as she pressed kisses to the back of his neck and slid her fingers through his dark hair. Excitement, relief and joy all fought for supremacy in her body. When the door finally pushed open, they fell inside and she sought out the full attention of his mouth. She was vaguely aware of him kicking the front door closed, only slightly noticing the noise it made. All her focus, all her attention was on him, his lips, his hands and her own struggle to undo the buttons to free his body from his clothes.

'My room,' she mumbled because the stairs at that point seemed like an insurmountable hurdle for her legs, which were rapidly losing tension. Teo didn't argue, keeping his lips on hers as they shuffled down the corridor to her room.

Her mattress when they reached it was like a relief. An oasis. His shirt came away easily from his shoulders and back, his trousers, even more so. But he struggled with her dress. The straps were tied in a tight knot at the back 'This dress will be the death of me,' he said.

Wait until he sees what's underneath it, she thought.

She knew the moment that he had from the groan that left

his body. The lacey bra, the almost non-existent underwear she had purchased to wear underneath it. Worth every penny.

'I'm never going to be able to forget these, you do know that don't you?' he mumbled as he kissed her neck.

'That may or may not have been my intention,' she said as she glided her hand down his underpants, feeling her way around him, exploring what lay beneath them. Before sliding her hand inside as she watched the look on his face change from excitement to the grimace of delighted pain. Cara ran her hands over the light hair on his hard chest, brought her lips to his nipples and felt his body tense beneath them.

She loved every moment of this, every sound, every touch, every ripple of desire that shivered through her and took her breath further and further away.

She caught her breath as Teo fumbled for his wallet and protection. She took the packet from his trembling hands and ripped it open herself. Her fingers were only slightly less shaky than his and as she sheathed him, he covered her hands with his, stilling her. Holding his breath.

'Cara, are you sure?'

'Oh, Teo, I've never been more certain.' Cara pulled Teo's strong frame back to her, every part of her aching, needy and ready. He kissed her lips, her neck, her breasts and she cried out.

'Now, Teo, please now.'

When they finally came together, Teo sucked in a deep breath and held it as she began to move. Finally, finally she felt him relax and move with her, rubbing and pressing all the right places, saw the concentration on his beautiful face.

He broke seconds after her.

He's been waiting. He's been waiting for you.

Cara rested her head on Teo's chest. With his arm around her, holding her snuggly against him she felt herself drifting back to sleep. He really did make the most relaxing pillow.

Teo shifted and placed a kiss against her forehead. 'I hate to do this but we need to get up. I've got meetings.'

Teo rolled away and she groaned. He was too comfortable; this bed was her new favourite place. Teo pulled on a pair of shorts.

'I'm going to be as quick as I can and then I'll come right back here, I promise.'

Cara rolled onto her back and groaned again. She had to get up too; she'd agreed to take the producers to the Alcázar. It wasn't an official part of her job but she'd offered to play tour guide to help keep the relationship on track while Teo and Val attended to some of their other work. She'd been pleased when Doug and Jerry had accepted. But that had been yesterday. Before.

Before she knew what making love with Teo would actually be like. And to be fair, if she'd known all along the kind of things Teo could do with his fingers, let alone his tongue, she wouldn't have been able to get anything done for the past few weeks.

'I need coffee. If you're going to keep me up all night, you'll need to make me a bucket.'

'Oh, I kept you up? I thought it was the other way around.'

He knelt back on the bed and kissed her again. Cara opened her mouth and deepened the kiss, pulling him back to her, but he pulled away.

She groaned again but this time, got up. If Teo was leaving the room there was no point in her staying. She grabbed her robe and pulled it around herself, with nothing underneath. Maybe she could convince him to come back to bed for a short while before they left for the day. But after some coffee. Her body was relaxed, boneless and happier than it had been in months, still buzzing from the places he'd taken her last night.

Cara followed Teo out of the bedroom, still thinking about

the things he'd done. She wasn't paying attention and walked straight into the kitchen before she realised that the room already smelt of coffee. And eggs. And fresh bread.

The table was already laid and Alba was at the sink.

'Oh, good morning to you both.' She smiled at Teo, who was wearing only shorts and Cara in an open robe that she hastily tied up. Alba didn't look the slightest bit surprised, let alone shocked.

'We got back late last night. I thought I messaged you, but I realised this morning the message didn't go through,' she explained.

'It's...' Teo stumbled over his words and the back of his neck reddened.

'This looks great, thank you,' Cara said, sitting down. 'How's your daughter? I was getting very worried. She's been ill for *so* long.'

'She's so much better, thank you. But then it went through the entire house.'

Cara wondered if they'd ever know the truth. Teo certainly thought Alba's absence was contrived. It was a remarkable coincidence that she'd returned this morning. Of all mornings.

'I hope you've been managing. I'm so sorry to leave while you were staying.'

'We've been managing just fine,' Teo said, sitting with his back straight, his jaw tight. He had changed back to old Teo. Proper Teo. Professional Teo.

'Yes, we've muddled through,' Cara confirmed, trying not to laugh.

Alba left the kitchen, not even bothering to hide her own smirk.

Cara put her hand on Teo's strong thigh and squeezed. 'Relax, it's just Alba. Besides, I bet she knew this was going to happen before we did.' Cara pointed back and forth between them.

Teo leant closer. 'You know it's not that simple,' he said.

'I know.' She did know what he meant. It was Teo's pathological need for propriety. 'But it also isn't complicated either. This, you and me, we both know it's just for while I'm here. We know it's nothing more than that. Who cares what she thinks?'

'It isn't Alba I'm worried about. You're my employee.'

'Only until the deal with the producers is finished.'

'But still.' Teo buttered his bread with such force he ripped a hole in it.

'You don't want anyone to know? About us?' She asked the question but was then, suddenly, afraid of the answer.

'I want to shout it from the rooftops,' he whispered. 'But I don't think that would do either of our professional reputations any favours if our personal relationship became common knowledge.'

Cara blushed at the thought of Teo standing on his roof yelling to the entire square and the streets beyond that they had made love. She'd think more about that image later, but he was right. Discretion was not a bad idea. He wasn't suggesting secrecy, just caution.

'Yes, that's true.' The chances of any of her clients finding out about her relationship with Teo were slim but not non-existent, and she preferred to keep her professional and personal lives as separate as possible.

'And it wouldn't look great for the deal if the producers found out,' Teo said.

'I doubt it would be fatal, but it wouldn't be a good look.'

She understood exactly where he was coming from, maintaining professional appearances was important to her but even more so to Teo.

'So you're okay if we keep this, not secret, but discreet?' he asked.

'Yes, that's sensible. And besides, what is there to tell?

We're two consenting adults enjoying one another's company. It's no one else's business.' She leant towards him and kissed his cheek. Her entire body sighed. He smelt and tasted wonderful. She wanted to devour him and not the breakfast laid carefully out in front of them.

She kissed him again.

After a cursory glance at the door, he kissed her back.

It was an effort to pull away from the kiss. Even more of an effort to get ready for the day. Teo kept pulling away to go up to his room to change but Cara nudged him back with kisses and caresses and talk about what she was planning to do to him when they got home that afternoon. They compromised, agreeing to another kiss once they were both dressed. And again once they were out the door.

By the time they arrived at the Verdadero offices in the luxury Torre Sevilla building, they were both late for their appointments. And she didn't care at all. She should care, after all she was invested in the deal going through as well. Maybe not as much as Teo, but she'd be devastated if it didn't get over the line. So when he parked the car in the underground car park and reached over for another kiss, she held him back with a hand.

Doug and Jerry were waiting for her in the expansive Verdadero reception area, but had coffees in front of them and were chatting away with Teo's assistant, Amaia.

'I'm so sorry, the traffic was awful this morning,' Cara explained, but happily Doug and Jerry didn't seem concerned.

The three of them took a car to the Real Alcázar, the stunning royal palace in the heart of historic Seville. Amaia had booked them skip-the-queue tickets.

The Alcázar was the first place Cara had visited on her first trip to Seville and had been awed by the history and the beauty of the medieval Islamic palace. It was no different this time around, the detailed lattice work, the colourful mosaics, stunning tapestries, each room and courtyard more stunning than the last.

They were standing in the Hall of Ambassadors admiring the magnificent golden dome, when another sight knocked the breath out of her: Teo striding towards them, a smile on his usually reserved face.

She wanted to reach for him and sensed his hand moving towards hers but they both held back.

'What are you doing here? I thought you had meetings,' she asked.

'They finished earlier than expected.' He smiled and she wondered for a second if he was telling the truth. He had to be, surely. Mateo Ortiz would never play hooky. Or lie.

He greeted the producers with another smile and the four of them completed the trip around the palace, with Teo pointing out the different architectural styles, small facts only locals would know, his pride in his city apparent to all.

A hand brush when no one was looking. A knowing smile. An 'accidental' bump. Her body was burning up by the time Jerry suggested lunch and the four of them sat down at a nearby restaurant.

Jerry claimed the seat next to her and Doug opposite, leaving her crestfallen even though she knew it was probably for the best. Teo was charming but it was an effort to keep her mind on the conversation and off the man speaking. And how he looked without his clothes. And the sounds he'd made. And the look on his face when he had made her climax for the second time. And the third.

Cara had to be alerted back to the present when it was time to leave, so distracted she'd been by memories of the previous night.

'I'd better get back to the office,' Teo said, and she tried to ignore her disappointment. 'Can I give you gentlemen a lift?'

Doug and Jerry declined the offer and left Teo and Cara

outside the restaurant. Once she was sure they'd turned the corner out of sight, she finally, finally, picked up Teo's hand. Strong, comforting, exciting. She stepped up to him. Their bodies separated by a whisper. 'It's a shame you have to go back to the office,' she said.

'I don't,' he whispered into her ear, sending a thrill down her body.

'But you said…'

'I fibbed. I don't have any commitments this afternoon.'

'None?'

'Well, just one.' He smiled and oh how she loved seeing Teo smile. 'I have a commitment to you.' He pressed his mouth against the side of her neck and her insides leapt, wild with anticipation.

A week later Teo sat in his office, staring at the papers on the desk in front of him. It might have been a week, he wasn't sure. Days and nights had blurred together in an erotic, exciting mix. He was awake in the night, asleep in the day. He didn't know what was up and down any longer. The only thing that kept him centred was Cara. Everything seemed to begin and end with her.

Except this contract. This deal. That was now in front of him and had been for hours. Or was it minutes? He was no longer sure of anything.

Particularly his own feelings.

I'm not going to break. You won't hurt me, Teo.

But what about me? Am I going to hurt me?

No. He wasn't. They had agreed their relationship was physical only. Not to mention short-term. They were old friends who shared an unbreakable bond. But it wasn't more than that. What Teo was feeling was happiness and joy. And the endorphin rush that came from having a lot of very good sex. It wasn't nothing, but it wasn't more than that.

Val sauntered into Teo's office without saying a word, much less knocking. This was normal for Val. If you happened to be looking for him, the last place you would ever check would be Val's own office.

'What's up?' Val asked, sitting in his usual chair.

'I'm just looking over the final contract. It seems to be all there, but something's still bugging me.'

'Teo, it looks great. The lawyers have looked over it ten times, you've gone over it twenty. Sign it. Celebrate!'

He pressed his lips together. 'No. Something's off. I'll figure it out.'

'Could it be the fact that once you sign this contract, the lovely Cara will be leaving Seville?'

Teo scoffed. 'She was always going to leave. That was always the plan.' The studio had put some loophole in the contract somewhere. There must be a typo or two to find. *Something*. If he'd been paying closer attention, instead of daydreaming about Cara, he would have found it by now.

'But I don't think the plan was for you to become so close to her either.'

Teo didn't like what Val was suggesting. He and Cara had been very discreet, not even Val would have picked up what was going on between them.

'You've become close to her too,' Teo said.

Val laughed. 'Sure, but not in the same way you have.'

He should deny it, but the weight had been pressing so heavily on him he couldn't, and what was the harm if Val already seemed to know?

'Say, theoretically, if you wanted to date your dead friend's ex-girlfriend, what would be the problems with that?'

'If by *your dead friend*, you mean Pablo, who has been dead for ten years and if by *ex-girlfriend*, you mean Cara, then nothing except your own complexes.'

'That's not true.' It wouldn't be right. It would *never* be right.

Val's face turned from amused to serious. He rose and walked to Teo's desk and stood next to him, forcing him to look up. Val placed his hands on Teo's shoulders.

'Pablo is gone and not even recently. Apart from anything else, you've spent the last ten years dedicating your life to his work and building an institution in his name. No one could accuse you of doing anything wrong as far as Pablo is concerned.'

'But this is Cara. The love of his life.'

'And so what? Did you ever wonder if it could actually be a good thing?'

'How?' Teo's voice was strangled. He was betraying his friend. And not just anyone, but Pablo, who had been the first person to accept him after his father's crimes. Who had trusted him with his creations.

'Because wouldn't Pablo have wanted her to be with someone he loved and respected?' Val asked.

Would he? Each time Teo let himself think something like that, he'd wonder if it weren't simply wishful thinking. Pablo had loved Cara so much, wouldn't it break his heart to know that Teo had stepped in?

Val continued. 'Besides, what Pablo might have thought is irrelevant—because he's not here. And apart from anything else, what Pablo may or may not have thought is hardly the most important thing.'

'What is?'

'Oh, Teo, I despair of you. I'm hardly a relationship guru, but seriously?'

If it were so obvious that Val—terminally single Val—could see it, then how low had Teo sunk?

'The most important thing is how she feels. How does she feel?'

'She thinks it should just be a temporary thing.' Teo sighed. Cara's heart was not for winning.

Val raised an eyebrow. 'Interesting.'

'Is it? How? It suggests to me that the whole thing is impossible.'

Val smiled. 'It suggests to me that you have done more than just think about how you feel. When did she say that she thought it should be temporary? At the beginning?'

'Yes. We were honest with one another when we…um, started.'

Val bit back a smirk. 'And since then?'

'Well, no. Because the deal was that it would be temporary.'

'Sometimes deals change. This started as one movie and turned into the option of three.' Val pointed to the papers on Teo's desk.

'It's not the same.'

'No, but it's not that different.'

Teo snorted. 'This is a business contract, I'm talking about…' He couldn't even say the words. Love. A relationship. Commitment. How could Val even compare what was in Teo's chest to the papers in front of him.

One was just a deal. A big one, but still just a deal.

Cara was so much more than that. Teo wanted to bury his face in his palms and sob.

But he couldn't, not even in front of Val.

How had he got himself into this situation? How had he managed to get himself into a place where he was falling for Cara? Where he was risking absolutely everything. His reputation, their business, and most of all, his heart.

'But, Pablo,' Teo said.

'Pablo would be happy for you both! Ah, it isn't Pablo you're worried about, is it? It's what everything else will think.'

'No.' *Yes*.

'You're worried people will think it's wrong. That people will think less of you. That they will think you've betrayed your friend.'

'I can't afford to ruin my reputation. *You* can't afford for me to ruin my reputation.' Their employees couldn't afford for him to do that. The millions of children supported by programs run by the Pablo Pascal Foundation couldn't either.

Val laughed. 'I think both our reputations can withstand you being in a consensual, mutually caring relationship. The only thing you have to worry about is what Cara thinks.'

Val was logical. Calculating. Mathematical, but what did he know about relationships? He was just as clueless as Teo.

Besides, Cara thought it was temporary. And he couldn't ask her, because what if that made her uncomfortable? He didn't want to ruin any chance of an ongoing connection and if he reneged on their agreement, he'd be doing that.

There was a knock at the door and both men turned. It was Cara, looking gorgeous in a plain black suit, her hair tied back and a lick of red lipstick. Her professional outfit. She thought it made her blend into the background but, as far as Teo was concerned, when she was in the room the rest of the world fell away.

Even if she wasn't in the same room as him, just the thought of her had the same effect.

'I'm about to head home and just wanted to let you know,' Cara said.

'Come in, Cara, come in.' Val gestured for her to enter.

Teo had a bad feeling about what was going to come next.

'How are you enjoying Seville?' Val asked but he might as well have hired a skywriter to tell Cara he knew about their relationship.

Cara looked from Teo and back to Val. 'Just fine?' she answered.

'Great, great. And where are you heading next?'

'Brussels. My next job is lined up for next week.'

'That's terrific, you'll be able to come to the ball after all.'

'The ball?'

'You know, for the foundation. It's this Saturday. Five days from now.'

'Oh, I don't…'

'You don't what? You are coming, aren't you?'

'I…' She looked back to Teo and the confusion on his face.

They hadn't revisited this conversation since early in Cara's stay when Val had first brought it up.

'You should come.' Teo's voice was rough.

She narrowed her eyes, as well she should. That was not a way to issue an invitation. Because he hadn't intended to ask her. He hadn't intended for her to come. The ball was about the foundation, which of course was all about Pablo.

'It's alright, I don't have to. If you don't want me to.'

'Of course I want you to. I didn't mention it earlier because I thought you would have left Seville by now. But you should definitely come.' Did he sound sincere enough?

If she came to the ball, she'd naturally be his plus-one. And then everyone would know that he was dating Pablo's ex. The thought made a bitter taste in his throat. And yet he was still foolish and selfish enough to want her there.

Val's invitation was far more generous. 'Of course you should come. I won't accept no for an answer. And if Teo hasn't asked you already, you can be my plus-one!'

They both looked at him, Cara's face was confused and hurt, Val's amused. Cara go to the ball, but with Val. Teo's throat constricted. It was unthinkable.

'Saturday night, shall I pick you up?' Val asked her.

'No need. Cara can come with me,' Teo said, then quickly turned to Cara, his face aflame. 'If you would like to come with me, I'd be honoured.'

'Thank you, I'd love to,' Cara said, not quite able to meet his eye.

Val clapped his hands. 'Fantastic, it'll be a great night.'

Cara looked between the two men, still uncertain, and nodded.

'Okay, good night. I'll see you back at home,' she said to Teo.

They both watched her leave. Val at least had the decency not to say anything more.

Teo stayed at the office much longer than he had been lately, far longer than he needed to. It was nearly eight when he arrived home. Cara was sitting in the living room, the television was on low and she turned when he entered.

'I'm sorry I'm late.'

'No need to apologise, you don't owe me an explanation.'

'Except I do. I was finalising the deal. Signing it.' He pulled a bottle of champagne out from behind his back. A peace offering and because Val was right, it was worth celebrating.

Cara whooped and ran to him. 'Congratulations! That's great news.'

'Yes, it is.'

'Yet you don't seem happy.'

'No, I am happy. I'm often like this, when a deal it done. It's somehow anticlimactic.'

'And you're worried about whether there are things you missed. Things you didn't think of?'

She knew him so well. How had that happened after only a few weeks?

It hadn't even been a month. It felt like no time at all and yet he also couldn't remember what his life was like before he'd received the phone call from the hospital.

He opened the bottle and Cara found the glasses. Working together as always.

'To Hollywood.' She touched his glass to hers.

'To Hollywood.' He sipped the wine and the bubbles hit him with a realisation: This was nice. It was good to celebrate with someone, even in a low-key way like this.

Especially if it were a low-key celebration like this.

'You've done such an amazing thing,' she said.

'We couldn't have done it without you.'

'I don't mean this deal. I mean the whole thing. Verdadero. The charity.'

'It's all Pablo's.'

'Are you mad? It isn't Pablo. It's you. And Val as well, but the way the company has been managed, the way you've steered it, that is all you.'

He shook his head,

'Are you being modest or do you truly not believe what I'm saying? Be honest.'

'Neither. The first game was designed by Pablo. And the coding, all the software development, that was down to Val.'

'So, you're saying that Val and Pablo on their own, created all of this?' She opened her arms wide. 'You think Val could have done this deal on his own? Any of it?'

'Well, a lot of it.'

She smiled. 'I adore Val, he's undoubtedly brilliant, but he can't organise his way out of a paper bag. This is all *your* doing.'

'We're a team.'

'Okay, but you're a very important part of the team. Essential in fact.'

Teo had never allowed himself to believe he was successful. He was a helper, a facilitator, because the sons of criminals didn't get to be successful. The sons of liars had to try ten times as hard as anyone else to be trusted.

They sat on the sofa together and drank the champagne.

'I'm sorry you were forced to invite me to the ball,' she said.

Teo shook his head. 'Not at all.'

'Answer me this, then, am I going, or going *with* you to the ball?'

He tried to pretend he didn't know what she was getting at. 'We'll go together.'

She raised a pointed eyebrow. 'I don't have to go, you know.'

'Of course you do.'

'I don't want to go if you don't want me to go with you. It wasn't part of our arrangement.'

Their arrangement. Val was so wrong. Cara did still expect them to stick to their original deal. A physical relationship. While she was in Seville. That was all. Their arrangement didn't involve going as his date to a very public event.

'Of course I want you to be there.'

That was the truth, he did want her there, at his side. The problem was the thought of it also made him squirm.

'Will I embarrass you?' she said softly.

'What? No! Cara, no. It isn't that. Look, I know I haven't been as open about the ball as I should have been. It's only because I don't want things to be awkward for you.'

'Why would they be?'

'Pablo's parents will be there.'

Her shoulders dropped. 'Oh, I see. No, it's okay, I've actually been meaning to get in touch with them.'

'I didn't want to upset you. I know you loved him.'

'Yes, but it's in the past. If anything, I think going would give me a sense of closure. And…why are you really so keen to talk me out of it?'

'I'm honestly not. I didn't want to bring Pablo up, shove him in your face. The charity is dedicated to him after all.'

She laid her hand on his arm, a simple act but he felt as though she controlled him completely. He could no more push her hand away than fly to the moon.

'I don't want to promise you anything I can't give you.' Teo's throat was tight.

She nodded.

'I don't want to hurt you, not ever. I want to be honest with you.'

'And I appreciate that,' she said.

'And going public with our relationship, well, we talked about that, didn't we?'

'At the beginning. Yes. And I suppose nothing's changed?'

'Of course things have changed,' he said.

Everything had changed. She'd upended his life. But in a week, she'd be gone. That was the arrangement.

'Like what?' her eyes sparkled.

'Like you are recovered from your surgery.'

'That's true.' She nodded.

'And I now do this.' He pressed his mouth to hers.

Cara melted into his arms. Some things had changed. Even he had a little. But had they changed enough to make her want to stay?

CHAPTER TEN

TEO TOOK THE empty glasses and champagne bottle in one hand and Cara's hand in the other. He tugged her off the sofa and towards the staircase.

'Upstairs?' she asked.

'Can you manage?'

'Of course, I might have weeks ago.' But she hadn't asked and he hadn't offered. Downstairs had everything she'd ever needed—her room, the kitchen, the comfy living room and the formal living room, and Teo's study. Downstairs was already a massive house.

Upstairs was Teo's private domain and she sensed, like his heart, that wasn't something he was ready to trust her with yet. If he ever would be.

'I was beginning to wonder if you have your first wife locked up here.'

Teo's mouth gaped.

She laughed. 'It's a reference from *Jane Eyre*.'

'Ah, I haven't read it. It doesn't feature too prominently on Spanish school curricula,' he said as he led her upstairs.

'The hero, Mr Rochester, has locked his mentally ill wife upstairs in his mansion. Jane only finds out after she agrees to marry him when she's at the altar.'

While recounting the plot of *Jane Eyre*, Cara surreptitiously checked out the hidden story of this house.

'I'll give you the tour, if you like. You can check the bedrooms for ex-wives. So, he imprisoned one woman and then tried to marry another? And he's the hero? They end up together?'

'Yep.'

'Even though he locked up his wife, she forgave him?'

'It's a two-hundred-year-old story. But yes. I guess people forgive a lot of things.'

'But *that*?'

The upper floor also circumnavigated the courtyard below. Cara counted three or four large empty rooms. Each time Teo opened a door Cara said, 'Hello? Anyone here?'

Finally, he opened the door to the one room that did seem to be occupied.

The room had high ceilings and arched windows. It was open and airy yet still welcoming and comfortable, with white furnishings and dark exposed beams on the roof. The light was low, only a single lamp lit the entire room, bathing it in a seductive red glow.

Teo entered but she stood on the threshold. This was Teo's room, his own space.

'You have a lot of bedrooms,' she said. It was all she could think to say. She didn't want to dwell on the fact that once she walked into Teo's room something would change. She wasn't sure what, only that something would. Teo was trusting her with his own space.

He shrugged. 'They came with the house.'

She counted two, three large rooms. This was a house built for a family.

'What do you think you'll do with them? Do you think one day you might have children?'

'It isn't something I've thought much about. I can't quite imagine it.'

She bit her lip. She thought she felt the same way, but

these empty rooms bothered her in a way she couldn't put her finger on.

'Do you think…you will ever have children?' he asked.

'I don't know, also I haven't really thought very much about it.'

Only theoretically. Only in the way you might think about winning the lottery. Or travelling into space. Things that were possible, yet seemingly highly unlikely to happen to her.

Because if she had children, she'd have to give them a home. And ideally, though not necessarily, she needed a partner to have them with. And she certainly couldn't carry a child around with her as well as her backpack. So with so many obstacles to overcome, it really wasn't something she'd given much thought to.

Teo didn't press for a longer answer for which she was grateful. He put the champagne glasses and bottle down on a low table near an armchair and walked back to the threshold, where he slid his arms around her and pulled her tightly to him.

Teo pressed both his lips to her lower one and tugged gently. She opened her mouth yet Teo still kissed everywhere but her lips; her earlobes, her neck, her temples, until finally he brought his mouth back to her hungry lips.

They moved into his room and Cara pulled him to the bed, desperate to feel him on top of her. But he kept them standing, as he kissed and caressed his way up her arms and down her shoulders, over her body, removing her clothing as he went.

It felt as though her insides were unravelling. It was like this with Teo, slow, teasing, she was impatient but he seemed to have all the time and willpower in the world. It made her desperate and satisfied at the same time.

Finally, he pulled her to the bed and onto him. Teo's confidence was a turn-on, but his vulnerability made her heart ache. She'd never known anyone like him, someone who could embody so many contrasting traits all at once. Strength, openness, calmness and passion. He took her breath away, when he was tracing soft circles on her breasts as he was doing now, and even when he was standing on the opposite side of the room, fully dressed. A single, easy smile on his beautiful face could suck every breath of air from her.

As he did now. And more. The air smelt like him, the whole space felt like him. And she wanted to stay there with him forever.

Neither of them set an alarm and they both slept late, satiated and relaxed to their bones after the night before.

'You're on holiday. You don't work for me anymore. What will you do?'

'Some preliminary work for Brussels.' The Brussels job was expected to go on for two weeks but she had to sort out her arrangements after that. She'd been offered a job in California and another in Singapore. The Californian one was straightforward but she'd never been to Singapore and she loved the idea of going. Given the languages she knew, most of her work tended to be in Europe and the USA. She'd love to see more of Asia.

The email had come two days ago—a lucrative high-stakes deal with six different parties. Three languages. She should have jumped at it.

So, take the challenge. Go for it!

'What's up?' Teo asked her.

'Why do you ask?'

'You're biting your lip as though I don't feed you enough.'

Cara licked her lips, realising what she'd done.

'Nothing,' she said.

Teo raised an eyebrow. She wanted to talk to him about her dilemma but that would mean talking about *after*.

After she left.

They would both have lives after she left, Teo with his movie and Seville.

Cara with…maybe Singapore.

A year ago, she would've hit Reply to the email accepting the Singapore job with a 'Hell yeah,' but now? Now her fingers didn't seem to be able to type at all.

Because Brussels was close. It was in the same time zone. But Singapore was a hemisphere away and the thought of that made her chest tight.

She didn't want to go. Not next week.

Not ever.

You can't stay. Apart from anything else, Teo doesn't want you to. This is a temporary thing for him. Teo is even less capable of trusting someone than you are.

He has to read every contract fifty times, he's so convinced someone is out to trick him. He won't do anything unless he's checked the contract half a dozen times.

She knew why he was the way he was. His father's betrayal had caused a wound that may never heal, but understanding why Teo was the way he was didn't mean he was any more likely to change.

It was a shame because if he was willing to trust her then maybe, just maybe, she might be willing to trust him.

The idea of trusting someone made her heart rate spike, but this was Teo. Loyal, proper, steadfast Teo. Teo, who Pablo had respected more than anyone in the world. Teo, who she in turn trusted more than anyone alive.

Teo, who made her laugh, Teo, who had sparked a desire in her she couldn't remember experiencing before in her life.

Teo, who she longed for so much even when he was in the same room as her.

Could she love him? Was this what love felt like? Or was this just what regret felt like? Or was she just anxious because of Pablo, of seeing his parents? Of leaving Seville for the second time? Whatever this emotion was, it had her jittery. Her hands shaking. She pushed her coffee mug away.

'Cara?'

Teo's voice brought her back to earth and snapped her out of her thoughts with a jolt.

'What?'

'You were a million miles away.'

She nodded. Yes, she was. Imagining herself in Singapore. Far away from Teo. She clicked her laptop shut.

'Sorry, what did you say?'

'I asked if you're okay?' A frown creased his gorgeous brow.

No, she couldn't tell him. That wasn't their arrangement. Besides, she didn't even know where she'd start. She was tired, that was all. She was hardly in a good space to be thinking straight, let alone making any decisions.

'I'm fine, just tired. Someone kept me up half the night.'

He smiled. 'I'm very sorry, though I don't remember hearing any complaints.'

No. Her exact words had been *More. Don't stop.* And *Don't you dare stop.* Her muscles clenched at the memory.

This wouldn't do. None of this would do. She pushed her chair back.

'I just need a walk, some air before the day gets too hot.'

He stood as well.

'Cara?'

'Yes?'

'You can talk to me, you know.'

'About what?'

'About whatever has made you jumpy.'

She smiled and nodded, but she didn't agree at all. Teo was the last person she could talk to about the fears and emotions suddenly rippling through her. Because even though she didn't want to leave, he'd still be able to let her go.

* * *

The fan was no match for the heavy afternoon air. They lay as they had fallen after making love, with their heads at opposite ends of the bed, top to tail. It suited him to be close to her, but not too close. He didn't want to have to look into her eyes, afraid of what his might reveal. But at the same time, he wanted her within hand's reach, touching distance. He was afraid of what lay ahead, but at the same time, terrified of her leaving.

Three days.

Three more days.

So all he could focus on were her two pretty feet and her toes wiggling as she chatted to him.

I wonder if she knows that her feet are as expressive as her hands?

Her nails were painted a bright pink, and one even had a tiny picture of a flower painted on it. Her feet were a contrast to her hands, which were on public view and neat, unadorned. Professional.

It's my job to blend in. I'm not meant to stand out.

An impossible task for someone as beautiful as Cara.

And then there was her tattoo. He traced it with his index finger. The sea turtle.

'You like turtles?'

'You don't?'

'I like turtles just fine. But I don't think I'd like one as a pet.'

'Of course not, they belong in the wild.'

'And I don't know that I love them enough to get a tattoo of one.'

'Ah, yes, well that, my friend, is how we're different.'

Friend? Two weeks ago, the word would have made him smile, now it crushed him.

'Turtles have their home on their back. They are self-contained. They have everything they need.'

'Like you,' he whispered.

'Yep. And of course it's cute.'

Cara would never stay in Seville, even if he begged. She'd never lose her shell. Or her backpack. She couldn't. She was that turtle.

The next morning, they lingered at the kitchen table, breakfast long eaten. She was reading something on her laptop; he was making an unhurried start on his emails.

He'd miss this. His days were so much nicer when she was near. Even as they were now, in silence but working alongside each other. Everything was better.

'Oh.' Cara gasped.

'What's happened?'

She stared at her screen and he watched her face turn from shock to grief.

He felt her pain in his gut, even though he didn't even know what was wrong.

'It's an email from my lawyer.'

Anger began simmering up inside Teo but he kept his expression as neutral as possible.

'What's happened?'

'They've heard from Liam. Oh, Teo.' Cara slumped over her laptop, face in her hands. Teo stood and wrapped his arms around her. She pushed her laptop towards him with the offending email open.

Teo scanned it. The lawyers appeared professional and sympathetic but the news wasn't good.

Her half-brother had sold the family home. That, in itself wasn't great but the next line was heartbreaking. It had been sold to a developer who had already demolished it to build six condominiums.

'I wasn't expecting great news, I wasn't expecting him to give in, but I wasn't expecting this,' she said.

'I'm so sorry. I'll get my own lawyers to look at it. We'll fight for a share of the proceeds.'

She pushed him away.

'It's not about the money. It's about the house. It's the only home I've ever had. And he sold it! Without even telling me!'

'I'm so sorry.' He was gutted for a house he'd never seen. 'We can fix this.'

She smiled but shook her head. 'We can't, Teo. Not with all the money or will in the world.'

'Then we'll…'

'What? You know there's nothing to be done.'

She'd lost more than a house; she'd lost the only home she would ever have and nothing he could ever do would replace that.

You could give her a home. Here.

He was still reeling from his own thought when Cara pushed back her chair and stood.

'I think I need a walk.'

'Do you want me to come?'

She shook her head.

He hated to watch her go, hated seeing her pain.

He could give her a home. He wanted to, but she was a turtle. She'd never stay in one place now.

'You don't have to do this alone. I'm here. For anything you need. I can fight for you or sit with you. Anything.'

Cara turned back to him, rested her hand on his arm and squeezed.

'I know,' she said, but she turned and left anyway.

Teo dropped back into his chair. He could help her. Couldn't she see? She could trust him!

Trust you to what? To look after her. Feed her? He couldn't even fix this. Her house. Her brother. Besides, why would

Cara trust him? He was a doer. An organiser. He wasn't brilliant.

Like Pablo.

'Oh, I thought you'd both left,' said Alba. His housekeeper began cleaning up the breakfast dishes.

'Cara's gone for a walk. I'm on my way out.' He stood again.

'She didn't look happy.'

Typical Alba way of digging for information.

'She's just had some bad news. She just found out her childhood home has been demolished.'

Alba nodded but didn't seem too concerned. 'Houses come and go.'

He laughed. 'Sure, but this one we're standing in is at least a hundred and fifty years old.'

'Sure, but it's been home to many people before you. Home isn't a building, it's what's in your heart.'

He knew this, but it would be a totally insensitive thing to say to Cara at this moment in time. Cara's house was more than a home, a safe refuge, it was her parents, it was her childhood. It was all her formative memories. And to lose it because of a betrayal by her closest relative was really heartbreaking.

And he couldn't fix it.

She doesn't need you to. She's independent.

'This would make a nice home for her,' Alba said.

Teo laughed. 'Wow, you're not holding back.'

She shrugged. 'Why would I do that? She leaves the day after tomorrow, so you'd better get your act together.'

'I don't need to get anything together. She's going to leave. She has another job to get to.'

This isn't the home she wants. She wants the one that's currently a building site for several condos.

Besides, why would she trust you? You're betraying your oldest friend by being with her and your father was a criminal.

'You worry way too much about what other people think. The only thing that matters is what you think,' Alba said.

It reminded him of Val's words: *the most important thing is how she feels.*

His feelings, her feelings, they were two independent souls. It would be impossible to make it work.

She was a turtle, and he built castles with other people's dreams.

Cara took the same route she and Teo had been accustomed to in the evenings. It was different in the morning, cooler, quieter. The street-sweepers were still at work on the streets, many of the shutters still closed. Her feet knew the way though. The same circuit to the local park and back. She'd only been here a few weeks and yet she had a routine.

Having a routine, being comfortable in a place, usually made her restless. It meant she was in danger to settling down. Of stopping. Of slowing. But now, there was nowhere to go back to. No home. No Woods Hole. No parents. She picked up her pace and walked faster. She'd choose a different route today. She wasn't going to settle anywhere. She turned a different corner.

Cara strode on. Her body felt strong, fully recovered now from the appendicitis, and the surgery a distant memory. She admired the unfamiliar streets, the new, different square with its unfamiliar church. And on she went, down another old alleyway, past a new park. This was good. This was how she lived, a new vista around each corner. Always something else to discover. It was good, she was fine. And she didn't need her house.

Cara's mouth was parched, she realised too late she should

have taken a hat with her, the sun was getting higher and the air warmer. It was time to head home.

She turned and began to retrace her steps.

Except…the streets were not familiar. She reached for her phone to find her route home but her heart rate increased as she felt over her body and couldn't locate it. She felt herself again but it still wasn't there. She hadn't taken her bag and had left Teo's house without anything at all.

She didn't have her phone with her. She didn't have a map.

She had nothing. And was tired and thirsty and felt like a good cry. She walked around another corner and a large church came into view. She recognised the Basílica de la Macarena, a place she'd visited a decade ago and realised how far away from home she was.

After weighing up all her options she walked into a souvenir shop, told the woman she was lost and asked if she could please use her phone for a call. Seconds later she was speaking to Teo.

'Hi, it's me. Cara.'

'What's wrong? Where are you?'

'Lost.'

'Where? I'll come and get you.'

'I'm sorry, I left my phone at home.'

'Don't apologise. Where are you?'

'The Basílica de la Macarena.'

'I'll be right there.'

She handed the phone back to the woman.

Teo did arrive quickly, or so it seemed. Cara hadn't even had time to think of an explanation for getting lost, but as soon as he arrived, she realised she didn't need one. He jumped straight out of his car and went to her, enfolding her in a tight hug.

'I'm sorry,' she said into his chest.

He stroked her head. 'Please stop saying that.'

'I forgot my phone.'

'I understand, you just had some awful news.'

His understanding and lack of blame made her press herself closer to him. She hadn't realised how worried she'd been to have been lost until he was there, holding her. His familiar body a sanctuary.

'You can call me anytime, anywhere, I will come.'

She didn't doubt that he meant those words, yet once she pulled away and they got into the car, she felt foolish all over again.

She would never call him for help again. She mustn't. Because even though her feelings for Teo were becoming increasingly strong and heavy to bear, Teo didn't feel the same way. As best she was a short-term fling, at worst a responsibility he owed to his oldest friend. Either way, it wouldn't be fair on either of them.

Cara sat on the edge of her bed, wrapped in her robe, hair still damp. She should start getting ready. She should be excited about going to a ball, but she didn't seem to be able to muster the energy or the motivation to dry her hair or put on her make-up.

This deep sense of exhaustion had been with her since yesterday and the news from her lawyers. It didn't help that this was her last night in Spain. It felt as though the last month had finally caught up with her, the surgery, Teo…and now Liam.

You'll feel better tomorrow, once you're on the road again. You'll feel like yourself.

That was all it was. This time with Teo had been great, but it hadn't been real life. She'd been unwell, and that had wreaked havoc with her emotions. No wonder she was feeling drained. And confused. It wasn't because she was developing feelings for Teo. It couldn't be. He was cold and distant Mateo Ortiz. Pablo's grumpy friend.

And yet, she was thinking about him. All the time. Even in her dreams.

Get some distance from him and you'll forget him soon enough.

Because she had to. Because whatever she might or might not feel for Teo, he was not remotely in the same place as her and probably never would be. The fact that he didn't want her to come to the ball proved this and was probably why she was still sitting on her bed in her robe.

There was a knock at the door and her heart hitched. She could tell him that she'd changed her mind, that it was better if she didn't go. He was right. It would be awkward for both of them and why put themselves through it when they both knew that tomorrow she'd be getting on a plane. He didn't want her there, not really.

But it wasn't Teo. It was Alba. 'I've come to see if you need any help getting into your dress, but look at you, you're not even close to being ready.'

'I'm not feeling the best.'

'Nonsense. This is just big night nerves. Everyone gets them.'

Not like this.

Alba started fussing around, clearing room on Cara's dresser and pulling up a chair. 'Let's get you sorted. Come on, you sit here and do your make up while I do your hair.'

Cara did as she was told and sat down in front of the large mirror.

Out of nowhere, Alba produced a blow-dryer and a brush and went to work, sectioning, drying, curling.

'Are you going to wear it up or down?' Alba asked.

'I wasn't really sure.'

'Then let's see how it looks down, if not, we can do it up. You'd better get going with your make-up.'

Cara was shamed into picking up her bag and sorting through it for a moisturiser and a primer.

'Not that you need much. Love, you never do, but I expect you want to feel special tonight.'

Cara did want to feel special tonight, but no amount of make-up was going to fix the heavy ball in her stomach.

'It's just another night,' she mumbled.

'Then why are you so anxious?'

Had she told Alba she was nervous? Or had her behaviour just hinted at it?

She wasn't nervous about the ball as such, more about the knowledge that this was her last night in Seville. Her last chance to say something to Teo. But what on earth would she say?

I think I might be in love with you. Does that scare you?

She knew his answer even before she asked the question. Oh, he cared for her. Just not enough.

'I'm more sad than nervous. I'm leaving tomorrow.'

Alba said nothing over the roar of the hairdryer. She worked Cara's hair while Cara paid special attention to her make-up. After Cara finished and finally focused away from matters of eyeliner and contours, she looked at Alba's work. Her golden hair fell down in luxurious shiny waves. She gasped.

'I can never get it to look like that. How did you do it?'

Alba shrugged 'I have three daughters and six granddaughters. I've had some practice. Now should we get you into that dress?'

The gold dress was hanging from the top of the wardrobe. It was gorgeous, but what had she been thinking buying it? And all the other things she'd bought while she had been here. She couldn't take any of it with her. None of her new things would fit in her backpack. Besides, what use would a red flamenco dress be at business meetings in Brussels or Singapore?

Alba brought the dress over to her and helped Cara step into it. Alba adjusted the neckline, instructed Cara to hold her bust in place and then zipped it up at the back. She stepped away and let Cara look at herself in the mirror. Alba clutched her hands to her chest. 'Beautiful.'

Did she look beautiful enough to make Teo fall in love with her?

Nothing you can say or do will make him do that. You could be the most beautiful woman in the world in the most beautiful dress and he still wouldn't love you.

Her eyes began to fill but she swallowed the tears back down. Alba interpreted her reaction as regret, instead of heartbreak.

Teo's kindness and care over the last day since she found out about the house had been amazing and only made her pain worse. Dropping everything to come and pick her up when she'd gotten herself lost. Holding her, just being with her.

'You don't have to leave, you know.'

'I do. My time here is over. I'm well again, I have another job to get to.'

'So?'

'So I have to leave.'

Alba shrugged again.

Maybe you don't have to, her shrug suggested. Maybe, just maybe, if she told Teo what was on her mind she could stay?

'I don't want to stay,' Cara said, answering a comment Alba hadn't even made.

'Fair enough. Who would want to stay here, in this beautiful house? With a wonderful man.'

Cara shook her head. No. It was time to move on. It wasn't unusual to feel regret about leaving a place but that regret always dissipated when she arrived somewhere new and found a whole new set of things to explore.

Just like she would tomorrow evening when she arrived in Brussels. Teo would start to become a memory. Just like her parents and Pablo and her house. Something that existed in the past only.

Only right now she couldn't imagine ever forgetting him at all.

CHAPTER ELEVEN

CARA EXPECTED THE ball to be held inside in a generic conference space, the likes of which she'd seen all over the world, but this was not that at all. The ball was being held in the large courtyard of a grand hotel, surrounded by arches, decorated in mosaics and carved in fine Moorish detail. They stood under the sky and a canopy of fairy lights, strung across the courtyard. The music was loud enough to dance to, but not to interrupt the conversation. The whole place smelt of Seville and its famous perfume of orange blossom and jasmine. It was magical.

The weight in Cara's stomach grew a little heavier. She should just enjoy the evening, live in the moment, but her future began tomorrow and it was difficult to look past that.

A voice called from behind. 'Teo, darling!'

Teo dropped her hand like it was on fire, stood ramrod-straight and they both turned in the direction of the voice. It was a middle-aged couple, a head shorter than her and Teo. Well-groomed, looking expectant.

Pablo's parents.

Pablo's mother and Cara recognised one another in the same blink. Señor Pascal's memory was not as clear as his wife's because he said, 'Teo, my boy. It's so lovely to see you. And who is your date?'

Teo recoiled subtly, and Cara cleared her throat. 'Señor

Pascal, it's Cara McCartney. I'm not sure if you remember me. I used to be friends with your son.'

Señor Pascal's mouth dropped but his wife leant in to kiss Cara on both cheeks.

'Cara, darling, of course we remember you. We're simply surprised to see you.'

'I'm sorry I didn't let you know I was here. It's been...well, my visit hasn't exactly gone to plan.'

Señora Pascal touched Cara's arm. 'It's a lovely surprise, don't get me wrong.'

Cara explained the circumstances of her visit, how she had come to be staying with Teo, her agreement to work for him. 'I'm very glad I had the chance to see you both tonight.'

Cara was aware of Teo's posture becoming increasingly stiffer next to her. She hardly dared look at him and certainly couldn't show any affection. It was as though a glass wall had risen up between them. Bulletproof. Impenetrable.

'Could you all excuse me? I have to greet a few people and I'm sure you have a lot to catch up on,' he said.

And he was gone. Leaving her alone with Pablo's parents.

'It's been too long,' Señor Pascal said.

Since the funeral, Cara thought, but didn't say it out loud.

'How have you both been?' She regretted the question as soon as it was out of her mouth. They had lost their only son, that wasn't something anyone moved on from lightly.

Señor Pascal slipped silently away and Cara wanted to disappear into the checkerboard tiles beneath her feet. Cara's loss had been deep as well, but she'd been young. Her relationship with Pablo had been intense, but short.

Señora Pascal squeezed Cara's arm. 'Oh, you know. We still have our bad days. We never forget him, but we've learned to live with his loss. And evenings like tonight, they are hard, but also very wonderful.'

Cara nodded. She knew exactly what Pablo's mother

meant. 'Yes. What Val and Teo have done in Pablo's memory is amazing, but it must bring everything up as well.'

'Yes.' She sniffed back some tears. 'Oh, don't mind me, I just didn't expect to see you tonight. And you must think me so rude, what have *you* been doing with your life?'

Señor Pascal reappeared at their side. Far from being upset, he brought over three champagne flutes and handed them to Cara and his wife with a smile.

'Cara, it's truly wonderful to see you.'

She caught them up on her life for the past decade, on her work and her travels.

'You were always welcome to come and visit,' Señor Pascal said.

'But we understand that the accident was traumatic for you too. We were—are—always there for you as well. Even though Pablo is gone,' added Pablo's mother.

Cara felt pressure build behind her eyes, in her nose. She sniffed it away as well but Señora Pascal pressed one of her tissues into Cara's hand.

'Thank you. That means a lot.'

That was an understatement. Why hadn't she gone back to see these wonderful, generous people?

Because they were more of a family to you than your own and it hurt too much to rely on them. They aren't your family and never can be.

When she'd left Seville the day after Pablo's funeral, she'd flown straight back to the States and her next semester of college. She'd been fleeing from something then. This time she had the opportunity to say goodbye to everyone and the city of Seville properly.

'I'm leaving again tomorrow, but I promise I won't leave it so long again between visits,' she said.

'Tomorrow?' Pablo's mother asked. 'But when will you be back?'

'I don't know.'

The Pascals exchanged a look.

'I envy you, Cara. The freedom to go where you want to go, to do what you want.'

She smiled. Yes. She had all the freedom in the world, didn't she?

Then why did she feel so sad? Freedom was wonderful, yet it could also be lonely.

'You can do anything you want to do,' Pablo's mother said.

And in that moment, Cara realised she was right. She could do anything. Besides, what did she really have to lose when she'd already lost everything? Her parents, her home.

If you're going to leave anyway, shouldn't you just tell him how you feel?

The Pascals were telling Cara all about the work of the foundation but she couldn't concentrate. She'd decided. After days of confusion and sadness, she suddenly knew what she needed to do.

Teo mingled with the guests, caught up with people he hadn't seen since the year before, but his body remained on the watch for Cara. She spoke with the Pascals for a while but then she was on her own.

You're her date, you have to go to her. It's rude to abandon her like that in a crowd of people she doesn't know.

He wanted nothing more than to be at her side, except… when he was next to her, he felt all the eyes on him, the camera flashes pointed in their direction. Everyone naturally wanted to know who the beautiful woman he'd brought with him was. Of course they did. She lit up the room.

'Who is your beautiful friend?' asked a woman who headed up one of their literacy programs.

'Her name is Cara McCartney. She's an interpreter, working with Val and I for a while.'

The woman smiled. 'She was talking to Pablo's parents earlier. Does she know them?'

Did nothing escape these people?

'Yes, she is an old friend of Pablo's.'

'Ah, I see.'

Yes, Cara would always be Pablo's ex. Pablo would always be the reason for their connection.

'You should go to her, instead of talking to an old lady like me.'

'Nonsense. It's lovely to see you,' he said.

'You don't have to be working all the time, Teo. You are allowed to enjoy yourself.'

The woman slipped away, no doubt to spread the news that the beautiful woman in the gold dress whom Teo had brought to the ball had a connection to Pablo.

He'd seen the look on Emilio Pascal's face when he'd noticed him holding hands with Cara. He'd seen the way Anita Pascal had looked at them both. Shocked. Surprised.

None of that was meant to happen. He hadn't meant to flaunt his relationship with their dead son's girlfriend in their faces. Especially not at the Pablo Pascal Foundation Annual Ball.

But none of these thoughts stopped him from winding his way through the crowd to where Cara stood, alone.

'Are you okay?' Teo leant in to whisper to her but was careful not to touch her.

'Yes, I mean, it was emotional talking to them, but I'm okay.' Her eyes were tinged with red and she was clutching a wet tissue. He *knew* bringing her here was a bad idea.

'I'm sorry you had to see them. If you need to leave, I understand.'

'Why would I leave?'

'Because the Pascals are here, seeing them has upset you.'

She took a deep breath. 'I've told you, I'm not going to break. It was good to see them, really.'

But she was upset. And he hated that it was his fault.

'You don't have to put yourself through this.'

She looked at him directly, held his attention with a glare. 'I'm not putting myself through anything, I want to be here. I can handle this. It's emotional, but it's also really, really good to see them after all these years.'

Teo frowned. 'Do they know about us?' he asked.

He knew instantly from her expression that it was the wrong thing to ask.

'I didn't tell them anything but I have no idea. And so what if they do?'

'Cara, I hardly think you and I flaunting our relationship in front of Pablo's parents is a good idea.'

'We haven't flaunted anything!' she hissed. 'I haven't told anyone anything about us and we haven't so much as brushed against one another since we arrived. Do you want me to stay?' She looked hurt, but this could be the out they both needed. If she was upset maybe she should leave.

'I want you to do what's best for you.'

'I know that, Teo. I know you are selfless to the point of stupidity. But I'm asking you what you want. Forget for a moment what you think I want or what you think the right thing is, what do you want?'

The most important thing is, what do you want?

'I want what's best for you.'

'Gah, Teo. No. This is never going to work if you can't be honest. If not with me, at least with yourself.'

Teo drew a breath to argue, to tell her that he was so honest with himself about his shortcomings, about his failures, about everything, that if she knew some of the things he told himself she'd think he was too honest.

But he didn't because they were in a crowd of people and also because at that moment Val appeared at their side and greeted Cara with a kiss.

'Great night, well done,' he said to Teo.

'Well done you,' Teo replied.

Val snorted. 'I did nothing, we all know that when it comes to organising things like this—or organising anything in fact—that you are the organiser.'

He was just the organiser. Great. Now he felt even smaller than he had moments before. Val and Pablo were the geniuses, he was just the organiser.

A woman, a stranger, appeared at Cara's side and asked about her dress. Cara's attention turned and the women began talking.

'You're setting tongues wagging.'

'What do you mean?'

'Everyone wants to know who the beautiful woman in gold is.'

'And what have you told them?'

Val pulled a face. 'The truth.'

'Which is what exactly?'

Teo's hands tingled as his adrenaline levels spiked.

'That she used to date Pablo—'

'You lead with that?'

'Why not? This is the Pablo Pascal Foundation Ball in case you hadn't noticed. What should I have said?'

'That she's been working with us, perhaps?'

'Or that you're head over heels in love with her?' Val whispered.

'What?'

'I didn't say that. I wanted to. But I didn't.'

'Good, because it isn't true.'

Val laughed. 'Sure, besides, I think everyone can make their own mind up.'

'What do you mean?'

'You may as well have a neon sign above your head. Everyone's noticed it.'

Teo's jaw was tight. His hands clenched. He wanted to get out of there before he exploded. Val was way out of line…

'Is she still leaving tomorrow?'

'Why wouldn't she?'

'Because you might have asked her to stay.'

Teo scoffed. 'She can't stay. She has a job in Brussels.'

'But after that?'

'After, she goes to her next job, and the next. She doesn't live anywhere.'

'So, that's perfect. She could live here.'

She could, he was right, base herself in Seville, and travel from Seville to anywhere she needed to go in the world.

But that would mean he'd miss her when she left. And it would mean his life would become further linked to hers. And people would talk, like they were doing now, about how he was sleeping with his dead friend's ex. About how he had profited from Pablo's creations and now was stealing his girlfriend. About how Teo Ortiz was not the upstanding proper person he tried to make everyone believe. How he really was a thief. How he really was no better than his own father.

Cara made small talk with some other guests, Teo spoke to Val and them some others, but they stayed where they were, in their small circle in the courtyard. Even with their backs turned, she still knew where he was. Her body felt it. Attached by invisible strings that were impervious to all the people coming and going around them.

Her anger from earlier had left her, it had only simmered. Teo wasn't ashamed of her, he was only worried about what other people thought. He was worried about upsetting the Pascals.

But Cara wasn't. Not now she'd seen them.

Yes, they probably did suspect that she and Teo had become close and not only were they not upset, they were delighted.

But it was no use trying to tell Teo that. He had to realise this himself.

If she could make the leap to trusting Teo, then couldn't he? If she could take a chance, surely Teo could as well?

She had to tell him. She was running out of time.

Cara excused herself from the woman she was talking to. She wasn't going to wait another moment. She had to do it now, before she lost her nerve. Teo was with Val and a few other people, so it was easy to go up to him, take his arm and excuse them both from the circle.

Teo didn't protest, she knew he wouldn't, that would only create more interest in them and that was the last thing he wanted to do. She led him to a quiet corner of the courtyard, beside large potted orange trees.

'Are you alright?' he asked.

She bit back a smile. 'I'm fine. I'm good in fact. Great.' No, that was overstating things. Whether she was great would depend on his reaction to what she was going to say next.

'Teo, I love you. I'm in love with you. And I thought you should know, before I leave.'

Teo's jaw dropped, shock crossed his face but in a second, he restored his neutral expression.

She'd been so sure that telling him was the right thing to do, she hadn't thought of what would happen next.

Of this moment.

She hadn't expected him to say, 'Thank you for telling me.'

'Thank you?' Was he serious?

Yes, this is Teo, he's always serious.

'Do you love me?' she prompted. She had nothing to lose.

'Cara, I…'

'It's a yes or no question, Teo.'

'It's more complicated than that.'

'How? Yes or no. Do you have feelings for me?'

'Of course I do. You know I do.'

'And do you love me?' Why couldn't he just admit it? If he loved her, they could figure things out, they could come up with a plan for the future, something that worked for both of them. If he loved her, they could do this together, but as long as he held back on her, they couldn't.

Teo grimaced and her heart fell.

'Because, Teo, I love you. I love you deeply and surprisingly. I love you so much and I don't want to live without you. But I can't do this alone. I need to know if you feel the same way. Or if you think one day you might feel the same way.'

'Cara, can we talk about this later?' he said and her knees buckled.

'There is no later. I'm getting on a plane tomorrow.'

'Just not here.'

Of course not, not when other people were around.

'I'm telling you I'm prepared to be wherever in the world you are. I'm prepared to upend my life. And you…'

Even if he couldn't name it, what they had was love. There was no other word—not in any language—to describe it.

'Cara, you know it's far more complicated than just saying three words.' He spoke softly.

But it wasn't. It really was just that simple.

'Here you both are!' Jerry's booming voice made them both turn. 'Teo, Val's looking for you. They need to start the speeches. And I promised this beautiful woman a dance.'

The last thing Cara felt like was dancing, but at least she didn't have to stay and listen to Teo tell her that he didn't love her. And that she had been right all along, she would always be alone.

Teo watched as Jerry led Cara away to the dance floor. His heart was still in his throat. She loved him? The thought should have made him fly, except just thinking about his response to her made him want to crawl into the nearest hole.

Unfortunately, standing on a floor of UNESCO-protected tiles made this impossible. Particularly as in a few minutes he was expected to stand up in front of two thousand people and talk about Pablo. Especially since Pablo's parents were walking towards him now.

'It's so lovely to see you with Cara,' Anita Pascal said.

He opened his mouth to deny it. But lying was even more difficult than telling the truth.

'You're not upset?' he asked.

'Why would we be?' Emilio shook his head.

'Because of Pablo.'

'That's exactly why we're pleased. We know he would be too.'

'Would he?'

'Son, you know better than anyone what a remarkable person Pablo was. He was many things, but he certainly wasn't petty or jealous. He would want you to be happy, and Cara as well.'

'I've taken everything from him. I owe him everything.'

'You owe him nothing. You didn't take anything from him, you grew his ideas, developed them, built them into a wonderful thing.'

'Two wonderful things,' Anita added. 'The company and the foundation. You didn't steal his idea. You grew it. With Val. Pablo wanted this business, he'd be so grateful that you made it what it is.'

'Look around you,' Emilio said. 'Everyone here knows you loved Pablo. Teo, you have nothing left to prove. We all know the business and the foundation wouldn't exist without you. You may have built it with your friends' skills and creations, but it wouldn't exist without you. You are as integral to all of this as they are.

'Besides,' continued Emilio, 'no one thinks you've stolen Cara. Heavens, that girl has a mind of her own.'

Teo smiled.

She definitely did. And it was one of the many reasons he loved her.

He loved her. And he had to tell her. Immediately.

Teo sought Cara out on the dance floor but couldn't see her golden dress anywhere. With dismay, he noticed Jerry standing with Doug to the side of the dance floor.

'Where's Cara gone?' Teo asked the men.

Jerry shrugged. 'She said she had to leave.'

'Leave?'

'Yes, she said goodbye, told us how much she'd loved working with us and wished us well.'

Damn.

'It was only a few moments ago, I'm sure she hasn't left yet.'

Teo wasn't. He couldn't blame her for getting out of here as soon as possible, especially after he'd just behaved so badly.

Thank you.

What had he been thinking?

He'd been thinking of his own hesitation, his own issues. When he should have only been thinking of her. He should have pulled her to him and promised to love her forever.

Teo was tall enough to see over many heads, but his height was not a match for the crowd. He had to go higher.

He climbed the first half of a nearby staircase and searched for the gold of her dress and the golden flames of her hair.

There she was. At the other end of the courtyard. Heading to the exit. Instantly realising he'd never be able to weave his way across the heaving dance floor to catch her, he climbed the rest of the marble staircase and ran along the length of the balcony.

There she was below him, just about to disappear underneath it and out of the ball.

'Cara, stop! Don't leave.' *I love you*.

She didn't stop and he now realised there was no staircase back down to the courtyard at this end.

There was no way he'd get down in time to stop her.

You'll catch her at home.

No. That wasn't good enough. Teo went to the balustrade and leant over it. 'Cara! Cara McCartney!' he cried.

Some guests stopped and looked up but Cara didn't.

'Cara! Cara! Someone stop that woman in gold!' he yelled again.

A few people looked around but no one close enough to catch her. The music drowned out his voice.

A metal box caught his eye. The circuit board. Could it be the power? All the power? He flipped it open and scanned the board. He only had an instant and flicked the switch marked 'Power 1.'

There was the clack of electricity turning off and music winding down. The place was quiet but for the voices, which all wondered what was going on.

The only lights that remained on were the fairy lights, strung across the courtyard, presumably on a different circuit but he couldn't think about that now.

'Cara, Cara, please stop.'

But she had already, like everyone else, frozen to the spot where she stood and was looking around to see what was wrong.

'Cara, please don't leave,' he yelled.

Her eyes found his and even from this distance he could tell she wasn't convinced.

'Don't leave. Not now. Not ever.'

She stood still, and he was now aware that everyone else had seen who he was talking to.

'Teo, are you serious?'

'I am serious, deeply serious. I love you and I want you to stay. Forever.'

He was aware of everyone in the ball looking from Cara to him and back again, but all he saw, as the rest of the world and all his concerns and worries fell away, was Cara standing where she was, nodding. And smiling.

Cara's limbs were weak. Every set of eyes in the courtyard were on her but she only had time for one pair. She pushed her way through the crowd to the nearest staircase but it was like wading through mud. Everyone wanted to greet her and give their best wishes but she couldn't get to Teo fast enough.

What on earth had he been thinking? Declaring his love from the balcony? In front of everyone? One minute he was telling her it was impossible, the next this. She should…she should…but the heartache she'd felt five minutes ago was all forgotten. He loved her. He loved her enough to tell the world. He loved her enough not to care what the rest of the world thought.

With a loud snap, the big lights came back on. Cara squinted, momentarily losing her focus on the staircase.

But then there he was, bounding down the last steps in a single leap and heading in her direction.

When they finally reached one another, she fell into his arms and he pulled her tight.

'I'm never letting you go again,' he whispered into her hair. 'I'm so sorry I was such a fool.'

'You were a fool, but I understand it. I understand why. It's been difficult for both of us. I should've told you earlier how I feel, I should have let you know about my feelings and my fears.'

Teo shook his head. 'I held back too. I held back for so long. I could hardly expect you to tell me how you felt when

I was so adamant I wasn't looking for anything serious. I'm so glad you told me. It was the kick I needed, even if it did take me a moment to realise.'

Cara shook her head. 'I wanted to tell you for ages but I couldn't find the words. And tonight's my last night. I panicked. I should have realised that you were already anxious enough about tonight. I could have chosen my moment better.'

He laughed. 'Oh, Cara, you can tell me how you feel anytime and anywhere.'

'Kiss her! Kiss her!' The voice came from across the courtyard but was unmistakenly Val's. A cheer echoed around the four walls of the courtyard.

Teo looked at her and her insides swooped. This was it.

'May I?'

'Oh, Teo, I wish you would.'

A smile broke across his beautiful face like the clouds parting and the sun shining through. She loved his smile, but his smile when it was for her was her new favourite thing in the world. Teo brushed her cheek with the back of his fingers, pushed her tears away with the soft pad of his thumb. She slid her arms around his neck and let herself fall into his gaze. She was aware of one of his strong arms sliding its way around her back, holding her up.

He'll never let you fall.

And when his mouth met hers, she knew he was the last man she'd ever kiss again.

EPILOGUE

It was another perfect spring evening when Alba helped Cara get ready for her wedding in the guest bedroom of the pink house.

Cara had long since moved her life upstairs to the room that was now Teo's and hers. One of the other rooms was now her study where she ran her business, an agency for freelance interpreters, which had become more successful than Cara could have imagined. She still did jobs herself, but picked and chose depending on the client, the job and the location. Teo sometimes went with her, especially for longer jobs. Together they had been to Buenos Aires, Montreal and Singapore.

But each time she returned to the same place, the pink house on the square in Santa Cruz, Seville.

Anita and Emilio Pascal walked Cara from the guest bedroom out into the courtyard where Teo was waiting with his mother, brother and sisters, and a small group of their friends, including Alba and Geraldo.

After celebratory drinks, the party walked the small distance to a restaurant they had hired for the intimate reception, Cara and Teo both adamant that Alba was a guest at this occasion. The speeches were short. Teo thanked everyone for coming, and Cara gave a toast to the people who weren't there in person but who she knew would have been delighted for them, her parents and Pablo.

And later, when they had returned to the pink house, and made love for the first time as a married couple, Cara said, 'I have to show you something.'

Cara rolled over, sat up and lifted her foot to show Teo.

'You got another tattoo,' he said.

Her smile was shy.

'Another turtle. You must really love turtles.'

Why would she get a second house-carrying-creature on her gorgeous skin? Especially now her backpack was stored away in one of the many cupboards of the house.

'It has a mate. A turtle friend.'

Ah, it was starting to make sense.

'My turtle isn't alone anymore. It still carries its house with it, but now it has a forever friend.'

She looked at him, her eyes expectant and he pulled her to him.

He didn't need reminding of her love, Cara was already tattooed over every inch of his body. But he loved the second turtle. He loved being her best friend, one half of a pair.

'I have something for you too.'

They had made a pact of no gifts; guests were invited to donate money to the foundation in lieu of gifts.

'We said no presents!'

'This isn't from me.'

'Then who?'

'I wasn't sure when to give it to you, but here goes.'

Teo rolled over to his bedside table and rolled back holding a velvet box. Long and large. It looked like a jewellery box, yet her wedding and engagement rings were on her finger.

And he said it wasn't from him.

She took the box and lifted the lid.

She gasped. Not quite believing what she was seeing.

Teo looked at her, expectantly. Maybe a little anxious.

Her mother's jewellery.

Her mother's treasures. The last time she had seen these was when she'd foolishly left the box behind at the Woods Hole house before going to college.

A small pair of ruby earrings, several gold chains, and her mother's wedding and engagement rings.

'How?'

'I got in touch with Liam.'

Cara's stomach churned.

'And he…he just gave them to you?'

'I told him that they would make an excellent wedding present for you.'

Cara had sent Liam an email letting him know that she and Teo were engaged, but hadn't extended an invitation to the wedding. She'd let him know where she was living, more for the sake of her niece and nephew, should they ever wish to contact her in the future, but she didn't want Liam at her wedding. And Teo knew all of this.

'And he just let you have them? Oh, Teo, you didn't buy them?'

Somehow the idea of having to pay for her own mother's things made her ill.

'No. But I was firm with him. Gently reminded him that you could still take him to court.'

Cara had no intention of doing so, she didn't want to fight anymore; she'd never forgive Liam but it was better for her and her future if she just moved on.

So to have these. Her mother's jewellery…

Teo picked up a ring, set with a large pearl and Cara's throat closed over.

'That was her engagement ring.'

'Oh, darling.'

Teo went to place it back in the box, but she said, 'No, I want to try it. Pearls need to be worn.'

Together they tried the ring on each of her fingers to see

if it would fit. Finally, Teo slid it onto the ring finger on her right hand where it sat perfectly.

'A perfect fit,' Cara said.

'Just like us,' Teo said, and he kissed her.

* * * * *

*Look out for the next story in the
Cinderellas in Seville duet*

Match Made in Seville *by Michele Renae*

Available now!

*And if you enjoyed this story, check out these other great
reads from Justine Lewis*

Italian Tycoon to Remember
Dating Game with Her Enemy
How to Win Back a Royal

All available now!

MATCH MADE IN SEVILLE

MICHELE RENAE

MILLS & BOON

CHAPTER ONE

THE VASQUEZ ESTATE, nestled in Seville's barrio de Santa Cruz, boasted an Instagram-worthy lush courtyard. Amber Martin strolled over the tiles curving along the shaded path. Birds chirped. Sweet orange blossoms bursting on the half-dozen potted trees perfumed her senses as she inhaled. Water bubbling in the center fountain tugged a rare smile onto her lips.

Had she stepped into a dream?

Until today, her passport had only marked France and the US. This was her first official assignment as a lifestyle consultant for Lux Love, the elite dating service that guaranteed an ultimate love match for the rich and famous. Yes, even the seemingly privileged needed help finding a lifelong companion.

Amber's job involved assessing the client's lifestyle from living environment, personality, hobbies, communication and so much more. Their bespoke matchmaking never paired two people who did not match at less than 90 percent.

It was a big task to undertake, but Amber was ready. It had been years since she'd lost her job as a paralegal because AI had made her position obsolete. Since then, she'd worked for a few small boutiques back in Minnesota, her home state, but hoped to someday utilize her research and communications degrees.

Last year she'd gotten the job as an assistant to an assistant to Colette Bellerose, international style icon, and founder and CEO of Lux Love. In Paris! Thank you, Aunt Judy, who had known Colette and mentioned Amber's desire to learn in a foreign country. Sure, at the time, Amber hadn't an interest in matchmaking, but no sane woman would refuse a job in Paris. Over the past year doing research and data entry for Colette, Amber had watched, trained and prepared for when she would be given her first client.

Don't let Lux Love down, Colette had said over the phone while Amber had been boarding a red-eye to Paris. When she'd heard about the job, she'd been in Minnesota visiting her dad. It had been too late to change her flight, so she'd flown to Paris-Charles de Gaulle, then immediately hopped a flight to Seville. It was now seven in the evening, Spanish time. The entire day had been spent in the air and in TSA check lines. In total she'd been awake for—no. Doing the math would only depress her. She'd considered calling and arranging to meet Senor Vasquez tomorrow after she slept off the jet lag but she didn't want the client's first impression of her to be canceling an appointment. She could push through the exhaustion for a brief introductory meeting.

The last thing Colette had warned her before boarding was: *Don't fall in love with the client.*

Amber muttered now as she approached the front doorway of the client's villa. "Who does she think I am? I won't fall in love. I don't *do* love. Love is…"

For everybody else. She'd never met a man who could challenge her intellectually or hold her interest for more than a day or two. And with her parents' divorce only three years in the past, she was still clinging to the realization that love couldn't last.

As well, self-aware as she tried to be, she knew her emotional IQ needed tending. And that actually made her perfect for the job of matchmaker. She was able to stand aside and observe the client's life, make notes, suggest ways to improve his or her profile and gain a match. All without becoming emotionally involved. She'd ace this job.

With an adjusting tug to her red Anne Klein suit—she'd had her colors done; it was her power color—and gripping her CHANEL purse tightly, which she'd be paying off on her credit card for years!, she rapped the guitar-shaped brass door knocker.

The owner, Valentino Vasquez, was not a musician that she knew of. There had been some mention of flamenco dance in his preliminary survey. Trying to get some sleep during the flight to Paris so she could be attentive and alert for her first big job had failed. She could never sleep on a plane. But it had given her time to study Vasquez's profile. The thirty-two-year-old Spanish native was a billionaire CEO—along with his partner, Mateo Ortiz—of the virtual reality gaming corporation, Verdadero. That meant *truth*, or *real*. Valentino was the coding genius of the pair. He'd called Lux Love two days ago requesting a match, which had set the vetting process into motion.

The comment section regarding his reason for seeking a match had been blank. Not an issue. Amber would learn everything about the man and get to know him better than any family member could.

The door opened to reveal a short woman of indeterminate age. A gush of rose perfume exuded from her body. Silver streaks highlighted her pulled-back black hair. Rounded shoulders and an apron over a plain brown dress. A housekeeper or chef? The woman cast her gaze over all five feet eight inches—in heels—of Amber but she didn't say anything.

"Hola, I'm with the agency," Amber said in Spanish. "Senor Vasquez is expecting me. I'm Amber Martin."

And…that was about as much Spanish as she could wield conversationally.

With only the one year of middle school Spanish under her belt, Lord help her if she was to converse with the client in Spanish.

"*Sí*, Emmer."

"Uh… Amber." A glance to the side revealed an open closet spewing a tumble of shoes, coats and outer gear. Amber began mental note-taking. Messes like that screamed disinterest or neglect. Or possibly the need for a cleaning person.

"*Sí*, come this way." The woman spoke rapid Spanish. "Senor Vasquez is at office. I show you to the work."

Senor Vasquez was still at work? She'd made an appointment via text for this evening; had overtipped the cab driver to step on the gas. Granted, it was an unusual time of day to meet, but Vasquez had texted it would be perfect. She could meet him, give him a rundown of what to expect and then retire to the hotel, where she'd had her luggage sent, and crash.

Amber followed dutifully as the maid led her through the house, across an inner courtyard open to the sky that mirrored the outer courtyard and up a stairway. She was no architectural expert, but this place screamed traditional Spanish influence with the cream-painted walls and tiled columns. Bright tiles on the floors and walls. Lots of plants in huge terra-cotta pots. And an airy openness that made her heart sigh. If she had the money for a place this grand, she would certainly indulge herself.

Someday she would.

The housekeeper directed her to walk through a door. "It is inside." The woman's phone buzzed in a hip pocket, which she patted. "I will leave you. I have my stories."

"Gracias—" Amber flinched as the door closed in her face. Really? "Not the friendliest."

Making friends with the staff wasn't necessary. Not yet. The housekeeper could provide insight into Senor Vasquez's life. She'd talk with her, and any other staff, only with the client's permission.

Strolling down a short hallway, she walked into… "A closet?"

Three times the size of her bedroom in the 9th arrondissement flat, which she shared with two other Lux Love consultants. It looked like a showroom, or a designer clothing shop. Well lit with dark woods and suede-lined walls. Three of the walls were shelved, racked and…impossibly messy. A vanity with a mirror and scattered grooming products occupied one wall. In the center of the room stood a marble-topped counter where a few watches had been laid out on a black velvet cloth. Beside that were tossed unmatched socks and…she averted her gaze from the boxer shorts.

Yes, she'd been briefed that her role in vetting the client could become intimate, in a manner. She would need to learn everything about Senor Vasquez's life. That included ticking off items regarding his sexual preferences.

Amber turned, taking in the clothing, which seemed a mix of expensive suits—thankfully, hung—and T-shirts and sweatpants. A little odd the housekeeper had taken her here to begin her work. Perhaps it was a passive-aggressive means to showing Amber where the worst problem was?

Her shoulders tightened as taut as violin strings at the sight of clothing piled here and there, the leather shoes scattered, the— "That silk tie must be worth a fortune."

Plucking up the crumpled pink silk, she smoothed it out before hanging it among many others displayed on a wall. The man needed a closet cleanup. She would note that on her to-do list. But why didn't the housekeeper take care of his things?

"Weird."

Messiness was not a deal-breaker, but this sort of disarray usually came from a lifelong habit. She'd do her best to gently but firmly guide him toward a tidier home. No woman wanted to marry a little boy who expected her to clean up after him.

But *she* also had to remember that one person's mess was another person's comfort. And messy people often matched to one another. Lux Love never tried to match an exact replica to the client. And truly, opposites never paired well. A happy medium always proved best.

If Vasquez wasn't home, she didn't want to start sorting through his things without his permission. She'd text him; possibly he was on his way home. Pulling her phone from her purse, she strode back to the door and—it didn't open.

"Locked?" She tried again. The knob twisted but didn't click open. "Did she purposely…?"

No. The housekeeper had no motivation to lock Amber in. It must have accidentally locked. A muscle twinged across her shoulders. This day had been too long.

Returning to the closet, Amber realized she wasn't hot from the stifling confines—the AC was on and it felt rather nice in here. But rather…she was so tired.

She tapped the phone screen but it remained dark. Out of charge? Seriously?

She'd had her bags—with the phone charger inside—sent to the hotel. Eying the outlets set around the center table, she wondered if there was a phone charger in one of the drawers. After a quick check, she didn't find any.

A glance to the mirror on the opposite wall displayed a frustrated, tired woman who was trying to hold it together on her first big job. "This has to go well," she said to her weary reflection.

Failure never earned the gold star.

Plopping on to an ultracomfy chaise longue before a narrow window that overlooked the inner courtyard, Amber shook her head. She could imagine Colette shaking her perfectly coiffed head and muttering how she should have sent Chantelle instead.

Amber would not tell her boss about this little misstep. Senor Vasquez would find her soon enough, if the housekeeper didn't come looking for her before that.

Life was all about achieving and moving forward. One step higher on the career ladder. One more credit card bill paid. Challenge was what nudged her out of bed in the morning. She could do this. And she would.

A yawn preceded a sigh, and then...

Val Vasquez strolled through the kitchen and grabbed an electrolyte drink from the fridge. His housekeeper kept all the necessities in stock. She knew he liked to jog home from work. Even if it was after dark.

He tilted back the lemon-flavored drink in a long swallow, then swiped the back of his hand across his mouth. Leaving the lights off, he sprinted up the inner courtyard stairs. The lush orange blossoms scented his house with a honey-citrus perfume.

Once in his bedroom, he tossed his sweaty shirt to the floor and aimed for the bathroom. A cool shower was in order.

Five minutes later, he wrapped a towel around his hips and entered the digital code on the closet door. He kept valuables inside so security was necessary. He entered the closet to grab a pair of linen sleep pants. Why were the lights on? Had they been left on since morning?

"Whatever." He veered toward the pants section.

But what was that? He spied something on the chaise before the window that overlooked the courtyard. Had Maria let in Emmer, the watch repairman? It was late to still be here. And he was…sleeping?

Who would take a nap while working? He glanced to the other door that opened to the hallway. The knob always jammed; something else for security to fix.

Wandering over, he deftly avoided a heap of dirty clothes with a jump to the side. He leaned over the chaise to jostle Emmer awake but retracted his hand before he could touch.

"A woman?"

CHAPTER TWO

SOMETHING NUDGED AMBER AWAKE. She shook her head. Winced at a kink in her neck. Opened her eyes.

A man leaned over her. He swept his fingers through his hair. Rich, curly dark hair that fell over one deep brown eye. Light glinted like jewels in his soft irises. So captivating. Did she...know him?

Wait. Was she—had she been sleeping? And a strange man loomed over her.

Amber startled upright on the chaise, swinging her feet to the floor. Where was she? *Closet.* She'd been...yes, locked inside. Had sat down because... *Jet lag.* And the man...was he...he wore but a towel!

"Oh no. I, uh...was not sleeping. I, uh, Senor Vasquez?"

"In the flesh."

He splayed out his arms as if to say *Look all you like.* Amber tried desperately not to, but...*abs*. Many rows of abs. So hard. And tight. She narrowed her gaze and started to count—

"You are not Emmer Ruiz."

Emmer? Where had she heard that name? Ah. "No, it's *Amber*. Amber Martin. I don't know any Emmer."

"Emmer is the name of the watch repairman that I assume Maria thought she let into this room. But the watches haven't been touched. And you are a sleeping beauty."

"I'm so sorry." Jumping to stand, she stepped near the window, hand fluttering nervously to her chest. A yawn was unpreventable. How long had she slept? "I was locked in. I wanted to call your maid to let me out but my phone is dead. I'm Amber, with Lux Love. We had an appointment this evening?"

"I thought that appointment was tomorrow?"

"I just spoke to you last night—er..." What time was it? "I'm...sorry, I don't think I made a mistake in the day..."

He tapped the watch on his wrist. "I never get things on my calendar. I think about it and then...eh. I got you switched around in my head with the watch repairman. Sorry."

"That's..." So not acceptable for his dating future. She could not abide a disorganized man.

Oh yeah, Amber? You're not here to vet him for yourself.

Right. She clutched her purse to her stomach.

"We all forget on occasion, Senor Vasquez. And it was a last-minute appointment. I didn't mean to nap in your home, but when I couldn't get out..."

"Not your fault. That knob needs to be fixed. And I always lock the other door on the bedroom side." He gestured to the mirror hung on the wall, which acted as an illusion that did not scream *Door right here!*

"I hadn't noticed that door. Anyway, once I sat down... jet lag attacked. I've been traveling all day. Started in Minnesota."

"That's a long haul. I did assume you were American from your accent."

Nodding, she put a palm over her mouth as she yawned again. Seriously. She just needed a real bed and some uninterrupted sleep. "My flight, which I hadn't had time to change, took me to Paris, and then here. It's been a whirlwind, to say the least."

"Don't worry about it, Senorita Martin." He wandered around the center console and shoved a random pile of boxer shorts to the floor. Cast her a glance. Like he thought she'd *not* seen that?

"Uh…" Her eyes kept landing on his impossible abs. *Likes to work out* would definitely be noted on his profile. Amber rubbed a hand along the back of her neck. "I know this is a very strange beginning…"

His biceps flexed as he waved his arms back and forth, meeting before his hips in a fist bump. Nervous energy? She knew the feeling!

"Just got home from work," he said, smoothing a palm across his bare abs. "It's, uh, almost midnight."

"What? Oh my gosh." That the client had found her sleeping in his closet! And it was so late! "I can't believe I slept so long. I should leave. We'll reschedule our initial assessment for tomorrow. I'm so sorry, Senor Vasquez. I—this is not like me at all. I'm much sharper. Totally reliable."

Futile attempts to keep her eyes from his abs were just that—futile. He didn't seem the least embarrassed.

"Don't worry about it. You're here for about a week?"

"Yes, a week. Or so. However long it takes to complete your compatibility assessment and…to get you matched."

"Assess all you like. I have confidence your AI will find my true love."

"Yes, true love." Delivered by artificial intelligence. Oh, how Amber despised AI. It had taken her job, after all. Yet despite that annoyance, she would only speak positively about its ability to delve into the realm of romance and love for the client. It was what the job required. "What everyone desires."

He cocked his head at her. "I don't have to know you to

judge from your tone that you just lied to me. Don't you believe in love, Amber?"

"Of course, I do." Mercy, she was so tired. Not top of her game. He'd easily sussed out her lie. "And you will too once the algorithms report back with your perfect match."

"I'm excited to begin the process. I called Lux Love because I don't have the time to do this on my own. And I'm over swiping left or right."

The norm for a man of his income level. As well, those who were financially gifted required a vetting service to weed out the gold diggers and transactional seekers. Unless of course, that was the sort of relationship the client sought.

"Please consider my home your home while you are here. I like to know my guests are treated as family."

"Gracias."

"You'll stay in the guest room while you are working?" he asked.

"Oh." Amber gestured toward the narrow window. "I have a room at a nearby hotel."

"Nonsense." A swipe of his fingers through his hair dispersed some hanks from his eyes. Dark irises that she couldn't get a good read on. But his smile distracted from that assessment. Genuine but a little nervous, to assess his fidgety movements. "There are so many guest rooms in my home even I don't know how many there are. I've had Maria prepare one for you. It'll be good to have you on-site, and you'll save some expenses."

"My boss would certainly appreciate that. And it is very late—"

"The guest room it is," he interrupted.

"But I've had my suitcase sent to the hotel."

He tapped his watch and spoke into it in Spanish, which Amber was able to half-decipher. "Maria, are you still awake? Come bring Senorita Martin to one of the guest rooms, will you? No, she's not Emmer, she's Amber. *Amber*. Like…the tree resin." He winked at her. A comment from Maria sparked him to correct her. "No, the orange trees don't need trimming. Come to my closet, Maria."

Amber looked to the door, possibly for escape. She'd just experienced the absolute worst possible way to meet the client. Colette must never learn about this less-than-promising beginning.

"My housekeeper will be right up."

"I hope you didn't wake her. I can find the room on my own."

"No worries. She stays up late watching her stories. Let her know which hotel your suitcase is at. I'll have my car pick it up for you." He scratched the back of his head. Could he have a manner that did *not* draw her gaze to those killer abs? "There's some grass in the courtyard. You can access it from any of the guest rooms."

"Uh, grass?"

Valentino's smile was sweet but salted with a curl of sensuality. "Take off your shoes and ground yourself. It's good for jet lag. It's what I do after a long flight. Works like a charm. So we can begin tomorrow?"

"Of course. I'll want to tour your home, take things in." *Assume control.* "Everything I observe will be entered in our database to complete your profile."

"Usually I wake at five for a jog, then head in to work after the sun has risen."

"Oh."

He smirked. "You've got free rein of the house. Do what you need to do. I'll check in with you at a more fitting hour to see if you have questions?"

She nodded. "That sounds great. I appreciate your hospitality, Senor Vasquez."

"It's gotta be Val if you're going to move in for a few days."

"Val. Of course."

"And you are Amber."

"Tree resin," she said and then burst into a big sleep-deprived grin.

He winked at her just as Maria called down the hall. "She'll get you set up. Don't forget to ground!"

Val watched the woman in a sleek red suit with sleep-mussed hair—he hadn't pointed that out to her—walk out, noting she clung to her purse as if it were a shield. Her legs went on for days. And despite her slim hips, she had the sexiest wiggle to her backside. She was going to spend a week with him to ensure he found the perfect match?

Something he didn't have the time, or social IQ, to do on his own. All the apps he'd given a try never showed the real person. Everyone lied about something. But the Lux Love service was something he could get behind. They utilized proprietary algorithms to find a match. As a gaming coder, he trusted algorithms.

He'd been told the Lux Love lifestyle consultant would assess his home, workplace, his every move. As a consultant, she may even suggest tweaks or slight lifestyle changes that may enhance his dateability. She would even go out on dates with him to assess how he treated a woman. That was all fine with him.

It wasn't going to happen naturally. So when all else failed, AI had his back.

With one last glance to catch the towel-clad backside of the finest Spanish billionaire she had ever met—admittedly, the only one—Amber followed the housekeeper's rapid steps. Maria curled down the grand staircase and they crossed the inner courtyard. Another bubbling fountain? More tiles? Terra-cotta planters? Love it! The home's decor held immense visual appeal for Senor Vasquez's future match.

But Amber knew that was all surface. The true measure of a perfect match lay in understanding her client's emotional wants and needs. Body language was an excellent indicator of emotion. Valentino's body language had been easy and sensual yet a little anxious. Of course, their meeting had been out of the ordinary.

They continued around a corner on the ground floor and down a hallway, then Maria opened a door, flicked on the inner light and gestured for Amber to enter. The spacious room drew her inward. Bright curtains were pulled back to reveal the solar lights set here and there in the courtyard.

Grounding? Was the man into that woo-woo stuff? She wouldn't expect that from a tech genius.

"Is good," the housekeeper stated. Not as a question.

"Yes, it's—yikes!" Amber jumped back after almost stepping into the large taxidermy head of a bull. Stuffed and mounted on a massive wood plaque. The horns were tipped in gold. It sported a large ring through its nose. "What the… Uh, is this…?"

She turned but Maria was gone.

Shaking her head at the dispassionate maid, Amber stepped wide around the hideous thing. It had been set on the floor in the corner of the room; the big black glossy eyes focused directly on the bed.

Hands to her hips, she took a step back and wondered if she could ask for a different room, then thought better of it. She was a solutions person. This? A challenge to be met.

She spied a blanket spread across the end of the bed. With a grand swing, she managed to cover the bull's horns and… Those eyes still held her in uncertain panic.

"You are going elsewhere," she said with a waggle of her

forefinger at the beast. "And then, to tackle the rest of this place. And…"

The man had stood before a complete stranger in nothing but a towel. Valentino Vasquez certainly wasn't modest. Had he been goading her? Looking for a reaction? Some men were so full of themselves they thought the entire female population wanted them. She hadn't sensed that from Valentino. Val. And she wouldn't lodge a single complaint against studying his body.

On the other hand, she was not here to assess his physique. Beyond checking the box that he appeared healthy.

"A fine specimen," she whispered. The sudden wave of heat that rosed her neck and cheeks could not be a blush.

Amber Martin was *not* attracted to Valentino Vasquez.

Colette's voice echoed in her head: *Don't fall in love.*

"And don't forget it."

Because love was fickle and never lasted. And after trying to console her dad during her recent visit, who still had not gotten over her mother, heartbreak was not something Amber wanted to experience.

CHAPTER THREE

AMBER SLEPT WELL despite the watchful eye of the bull. Today she would go through Val's house to get a feel for his environment. Most would believe it wasn't necessary to go so deep into a person's life just to make a match. Did the match really care if his sheets were flannel or silk? If his toothpaste was all-natural? And were those tiles in the courtyard mass-produced or handmade here in Seville? It was Lux Love's dedication to detail that had garnered them a 98 percent success rate.

Amber's boss never talked about that 2 percent. She did wonder about it but would never ask. Inappropriate. And… they couldn't get it right all the time, could they?

Well. She did expect that a computer should make that a 100 percent with ease.

Now she stood out in the courtyard barefoot on the grass surrounding the orange trees. Having discovered a plate of fresh fruit, coffee and toast waiting for her in the kitchen, along with a text from Val: Left for a jog at five a.m. Feel free to go through the house while I'm at work. As well, he'd given her the code to his closet. Just in case, he'd noted and ended with a smiley face emoji.

She would not carry that humility of getting trapped in his closet. It had happened. She had not seen *all* his anatomy. Unfortunately. Nothing she could do now to change that inauspicious first meeting. Move on.

But as well, check the box for *thoughtful* and *kind*.

Wiggling her toes in the cool grass, she gave herself a gold star for insinuating herself into the client's home. Colette preferred on-site vetting, but her consultants booked hotel rooms first. If offered, they gracefully accepted to stay in the client's home, or guest house. And with the Lux Love clientele's income, that was generally offered.

Valentino Vasquez should be an easy match. Who could resist that muscular, dark drink of sexy? His voice oozed a playful sensuality. Amber shivered to think of it. Or was it the play of the grass across her bare toes that gave her the chill? No, the right tone of voice always did it for her. And his dark hair and beard stubble. Perfect playground for someone's fingernails to glide over. Explore. Dash a finger across his lips?

Straightening and shaking her head, she admonished herself for a slip into daydreams. She was not here to drool over the client. Swooning over a man was beneath her. She would note all the man's physical pluses on her assessment. And really? A person's exterior was just for show. What really mattered were the insides, and that included all the messy emotional stuff that, admittedly, she wasn't tops in relating to.

Stepping back into her heels, she gave her bouncy curls a flip with her hand then strolled inside. Her suitcase had been waiting outside her bedroom door this morning. Thankfully, she'd packed a linen dress for her visit to her dad, because it had been an unseasonable sixty degrees in Minnesota—crazy for the end of March. She visited her dad twice a year to catch up, but also to have coffee with friends from her hometown. Eddie Martin was an electrician who kept himself busy with work and outdoor sports like fishing and hockey with his friends. But he had been heartbroken when her mom announced she wanted a divorce three years ago. The pain in his eyes was still evident. Amber suspected her dad would never remarry. But she did hope he'd find a way toward seeking female companionship. There was nothing wrong with beers with the guys, but he had mentioned how he missed going to the movies and having dinner out.

Mom lived in Canada; she and Amber hadn't seen one another in years. They were both still cooling off after what Amber considered a mutiny from what she'd thought had been a fairy-tale romance of twenty-five married years. The luster had been wiped from her mom's veneer. She'd not been the perfect wife, after all. The divorce had crushed Amber's heart and made her believe that love could never be real. If two people could part after living together so long? Why risk even entering into a relationship in the first place?

But right now, in order to do her best at the matchmaking gig, Amber had to set that heartbreak aside.

The entire Vasquez villa smelled like an orange tree orchard. It was going to be quite a letdown to return to her tiny space in Paris that backed up to a brick wall. But still. Paris. A girl could never argue with that cosmopolitan address. Even if it was merely a closet. And paying rent put her in debt.

She picked up the Lux Love–issued tablet she'd left in the kitchen and decided to go through the house room by room. It was surprising what could be learned about a person by taking in their surroundings. Artwork was a big personality tell. While furniture and the colors and textures within the house were considered, many men of Val's wealth used stylists, minimizing its importance. She would even spy on his television watch list. All sports and no movies? Only documentaries? Romances and action-adventure? All necessary to get a thorough understanding of the client.

First confirming the housekeeper wasn't around, she then opened some kitchen cupboards to get a feel for what foods Valentino Vasquez liked to eat. Hmm, there were a lot of orange preserves in here.

Val stepped out of the lounge chair he'd designed to optimize his working conditions. A comfy chair, it sported a full-body massager, heat and cold adjustments, and was equipped for VR with haptic sensors. When not sitting, he stood on the hologram platform amidst a literal digital representation of his work. Thanks to the room's biosensors, he could type and move code around without haptic gloves. It was action-movie futuristic stuff, but not really. This was today's technology, and he loved playing with it. But there was also an hourly alarm to alert him to give his brain a rest. Otherwise, he could get lost here in "the dark room," and may emerge in the middle of the night. Been there. Done that far too many times.

His brain worked best when immersed in chaos. He rarely grounded himself like he'd told Amber to do last night. But he should. He wasn't going to find a life partner by spending 75 percent of his time here in the dark room. Or was it eighty? He didn't want to do that math.

A glance to his watch confirmed it was lunch time. The cafeteria catered from local restaurants and always offered something delicious. As he left the room, he said goodbye to Hal, the AI he'd programmed to help him code and which biomonitored the entire dark room. Hal could tell him he was going to get a cold before Val even knew it. Everything about the Verdadero headquarters was designed for health. Both he and Teo were sticklers for working out, staying healthy and…

Teo had fallen in love last year. He'd found his person. And had married her recently. And that had poked at Val's heart in a manner he hadn't expected. Made him examine his life. What little life he had away from the office. He wanted that happy, smiling, confidant stride Teo had. And after years of devoting all his time and talent toward Verdadero, he wanted to start focusing on his needs. Was it possible? What *were* his needs?

The main need had risen to the fore after missing his regular weekly dinner engagement with his dad last week. Luis Vasquez had wanted to introduce his son to a niece of a family friend. His old man was always trying to get him married off. To start a family. To preserve a family legacy steeped in cultural traditions. And Val didn't mind; it distracted his dad from bemoaning his son's job.

You have so much talent! Luis Vasquez often accused his son. *What is this coding? It is not a traditional skill.* And then his dad would make that scoffing noise and the gesture of dismissal the old man should patent. Luis had actually once told a news reporter that his son had been lured away from dancing by the selfish pursuit for money. Seriously!

His dad was a former bullfighter. Luis once lived for the adulation, the cheers from the crowd. He'd married a beautiful Andalusian flamenco dancer for love. Since Val could walk, his mother had influenced him to take up flamenco dance. He loved the movement, the expression of a story that was steeped in Andalusian and Sevillian history.

There were times Val wondered if he'd made the right choice leaving dance for coding. It hadn't been for money; but, oh, how the money had flowed. He did enjoy his job *and* he worked with his best friend. Who could ask for anything more?

He could. He wanted love. And to start his own family. And sure, he could assuage the guilt his dad instilled by marrying a Spanish woman.

But he'd missed the dinner date. Why could he never remember to schedule appointments in his calendar? Luis had called and chewed him out. Val had given the usual excuse: working. So when Teo had sent him a link to Lux Love a few days later, Val had immediately called the number and spoken to the owner, Colette Bellerose. He was ready to get serious about finding love.

But what a tease that they'd sent a gorgeous woman to live with him for days to vet him for the service. And to find her sleeping in his closet? That seemed far off course from a professional dating service, but he did understand she had been jet-lagged and had appeared embarrassed. He'd decided against trying to speak to her this morning. His hours were too early for most humans.

She would go on dates with him to see how he treated a woman? Fair enough. But also, not fair! How to keep from staring at her bright red lips? From pushing his fingers through that bouncy dark hair? Sleep tousled, it had been so…touchable. But he'd read that clutched purse as uptight. That would have to change. No one spent any amount of time with him without letting down their hair and eventually going for a jog with him.

It was his nature. He was *inquieto*, as his mom used to describe his need to always move, always be doing something—creating, running, dancing, coding, whatever was to hand. He couldn't sit still for long. Even when coding, he paced the holo-platform, gesturing, jogging, shadowboxing. He kept a jump rope in the dark room for quick bursts of adrenaline. And his brain insisted on remaining in the game, short-circuiting his focus and constantly alerting him to new tasks, experiences, tastes, conversations—whew!

He tired himself out some days.

"Val!"

At the sound of his partner's voice, Val jumped into a spin and waited for Teo to catch up with his backward steps. "Heading in for some gazpacho. Join me?"

"Always." His friend since middle school was taller than him, a good-looking guy and very driven. Teo was somber to Val's goofy. And always dressed impeccably.

Val had tried to do business suits but his constantly-in-motion body struggled with the strict confines, so he went with jeans and a T-shirt most days. But a nice T-shirt. So what if it had a few wrinkles?

Teo opened the glass cafeteria door and held it as Val dashed inside. "How's the StarCloud project coming along?"

"With all our games now being considered as potential movie projects, I want to go over everything with a fine-tooth comb." They'd signed a deal with a major movie studio last year to put *Matador* on the big screen. Their former partner, Pablo, who had died years earlier, would be so proud! "How about you? What are you working on?"

"This and that. Marketing the latest VR gaming centers we opened last month in Japan. You remember there's the foundation ball in less than two weeks, right?"

The men sat at their usual table and with a gesture to the chef from Teo, they knew they'd be served.

Val leaned back and put his foot up on an empty chair. His favorite trainers were getting thin on the rubber soles. They were about the only material item he enjoyed shopping for. "I forgot about the ball."

"I knew you would." That smile was the one Teo always gave Val when he knew his friend's brain was juggling half a dozen balls.

Val nodded thanks to the chef, who delivered their meals personally. "What's the focus for this one?"

Every year Verdadero held an elegant ball to thank the

supporters of the Pablo Pascal Foundation. One third of Verdadero's profits, Pablo's share, was placed in the foundation. It was their way of giving back to the community they loved and to honor their departed friend Pablo, who had been killed in a tragic hit-and-run crash; the driver had had a medical emergency. Twenty-two had been too young to die. But Pablo's legacy would live forever through the foundation and in their original game, *Matador*.

"Your suggestion, actually," Teo said. "Remember the meeting after the last ball when you said we should donate to local schools to pay for music education and instruments?"

"Oh yeah, that was my idea. Cool. It's time to dig out my tux."

"And consider having the shirt ironed, eh?"

Val matched Teo's smirk. Maria—she tried to keep up with him but laundry was not her forte. Nor was housecleaning. But she could mix up a to-die-for sangria.

"Cara is excited for the event. It'll be her first one as my wife."

She and Teo had married recently after dating a year. Cara had once dated Pablo. After the car accident and following Pablo's funeral, she had disappeared. Then last year she'd shown up in a Sevillian hospital in need of a place to stay while she recovered from surgery to remove her burst appendix. Teo had taken her in. And that was another story entirely.

Val high-fived his best friend across the table. "She's good for you."

"Too good for me," Teo said. "She makes sure I don't get bogged down in work and that I laugh at least once a day. But am I good enough for her?"

"Never." Val chuckled. "But I won't tell her that."

"Do keep that to yourself. So what about you? Did you look into that matchmaking service I suggested for you?"

"There's a consultant at my home right now, going through it with a fine-tooth comb."

Teo slurped in some of the chilled soup. "What's that about?"

"They pour over my entire life in order to match me to the perfect woman."

"Do you *really* want a perfect woman?"

"Absolutely not. Perfect would be too much. You know what I really want?"

"A gaming partner who won't complain about your dirty boxers strewn all over the house?"

"Is someone like that available?"

They both laughed.

"No, what I really want is goose bumps love."

Teo nodded, knowing. They'd both listened to Pablo when they were teens talking about all the women he was going to love. Pablo had been geeky Val's inspiration and a mentor on how to approach girls. According to Pablo, the only way to know if you were really in love? A guy got goose bumps when he kissed the one.

It hadn't happened yet. But that was the measure Val intended to use.

Perfection was always her goal.

Amber had strived for it her entire life. From getting straight A's in school—the rewards were cash from her parents and a new laptop—to wearing trending clothes, even if she had to budget and find dupes or thrift, makeup and hair. She had to do things right. The perfect way. Or it wasn't worth doing at all. And so what if others didn't understand her quest for perfection? All that mattered was that metaphorical gold star she got when she knew the job had been done right. More so now that she was competing against her parents' failed marriage. They had lost their gold star. Amber was determined to keep hers.

Her shoulders dropped as she stood in the guest bedroom staring at the massive stuffed bull's head. There was a fine line she tried to balance between overzealous control and a breathable state of not-quite-control, yet it wasn't that easy. Perfection had been brewed into her veins by her professor mom and electrician dad. She didn't know how to let her hair down and relax. And that taxidermy head was not conducive to relaxation.

Her phone rang.

"Colette, how are you?"

"Amber, *chère*, you are in Seville with the client." Colette wasn't one for niceties; she always got right to the point. Unless you met her in person, then the double-cheek kisses and surface-level praise were de rigueur. "How was the initial meeting?"

In the closet and with a half-naked man? She couldn't tell her boss she'd fallen asleep on the job before the job had even started. The bull's glossy stare seemed to accuse her of that slipup.

She turned her back to the beast.

"Senor Vasquez keeps odd hours, so he was home late last night and out the door before the sun rose this morning. He's given me free rein in his villa and I've spent the day assessing the place."

"Any issues?"

"Other than a severe lack of tidiness, nothing stands out. The expected expensive artwork and furnishings. Electronic gadgets and toys everywhere." A superior coffee maker that she had merely told what she'd wanted and it had delivered. "Also very cozy and traditional. I like it." She straightened, realizing she'd interjected her own feelings. "I mean, it's a lovely home. But I may suggest he hire a housekeeper."

"I thought he already had one. His survey lists a chef, gardener and maid."

Yes, Maria. Amber wasn't sure what the woman actually did around the house. She'd only seen her in the kitchen at lunchtime, sitting at the table watching a portable television. She'd barely lifted her head to tell her to help herself to the pantry items. Or at least, that's how she'd interpreted her rapid Spanish.

"It's the first day," Amber stated, unwilling to let on that she hadn't gotten a grasp on the job yet. "I'm just sitting down to fill in data on the assessment."

"Have you scheduled a date with Senor Vasquez? We mustn't waste time, Amber. We don't want to impose on the client longer than necessary. Efficiency is key."

"I'm very efficient." And she expected the validation for that. But she hadn't looked ahead to the date part of this assessment. And that wasn't because this was her first time in the field. She was…a little nervous? Unsure about doing the fake date thing with such an arrestingly handsome man? "I'll…we'll go out tonight so I can get a feel for how he treats a woman."

"Excellent. Keep us updated. I'll be following your progress as the data comes in."

"Of course."

"Ciao."

"Yes, ciao," Amber muttered but Colette had already hung up.

Her boss was a stickler for keeping the budget down, but she also strived to keep an elite face to the company. Which required her consultants to dress the part, checkbook groaning. Necessary, considering their clientele. Invited to all the hottest parties, Colette often mingled with the rich, celebrities and even politicians. But behind the scenes she was all business and aiming to move that 98 percent match rate up another number.

Amber dialed Val and when he didn't answer, she texted: Would you like to get something to eat tonight? Work date?

He answered quickly. You going to study me?

Of course.

Sounds intriguing. I'll be home early, around seven.

See you then, she texted back.

She wandered to the patio door and stepped out, taking off her shoes. Her skin tingled, soaking in the citrusy scent. Muscles shivered from a cool breeze. She was going on a date with a man she'd met briefly last night. In a towel. And she'd taken that time to count his abs—an eight-pack—instead of holding a witty, informative conversation with him.

Who would have ever thought a girl who had once aspired to sit in dusty old law libraries researching for her bosses would see herself in such a situation? It hadn't been in her life trajectory. So did that mean she was adaptable?

"Don't get carried away," she muttered. "The last thing you want to do is let your hair down and…" *Have fun?* "…screw up this job."

CHAPTER FOUR

EXITING THE SHOWER after work, Val wandered into his bedroom with a towel wrapped about his hips. He rubbed another towel over his wet hair. Arriving home around 10:00 p.m., he'd found Amber sitting at the kitchen table rapping her fingers on the surface. That look she'd given him had felt like a parent admonishing a child. Had she studied under Luis? Ha! So he'd been three hours late. Yes, he knew he couldn't do that on a *real* date.

If he were honest with himself, it wasn't because he couldn't remember to schedule appointments or to leave work at a reasonable hour—it was just that his priorities were focused on work. He didn't know how to move *personal life* up on that list.

Kind of weird to think that Senorita Martin was meticulously scrutinizing his life, both personally and professionally, to find him the ideal partner.

The one woman for him. His person.

Was she out there?

Changing into casual slacks and a black dress shirt, he then studied his face in the vanity mirror. Needed a shave, but he'd not known his face without the dark stubble since he was a teenager. Giving his hair a vigorous scrub with his hands would help it to dry. He kept it trimmed along the sides and back and let the top do its thing. A woman had once told him in a sultry coo that it was bed-tousled. Ha! The sight of his messy morning hair would have made her laugh.

On his way to the main level to find Amber, he passed Maria resting in the inner courtyard under an orange tree. The mini TV was propped before her.

"How's the family, Maria?" he called as he strolled down the stairs.

"Eduardo and Catalina are having an affair."

"No kidding?" He jumped from the second to the bottom step to the tiled floor. "That's not good."

"Oh, it's delicious."

He smiled to himself at his housekeeper's giggle. Over the years, he'd gotten to know all the names of the soap opera characters that kept Maria's attention. "I'm heading out, Maria. Don't wait up for me."

He always said that to her when he left. She wasn't his mother, or even his grandmother, but she was a sort of matriarchal substitute. His mother had passed away when he was seventeen. He'd not known grief until then; he'd felt her absence as a genuine ache in his heart. He was thankful for Teo and Pablo—they'd helped him to rise above that grief. Yet as he'd entered university, he struggled with leaving dance behind. The one thing that had bonded him and his mother. It had been Maria, who had worked in a local café near the campus, who had taken him under her wing, chatting to him as he'd burned late hours studying in the back booth. When he'd bought this villa, he'd gone in search of Maria and learned she was doing housekeeping. Good woman, that Maria.

Amber spun out of the kitchen in a knee-length blue dress that more than hugged her body. It wrapped its metaphorical arms about her and made love to her. She wasn't a curvaceous woman, but something about the way she held herself, chin up, shoulders straight, radiated confidence. Her hair was so shiny. Val wanted to touch it, see if those curls might coil about his fingers. And how perfect was her mouth? The bright red lipstick screamed that her mouth had been made for a kiss.

"Senorita Martin." He bowed slightly. "Nice to finally meet you. Er…in the proper manner. My apologies for last night. I hadn't expected to find you—"

"Awake and upright? Already forgotten," she rushed out. She extended her hand for him to shake. The greeting was too formal. He stepped in and kissed both her cheeks. She slipped back, a little startled. "I, uh… Nice to meet you too, Senor Vasquez. Despite the three-hour lag." She wasn't going to let him forget about his lateness. "And thank you for giving me the run of your home today while you were at work."

"Did you find what you were looking for?"

She tilted her head in question. "I wasn't snooping, or anything like that. I noted how you live. If there are possible areas for improvement—"

"Improvement? You don't like my casa?"

"It's lovely. The artwork tells a lot about a man."

"You think so?" Val turned to the Dulk mural on the wall behind him. "How do you know that wasn't there when I moved in?"

"Generally, when someone with your kind of money moves into a house, they usually make it their own. Including the artwork. I can't imagine you'd be content with another person's tastes."

"Unless they match my own?" He shook his head. "I'm teasing you. That's my favorite work." He gestured over his shoulder. "Dulk is an urban artist. He worked directly on the wall with spray paints and oils. The fish on the leash always gives me a chuckle. You like the modern artists?"

"I'm not into art all that much. I wouldn't know a Picasso from a Rembrandt."

"Oh, you would. But now don't think I'm going to forget you mentioned something about improvements? To my home?"

"I shouldn't have put it that way. Well. I'm looking at your home as if I were a potential match. Women like a tidy home. Everything in its place. How else to know what belongs and what doesn't?"

Val smirked. "That's what a cleaner is for."

"That's what I've always understood, but..."

That she let it hang was a play, inviting his move. So Maria did not pull her weight around here. It didn't bother him at all.

Val snagged a pair of black loafers from beneath a stack of unread newspapers that were creeping out from the foyer closet and slipped them on. "Maria is non-negotiable. She stays. No matter what."

"Is she...family?"

"Yes. Uh...not by blood, but she's been with me since I got this place six years ago."

Amber made an adjustment to his shirt collar. Comfortable with him already? Or some kind of neat freak? He guessed the latter. Everything about her was exact and tidy.

She splayed her fingers and stepped back, obviously realizing her faux pas. That moment of self-realization tickled him. Like she wanted to relax and go with the flow but had to stop herself. He'd not known such a restrained person as she. Interesting.

"I shouldn't have presumed," she said. "Whatever help Maria provides is certainly worth it if she's like family to you. But an occasional stop-in from a cleaner..."

"I can look into that. I'll add it to my list of things to do."

Which needed to move up on his priority list. Hell, what priority list?

She smelled like the orange blossoms with a hint of warm spice. The urge to wrap an arm around her waist and pull her closer was so strong he had to inwardly admonish the lusty thought. No flirting with the consultant! "Too many wrinkles?"

"Just the one right here." She pressed her fingers over his shoulder. "If I buy you an iron..."

"I do know that I own an iron. One talent Maria has is she puts a nice crease in my boxers. You gotta love that."

"Well then." She stepped back, hands to her hips in assessment of her handiwork. "Creased boxers. I'll add that to your profile."

"Really?"

She shook her head. "No."

"Ah, so you've some funny in you." He hooked an arm and she threaded hers with his. "I'm completely in your hands tonight. *Matchmaker, matchmaker, make me a match,*" he sang as he opened the front door and led her through the courtyard to meet the waiting car.

"*Catch me a catch,*" she sang in response. "I love *Fiddler on the Roof.*"

"Yeah? I like the old musicals, too. Great way to divert my brain from code during an afternoon break." He opened the car door for her. "Your carriage, my lady."

"Why thank you, good sir."

Once inside, he noticed Amber's dismay at the instrument-free dashboard.

"It's driverless," he said. "The AI does it all."

"Oh. AI. Of course. Yet one more thing set on taking over the world."

Val smirked. "And I'm happy about it. Buckle up. We'll be there in no time."

* * *

Sitting in a car that drove itself was unnerving. Val hadn't once touched the steering wheel. In fact, he'd slid his seat back and leaned an arm on the side door. Amber twisted her fingers under her thighs as he pointed out sights along the way. Oblivious to the worry they could crash at any moment.

Get over your annoyance at AI, Amber. It wasn't so much that she hated it. If the car were suddenly presented with an accident situation, would it choose to swerve to avoid a pedestrian, thus saving its occupants, or go straight ahead, possibly killing an innocent?

Oh, she had to stop thinking about it. *Concentrate on the sexy man. Take notes for his future wife. Do your job.*

Soon enough they'd arrived, Amber grabbed the door handle, eager to get out of the bizarre car, but then she relented. Would he run around and open the door for her?

When her door opened, and Val offered his hand, she took it, mentally noting that this one was a gentleman.

CHAPTER FIVE

ONCE AT THE RESTAURANT, Val got out of the car and swung around the back to open Amber's door and help her out. When she started to walk, he hooked his arm in hers and strolled her through the front door. The gentlemanly moves startled her. Amber hadn't been privy to such an act of chivalry. Ever. This was definitely going to make his score soar.

The restaurant was cozy but classy. At sight of Val, the maître d' escorted them to a table on a private terrace set near a fragrant flowering vine. Though the temperature had fallen, a nearby open hearth kept the area warm. Candlelight glittered. Somewhere, a soft melody was sung by a live singer. The waiter filled their wineglasses. Amber already felt more special than any date she'd previously—

She had to check herself. *She* was not on a real, romance-possible date with Val. This was a business date so she could get a feel for how the client treated a woman. And it hadn't started out on the best foot. She'd waited for him for hours.

Upon sitting, she'd set the tablet to her left, opened to the notes page.

"Does that tablet come along for the ride all the time?"

"I am on the clock." Amber sipped the crisp wine. "There're thousands of data points to complete your profile. I'm not much of a techie, but I know our proprietary AI is the key to Lux Love's success rate."

"Ninety-eight percent is nothing to sneeze at. Yes, the more data you enter, the finer and more accurate your results will be. But let's pretend this is a real date, *si*? I haven't been on a date in a while and—honestly, it's a rarity I get to relax and talk to a beautiful woman."

The comment should make any woman glow but Amber couldn't recall ever blushing. Though the feeling of warm acceptance was awesome. Even if it was fake, she could enjoy the compliment. And, very well, she needed to relax a little in order to take in the full experience.

"Right. This should be like a real date." She tucked the tablet in her purse. "Sorry. I'll take notes later. I…just like things to be perfect."

"Perfection is unobtainable."

"I don't know." The way the candlelight glinting in his dark irises was surely some sort of romance addict's prompt to fall into them. Amber halted her fall by sitting up straighter. "Ahem. I'm sure I can touch perfection. It's on my life trajectory."

"Your life trajectory? What's that about?"

"This date is not about me."

"But it is." He leaned forward, propping his elbows on the table, totally at ease in his body. "I like to get to know a woman when I take her on a date. Not talk about myself."

A man interested in something other than his stunning bank statement and remarkable intellectual feats? Intriguing.

"Fine." She could play along. And really, providing personal anecdotes would make the client more open to sharing his personal details.

Amber teased the stem of her wine goblet to distract her interest from his gaze. She'd once watched a movie set in the Regency era where the heroine had described the hero's eyes as brooding. She hadn't understood what that meant. Until now. Val's dark, heavily lashed eyes were definitely broody. Like sex simmering, waiting for the right moment. To...what?

Oh, she just wasn't tops when it came to dating. Once upon a time, she'd believed in love. Looked forward to the man opening her car door and treating her like a queen. Since her parents' divorce had shattered that belief in love? Her idea of a date was to be set up by a friend, go out for drinks and if both were willing, a few hours of making out and sex. Always at his place. And she always left right after sex. She didn't do the snuggle. Too awkward.

But none of that personal stuff would be revealed to a client. Unnecessary.

"My life trajectory," she announced. "Pay off my bills. Paris is very expensive. Start my own business. I'm not sure it has to be matchmaking related. It has to play to my strengths."

"Your strength is *not* in matchmaking?"

Oops. Shouldn't have mentioned that one. "Well, of course." Amber fiddled with the goblet stem. "Or else I wouldn't be here right now. I'm skilled in reading body language." Two days of utilizing it so far! "Your relaxed position means you are open. Easygoing. But as for the rest of my trajectory—" Yes, distract from the sad truth that she wasn't the best person to know and recognize love. That's what the algorithms were for. "—I want to own a home. Either in a city or suburbs. I'm not picky. But I prefer international as opposed to the States. I'm loving Spain so far. This spring weather is great, but I've heard Seville is like a frying pan in the summertime."

"You have to know how to live. Rise before the sun, spend the sunny hours inside with the air-conditioning, and siesta in the afternoon. It's all good. But one thing I didn't hear in your trajectory was mention of romance."

"Romance?"

Watch it, Amber. That tone of disgust is not putting a good light on Lux Love.

"Isn't that what life is about? To love and be loved?"

Could the man be any more compelling? His eyes…lured. She couldn't look away from them. And then his whole face came into view and his easy body language held such a teasing appeal. He wasn't trying too hard. Wasn't spouting numbers and successes like most men were wont. He seemed genuinely interested in the topic.

"Love has its merits," she said by rote. "I suppose."

"Wait." Val laid a hand on the table, skimming her fingertips that rested on the base of her wine goblet. A practiced move? Subtle touching could clue to seeking control. "A consultant from a matchmaking service is telling me that love *has its merits*?" One of his fingers tapped one of hers. "Do you even believe in what you sell?"

"I didn't mean it that way." Not the way to sell the company. She could hear Colette firing her right now. "I just… well…" Exposing her private life wasn't necessary to matching this man to another woman, but… His finger tapped hers again. A little tease or a touch of assurance? Amber sighed. "Love is personal to me. I don't share intimate details on a first date."

"I'm trying to get to know you."

"But only for fake. This isn't real, Val."

"I know that, but I'm trying to be myself and you are making that difficult."

"I'm sorry. I…know."

By all means she had to win the client's trust. She was his first match after all. Client to consultant. And this was part of the job. Letting her hair down metaphorically and playing the role of a date.

"You're right. You are only asking questions you would ask any woman on a date. Trying to get to know her. See if there's something about her that sparks your interest."

"Exactly."

"Honestly?" Dare she confess? He seemed good-natured about all this. "I've been with Lux Love for a year. I've watched and learned. But you're my first field assignment. So, please, don't say anything to my boss about my slipups, most especially our first meeting. I was mortified."

"To see me in a towel? I'm not sure how to take that."

"That eight-pack you have is fabulous. I mean, that I noticed."

That grin. Like a kid who'd just scored a whole bag of chocolate and didn't have to share it. It was cute, and it suited his easy charm. Oh, how his dates were going to love him. "For future reference, I'll try to wear clothing every time we are together."

Way to spoil a girl's daydreams.

"Clothing is good for client-consultant interactions. But on a real date, I'm sure you can let that rule slide."

He tilted his head in surprise.

What had she said? Oh! Amber had never been so flustered by a man's presence. He was all around her. Comforting but also tinged with a seductive tease. "Sorry. I'm trying to be perfect—"

"Amber." Val took her hand. His touches had a duty. To relax her, to make her feel grounded and comfortable. Mission: Scrambled! "Let's set perfection aside for the night, *si*?"

The man held her gaze longer than a few seconds, which breached a certain level of propriety and crooked a finger, luring her toward something more intimate.

"Amber?"

Beyond her thundering heartbeats she wrestled with her brain. *Be in the moment. Take it all in. Just pretend it's a date. A real one.* That was the only way she'd ever get a peek inside who Valentino Vasquez really was.

"Can we start over?" she asked.

Val released her hand and raised his wine goblet. "Hola, I'm Valentino Vasquez. Everyone calls me Val. *Encantado a de conocerle.*"

"Pleasure to meet you as well, Valentino. I'm Amber Martin. Er…well, you know, like tree resin."

His laughter was hearty and deep from his chest. And Amber couldn't even feel embarrassed by his reaction.

"You make me laugh, Amber. I like that."

"Pretty sure I don't have a humorous bone in my body."

"Everybody has one or two. I'll find them all."

Oh, would he? And how exactly did he intend to do that? By word or by touch? The thought was so arresting, she was thankful when the waiter arrived tableside with their meals.

Val requested more wine, and then took her hand again. "Join me to say thanks for this meal?"

A religious man? Or simply thankful for the things he had. Nice. Amber nodded and silently said a *thank you*.

When Val dove into the food, he growled appreciatively. "This is so good. I love it when someone else cooks for me."

"Isn't that always?"

"You got me there. I appreciate that my bank statement allows me to afford a chef."

"Do you want a wife to cook for you?"

He forked in a bite of his food. "If she wants to, that would be great. If not? There's the chef. I'd never want a woman to do anything just to please me."

"But some people's love language is acts of kindness toward others. So a woman may like to cook for you."

"I'm good with that. How do I know what *my* love language is?"

"I'll let you know once I figure it out." The assessment included a whole section on just that. "I think I could get used to a personal chef."

"Much better than all those potato omelets in college. Ugh."

"Is that where you met your partner, Mateo Ortiz?"

"We've been friends since secondary school after the councilor assigned me to tutor Teo and Pablo in maths."

"You all went to the same school?"

"Yes, we grew up in Triana. It's an older Sevillian barrio steeped in tradition. I was so thankful for that tutoring setup. Met the best friends of my life."

"And where is Pablo now? You listed him as a founding partner of Verdadero in your survey. But I noticed he's not mentioned as a fellow CEO?"

"Pablo passed away eleven years ago. He was hit by a driver who suffered a medical emergency."

"Oh, I'm so sorry. I didn't realize. I should have known." Why had that important detail not shown on the survey? A background check should have uncovered that.

"I didn't include that information in the survey because it's not necessary to finding a wife. Although…" Val leaned back in his chair. "Pablo was the one to show me how to be comfortable around girls. And it was his artwork and idea for a storyline that we developed into our first VR game, *Matador*. He was so talented. Kindest man you'd ever want to know."

"You must really miss him."

"*Sí*. We honor him every year with a fancy ball in his

name. The next one is in under two weeks. You'll have to attend."

"I'm not sure I'll be here that long. This process generally only takes a week or so."

He lifted his wine goblet for a toast. "Here's to making it last as long as that *or so* can be."

Charmed by his compelling manner, Amber clinked glasses with him. He wanted her to stick around for weeks? That would make this one very long assignment.

Yet, the thought of spending time with Val wasn't unpleasant. Sitting across the table from him, dining on fine food and wine did not feel at all like work. She could almost place herself in the position of some lucky woman who may become the man's future wife.

Actually, that would be helpful in her assessment. If she reacted to him on an emotional level, then any other woman should as well, yes?

Look at you, Amber, acing this assignment.

"Tell me about that mention of dance in your survey," she said. "Is it something you enjoy watching?"

"I studied flamenco dance for a long time."

He danced? Interesting. "Why did you decide to make the switch from dance to coding?"

"My friends and I had an idea for a video game that we were eager to create. I started coding for it while also dancing. After my mom died, I couldn't bring myself to dance anymore. I made the decision to set dancing aside right after entering college. My father will never forgive me for that choice."

"Oh?"

Val shrugged. "The old man is traditional. A *baille*, or male flamenco dancer, is the epitome of masculinity to him. He's a retired bullfighter. Ultra masculine. But also steeped in Spanish tradition, you know? It is a tremendous guilt I carry, trying to please him."

"Doesn't the fact that you've made a fortune turn his head just a little?"

"Not at all." Val cut into his steak. "He thinks I've sold out to some robotic future that is going to overtake humankind. Ha! Well, you never know, eh? Anyway, I've always been a geek. Never attracted the girls in school because I hadn't a clue how to speak that language."

"What language is that?"

"Love and romance, of course."

"But you said Pablo taught you how to be comfortable around girls?"

"Yes, he taught me the finer points to being 'a ladies' man.' Yet I still question myself every time I go on a date. I always think no one will get me."

Really? Even with all his money? Amber checked herself. She had come to understand that the Lux Love client list was different than most in that their money could attract all the wrong people. "That's why I'm here. To get you."

He laid his hand over hers. "Which is why I'm putting my trust in the matchmaking service. Algorithms, I trust."

Algorithms. All to do with an artificial intelligence. It had made her job with the law firm obsolete. And everywhere she had applied asked if she could work with AI. Going in, she hadn't known Lux Love relied so heavily on AI to match clients. The lack of personal touch offended her. But she wasn't going to quit. Paris! And from what she'd seen over the past year, the AI did seem to have a talent for matching people. But she was never going to start engaging with a chatbot. Abhorrent.

"How much do you work now?" she asked.

"Every day, except Sundays. All day. And, very well, some Sundays as well."

"What time to you get in to work?"

"It varies from six to ten in the morning. Then I sometimes don't return home until after dark. Well, you saw last night was late."

"And tonight was no early return either. That's a very long workday. Making a match is one thing, Val. It's *keeping* that match that requires effort. Honing a relationship, and…working less, as you've already realized."

"My partner, Teo, is always telling me to work less. I don't even need to code. We've got many talented coders. And AI does a lot of the heavy lifting. But I can't seem to let go of it. I need to check their work. Make sure it's up to my standards."

"And is it?"

"Always."

"Then perhaps you need to accept that the job is being done well and that if you don't always have the opportunity to check their work, it'll be fine." Yet she could relate. Amber always checked her work over and over. No gold star for less than perfect! "Do you think I could tag along to your office tomorrow?" she asked. "Get a feel for your work life?"

"I'd love to show you around Verdadero. You want to tag along on the five a.m. jog too?"

Amber winced over a sip of wine.

"Had to try. I'll return home around six to pick you up."

She was an 8:00 a.m. riser. But this was her job, and she would do it to perfection.

"Six it is. Do you jog every morning?"

"Even in the rain, which is rare around here. Gets the blood rushing through my brain. I come up with the best ideas then."

The waiter arrived with dessert. Val shrugged. "What's a meal without a decadent dessert?"

Chocolate and cherry sauce? Oh, she was liking this man more and more.

Val suggested a walk along the river, which wasn't far from his villa. They strolled on a sidewalk canopied by the city's abundant orange trees.

"Your profile is filling in nicely," Amber said. "But we need info on what you want in a woman. Looks, personality, education, career, values. All that stuff. You willing to go through the list?" She tugged her tablet from her purse.

Val shoved his hands in his pockets as they walked. "Fire away."

"Okay, let's start easy. Looks."

"No, no. I'm not going to give you a description of what attracts me because I don't know until I know."

"Oh, come on. You don't favor blondes over redheads? Slender over muscular? Petite over tall?"

"Never think about it too much. I like all sorts of women. I don't judge a book by its cover, height or weight. Though, I suppose I should have checked *Spanish national* if I want to please my father. Which I do. And yet… I do adore dark brown curls."

His wink startled her. *She* had dark brown curls.

"Don't overthink that one. Next question," he said.

"Fine. Open to all appearances with a preference for Spanish." She made a note in her file. Hard not to feel self-conscious over her hair now. She pushed a hank of it over her shoulder. "How about occupations? Do you prefer a career woman? You seem to be looking for someone more traditional, so perhaps you prefer a woman who cooks and cleans and kisses you on the cheek every morning before you head off to work?"

"Is that an option? The cheek-kissing part? That would be cool."

"You're cute, but I'm trying to do my job. Cheek kisses are on the table," she said as she noted that. "What about her job?"

Val shrugged. "I am traditional in that I believe a woman shouldn't have to work to help support her family. I make more than enough money to cover a household so...a job isn't necessary. But."

She lifted a brow.

"If she enjoys working, I'm not going to tell her to stop. People take satisfaction in working. Especially work that plays to their passion."

"Passion is important," Amber said, because it sounded like the right thing to say. She wasn't sure if she had a passion. Even this job had been merely a means to move to Paris. It hadn't been because she'd been interested in matching people. Becoming a romantic fairy godmother, of sorts.

Yet, was that her future with Lux Love? For some reason, juxtaposing the algorithms with actual feelings and emotions never sat well with her. Was there a way she could bridge that gap and make things more personal for her clients?

What were they talking about? Passion. What would real, romantic passion feel like? And could AI ever find that for another person?

"Still taking notes?" Val's voice jarred her from her mind wandering.

"Uh, sure." She tucked away the tablet in her purse and inhaled. "It smells so good here under the orange trees. As does your house. You must miss it when the blossoms have dropped and lost their scent."

"A woman I once dated had an essential oil cologne crafted for me using *azahar*, the orange blossoms. I use it occasionally."

"What a lovely gift."

"*Sì*, I didn't know how to return the favor so I bought her a Vespa."

Amber's jaw dropped open.

"I know, right?" Val shrugged. "Our family has never been big on gifts. I don't know how to do them. They take a lot of thought. Do you think I should do gifts? For my dates?"

Being asked for guidance made her stand up straighter and a warmth curled in her chest. "Women do like gifts, but we don't need diamonds. Or Vespas. Simple things to show you notice are nice."

"I can do that." He leaped, tapping the canopy of leaves above them and landed before her. "Here." He twirled a big white blossom. "Just a little gift. Can I put this in your hair?"

"Uh…"

He stood close enough to inhale and oh, what a delicious man. Whose every spoken word and action made her realize how miserable her dating life had actually been up to this point. Lack of attentive lovers? Check. Never being able to maintain a relationship beyond a week or two? Unfortunate check. Passion? Not a single check. Allowing a man to touch her so casually without flinching? There was a first time for everything.

"Beautiful." Val's eyes dropped to her mouth. He lingered there, studying her as if she were the dessert they'd shared at the restaurant.

Panic curled at the base of Amber's throat. This felt very much like a go-in-for-the-kiss moment. Completely unacceptable for a Lux Love consultant to fraternize with the client. And yet…

What would his kiss feel like? To breathe him into her skin and taste his mouth… Hug against his strong frame and soak in his warmth like a starved kitten. It wasn't that she was against romance so much as she'd just never had a talent for it.

Suddenly, he stepped back. "Sorry. I, uh…" He rubbed his fingers along his jaw in an embarrassed move. "That was inappropriate. It felt like a kissing moment. *Sí?*"

Oh, yes, please yes! "A little."

"If this were a real date—"

"Oh, of course, I understand. Don't worry about it. I'm not offended." At not getting a kiss or that he'd thought she'd want one? What a liar, Amber!

"It's just that your lips are made for a kiss," he said in all seriousness.

"Oh my." Exhaling, her shoulders dropped. Her hair felt heavy on her shoulders, so…curly and dark. Like some kind of romance heroine. She'd never swooned over a man before. Had never stood in a moment like this. *Time to learn, Amber*.

"Whew!" Again, Val put some distance between them with a bouncy step and a bat at the low-hanging leaves. "Change the subject, man. I don't want to make you nervous." He bounced on his toes, shaking out his shoulders. Regrouping, in a manner. He gestured outward. "This is what I brought you here for. Check it out."

He led her through an aisle of trees to stand before a wrought iron balustrade that overlooked a drop to the river below. The dark blue velvet sky was sprinkled with stars. Breathtaking.

"I'm surprised you can see stars in the city," she said.

"You can always see the stars in Seville." He stood beside her, their elbows nudging. The heat of him overwhelmed her. The orange blossoms perfumed the air, giving her a woozy sort of contentedness. "This is why I will never leave Spain. It's so beautiful here."

"So you won't move for the woman you'll eventually fall in love with and marry?"

"It'll be a tough haul getting my feet off Sevillian soil."

"Noted."

"Stop taking notes, Amber. Just close your eyes and inhale. Then look to the glittering sky."

A romantic suggestion. She was going to make a note of that—later. Closing her eyes, she inhaled the *azahar*.

Had she just been thinking about swooning? Tossed her hair over a shoulder like…? Ha! And yet, he'd almost kissed her.

What was that about?

Best to focus on how securing this man his perfect match would get her a raise and pay those bills. It was all for her life trajectory. And his charming touches and gazes would never make her blush.

She was *impervious* to his charm.

"And don't forget it," she whispered to that wanting part of her that had surprisingly fluttered to life.

CHAPTER SIX

SHE WAS ADORABLE when sleeping. Val leaned over Amber's bed, hesitant to wake her. He'd already carefully pulled back the curtains from the window. If he were suave, he'd have swept her off her feet and into his arms already. Or at least, been more convincing last night. That stars-by-the-river moment had gone all wrong. He'd forgotten himself and had wanted to kiss her. That may work on a real date, but—this was like playing house and not getting the bonus of intimacy.

Could she feel the same? No, she was a trained professional. And he had contacted Lux Love for a reason. He trusted the algorithms. And in order for them to work, he had to play along with everything requested of him and provide all the data. So he could find the woman who would earn an approving nod from his dad. And that did not include being distracted by the sexy consultant.

Daylight was draining away. If the professional wanted to accompany him to work today to see that side of his life, it was time to get this show on the road.

"Sleeping Beauty!" he announced with the élan of a carnival barker.

Amber startled upright and caught her palms on the pillow. Hair tousled over her face, she looked around.

"Sorry," Val offered. It wasn't the kindest move. When was the last time he'd had a woman sleep over at his house and he *hadn't* slept with her? This situation was odd. But also kind of fun. "Had to be done."

Discombobulated, she slapped a palm toward the nightstand to grab her phone. "What time is it?"

"After seven."

"After—I set my alarm for six." She brought the phone closer to her face. "I hit snooze three times?"

"Sometimes the brain doesn't register those hits. It's that hypnopompic time of the morning where your memory plays tricks on you."

"Yes, that state of dreaming just before a person wakes. My apologies. I'm never late. I can't believe…"

Pushing the hair from her face, she looked at him. Her jaw dropped open. She clasped her arms across her chest. The blue-striped cotton pajama top and pants she wore didn't expose anything, but he sensed her sudden embarrassment.

Val turned and made to study the horns of the stuffed bull's head. "You know it is a great honor to receive such a gift from a matador?"

"Is that so? Did the bull win or lose? Either way—no. Don't tell me. I know it's a national tradition in Spain but if you ask me it's…" She gestured with a dismissive fling of her hand. "Do you always hover over sleeping women like that?"

"Not always. Sometimes I stare through their windows in the middle of the night." Her reaction was the expected shock. Val laughed and shook his head. "It's too early for my humor. Sorry. I'll leave you to get ready. Work is waiting."

"Yes, uh…give me half an hour."

"Is that all? I've never met a woman who can get ready in less than an hour."

Her eyebrow lifted in challenge. "Then make it twenty-five minutes."

"Deal." Val tapped his watch and set the timer as he strolled out of her room.

* * *

Amber made it in twenty-two minutes because that was how she rolled. Always up for a challenge. Shower, makeup, a tousle of her curly hair—no need to wash it. The linen sundress topped by a cashmere shrug was perfect for the weather.

The Spanish sun hit differently than in the States. It was golden and full and it felt as though her skin were sucking it in, starved of vitamin D following a long Parisian winter. And the air here wasn't like most big cities. It felt ancient, as if it possessed secrets never told, even through the centuries.

A bit of the fantastical slipping into her thoughts? Why not? Just because she was officially on the clock didn't mean she couldn't enjoy her surroundings. But she was thankful she'd missed the requisite jog. Val's car had driven them to his work, which was just across the river.

The Verdadero office occupied the top three floors in Torre Sevilla, the tallest office tower in Spain. Status symbol? Check. Val introduced Amber to Amaia, the receptionist who sported a pink bob, and who seemed to be handling three calls via her headset, pouring coffee to hand to Val and asking Amber if she took cream for hers. Amber loved her instantly.

"She's efficient," Val commented as they strolled through the halls that were a mix of grayish woods and steel. Masculine and modern. Spare in design. And lots of curved windows. Val peeked into his partner's office but Mateo Ortiz wasn't there.

"He's recently become a nine-to-fiver," Val commented as he gestured to another office across the hall. "That's mine, but I rarely use it. Too…office-like."

Sipping the coffee that tasted as if it had been freshly brewed from beans picked directly from the plant, Amber asked, "Isn't that what an office should be?"

"Sure, but stark walls and a desk are not me. I work in the dark room. It's my safe place."

That sounded both intriguing and a little worrisome. "What do you have to be kept safe from?" She followed his casual stroll up a stairway to the next floor.

"Interruptions." He cast a grin over his shoulder at her. "When I'm in the zone, I like to fly."

She knew his job involved sitting before a computer and typing mind-boggling lines of code that she couldn't begin to understand. And yet... "Doesn't AI do a lot of that nowadays?"

"It does, but someone's gotta tell the AI what to do. I do a lot of visual scripting and gesture-based coding, but good old-fashioned text-based coding is still the workhorse. In here."

Val opened a door that led into darkness and waited for her to enter. Amber paused on the threshold, clutching the coffee cup. This was the first time she'd felt the slightest bit of unease around him. He wasn't kidding about a dark room. "No lights?"

"When you step inside Hal will adjust to your presence."

"Hal?"

"The AI. A little *Space Odyssey* humor there. Go on. Hal won't bite. I don't think."

The man did try at humor. Amber had noted that in his assessment this morning after her rude awakening. Though, she had been the rude one missing their 6:00 a.m. wake-up call. And really, the joke could be very funny, but she had no context when it came to cyber stuff.

Stepping inside the cool room, it suddenly flickered and took on a greenish-white glow that made her feel as though she were standing inside a vast computer system. The entire far wall was a massive screen that scrolled code and looked like something from *The Matrix*. A huge easy chair sat before a black circular platform in the center of the room. The opposite wall featured a console with dozens of large monitors, keyboards and all the techie stuff she couldn't begin to name.

"This is where I work." Val slid a palm along the back of the leather chair. "My home away from home. And this is the captain's chair."

"It's certainly…" Cold. Busy. Unreal. Futuristic. "Exactly what I would expect for a man who codes for a living." But so opposite from the warm, charming man she was getting to know. "Quite fascinating. Why so dark?"

"The lighting is designed for optimal viewing and minimal eye strain. No blue light. Lots of healing yellow and red. It changes throughout the day and according to the inhabitant's biorhythms."

"The inhabitants? Even…me?" Amber scanned around for hidden cameras.

"Yes, you crossed a bioscanner upon entry. Hal is monitoring your every move."

"Creepy much?" She rubbed a palm up her arm, feeling the unease return. "And where was the informed consent?"

"Sorry. I don't often bring in visitors. I should have told you before entering. You can leave?"

"No, I'm fine. Not like we're not being recording everywhere we go and in every business we visit."

"You're not wrong."

Again, she scanned the walls and ceiling. "Is Hal recording everything we say?"

Val offered a sheepish shrug, which she took to mean *yes*.

With a gesture of his hand, the area above the circular pad suddenly filled with scrolling code. Very *Matrix*-like! Smiling, Val strolled to a wall where what looked like VR goggles were hung. Along with gloves and plastic swords and elaborate plastic guns. "Let me show you what I do. Have you ever experienced VR?"

"No." Amber reached out to touch the scrolling code and her hand moved through it. Fascinating. She had never gotten into video games. Not even *Words with Friends*, which was her dad's favorite time-waster. Save for her phone and a few social media accounts, she was as low-tech as it got. "But I'm interested in what you create."

"This is our latest prototype. Hope to bring it to market next year." Val held a silver visor toward her.

"It looks heavy."

"Nope. Made from ultralight carbon fiber. It's loaded with sensors, a gyroscope, accelerometer and cameras to track your movements. It's untethered so a person can move about freely. Are you…unsure?"

Beyond the need to learn more about what made the man tick so she could fill in his profile, the idea of standing beside him while they experienced altered worlds intrigued in a way that surprised her. Could she step into a fantasy world and be comfortable? Alone with this man who disturbed her personal boundaries with every slight touch he gave her?

"It doesn't hurt," he said encouragingly.

"I know that. I just…doesn't this mess with your proprioception? I don't want to fall on my face."

By all means she would never put herself in a position to be appear unskilled or embarrassed.

"We've haptic feedback sensors to counteract issues with bodily placement. Come here."

He held out his hand and she took it. Because every time he touched her it made her feel things she'd never felt before. And she was curious about those feelings. It happened again as he led her into the platform so they stood amidst the code. Being led by this handsome being who seemed so gentle and whose touch made her skin scream *More!* Would his touch make any woman feel the same? He did like to touch, make skin contact. It was so natural to him he probably wasn't even aware.

– Don't fall in love!

No. She wasn't that easy. And—when had he let go of her hand? She stared at her fingers for a moment. Lost.

"Do you get queasy easily?" he asked.

Queasy? From him holding her hand? It was more like a warmth in her belly that made her heart flutter. Her spine untense and—

Oh. No, he hadn't asked that. "Uh, no. I've a strong stomach."

The code moved over his face in flashes of light. She wanted to touch the numbers on his face, but she kept her hands to herself.

"Good. The biometry system monitors your position and provides haptic feedback so it shouldn't make you dizzy, but some people are susceptible to inner ear fluctuations."

He displayed a glove which looked more like a chrome skeletal attachment one would wear on the back of their hand, with soft black sensors that curved over the fingers. "The bioglove is something new we're ready to put to market this fall. It allows you to touch and feel virtual objects. So you'll give it a try, *sì?*"

After she set the coffee cup aside, he showed her how to put on the gloves. They were incredibly lightweight. They did make her feel a bit like Skeletor. Then he helped her put on the visor.

With a wave of Val's hand, the scrolling code disappeared, leaving them in the subtle green glow of the room. "I'll take you on a walk through an archeological dig. No games. You won't have to fire any weapons."

Amber shook her head, feeling as though that move unloosed her hair a little. In a metaphorical way. *Let it all fall down.* "Lead on, Captain."

His hand pressed firmly on her shoulder. "Don't worry. I got you. The on switch is right here." He tapped the side of her visor and instantly she stood in a cave. The sudden change in environment made her wobble. "You good?"

"Uh… I think so." She turned her head. It was as though she were surrounded by dark rocky walls and she could see down an aisle that opened into something bigger. "This looks so real." A shiver surprised her. "I almost feel the cool air."

"You do. That's part of the bio-enhanced experience. You don't need to walk, just stand still. If you move your hands, they'll move before you. And… I'm going to join you." Suddenly she could see a man's hand reach out before her. His fingers wiggled. "Our hand-tracking technology is next level. We've overcome self-occlusion and the uncanny valley effect. Try it out. Take my hand."

Always.

She reached out and saw her hand clasp with his and she… felt the warmth of his hand against hers. This was weird! But also incredibly interesting. The reassuring clasp of Val's hand gave her the courage she didn't realize she would need to experience a VR game.

"Do you trust me?" he asked.

Did she? *I want to.* "Lead the way."

Val preferred diving in and going for it. Like leaping out of a plane to free-fall into the Grand Canyon. Or standing in the eye of a hurricane. But his threshold for excitement and pushing the boundaries was higher than most. Blame it on *inquieto*. He loved to always be in motion. It's what kept him vital. Made him feel alive.

It was always best to start slow for someone who hadn't experienced VR, which is why he hadn't selected a war game for Amber's first run. Verdadero offered a number of exploration games they sold to schools and universities. They simulated actual places such as archaeological digs, underwater diving, a walk through an Egyptian pyramid—even a rainforest search for rare insects.

Amber had tried to hide her reluctance, but he'd sensed it. And not even in her straight posture, which was her norm. It had been in the tone of her voice. She'd needed him to step up, take her hand and guide her.

Soon enough, she let go of his hand and moved forward to explore all the interesting pictographs in the cave. As she stroked a finger over each one, the narrator explained the meaning. Val had the thought that he'd love to get his dad to try one of these walks. Maybe then he'd realize that Verdadero really was doing something good by teaching, and not just putting out shooting games. But how to even convince the old man to step inside Verdadero? He'd never visited the office, no matter how many times Val invited him.

"This is so cool! I can almost feel the mist from that water trickling down the cave wall."

Amber arrived at a short climb and she eagerly jumped over a stream and grasped on to some crevices in the wall. He stood below watching, her feet about level with his chest.

"You're doing well, Amber."

"Yeah?" She glanced down. "Whoa. I don't know. I feel like I'm going to fall."

"You can't physically fall in the game. It's only a simulation. But it may feel—"

He sensed her wobble on the platform beside him before he saw her let go of the rocky handhold in the game. For an inexperienced user, such a move could be terrifying. And they could lose proprioception, an awareness of where their body was.

Tearing off his visor, Val put out his arms to catch Amber as her body faltered and her shoulders swayed backward. He caught her back against his chest, nuzzling his face aside her neck. She smelled so good. No VR game could ever simulate scents. Though, he was working on that.

"Take off the gloves and visor. We're done," he said.

She did so, and still gasping, she turned in his embrace. A wobble set her forward. Crushing her against his chest, he held her in a hug to let her know he was real, that she stood on solid ground and was safe. It was a surreal moment. Many players felt lost and disoriented entering and leaving VR, yet he felt an unprecedented protectiveness toward her.

His fingers tangled in the ends of her curly hair. Softer than he imagined. The heartbeats thundering against his chest prompted him to hug her just a little firmer.

"I'm okay." Her fingers trembled as he took both her hands, unwilling to let her go until she found her bearings. "That was so realistic. I felt like I was falling. My body reacted. You…caught me."

"You wouldn't have gotten hurt in the game."

"I know but…might I have fallen in real life? Landed on the floor?"

Her eyes were so luminous. Trusting, yet worried. He wanted to reassure her that nothing could ever harm her. He'd never felt such a strong protective instinct for a woman before.

She pulled her hands from his and clasped them across her opposite forearms. A shielding move, but also, he suspected, quelling the racing adrenaline.

"It can happen sometimes. That's why this holo-platform is padded." He jumped on the bouncy surface. "You're still all in one piece."

"Thank you. I'm glad you were there to catch me. You were there." Her eyes brightened with that realization. Too quickly though she shook her head. "But that's enough for me. I got the idea of how VR works."

"I'll take you on a flight to Mars one day."

"I prefer good old terra firma. Whew!" She brushed the hair from her face and turned to look around the room.

Val wanted to hug her again. To feel her warmth and that delicious connection. Her lack of laughter suggested the experience impacted her in ways he should be cautious of. It was that need for control he knew she required. He could recall the first time he'd taken a VR walk. It had always been like flying to him. Something to crave, chase and never stop. Like dancing, but even more exhilarating.

"How about we get a drink in the cafeteria?" he suggested. "Some tea to settle your racing nerves."

"They're not racing," she protested a little too quickly.

"Of course not." She was trying hard not to appear affected. He'd give her that. "But I need some tea. Come on."

Over lemon-ginger tea, Val answered Amber's questions about Verdadero's beginnings. And about his decision to devote his life to coding over dancing.

"You studied flamenco dancing?"

"For years as a teenager. My mother was a professional *bailaora*."

"And how old were you when she died?"

"She passed away when I was seventeen."

"I'm so sorry. It's difficult to lose a parent."

"Do you say that because you've lost one as well?"

"Oh no, I mean, well…" Her posture tightened. "My parents divorced three years ago. After twenty-five years of what I had thought to be a perfect marriage. My mom decided one day she had fulfilled her soul contract with my dad and said it was time to move on to her next experience."

"Interesting."

"But nothing similar to your loss. I've never lost someone close so I can't relate. Should we get back to why you left dance for coding?"

"Of course." Much as he'd enjoy having a deeper conversation with her, Val accepted her gentle guidance to stay on focus. There were questions to be asked, data points to be filled out. "When Teo, Pablo and I created that first game, and saw some success with it, we realized we wanted to go big. I knew I couldn't dance *and* code because there's not enough hours in the day, so I made the choice to set dance aside. And, well, my mother's death made it difficult to want to dance also. As I've explained, giving up dance created the one sore spot between my dad and I. Coding is not something he understands. Flamenco? Now that is what a traditional Spanish son should do, especially since his mother was a dancer."

"Dancing must have bonded the two of you?"

"Oh, yes, I learned everything from my mother. She called me *inquieto*."

"Always on the move?"

"Yes. A jittery bouncer when I was much younger. She taught me to focus that energy into dancing. But I always say I speak three languages. Coding is my first language. Dance is the second, with Spanish a distant third."

"And English as well. You've been very kind to speak English with me."

"Your Spanish is not so good."

She mocked affront, but then laughed. "I do try."

"It is serviceable. It makes Maria laugh."

"Is that so? I'll make a note to brush up. So, the three of you went on to create Verdadero?"

"Yes, the three musketeers. Pablo was the artistic genius behind it all. Teo is the marketer, the salesman, the money man."

"And you provide the code."

"Standing on the holo-platform in the dark room is my happy place."

Amber sipped her tea. "A happy place for you. But not necessarily for any woman who wants to get your attention. You spend more time at work than at home?"

"I do."

"Do you have any desire to balance your work and private life?"

"Balance?" He winced. Sure, he understood what she was asking, but life was more nuanced. He held out his hand and tilted it. "Real-life wobbles, you see? I enjoy working. I don't have to code, but it makes me happy. I want to have a relationship. I want to fall in love. Take you and me. This is nice. Just talking. You're so attentive."

"Lots of people are good listeners."

"Maybe. But I like how you do it. Your body is open and you hold eye contact." He leaned across the table, grabbing her focus. "Do you know people don't even know how to look one another in the eye nowadays?"

"Yes, I've noticed. I suspect it's to do with always having our attention on the screen in our hands. Normally I don't have this tablet with me. I try to avoid screen time when I can. But your life is all about the screen."

"In a manner." It was so much more than a screen with VR. But to begin to explain the intricacies to someone who was more interested in his personal life? Val would not bore her with the tech details. "Hey, you want to duck out and get some *tocino de Cielo*?"

"I have no idea what that is, but the way you say it makes it sound like something I definitely need to check out."

"It's a sweet treat. Come on."

CHAPTER SEVEN

IT LOOKED LIKE FLAN, but apparently it was not. Called *tocino de Cielo*, which translated to *heavenly bacon*. Val explained to Amber that it was called that because of its resemblance to a slice of pork fat.

Weird as it sounded, the caramel custard treat had been delicious. The pastry shop they'd got it from reminded Amber of the Parisian hot spots like Angelina and Ladurée. The place had been packed with tourists so they'd taken their treats to go and now wandered riverside, Val's intention on the electric bike rental spot just ahead.

When he spied the two-seater—side-by-side pedaling—he bounced like an excited kid and gave her a goofy grin. The last time she'd ridden a bike had been in high school. And not that she was out of shape, but sharing the pedaling duty was fine with her, so they rented it and took off for a leisurely ride along the Guadalquivir. He pointed out statues and important buildings, then they strolled through a garden, past a duck pond under the shade of olive and palm trees, and paused at a gazebo.

Amber leaned her elbows on the stone banister. The pond glinted green and gold in the sunlight. Ducks floated in bliss. Some insect chirped. And the air held that ancient scent she couldn't quite place but could feel settle on her skin, as warm and mysterious as a subtle perfume. Or Val's touch.

Him holding her on the holo-platform? In the moment she'd been frightened. The experience had felt so real. Only focusing on Val's body heat, his calming voice, had brought her down. And a little too close to desire. She'd quickly stepped back from him.

She regretted that move now. But that regret battled with her need to keep their interactions professional.

"Is this park close to your home?" she asked.

"Not far."

"I would visit daily if I lived nearby. It's idyllic. Does your morning run take you through here?"

"All the time. This scenery reminds me of a masterpiece painting."

"But I thought you liked the moderns?"

"I do, but Verdadero once designed a game for the Louvre. It was an incredible learning experience familiarizing myself with all the artworks."

"I understand a movie is being made of one of your games?"

"For *Matador*, yes. We signed the deal last year. Very exciting."

"Do you get a part in the movie?"

Val laughed. "I didn't think to ask for one. But maybe, eh? That would be something new to try. Though I don't think I should be given a speaking part. I'll stick to the action."

"You do like to move and stay busy."

"Chaos is my calm."

"That's the weirdest thing I've ever heard, but..." That curly hair of his defied taming and sometimes plopped over one mischievous eye. It was all she could do *not* to reach out and flip it aside. "I can see that in you. You've got a lot going on in your life. If you had to slice out something to give you more time to focus on a relationship, what would it be?"

"Is that another question on your assessment?"

It wasn't. And yet, she was here to guide him toward—once a match had been made—*keeping* that match. "I'm curious."

Val leaned his elbows onto the railing beside her and looked over the pond. This easy companionship was a new experience for her. She'd never had a male friend. And her dates were not often spent conversing beyond dinner and discussing the latest Netflix series. Maybe she didn't know how to do small talk? A note to make on her own to-do list if she were ever to someday get serious about her dating life.

"I'm not sure about finding the time," Val offered. "Everything I do is done with purpose and makes me happy. Otherwise, it's a waste of time to do it."

"What about cutting back on your work hours? I think if you had someone in your life, that would be much easier to do than it is to imagine it now."

"You're not wrong. I've watched Teo do that for Cara, who is very important to him. I mean, the two just got married!"

"When was the last time you went on a date? Had a girlfriend?"

"Honestly? My dates are more like one-night stands. And I'm not proud of it."

"There is no shame in ensuring your needs are met." *Speaking for myself.*

"It's not like that. Eh. Sometimes it is. Most of the time it just doesn't feel right so I end it. I don't spend time with someone if it doesn't make me happy."

"Maybe you don't give those one-nighters enough of a chance? To get to know you? For you to get to know them?" Still speaking for—or at—herself? *Oh, Amber. This is not about you.*

"Possible. But I usually suss out quickly if she's just in it for my money. I hate feeling like a lending bank that never asks for repayment on loans."

"I imagine it's difficult what with your bank account. But you must have some specifics you require, because of that money. What is it you want in a woman?"

"No gold diggers. Obviously. I mean, I love to spend money on a woman, but if that's what they're in it for, it makes the gift so much less meaningful. That's why I avoid gifting."

"Flowers are nice." Still speaking for herself! But hey, there were a few simple things in life that appealed to most women. She wasn't going to push away any offering of kindness.

"What I really want is someone to challenge me intellectually." Val turned and leaned his elbows on the balustrade beside her. "And to never stop being curious."

Amber nodded. "I get that. Conversation and sharing experiences."

"It's not so much the words but the connection," Val said. "Resonating with the other person. I can tell if a woman is trying too hard or is attempting to put on an act to be something she's not. I want real."

Could he read her? She tried to remain aloof, a consultant dutifully recording details, but she was finding it difficult not to place herself in this faux dating situation.

On the other hand, she'd decided that was the best way to learn about the man. *So, go Amber!*

"Do you get a lot of women who only see your wallet?" she asked.

He chuckled. "I do. I don't mind that. I have a lot of money. Spending it to make someone happy doesn't bother me. But I'd never buy a person's interest or love."

She recalled the flower he'd pressed into her hair. The

moment had felt like some kind of Disney romance scene where the orchestra rose and the feels flowed. "You've a bit of the knight in shining armor in you. You did rescue me in the game."

"A man should never allow a lady to fall. And I mean that metaphorically."

"Oh yeah? What's a metaphorical fall?"

"Like not being looked at as the goddess she is or allowing her to fall from the pedestal."

Amber wrinkled her nose. "Maybe some women don't want to be put on a pedestal."

"You think?"

"I imagine it can be very challenging, even lonely, way up there with the man meeting your every need. We women—some of us, anyway—like to do things for ourselves."

"See, that's what I need to learn. I was raised in a family where the man was the head of the household. He worked. He took care of his family. Women weren't expected to also bring home a paycheck."

"But your mother danced professionally?"

"She danced for a local theater troupe. The pay wasn't much but that wasn't the point. She indulged her creative passions. My dad would have never expected her to contribute to household expenses. Because besides being able to dance she was also the housekeeper, the cook, the caretaker. She did it all and never allowed her dance engagements to get in the way of her taking care of her family. And in turn, my father treated her like the queen she was."

"That's nice. But I think there are a lot of less traditional women nowadays, and today they want to share in the household duties with the man. And the work requirements. Paychecks are validating. We women want it all. Can you get behind that?"

"I can." Not a convincing tone to his voice. With a tilt of his head, he asked, "Can you?"

"It doesn't matter what I like or don't like."

"Yes, it does. What is it you look for in a man?"

Treating her like a date and trying to get to know her better? Very well. She knew how to play this one. "One with a brain and who uses it," she said quickly. Amber shrugged. It was the truth. "Not on socials all the time. Funny. Athletic. Confident. Perfect."

"Perfection is overrated."

"Oh, I don't think so."

"Your standards are high."

"I am driven to succeed. And I'd like a partner who feels the same. I just…want someone who values me."

"I like that. You need to feel valued. Your presence, your emotions, your desires. Everyone needs to know they are accepted."

Those big brown eyes would never stop tugging at her heart. Er—some other woman's heart who would cook for him and kiss him on the cheek when he returned home from work, and who gave him lots of babies. Traditional stuff. It sounded…kind of spectacular.

"Don't get me wrong. I've never been treated terribly by a man," Amber confessed. "I guess I've never truly connected to a man."

"And *you're* a matchmaker?"

"Don't worry. The algorithms do all the work, remember?"

"Good ole algorithms. Still. It's sad that you've never connected to a man."

"Whatever."

"Whatever? Amber, please." He patted a hand over his chest. "You're making my heart break. Don't you want love?"

A sigh hid her need to scream at him that no, she just didn't believe love could last. "My relationships never seem to last long because I'm very...exacting. I like things a certain way. There. You got it out of me. I'm certainly not the woman for most."

"I don't know. I think you need tender loving care. Any man who is worth a morsel of humanity would see that. I like your smile, Amber. You don't wear it often enough." He put up a hand. "And before you protest that men shouldn't be telling women to smile, I get that. I just feel your happiness when you smile. It's genuine."

How to take that compliment without shoving the protest he'd soundly quashed right back at him? "Should we keep pedaling?"

"Let's drop off the bike and we can walk to my villa. It's been a nice afternoon, *si*?"

"It has. But you haven't worked at all today. Do you need to return to the office?"

"You did say I should spend less time at the office. I'd better start practicing if I'm going to attract a mate. What about dinner out again tonight?"

"Sounds..." *Necessary to get the job done.* "...great. But allow me some time to do a little work once we return to your place?"

"Taking notes on me?"

"That's what you hired me for."

"I was starting to forget that." He got on the bike, patting the seat beside him. "Your carriage, my lady."

As they pedaled to a bike return, Amber couldn't help think Val was the perfect man for any woman. She'd certainly pick him if she had the opportunity. But that wasn't how Lux Love worked. Val would be matched with a woman in the database.

Of course, Amber was in the database. Her account flagged as an employee so it never accidentally got matched with a client. It was a requirement all employees fill out a survey so they knew what the client experienced. And all the consultants secretly, on occasion, would run their stats against one of the clients. Colette wasn't aware. If she were, there would be a mass firing. Amber had done it twice for her roommates.

Amber couldn't resist wondering how she and Val would match. But the idea of checking scared her. What if they were a terrible match?

Worse yet—what if they matched perfectly? A girl who had lost all trust in love and who wanted to excel in her career trajectory wouldn't want to risk even checking.

CHAPTER EIGHT

Upon arrival at the tapas bar, Amber interpreted the Spanish-language sign on the door: No Wi-Fi. Talk to One Another. Tucking her ever-present mini tablet away in her purse, she decided to enter any new details later.

Val walked ahead to the bar as she took in the aged leather and wood furnishings, cozy confines and walls covered with black-and-white photos depicting Sevillian architecture. He'd said to allow him to get her drinks and something to nosh on. She liked that. A take-charge man.

Drawn by the savory scent of seafood and something tomatoey, she joined Val at the bar where he spoke with a couple older men who nursed drinks. They loudly and appreciatively bellowed "Ay!" as she stopped beside Val.

"This is Amber." He introduced her to each of the two men. "Emilio and Homer are permanent fixtures here. If you want to hear the best *cantaor* in all of Seville, here he is."

Emilio bowed his head. *Cantaor* was a singer.

"Nice to meet you both." Amber was about to offer her hand to shake but Val turned and handed her a plate of something, while he took up his own glass and plate.

He nodded toward a back patio that glowed with orange light and echoed out festive clapping. *Palmas?* The clapping that accompanied flamenco dancing.

Sniffing at her drink as she followed him out into a courtyard, she determined the alcohol level could probably run a car for an entire day. Best to eat first before sipping the libations. She was on the clock.

Date number two: Study the man's interactions with others.

A round of cheers greeted them. Amber took in the small courtyard paved with bricks and packed with men and women chatting, nodding, eyeing her. Anxiety level? High. Geeky smart girl so used to getting by on her own and never partying? Mingling and small talk? The horror!

The men clapped Val across the back and, with some, he exchanged cheek kisses. The Spanish did like to touch and make extended eye contact when greeting. Unsettling, but also heartening, if she was honest with herself. Everyone acknowledged her as they made way to a table tucked tightly among others.

"Is this a place you would take a date, Val?"

He slid onto a chair beside her, his elbow nudging hers. Everyone was packed around a small dance floor where a guitarist currently strummed. Behind him on a vine-covered stone wall hung a few more guitars, their wood surfaces faded or worn from decades of strumming.

"Of course. It's my favorite hangout."

"And the obvious next question is…" She wobbled the wine goblet between her fingers. "Do you always ply your dates with strong drinks?"

He smirked and shook his head. "It's orange wine. Locally made. Give it a try."

Amber sipped. Surprisingly sweet, almost honey-like, and it smelled of the orange blossoms that seemed to blanket the city.

"*Vino de naranja*," he said. "Made with oranges grown in my courtyard. It is white wine vinified with the orange peel in an oak barrel. I allow my neighbor to pick my trees clean and he brews small batches."

"You…supply fruit for bootlegger wine?"

"Yes. Maria makes jam with the oranges as well."

"That explains all the preserves in the pantry. So you're an orange supplier, a dancer. *And* you code for a billion-dollar VR gaming company?" Impressive. If not slightly quirky. "What else do you do?"

"Lots of things. I like to keep busy. And I've got to do something with all the oranges that grow on my property. Warning—never eat the oranges fresh from the tree. They are very bitter. But they make an excellent wine. It roses your cheeks."

Amber touched her cheek. Had she blushed? Had to be the wine.

Val nudged a plate toward her and she took a bite of the crunchy bread. "No, spread the tomato sauce on it and then some salt. You can get messy with it." He took her bread and showed her how to do it. A tiny saltcellar sat on the table, from which he generously sprinkled flakes over the bread. When he handed it to her, the juice from the freshly chopped tomatoes ran down his finger and on to hers.

Caught in his gaze—which, had she a match, might ignite and quickly extinguish to a long and wispy smolder— Amber tugged the bread from him. He licked his finger and winked at her. "Lots of salt is best. Good stuff."

A bite delivered a fresh kick of savory flavors. She wanted to lick her fingers too, but instead grabbed a napkin.

Val leaned an elbow onto the table while his other hand kept a clapping beat on the side of his thigh. A female dancer had taken to the small floor space before the strumming guitarist. She spun, her hips twirling while her head seemed to dart around so quickly it was as if she never took her gaze from the audience. Her expressive hands coiled and glided through the air. The pained look on her wilted-apple face spoke of experiences Amber could not relate to.

"It's a very emotional dance, yes?" she asked.

"Indeed. Steeped with centuries of storytelling. Each song can be traced to a different region and story. I favor the malaguena. It's a fandango style of dance attributed to the Moors. It's a kind of romantic form of the song."

"Is that so? Interesting."

She did understand the romance of flamenco, which included song, dance and the guitarist. There was something so energetic, yet earthy and commanding to it. Mournful, as well.

Someone slapped a hand on Val's shoulder. "Vasquez, you show us how it's done!"

"Ay!" He gave Amber's hand a squeeze as he stood. "I'll be right back."

He did not come right back. And Amber was perfectly fine with that.

The other dancer bowed and gave Val the stage. With a stomp of his foot, he assumed a pose, body stretched, one arm high and hips jutted forward. His head down, he appeared to summon a darkness. A note sung by Emilio wailed painfully, a call to attention. An invitation into that darkness. A cry from someone sitting at a table echoed a distant plea. They were in alliance. A family.

Suddenly, the food didn't matter. As the hairs on Amber's arms stood up, she leaned forward.

Val's first steps beat the small wooden stage while the guitarist's strums accompanied him. An older man sitting on a box drum thumped out a beat matching Val's stomps. While his upper body stayed still, he swished out his arms like a matador, snapping his fingers. His feet were another story, stomping, tapping, beating. A rapid thunder of zapateado. Fierce concentration etched his face. He personified what Amber thought must be the story he told. Angsty and commanding. Wailing yet hopeful.

The man had many talents. Amber didn't see any negatives about him. Besides the unkempt closet. And fine, the lack of a schedule and disregard for time. He seemed kind, vital, polite. Sensual. A part of the very cobbled streets and perfumed air that designed this old city. Authentic with an uncompromising dash toward the future.

All of a sudden he turned slowly, his chin down, arms arced. The fluidity of his body captivated her. Powerful like the bull, yet graceful. A protector who could stand before the bull, swing out the metaphorical cape. He walked in a circle and winked at her before he started a rapid succession of footwork. *Palmas* increased. A few "ays" were shouted. The singer intoned. The guitarist strummed madly.

And then with a final stomp and dust rising about his shoes, Val finished.

Amber's breath gasped out. She pressed a hand over her pounding heart. What a—was she turned on? Her hands felt…sweaty. Her breasts rose with her rapid breaths.

Another woman took Val's place as he returned to sit beside her. His sheepish smile silently asked what she thought of his performance. A little boy looking for validation.

What she wanted to do was grab him by the wrinkled lapel and…kiss him.

Whew! What was that about? Turned on by a man displaying his masculine physique with a few stomps of his feet? Really?

"Amazing," she finally said.

He shrugged, a good-natured dismissal of a wildly incredible talent. One of the elder gentlemen patted Val's shoulder and said something in rapid Spanish. He squatted beside Val's chair and the twosome began to converse.

"Uh…will you excuse me?" Amber wanted to give him the freedom to hold that conversation. And she needed some air. "I need to find something to drink other than wine or I'll be tipsy."

"I'll get you some water?"

"No, you stay. You might be called to dance again. I'll be right back."

As the guitar riffed into rapid fanfare, Amber snuck out of the patio and into the main bar where the air was clearer and she could breathe. It was rare she found herself utterly wordless over a man. Enchanted by his dramatic mating dance.

What was she thinking? He hadn't been trying to seduce her. Well. She'd felt *something* back in that courtyard. She would note that feeling but not on the assessment. That might raise a red flag with the AI.

At the bar she asked for water and the bartender filled a glass with ice.

"You are Senor Vasquez's girlfriend?" The woman handed Amber the water.

"Oh no, I'm vetting—er, his, uh…" It wouldn't be professional to reveal what she was here for. Client privilege. "I'm a lifestyle consultant." Which she was. "Here to…"

"Consult on Val's life?" the bartender guessed.

"A little? He is a bit disorderly."

The bartender laughed. "You've come to bring order to that beautiful mess of a life?" She shook her head and swiped the counter with a cloth. "No, no. You leave him as he is. That man is exactly as he should be."

Interesting. Amber had to ask, "Have you…dated him? I mean, to know that about him?"

"No, I am married, senorita. I just know Val. Everyone in

the neighborhood knows Val. He is a passionate man. About everything. You cannot bring order to passion."

Amber might argue differently. Everything needed to be arranged and put in its place. Passion was not necessary to creating such order.

"I'll remember that," she said, to be nice. "Thanks for the water. That orange wine might have put me under the table."

Amber wandered back to the patio doorway where the music had increased intensity. Val sat on his stool, both feet tapping and hands clapping. *Passion, eh?*

Catching sight of her, he smiled and beckoned her over. She couldn't avoid sitting thigh to thigh with him. While clapping, Val leaned in and touched his forehead to hers. A weird intimacy that she didn't want to back away from. And when he leaned back, he smiled. "Is good?"

Oh, yes, he was very good.

CHAPTER NINE

VAL HELD THE front door open for Amber. The night had chilled and she'd been glad she had worn a sweater, cropped as it was. As they entered his villa, he heard the faint tones of a malaguena echoing out from the kitchen. It was after midnight. Had Maria left her TV on before turning in? Sometimes the housekeeper did stay up late making bread. Yes, he smelled the yeast.

Before Amber could turn down the hallway toward the guest room, he stomped a few *golpes* and took her hand, walking her toward the inner courtyard. "Dance with me, Senorita!"

She tugged from his grasp. "Oh, I'm not a dancer."

No, but she didn't have to know the steps to move her body. Tension seemed to be the woman's natural mien. She needed to shake her lush curls and allow her muscles to relax. To feel her body as only dance would allow.

He stepped in time to the faint music, back arched proudly as a dancer must display. Performing some measured heel-toe walks, he approached her with a hint of defiance. A glowering look that was supposed to display the grief of his ancestors but—eh, it probably looked a bit threatening so he abandoned it. "Anyone can dance. It is a way to get to know your body, *si?*"

She shook her head. Rubbed a palm up one arm. Shy? He wouldn't press. But he wasn't ready to let her walk away from him. Sitting so close to her on the patio, feeling her body heat, inhaling her spicy citrus scent, there was no way he'd get her out of his senses. And he wasn't sure he wanted to.

"Flamenco is a lifestyle," he said. "It is said the *cante* or *bailaor* cannot perform without immersing themselves in the beat, the compas." He patted his chest over his heart. "It is all about the compas."

He walked purposefully around her, snapping his fingers *contratiempo* to show her the beat that he no longer heard from the kitchen. It now ran through his veins.

"Flamenco *is* a very sexy dance," she offered.

"You say so?" An easy smile boosted Val's confidence, the matador standing before a not-so-threatening bull. "Flamenco is *passion*."

"Right. I did hear someone say you were passionate tonight."

He did possess a passion for movement, telling a story, and entering the state where dance fused with emotion and his very atoms.

Val bowed his head and looked through his lashes at her. "One must rouse the daemon to truly dance as our ancestors danced."

"The daemon?"

"Duende." He calmly walked around her, studying the tightness of her shoulders. He didn't want her fearful of him, but he did want to see if she would soften, lean into his presence. The dance. The daemon within him.

Or just…smile at him. Give him some signal she wasn't offended by him. And that their interactions weren't all work for her. Did she never relent with her mental note taking? How to see inside the woman? To bridge the work side of Amber Martin to the personal side. Curiosity nudged at him.

"Walk slowly," he instructed. "Keep your eyes on mine."

She looked at him then quickly averted her gaze. A matchmaker who played it coy? Interesting. Also, he couldn't have that. Val snapped his fingers in *pitos* before her, bringing his elbows up and his hands out to direct her gaze, slowly, eventually, up to his eyes. He smiled at her, softening his stance. She tugged in her lower lip with her teeth.

"The *rosas* is the slower more serious part of the dance." He slowed his pace, his shoes brushing the tile floor. "It is a moment to take in your breath and touch your daemon. Thank it."

"Thank it?" She hadn't dropped his gaze. Her attentiveness turned him on. It softened her stuffy professional side. And made it easier for him to relate. They inhabited his realm now. The safety of flamenco.

"Thank the daemon for the dance. It is what keeps me vital." He finished with a short zapateado and then stomped the ground with both feet. "Olé!"

Out the corner of his eye, he noticed movement in the kitchen. Maria had slipped back from watching them. Val chuckled and ran his fingers through his hair. "I do love to dance."

Amber pressed a hand to her chest. Bewildered? "Whoever matches with you will have to love flamenco."

"That would be a good quality. Tell me, do you love flamenco?"

"It's incredible. I could watch it every day. Especially the way you move—oh." She stepped back from him. Finding her self-assigned place. Protecting a part of herself that he wanted to delve into. No longer under the spell of his daemon.

She fluttered her hand before her. "Boy, it's getting late, yes?"

It wasn't too late to kiss her. Val studied her expression. Teeth worrying at her teasing red lip. Eyes darting. She couldn't hold his gaze for more than a moment. He wanted her to look at him. To touch him as he touched her. Absently. Reassuringly. Kindly. Testing.

"Val?"

"Huh? Yes." He'd lost himself. In something that fascinated him. "Did you get more information for your assessment tonight?"

"I did. And I'll want to fill that out before turning in. Thank you for being so kind with your time, Val. I know you could be working instead of entertaining me."

"It is important to spend time with you."

"For the matchmaking," she said.

"Yes. For the matchmaking." And for himself. Because he'd not spent such a satisfying evening with a woman in a long time. He liked how he felt when with Amber. Without that tablet in her hand. "We should probably go on a few more dates, *sì*? So you can establish a thorough understanding of...who I am?"

"Feels...necessary."

He stepped closer to her. "It does."

Brown eyes. Soft. Liquid. Unsure. If he touched her, ran a thumb along her jaw and cupped the back of her head, he'd have to kiss her. Stake a claim to her lush red mouth.

Every molecule of his being swayed his hand upward...

"So good night then." Amber backed away, turned and rushed down the hallway.

Val clasped his fingers in a soft clench, so close to having touched her. Had he done something wrong? For her to flee?

Of course. He'd been treating her like a date, a woman he was interested in. She was a consultant, not someone he should look at in any way other than as a business relationship.

That was growing more difficult day by day.

CHAPTER TEN

AMBER ANSWERED THE call from her boss, Colette. "How's it progressing with Senor Vasquez? It looks like his profile is filling in nicely."

As usual, Val had left for work by the time she had risen this morning.

"It's going well. I've been on a few dates with him so I can observe his mannerisms and the way he treats a woman. Such a gentleman. And a very talented dancer."

Oh, that dance last night. If she'd been unsettled watching him dance at the bar among so many others, that private dance in the courtyard had taken her beyond…something. Why could she not place the feelings? She'd been around sexy men before. Could appreciate them for their looks and charm. But Val went beyond surface appeal. He fascinated her on a visceral level. Not sexual but, yes, she had found herself getting aroused. Had she never been seduced by a man before? Why did this feel so new? So…desirable.

Not that he'd been trying to seduce her.

Or had he?

"Remember the golden rule, Amber," Colette said. "Don't fall in love."

"You keep saying that, but I know you hired me because of my miserable dating history."

"I do recall you saying you loved love for other people but didn't need it for yourself. I don't want to begin to examine that statement. And you do have a certain astute detachment from emotion that I think works well for this job. But don't allow that to keep you from seeing into the client's heart. A consultant must dig deep."

"Of course."

Detached from emotion? Her? Check. Unless a sexy man danced a private flamenco before her. He may have almost kissed her last night. Why hadn't she let it happen?

Because she was a professional.

"Don't worry, Colette. Val is a remarkable man but my detachment from emotion won't keep me from digging deep into his emotional needs and values."

Colette's chuckle brandished an edge of disbelief that made Amber question her own words. Really? *Was* she attracted to Valentino Vasquez? She merely appreciated a man who checked off all the admirable qualities on the database. Any woman would be!

"It's been days," Colette said. "We need to set up the client with a date soon. But you must fill in the client's wants section. What does he want in a woman? Her looks, her career, her personal motivations? If you get that filled in, Amber, then we can start generating a search."

"Of course." She'd learned some of that already but had yet to enter it in the database. "I'll make sure it's completed today."

"Get on it, Amber. Report back tomorrow!"

"I will. *Merci*, Colette."

Amber clicked off and set her phone aside on the bench. She sat in the courtyard, shoes kicked off and feet nestled in the cool grass beneath the canopy of verdant leaves. Untethered by the breeze, orange blossom petals rained down. It was a heavenly spot. Grounding. Not something she would have ever tried in her lifetime. She intended to make bare feet in the grass a new habit.

Colette was already pushing for Val's first date? She really did need to step up and get that wants section completed.

She checked the time. It wasn't even noon. Would it be too forward to show up at his work with lunch? Probably. But she wasn't trying to pick up a rich man and stuff him in her pocket. She had a job to do. And he had been informed that conversations with Lux Love's consultant were part of the process.

With a decisive nod, she decided to stop by a restaurant for takeaway on the way to Val's office. She wouldn't bother Maria to cook. That woman… Nonnegotiable? Val really did need to hire a housekeeper. Who knew how to use a vacuum. And operate a washing machine.

Val set his visor aside and leaned back in the chair. The massage rollers gently eased his lumbar region while the body sensors read his biorhythms.

Blowing out a breath and shoving his fingers through his hair, he shook his head. He'd been working on the same line of code for fifteen minutes. Wasn't even seeing the letters and numbers anymore because all he could see were Amber's bright eyes. Those sensual red lips. Tugged by a white tooth when uncertain. And that look of interest she'd held as she'd watched him dance around her last night.

Maybe he wielded some charm in his arsenal after all? Pablo would be proud his buddy could loosen up in a woman's presence. And sure, he wasn't a total dweeb around women. To his surprise, he'd learned money softened his anxiety. Throw it around and that alleviated any nervous uncertainty on a date. It was just when he sought meaningful connections that he froze up. Emotional unions? That sucked away his confidence and reduced him to that awkward schoolboy all over again.

So he'd gotten what he'd put out regarding relationships. Surface-level experiences. Women attracted to what he could give them. Trips, jewels, Vespas. That was all so surface. His soul craved something different. Something real.

He rarely found himself daydreaming about a woman unless he was attracted to her. Amber made him look away from his work. He was so eager to see her that he wanted to go home immediately to spend time with her. Because once his match was found, Amber would leave. Or sooner. Apparently, the consultant walked away as soon as dates began. After she recorded every minute detail of his life and…

He had to chuckle to think of the lifestyle changes she'd suggested for him. Hire a new housekeeper? Not going to happen. Less work?

He liked to stay busy. It helped him avoid taking care of himself. He paid others to feed and clothe him. To schedule his life. To entertain him. No time. No desire. But that wasn't what he wanted to be. He should be in control of his own life.

He *could* work less. He didn't need to spend all day here at the office. Once upon a time he'd lived a balanced life; now, he was essentially a recluse. The more his father had pushed his son to find a wife and begin a family, the more Val had shoved back. He would not be told what to do!

Until he'd realized maybe it was time to start looking to his personal life. At thirty-two, he wasn't getting any younger. He didn't need to code all the games. He didn't even need to check the work of his fellow coders. They were talented. As skilled as he was in coding. He rarely caught errors. And if he missed them? Hal would find them.

Could his lack of perspective, stemming from being confined to this room, have been the cause for his unfulfilled life? Didn't he deserve a happy life? A family? Why did he feel as though he *didn't* deserve that?

It had nothing to do with Pablo being struck down so young and never getting to experience creating his own family. Maybe a small part of it was that. Had his mother's death given him cause to push away dance and anything that gave him a spark of happiness? It had for a while.

Coding was happiness when he didn't do it all day every day.

A man really needed to get away from this chair, communicate with those around him. Live. Allow some balance into his life yet still be able to wobble at will.

He did deserve a good life. And listening to Amber talk about his talents and attributes that would attract a woman gave him hope it was possible. And if that woman were like Amber? Smart, witty, easy to talk to. Their conversations were insightful. He enjoyed that. She did tend to pull back, keep to their business relationship when they went too deep, though. Expected. And she had to control the situation, he'd felt that too. This was her first time as a matchmaker? She was doing well.

They had more in common than not. Both geeky and slightly unsure about social mannerisms. He couldn't stop thinking about kissing Amber when she stood close and he watched her lips move as she talked. The woman...needed to be held. To be cherished. To be kissed soundly.

A knock at his dark room door startled him up from the chair. He commanded Hal to unlock and open it and there stood the woman of his daydreams. "Amber?"

She held up a brown bag. "I brought lunch. I suspect you may not have taken a break?"

"You suspect correctly. What's in there? It smells great."

"It's paella. I've never had the authentic Spanish version. It smells ridiculously yummy."

"You picked my favorite meal." He took the bag from her, kissed both of her cheeks—this time she did not pull away as if startled—then led her down the hallway. "We'll lunch in my office. I don't like to have food in the dark room."

"Sounds good. Have you seriously been in this room since dawn?"

"I have." That answer was beginning to make him feel guilty. He opened his office door and gestured she enter. "Was just thinking about…"

Amber. His heart rate was really zooming now. Good thing Hal wasn't connected to this office or the AI would suggest he reduce his stress.

"Yes?" she prompted. "What were you thinking about?"

"Uh, how I do need to cut down on my work hours?"

"Are you telling me or asking me?"

He caught her smile. "Do you think a man can change his ingrained habits?"

She arranged food containers and utensils on his empty desktop. "I'm not sure. I have habits that probably need changing. I also work too hard. Won't ask for help. I'm always trying to prove myself. If I don't get a gold star then I feel I've failed."

"I get that. A tiny bit of foiled paper. Gold stars, real or implied, make a person feel valued. Isn't that crazy? Our worth is directly related to our achievements."

She sighed. "To hear it put that way is a little sad. This one's yours." She pushed a takeaway box toward him. "I went with a version without seafood. I've never tried shrimp, believe it or not."

Val took the food box and then…he switched his with hers. She gaped at him. He shrugged. "Let's change up our routines, eh?"

She gave a little agreeing shoulder wiggle, fetched his box and sat opposite him at his desk. "Here goes nothing."

"Nothing doesn't really exist." He marveled over the rich saffron rice. "It's either a one or a zero."

"Isn't zero nothing?"

"Do you really want to get into this conversation?" He forked in some paella. "It's geek stuff."

"I have an idea of where it leads. Something about an absence of quantity?"

"Very good. And you must actually have nothing before you can assign the value of zero to it—yes, I recognize that glazed look in your eyes. I won't go into the mathematical weeds."

"Thank you. But keep talking about the stuff you are passionate about. It's relaxing to listen to your voice."

"It is?"

She laughed. "Sort of? It's very calm and sure. You are confident in body and your surroundings."

He was. Despite his belief he was not. But that she'd pointed it out made him relax a little more. It was easy being with Amber.

"Actually, I came by to pick your brain again."

"Haven't you mined everything out of it already?"

"If I took out everything, wouldn't nothing be left?" A lift of one of her brows challenged him.

"There would still be a hunk of matter that weighs approximately three pounds jiggling up here." He shook his head. "Still computing, still creating my passion."

"Yes, passion. Like your dancing?"

"Coding makes me passionate as well. It's not as dramatic as flamenco. But I still need to mine the daemon for coding on occasion."

She propped an elbow on the table and rested her chin on the back of her hand. "How so?"

"There is a story to all of the games we create at Verdadero. Emotion, drama, conflict, passion. It requires one mine deep."

"Even for ones and zeros?"

"Even so. Those ones and zeros must allow the player to feel and experience the game as if it were really happening to them."

Amber sat back. "Do you think someday people will sit around in their homes, VR goggles on all day as they experience things they can only dream of?"

"It's a possibility."

"Ugh. I hope not. I was replaced at the law firm by AI."

"Law firm? How come I didn't know that about you?"

"Because you didn't ask? Before landing the Lux Love job I was a paralegal. I'm a research addict. Turns out when it comes to research skills, AI is excellent and cheap. So… bye, bye, Amber."

"I'm sorry. We believe AI will take over the boring, mindless jobs that humans would rather not do, but there is validation in having a job and doing meaningful work."

"Yes, the gold star."

"So with a background in legal research, how did you land in matchmaking?"

"My aunt knows my boss. And she knew I wanted to travel. She put in a good word for me, and Colette took a chance on me."

"Matchmaking in Paris. That's almost a cliché in the romance department, isn't it? Yet you've indicated you're not a big believer in love?"

"I believe in love. I just—" she gave it some thought "—don't have high hopes it can persist. My best example of love was my parents' marriage. After twenty-five years they divorced. So…"

"Hey, at least they had the twenty-five years to learn and grow together."

"You're optimistically pragmatic. I find your background and desire for the traditional fascinating, yet you also live a fast-paced lifestyle that focuses on the future and technology. You're a dichotomy. In a good way."

"I'll take that as a compliment. You are as well."

"How so?"

"Doesn't believe in love yet she's fixing up people in love matches."

"I'm not doing the actual fixing up. I'm just filling out the assessment. It's all in the nonexistent hands of the AI. Of which, I certainly hope AI doesn't overstep and start moving in on romance."

"Too late. The AI companions available right now are designed to simulate real-life friendships and relationships."

"That's terrible!"

"Perhaps Lux Love will be matchmaking humans to AI sims some day?"

"Never!" She laughed at her passionate reply. "Sorry. I don't ever want to live in that world."

"Same. But it's a generational thing. Young people nowadays will be much less averse to the idea of a robot as a partner than you and I are. Still. I don't think a person will ever be able to exchange meaningful looks with a robotic companion. Just look at it as a helpful assistant."

Her eyes latched to his. He could look into hers all day. Sense her soft breaths, the subtle orange perfume lingering on her skin.

"Right," she said slowly, touching her lips. "And forget physical touch from some sort of robotic being. It could never be so gentle."

"Oh, it could. But no." Val quickly added, "No robot romance."

"I agree." Her mouth revealed her thoughts before she spoke them. That subtle tooth pull. Parted and expecting lips. Wanting. He could reach—

Amber shook her head. Val lost the enchantment.

"So back to your wants," she said. "You're open on the career front as well. How about personality?"

He'd been so close to touching her. Making contact. Probably for the best?

"You mean like giggly and fun as opposed to serious and exacting?"

She straightened her shoulders. She did swing from relaxed to serious in the snap of a finger. As shifting in her emotions as he supposed he was. But he tended more toward, hmm…passion.

Really, it was duende. Two souls dancing around one another with words and subtle expressions. It was that untamable something he needed and craved.

Val leaned forward, pushing his takeaway box aside. "I like a well-rounded personality. Someone who can have fun, likes to talk, but isn't an airhead and—if we're going to be real here, I'm not keen on someone who lives for shopping and being seen. You know, like those influencers whose lives revolve around getting likes and follows? Always with a phone recording their every experience. I want someone with whom I can converse."

"I agree," she said softly.

Had she fallen into his accidental enchantment again? What to do? Dare he kiss her? It…didn't feel right. She was wobbly. Off-balance. And he liked that, but he knew she did not. She needed to stay in control.

"No influencers," she noted with a dash across her tablet. "But what if you matched to one?"

"How could I? If you enter my wants in the database, the algorithms will do their job."

"You and your algorithms."

"I trust them completely. I mean, it all traces back to the original programmer, right? The AI is only as smart as the person coding it, feeding it the information. But I did my research on Lux Love. Your success rate is impressive."

"We are very thorough."

Struck by a sudden desire, Val leaned forward. "Are *you* in the database?"

"I am."

"Really?" He sat up straight.

"But we're not allowed to be included in searches. We fill out a profile to know what the clients' side of the experience looks like. Moving on…"

He didn't want to move on. He wanted to hack into Lux Love and put Amber in the search database for his match.

"Tell me about some of your past girlfriends?" The woman was certainly focused.

"Why? You want to dissect why the relationships didn't work out?"

She lifted her shoulders. "It can be helpful. Learning from one's past mistakes."

"You going to eat that?"

She forked a few pieces of shrimp into his box. "They taste great but I'm not as hungry as I thought I was. What about your mushrooms?" He pushed his box toward her so she could fork them out. "Thanks. So how many women have you dated seriously?"

"Seriously? Like more than a few months? One or two. Lots of one-nighters, weeklong hookups, things like that."

"What was your longest relationship?"

"Six months. About a year into university. I really loved her. Or I thought I did." Val set the box on the desk to give her his complete attention. "What even is love?"

"Right?" Amber leaned her elbows onto the table and caught her cheek against her hand. "It's hard to define. Numbers and bits and bytes are great, but ultimately, it's a soul deep thing, don't you think?"

"Possibly. Do you think your parents were soulmates?"

"Oh." Her wince alerted him the topic was touchy for her.

"I mean, parents aside, do you think there is a specific soul out there designed for one other soul?"

"I've never thought much about it, but I like that. Unless you count watching movies with princesses who find their prince charming. Doesn't everyone want that? But then again, love does have an expiration date. So…"

Her parents' divorce had worked a number on her. Val could relate. He'd given up dance following his mother's death. Heavy events like that tended to change a person's way of thinking. But he hated to think that Amber might never allow herself the freedom to open her heart when love stepped up.

"Have you ever been in love?" he asked.

Amber shook her head. "I don't think so. I've had boyfriends but they always…" She winced. "I don't like to risk intimacy with someone I don't know. I've never been with a man where I felt I could walk around naked and just…be."

He wanted to undress her. Touch all of her to see how she reacted. Would her back arch if he touched her stomach? Would a stroke along her throat make her sigh?

"*That's* your criteria? Being naked and comfortable?"

She shrugged. "It's a start, isn't it?"

"Interesting. There's the thrill of new love and being with someone but it gets old fast if all you share is sex."

"Right? Whatever happened to slow walks and holding hands?"

"I love holding hands."

"I've noticed you are a toucher. You like to make contact."

"Anything wrong with that?"

"Not at all."

"Listen. I know I'm a workaholic. That's usually the deal-breaker with my dates and girlfriends. I can't commit or find the time."

"You'd find the time if she was the right person for you. Work would slip your mind like scheduling appointments on your calendar slips your mind."

"Probably." He poked at his remaining paella. "So, if I catch you walking naked through my villa, does that mean you're comfortable with me?"

She laughed and choked a little on a bite of food. "Not going to happen. I don't think my boss would approve."

"*Sì*, but I would."

Amber's jaw dropped open, mid-chew. He'd caught her out.

Sitting back, she closed the lid of her empty meal container and set it in the takeaway bag. "Ahem. Back to the assessment. I like that you seem open to anything."

Val splayed out a hand. "I'm very adaptable and eager to be matched to most any woman. And I promise I will be fully dressed our first meeting."

"Good call. Not that your abs wouldn't serve as a perfect conversation starter."

Heh. So he'd made an impression on her that first night? She wasn't so staunch and emotionless as she tried to convey.

"I, uh, suspect we'll have a match for you soon after I've entered this info."

"Any more details you need on my preferences?"

"I assume your values should match the woman's. Trust, honesty, humor, loyalty. Anything else important? Why *did* you break it off with those two longer relationships? It wasn't just because of your work habits, was it?"

"One didn't want to get married, but she did want me to buy her a flat in Paris."

"A gold digger?"

"Yes, that's what you call it. And the other was…well, I imagined myself married to her. And we even talked about it one night."

"That's serious."

"It was. But she—no, it was me. Ultimately, I was scared to dive in. To step away from this singular life I have. It's a good life. I can do what I want, when I want, and don't have to answer to anyone."

"So why suddenly do you feel the need to settle down? You said something about your dad wanting a traditional marriage for you. You're smart enough to know you can't please others. Most especially family."

"I am smart. As are you. You know things about me even I have to give some thought to. No, contacting Lux Love for a match was not completely because of my dad's wishes. Honestly? I realized such an attitude of not wanting to answer to anyone was selfish. And not my true values. Teo changed when he fell in love with Cara last year. Not that he wasn't a good man to begin with, but a light sparked in his eyes. He became more…buoyant. Bright. I want that light. Does that sound silly?"

"That sounds downright romantic."

"*Si?*"

Amber clasped her hands on her lap and nodded, not meeting his gaze. "Lux Love will bring that buoyant brightness to your life. Promise."

Not selling it with her posture. Then again, she was Miss Impossible regarding love.

Dare he brainstorm how to get *her* profile activated at Lux Love?

CHAPTER ELEVEN

THE MOVERS LEFT after completing their task. Amber had called them. Another night with that bull's head staring at her was not conducive to a good night's rest. When she'd consulted with Val via text where to put it, he'd said "Wherever," that he'd didn't care.

Really? The man needed to be more involved in—well, everything in his life. He was too lackadaisical at times. So, now Amber stood in Val's bedroom. Staring at the bull's head on the wall. Was she taking this a little too far? Honestly? The bedroom was sparsely furnished with a massive king-size bed on a wood platform, and but a single square wood block as a nightstand for a lamp. No paintings, no decorations. It looked great on the wall. Gave the room gravitas. But it wasn't something she could imagine Val's future wife would enjoy staring at.

With a secret smile of success, Amber turned off the lights and left the bedroom. Not sabotage, she argued inwardly. Just…a welcome gift to his match.

By the time she landed in the kitchen, doubt attacked. What had she just done? Was she allowing emotions to hinder her work? That was a very personal move she'd just made. It screamed *jealousy* in a manner she couldn't quite figure out. She'd never been jealous before. And of a nonexistent woman, at that!

Grabbing a coconut water from the fridge, Amber shook her

head at her inner argument. It would be fine. She'd done nothing wrong. In fact, she'd enhanced the decor of the man's room.

Maria eyed her and said something she almost thought sounded like a curse. In… English.

Amber narrowed her gaze on Maria. The housekeeper lifted her head and resumed placing groceries that had been delivered inside the pantry.

"Sure, whatever." Amber strolled outside. She didn't notice Maria's sudden twist of head to look over her shoulder at her.

Val managed an evening away from the office. If he didn't spend time with Amber now, he might regret it. She would leave as soon as the computer spit out his first match. So he suggested a movie night and she eagerly accepted. That both bolstered his confidence and made him realize that maybe making time for someone else wasn't such a challenge. And the reward was far greater than perfectly vibed code.

The inner courtyard was private and lush. Val had the stone hearth installed when he had moved in. When he entertained, which was rare of late, his chef made fire-grilled pizzas and unique smoked drinks for his friends.

Now a low fire crackled. Amber gathered the takeaway boxes from the supper they'd just eaten, and when she asked if he wanted a beer from the kitchen, he said yes.

He stoked the fire and settled on the rug, leaning against the cushioned front of a big cozy sofa. The open courtyard looked up to that big azure sky he'd loved all his life. Stars twinkled. Everything felt ripe for romance.

And he was just daring enough to see if it might happen.

The night was sultry, even though the temperature had sunk. Her cashmere shrug had been a lifesaver for the cool spring evenings here in Seville. Amber soaked in the warmth from the fire, the lingering *azahar* perfume kissed with a hint of fire flame. Orange wine warmed her throat and loosened her muscles. She and Val sat on a huge woven rug before the fire, leaning against the sofa, looking up to the sky where the full moon was framed by the tops of two orange trees.

Everything about this evening felt unreal to her. From the luxurious courtyard and food delivered by a driverless car, to the heady star-kissed atmosphere, to the handsome man sitting so close their arms rubbed. And when he laughed at her story about getting lost on the metro for three hours when she'd first arrived in Paris, his hair had fallen over his eyes and she'd swept it away. One quick dash of her fingers.

Now a sneak glance found Val's eyes closed, head tilted back as if moon bathing. She'd not witnessed him embody such stillness. So there was a calm within the beautiful chaos. Had she unearthed that?

She'd take the credit, but only because she was feeling rather chuffed by her success with the man. And she would call it a success. Sure, the assessment was almost completed. But it was the gentle suggestions to change she had made that he'd taken to heart. Taking time off work? Check. Talking about himself on dates? Check. And the foyer had even been straightened of the mess. Had he asked Maria to do that? She hadn't noticed a cleaning woman checking in.

Colette should be pleased. Amber would ensure this eligible billionaire bachelor would be matched.

Here's looking to a nice commission for a job well done.

And she hadn't fallen in love.

For the most part.

"Hey, do you want to watch a movie?" Val suddenly asked. He tapped his watch and with a click, a large screen lowered from an overhang she'd thought simply part of the architecture. "Cool, right? Ever since I was a little boy in Triana I've always wanted one of these fancy hidden screens."

"Impressive. What movie are you thinking?"

"And oldie, for sure. I'll bring up the list and you can pick."

"Fair enough."

As he tapped away, she studied his grin. Innocent in that little-boy-who'd-earned-the-toy manner, but also so attractive.

How could a woman—any woman—not fall a little bit in love with the adorable tech CEO? There was something about the man that *tugged* at her. Something deep within that she couldn't name or place. He'd grasped hold of it and—

And really, if *she* didn't fall in love with him then who else would? Such feelings indicated she had a winner. Any woman could fall in love with him.

Maybe she was on to something here? Had Colette overlooked that tiny detail? The client should be lovable! So if a consultant responded to the lovable parts of their client, then excellent.

She wasn't going to overthink her logic. She'd learned who Valentino Vasquez was and she adored him.

"Which one?" he asked.

She scanned the list on the screen. "Of course, *My Fair Lady*."

"Love it. *Words! Words! I'm so sick of words!*"

"*I get words all day through.*" She continued the lyrics of what was one of her favorite songs in the show. The woman in the movie was so over pretty words from her gentleman callers. All she wanted was for them to show her that they cared for her, hungered for her…

It wasn't an empty sentiment. Any woman would want as much.

The movie began. The warm touch of Val's hand slid against her palm. She closed her eyes as their fingers entangled.

"I know what your love language is," she said.

"Yeah?"

"Touch. You like to make contact. Always. It's nice."

"Touch." He squeezed her hand. "I think you're right. What's your love language? Perfection?"

It hurt to hear that word because it sounded judgmental and foolish now. "No, I think it's…" *Not pretty words.* "…being seen."

"I see you."

She turned to meet his gaze. Always, a smile in his irises. And that seductive darkness. "Yes, you really do."

As they settled to watch the movie, Amber didn't pull her hand from Val's. And she didn't even think of the impropriety because throughout the movie they parted as each broke into song. At one point Val went to the kitchen to retrieve another beer for each of them and he returned doing a little dance to Professor Higgins's song. And as the credits rolled, their shoulders hugged, and Amber's head tilted against Val's.

Val stirred subtly. His dark brown irises danced across her face. His smile assumed charm mode. With a shy bow of his head, he then caught her stare again and said, "I want to kiss you."

Oh. Oh?

No. That…

Was exactly what she wanted.

He turned his body to face hers. "That's all I've been thinking about since Professor Higgins realized he's grown accustomed to Eliza's face. I've grown accustomed to your face, Amber. Your lips. Your mouth. Would a kiss taste like orange wine?"

"Val—"

"It's touch, Amber. My love language."

"Yes, but I'm working for you." Seemed the appropriate response for a professional matchmaker who must *never* fall in love with her client.

On the other hand, she had gleefully sung through an entire movie alongside him, batting her lashes during the cheeky parts, and sighing dramatically at the sad ones. And it hadn't at all been related to learning more about him for his profile.

Why was she forcing herself to resist something that felt real? Meant to be?

Because you want to show your boss you are capable and worth being promoted to a full-time consultant. Because you think that love can't be real? Or last? What if she did open up her heart to Val only to have her world and her heart crushed when finally, he was matched with a client?

All of it was too risky.

"We are adults, Amber. And I get that I am your client. But right now? We're just two people sitting under the moonlight, acting out one of the best movies ever made. I assumed this was a nonwork thing."

He leaned in closer, his eyes tracing her mouth with seductive scrutiny. She tugged in her lower lip. Touch? *Yes, please.*

"If you don't want a kiss," he whispered, "just say *no*."

When had a *yes* or *no* question been so difficult to respond to?

Amber struggled inwardly with the right and wrong of it. Her astute professional career girl screamed that she'd be messing up any chance of keeping the consultant position and ultimately paying off her credit card bills. While the softer, deeply guarded part of her reached out and made a gimme gesture with her fingers. She was so needy. Wanted real intimacy. With a man who related to her on a level she'd never experienced. He got her.

What was wrong with one little kiss? No one had to know. And really, it wouldn't equal insta-love to be eventually quashed by a breakup.

"Haven't you thought about kissing me?"

Yes! But not falling in love with the billionaire.

But again, not that a kiss required love…

"I will add," Val said on a breathy tone that seemed to mine deep from within his soul, "that no response will be taken as an affirmative."

Amber swore inwardly. She wanted this kiss. She wanted him to take her in his arms and…ravish her. She wasn't even sure what ravishing involved. But oh, did it feel acceptable.

"Very well." Val leaned closer. "No response. That means…"

She didn't flinch as his head moved closer. His eyes focused on her lips, which she parted, because a gasp was unavoidable. That hush of breath countered her rushing heartbeats. The flames crackling beside them played harmony to the electricity zinging through her veins. Ultra-alert, her skin prickled, growing receptive as his breath hushed over her lips.

Push him away!

The professional part of Amber Martin was just too much. Too perfectionist. Too people-pleasing. Too resistant to the emotions striving for release. For once in her life, she had to abandon the quest for seeking approval from others.

Or she'd never know the touch of Val's kiss.

Amber slid her hand along his neck and pulled him against her mouth. His hand cupped the back of her head. The kiss, hard and seeking, crushed and then did not, and then it sought again. Combustible as the flames. As grounding as a flamenco dancer's feet beating the earth. They clung to one another, chasing heartbeats and gasping sighs. Their urgency found a rhythm. Slower, but tight and insistent. He tasted like the local craft beer they'd been drinking. And his hard body against hers tempted her to arch her back, slide up a leg along his to feel all of him, as much of him as she could discover.

Because this kiss was an anomaly. It could never happen again. So she'd enjoy it while she could.

The kiss alternated between hunger and a slower exploration. Val's hand slid along her arm, and then against her rib cage, holding her. His thumb pressed up under her breast. A subtle connection that did not-so-subtle things to her body. They didn't part. How to force apart the north from the south? Yet, they weren't so much like opposites poles. She could geek out with him at the best of times.

Stop thinking, Amber.

This wasn't love. This was passion. What was that word he'd used? *Duende.* It was stirred in a mix of wanting, knowing and expressing that passion between one another. Sometimes a girl had to brush off her exterior armor and let the arrow pierce her softness. Because Amber had a softness that craved this moment. Despite the risk.

Val ended the kiss. Bowed his forehead to hers. Always connecting to her, skin to skin. "Had to do that."

He didn't say sorry. That word might have cruelly ripped out the arrow. For now, Amber wanted to leave it in. A love dart, of sorts. "I should…" Leave? What was she thinking? Now that she did start to think, practicality and propriety began to grip that arrow by the shaft…

As Val bowed his head to hers, she knew what was coming and—*push him away!*

Amber gripped Val's shirt lapel and pulled him to her mouth. She kissed him quickly. Once. Twice. But as the angel and devil struggled in a fistfight on her shoulder, she grasped some modicum of sanity, and pushed away from his delicious mouth.

Now that they'd kissed, things were beginning to click inside her. Things she'd never felt click before. And that was not a metaphor. Yes, arousal, but it was something beyond that. A weird sort of…knowing?

Had they begun something tonight?

No one would have to know. It wasn't as though Colette could see through the tablet and watch Amber's every move. Unless—no, she knew the camera on the tablet was only front facing.

So, yes. She'd kissed the client.

And she'd liked it.

CHAPTER TWELVE

AMBER WOKE TO a message from Lux Love. A 92 percent match had been found for Val. The woman, Carmen Alonso, even lived in Seville. A recruiter for a global charity organization, she traveled for her job and was leaving in three days for Ecuador. Would it be possible to set up a date soon?

Amber replied that it would happen. She'd report back with details later.

Tossing her phone aside, she knew she'd have to call Val because he was likely at work. Probably had been there for hours.

She traced her lips. Was he thinking of last night's kiss under the moonlight?

Why had she let that happen? It had been the most exciting, intoxicating, titillating—she ran out of adjectives. It had rocked her world.

And now Carmen, who was a freakin' charity worker, for heaven's sake, waited to go on a date with her man.

Not *her* man. Val. Valentino Vasquez. Her *client*.

"Pull yourself together, Amber. Do your job."

She'd kissed a handsome man. He'd wanted to kiss her. Had given her the option to refuse. Didn't mean they were going to make babies and live happily ever after. Sometimes two people kissed because they wanted to. They had sex because they wanted to.

"Sounds like a boring sex talk for teens," she muttered bleakly. Because she didn't get satisfaction from a hookup. It was so empty. She wanted more. She wanted that *duende* Val talked about.

She slid out of bed and paced the floor before the patio doors, which she'd left open all night, so blissful sleeping with a breeze dancing over her skin. She called Val and he answered on the first ring.

"*Buenos días*," he said. "Just waking?"

"You know it. Already deep into your code?"

"It's a living."

And what a profitable living. But also, a restrictive one when it came to occupying all the man's time. For heaven's sake, the man could retire. Never lift a finger amidst virtual code again! "You know what I said about working so much."

"I know. I'll try to be home at a reasonable time today, honey."

She rolled her eyes at the endearment, while part of her melted at the intimacy of their jesting conversation. Handsome man giving her a pet name? It felt better than it should.

"I've great news for you." She leaned in the open patio doorway. "We've found a match for you. Ninety-two percent."

"That's…good. I suppose."

He *supposed*? What did he expect? A one hundred percent match? Ninety-two was incredible.

"So what happens next?" he asked.

No mention of their kiss. At least one of them could stick to business.

But was that all it had been to him? Kiss the girl. Back to business?

Amber closed her eyes and shook her head. She was a professional. She would proceed professionally from now on. No more kisses!

"Now we set up a date," she finally said. A patch of grass caught her eye. She looked down at her toes. "Her name is Carmen Alonso. She actually lives in Seville but she's leaving town in a few days so…how about tonight or tomorrow?"

"Tonight would be best. Wow. This is happening fast."

"It's what you wanted, right?"

"Of course." Was that a touch of reluctance in his tone? And why did that perk her up, give her a hope that she shouldn't even wish for?

"Do you have any questions about Carmen?"

"Should I have questions?"

Yes, he should. He should want to know everything about her. Where she was born, lived, went to school, what she did for a living, what she did in her free time. What her thoughts about dating were, what her thoughts about handsome billionaires were. If she were a gold digger.

"I will forward her profile to you, so you can take a look over it."

"Sure, I'll see if I can find some time to look it over. But I'm not worried. I trust the algorithms. Set something up for tonight."

"All right." He was being too indifferent about this. Like it didn't matter. Like it wasn't going to possibly be *the* date that could change his life. "Can you at least suggest a restaurant to meet at?"

"Let's do the Trastienda."

The same place he'd taken her. The food was excellent. The atmosphere perfect for a first date. Was it his MO? Had *she* been just another date?

You are not his date! Ever!

Amber stepped out onto the grass. "Got it. How about seven?"

"That works. Will you send me a text reminder?"

Seriously? "Val, I'm not going to be here to send you reminders for every meeting or date you have."

"I know. I really need an assistant. I wonder if Carmen has ever done any such work?"

"She's a recruiter for a global charity organization. Don't even ask her if she does secretarial work. That's very condescending."

"Right. Uh, I gotta fly on this job. Seven, then?"

"Yes, and do me a favor and arrive at the restaurant ten minutes early."

"I'll be home by six to change. See you later, honey."

He hung up and Amber could but only stare at her phone. He'd used *honey* again. Jokingly? Absently? What was wrong with him that he wasn't over the moon about a potential match? He had contacted Lux Love for this.

And why was she letting it bother her so much? If he messed up tonight's date, that was on him.

Well. It was on her. Colette insisted her consultants continue their work until they were assured the client had found *the one* and marriage seemed imminent. It didn't require staying near the client, but making sure a second date happened, and following up with those first two dates to get feedback was vital.

Which meant, if tonight's date went well, then Amber was out. So why did she feel as though this client was going to mess up majorly? That she might even need to fix his tie or adjust his hair, as if she were a mother making sure her offspring were presentable before he stepped out?

"He'll be fine."

Tonight, Val could meet his match.

And all the time they'd shared, the fun they'd had, the laughing, the conversations would be over.

She swore softly under her breath. She was jealous of Carmen Alonso. The woman might win Val!

And the only way to remedy that was to remove herself from this situation. Consultants rarely stayed on after dates began for their clients. Communication was continued through phone calls. And she was a consultant who did her job as expected.

Amber retrieved her suitcase from the closet.

The bull's head on the wall opposite his bed stared at him. He *had* told her she could put it anywhere. Was the placement her idea of a joke? Amber didn't do jokes. And it wasn't funny.

Eh. It was funny. He may get used to it there. Though, he couldn't stop associating it with his dad. Not conducive to a good sleep or even a sexy liaison.

"Amber!" Val called down the stairway and made his way toward the guest room. At Amber's suggestion he'd gone with a suit. Good first impression. He didn't mind the white business shirt. It wasn't starched so he'd keep the coat on to hide the wrinkles. But this tie!

Amber's head popped out from her room. She saw him dangling the tie and shook her head. "Come inside."

He splayed out his arms in defeat. "I never wear ties."

"Seriously?" Her red lips pursed—lips that he'd kissed—as she perused the situation then started folding one end of the silk tie over the other. "You've got quite a collection of them in your closet."

"They come with the suits. Or they are gifts from women."

"Really? So the women you date read suit-and-tie kind of guy from you?"

"Right?" He winced as she tugged the tie too tightly, which prompted her to loosen it. "But I am capable of change. Last night, I was Mr. Relaxation."

"That you were." She met his gaze, tilted her head as if searching for something, then focused back on the tie.

Was she thinking about that killer kiss they'd shared? The one he'd not stopped thinking about all day? Had even lost his way during coding and Hal had prompted him to pay attention. That had never happened before!

Why couldn't he have kisses like that all the time? And not from any woman. If Amber were among the potential matches on Lux Love's database, would they match?

"Have you ever used your service?" he asked as she adjusted his tie.

"What? Lux Love? As I've explained, we're not allowed. I'm no expert with ties, but I think that'll do." With a pat of her hand to declare the job finished, she stepped back and, hands on her hips, looked him over.

He did love that authoritative pose she assumed. Trying to look all in charge but her soft red lips and wavy hair always gave her away. She wasn't so sour on romance as she liked to believe. And he counted kissing as romance.

A smart guy could hack into the system and add her file to the database—no, he wasn't a hacker. Not that he couldn't do just that.

Amber hadn't taken her eyes from him. Val asked, "What do you think?"

"Handsome, talented young billionaire looking for love? Who wouldn't fall for you?"

Assuming his best leading man swagger, he asked, "Would you?"

"Well." Hand to her hip, she surveyed his attire. "We have been on a few dates already."

"Did you fall for me? I mean..." If she were to play this game, he could as well. "...purely in the sense of you doing your job, seeing if a potential match would fall for me."

"Of course." She ran a hand along the back of her neck, then quickly gestured with her palm between them. "Only in the sense that I was a stand-in for another woman."

But he wished she was not.

"Yes, I could see any woman falling for you. But most especially Carmen. I've read her profile. She's a lovely woman with good values and a successful career. A ninety-two percent match is very promising."

Val noticed her suitcase open on the end of the bed. "Are you packing?"

"Yes. I, uh…well, tonight's date could be the one. Beyond the follow-up interview in the morning, you don't need me anymore."

"Yes, I do." He rushed over and tugged the suitcase from under her touch. "I mean…" *Needy much?* "I haven't taken you to see the Metropol Parasol yet. Or there's a cool old cathedral by the bullring. And the beaches in Cadiz."

"Val, we don't need to do the fake dates anymore. Your profile is complete. Now all you have to do is let the algorithms do the work."

"Algorithms." For the first time, he almost hated that word. Because finding a match meant Amber would leave him. There would be no more world-rocking kisses. No more midnight movies under the moonlight. No more wondering if he might take her on a virtual adventure into an Egyptian pyramid. Or to Mars! They'd never gone on a jog together! No more… Amber.

Amber pushed her suitcase aside to sit on the end of the bed.

Val sat beside her. He eased at the tie to loosen it.

"Still too tight?"

"I feel so confined."

"You don't have to wear the tie."

"I want to—" *Impress Amber.* Because she'd suggested it would look good. "No. It's fine. I can suffer through one date with a noose around my neck."

"Please, do not go into your date with that thought to drag you down. Are you nervous?"

"Of course!"

"You've never seemed nervous around me."

"Because you're easy to be around." He twisted and pressed his forehead to hers. "You calm my chaos."

Her moving away from him actually hurt his heart. "You are chaotic," she said as she stood and fitted her hands to hips. "But it's who you are. Nothing wrong with that."

"Really?"

"Really. Initially, I thought you were too erratic, too busy to slow down and take notice of the world. Let alone a date. But I was wrong. Just be Val. That's the guy Carmen will love. Think of our dates as practice. Just pretend it's me you're talking to, if that'll help."

"Why can't it be you?"

Val suddenly felt as though he were back in school. The awkward geek who could never get a girl. If Pablo were still alive, he'd have slapped Val across the shoulder, winked and told him *Go get her.*

But the *her* in question was named Carmen.

He could do this. He *would* do this. At the very least, his dad would be pleased to hear he was making a concerted effort at finding his future wife. And who knew? He and Carmen may hit it off.

"I should head out. Will I see you later tonight?"

"I don't know, Val. What if you bring Carmen home with you tonight? It wouldn't look good to have another woman staying in the guest room."

He gaped at her. She intended to leave *tonight*? But more

so… "I never do that on a first date. Sex on the first date is—you know that about me."

"I…did not. I just don't want to interfere in any manner. My boss would kill me if—"

If she what? Prevented him from seeing Carmen tonight? Actually let down her defenses and used her own advice to relax and enjoy their interactions?

She sighed. "Fine. One more day. I will need to do a follow-up interview with you in the morning. It's important."

"Fair enough. Then you have to stay. For the interview."

"Yes, for the interview. But if it goes well with Carmen, you must tell me. I reserve the right to leave you to romantic bliss with the woman of your dreams if that's what comes of tonight."

"Deal." He fist-bumped her, but he wished it was a kiss. "See you tomorrow morning."

"Good luck tonight!"

He paused in the doorway. He didn't need luck; he needed Amber in his arms.

CHAPTER THIRTEEN

ONE MORE DAY? Amber wanted another day with Val. Another chat. Another walk. Another kiss to end all kisses. Another movie night featuring them singing song lyrics at the tops of their lungs. Another standing in near darkness holding his virtual hand. He had caught her when she fell. It had been a storybook romantic moment that she hadn't known how to react to at the time, never having been a receiver of romantic gestures.

Was her dating life so terrible? Yes, it had been.

And why was that? Too picky. Too exacting. Expecting too much from the men she dated. Was her need for control stifling her reception to pleasure?

Her parents' divorce had affected her as well. But it shouldn't. That was between the two of them. She wasn't her mom or her dad. Why did she feel the need to blame her poor dating history on anything but her own shortcomings? Was she too focused on perfection? Even her mother had been able to set work aside and just be a mom when she had been home with Amber.

"I'm being too hard on my mom," she muttered. "She had her reasons for leaving the marriage. Reasons I shouldn't judge. I should give her a call."

She looked at her hand. Curved her fingers as if to hold Val's hand. He was smart, but he didn't wield that intellect as a front for his personality. It wasn't his label. He didn't label anything or anyone. He was his own man. Everyone around him was their own person. He saw everyone for however they wished to be seen.

And he saw her as pretty, smart and—kissable.

With Val, she didn't need to be perfect. She could be herself. And beyond the studiousness and quest for perfection, Amber was just a girl wanting to be loved. To be caught when she fell. To be kissed like the world was ending.

And the one man her heart had decided to pump for, she was sending out to meet another woman tonight.

"Ninety-two percent," she muttered. "Not the highest match."

Most of Lux Love's matches were 95 percent or higher. But as soon as the computer spit out a name above the 90 percent minimum, then it stopped its search until it was prompted to continue.

She picked up her phone and dialed Elise, who worked evening hours at Lux Love because she had a morning job at a patisserie. Elise brought home so many expired baked goods; they were still good to eat, if a little dry.

"Amber! How's Spain?"

"Delicious in all the ways you can imagine."

"I know! Senor Vasquez is one delicious bite. I see we have a date scheduled for him tonight?"

"Yes, he left a while ago. Headed out to meet his future wife."

"Fingers crossed. Or...?"

From Elise's tone, Amber sensed she had caught on to the reason for Amber's call. Elise was the closest she had to a best friend. Though they saw one another at work, their free time together was rare. But in those spare moments, they managed to convey their likes, loves, hates and quests. And the girl code bonded them by a common love for all men with a sexy accent.

"You want me to check your numbers?" Elise whispered.

Amber panicked at her lowered voice. "Is Colette in the office?"

"No, I'm all alone."

"Whew! You scared me. But...yes. Would you? Just for kicks and giggles. You know."

"Of course. Kicks and giggles. Whatever that means. Hang on."

Elise was Swedish and she often gave Amber the glazed-eye look whenever she used an American idiom.

"I'm running the stats. Want me to call you back as soon as I get results?"

That could take an hour.

"Yes, please?"

"Just for fun," Elise said. And Amber could almost hear her conspiratorial wink. "He is a sexy one."

"Too sexy. My reluctant heart is—oh, Elise, don't run the stats."

"Too late."

Amber knew it wasn't too late. All Elise had to do was execute the stop command. She was second-guessing herself. Knew this wasn't going to prove anything one way or another. If she and Val matched, then her heart could only break even more. And if they didn't match, then it would prove that Amber Martin would never find her man. Because she just couldn't loosen up and allow happiness to enter her life.

"Talk soon," Elise said and hung up.

Amber tossed her phone to the bed. It was early still but she wasn't in the mood for a walk. A shower would lift her spirits and then maybe a relaxing wander in the courtyard.

Carmen's smile was genuine and kind. Petite, blonde, very animated. Not overly gushy, but not shy either. She spoke with elocution and their initial handshake had been firm. A gorgeous woman; she would turn any man's head. The scent she wore was curious. Astringent with an undernote of floral. Val didn't like it, but he wouldn't say anything.

Throughout dinner they exchanged questions, volleying answers regarding work, hobbies, favorite entertainments. The usual. She didn't balk or wrinkle her nose when he drifted into the tech details about his work. Though she did wriggle in her chair when he mentioned his late work hours.

"I'm trying to change that," he added, as the waiter took away the empty bottle of red wine and replaced it with another. "I don't need to work as much but I do enjoy the purpose."

"Did you work today?" she asked.

"Every day but Sundays." Or most Sundays. He did try. Really, he did.

"You attend Mass?"

"When I remember. You?"

"Every Saturday evening and midweek if possible. It's important to me. But I'm willing to overlook your forgetfulness."

He shrugged and tilted back another swallow. "I don't want someone to view my worship schedule as lacking."

"I didn't mean it that way. Well… Faith is important to a healthy family environment."

He'd read that as he'd skimmed her profile. Didn't bother him. He'd grown up in a religious home and truly did wish to attend Mass more often. But…choices. His work was the most important thing in his life right now.

Save for finding someone with whom to share that busy life. Someone who didn't chastise him for it, even if she did like to suggest he work less.

Val smirked to himself. He didn't mind when Amber told

him what to do. He understood it was a part of her perfectionist personality. The need for subtle control. Something that didn't bother him. Because she wasn't perfect and that made her even more appealing.

"After I marry, I intend to become a homemaker," Carmen said. "I love what I do with the charity aspect of my job. But raising children is a job in itself and I feel taking on the role of homemaker would be immensely satisfying."

While he was saddened she'd give up such an interesting jet-setting career, he also understood raising children was a job that should get overtime and vacation pay. "Good for you. I'm sure your husband will be very happy about that."

Carmen raised her wineglass and said, "To a happy husband in my future."

Val clinked his glass against hers. Yes, but…he wasn't going to be that husband.

Clad in a striped-linen pajama set, Amber had taken a blanket out to the courtyard along with a goblet of wine. Not the orange wine. That stuff was capable of making her walk into walls!

Alone but for the discordant chirp of a hidden insect, she drifted into reverie. Would Carmen find Val as charming as Amber did? The only thing Amber sensed might not vibe between the two of them was the religion aspect. Val didn't seem overly religious. Amber had been raised Catholic but considered herself lapsed. But she was open to attending a service on Val's arm.

"He's not yours to fit into your fantasies," she muttered and tugged up her legs, settling against the cushy back of the lounge chair. "He and Carmen are probably laughing over shared interests and drinking wine right now."

Pouting would get her nowhere. Nor was it a good look on her.

Her phone jingled. Amber hesitated answering, but ultimately couldn't resist. "Elise, are you *still* at work?"

"I like to burn the midnight oil. I take my laptop out to the terrace and watch the Eiffel Tower twinkle on the top of every hour. And I don't have to work tomorrow morning. So… I got your results."

"Yeah?" Her heart suddenly thundered. It was just for fun. Really. But she and Val did have a lot in common. What if they matched in the nineties? "Tell me."

Elise's sigh did not bode well. "Sixty-two percent match between Amber Martin and Valentino Vasquez."

"Oh." Her heart suddenly quieted. Seemed to stop beating completely. She pressed a hand to her throat. Nodded.

"You okay, Amber?"

"Of course, I am. It was just a silly check. Right?"

"Right. But…*right*?"

Nothing at all felt right now.

"Amber, have you fallen in love with him? It can happen as quick as a blink."

She nodded. Then shook her head.

"Amber?"

"I—no, of course not. Don't be silly. This is my first consultation. I'm not so foolish as to jeopardize my job. Besides, Colette hired me because she judged me as too emotionless to ever match anyone. So make of that what you will."

"If you ask me, Colette is the emotionless one. She doesn't even notice Jacques pawing at her feet like a puppy."

The office took bets on how long Jacques could go until telling Colette he was in love with her.

"It's okay to lose your heart to the clients, Amber. It's happened to me."

"And what did you do?"

"He matched with a woman at ninety-five percent and they married three months later. That's what I did."

"But it hurt?"

"Of course, it did. Still does a little. He was so kind. Called me Sugarpop. So don't take this too hard. But also, don't be too hard on yourself."

"Thanks, Elise. I should go." Amber clicked off and set her phone far away on the bench where she had cuddled up under the orange tree.

She tugged the blanket up to her face to catch the teardrop that spilled down her cheek.

Val wandered into his home and strolled toward the inner courtyard where the solar lights beamed along the path to the stairs. Amber sat on a lounge chair, legs pulled up and a blanket around her shoulders.

A smile was irrepressible. She'd waited up for him? He liked having her face be the first thing he saw when he returned home.

She patted the chair beside her and he sat, loosening his tie. That felt great. A sniff tracked the astringent perfume Carmen had worn. She was still on him? He hadn't even gotten that close to her. Well, he'd kissed her cheeks in greeting and they'd hugged when parting.

"Makes me feel good to know that someone waits for my return home."

"Even after a date? Shouldn't that be the opposite? Like I was expecting your date to end poorly and—here you are. It's barely after midnight. What went wrong?"

"Is this the follow-up interview?"

She crossed her legs before her, assuming her take-charge mode. "Yes."

"All right. Nothing went wrong. Carmen was lovely. A beautiful person. We had a great conversation. We share many things in common."

Amber tapped her lower lip. "I sense there's a *but*."

He shrugged and leaned back, putting his feet up on the edge of a big terra-cotta pot, home to a massive palm. "I don't know. I didn't feel anything toward her. There was no spark. Her perfume was…"

"So strong." Amber winced. "It's all over you."

"Right? I'm going to have to send this suit to the dry cleaners. And when she said she intended to give up her career to become a homemaker once married, it hit me wrong."

"You don't want a wife to stay home with the children? I thought traditional was what you were shooting for?"

"Well, sure, but it was the idea of Carmen giving up a job that meant so much to her. Do you know she travels worldwide for charity?"

"I read that about her. Noble."

"It is. And I have nothing against stay-at-home parents. It just felt like such a loss to abandon the work that obviously gave her passion."

"How do you think she felt about you?"

"I think she liked me. But does it matter? I…don't want to see her again."

"Oh."

"I've failed my dad," he said. "But also, I've failed you."

"Not at all."

"But your algorithms…"

"Doesn't mean two clients are going to hit it off. We use a complex system to match people, meticulously examining all aspects of their lives. But there's a whole new level *beyond* the algorithms. Once you meet face-to-face and talk. The most important being will you match on a soul level?"

"Soul level?" He turned to face her. She wore striped pajamas that reminded him of summer and beach parties and not having a care in the world. He wanted that. "That's not something a computer can predict. Not unless you find a way to program it into the system. No. It's just not possible."

"Exactly. So the human element will always be necessary when it comes to matchmaking. And I mean—well, the soul level thing is not a part of the Lux Love litany so I shouldn't interject my own thoughts."

"Please do." He took her hand and kissed the back of it, studying her reaction. He could sense a flinch in the flex of her fingers but she didn't pull away. So he curled his hand about hers, holding it lightly but surely. Holding Amber's hand was so much nicer than holding Carmen's hand. And she smelled like everything that made him happy. "What does soul level mean to you?"

"I don't think a person can put it into words. Sort of like *duende*."

Exactly what he was thinking.

"It's a feeling," she said. "A knowing."

"Yes, a knowing. Like this person checks all the boxes and would make any guy a perfect match but…there's just that *something* that you can never fit into a tiny little box waiting for a check mark."

"The ineffable something," she agreed.

"Like the goose bumps."

She tilted a smile at him.

"That's the kind of love I want," he explained. "The kind that gives you goose bumps every time you see her because you know she's the one for you."

"That's a good way to put it." She smoothed her fingers over their clasped hands. "I'll inform the office to run the program to find you date number two."

"Thanks." He bowed his head over their hands and kissed her skin, lingering, inhaling as much of her as he dared. He wanted to keep the essence of her in his memory forever.

Amber shivered and he looked up as the breeze wafted her hair across her cheek. "I have to return to Paris tomorrow," she blurted out. With a gentle tug, she extricated her hand from his. "Once the client starts dating, my job isn't to babysit or linger."

What to say to that? This moment was so intimate. So easy. "I don't want you to go. I like spending time with you, Amber."

"Yes, well… Fraternizing with the paid consultant isn't getting you any closer to finding a match."

"Isn't it?" He stroked the hair from her face.

"Val. That's not…"

"Not what? How it works? Aren't you interested in me? Is there a rule against consultants dating their clients?" he asked.

"Of course there is."

"There shouldn't be." He touched the ends of her hair and twirled a bit around his forefinger. "You're the most interesting person I've met, Amber. Ever."

"Well, that's…" Her sigh settled heavily in his chest. "Val. The algorithms were the very reason you called Lux Love. You trust a computer program to do its thing and to pick the perfect match for you. And, I only want what is best for you. So, don't make this any more difficult than it should be. I'm…going to bed. I'm sorry your date didn't work out tonight."

Her leg skimmed his arm as she rose and walked away from him. The sensation raised a wave of goose bumps on his forearms. And all Val could do was smile.

CHAPTER FOURTEEN

VAL PACED BEFORE the stuffed bull's head.

He wasn't sure how he was going to keep Amber in Seville. He was not ready for her to walk away from him. Algorithms or not. She wanted what was best for him? There was something between the two of them. And she felt it, too. But for some reason she was too afraid to admit to that shared feeling. Was it because of her job? Did she put that over him? As an employer, he would expect employee loyalty.

But as a man he wanted her to be real, to show him exactly how she felt about him. To kiss him with all her heart and soul.

They needed more time. He wanted to show her how he felt about her. Do more things with her. All the things. Spend every moment of every day with her. Holding her hand. Sitting quietly beside her—a feat for him, but so easy when in her presence. Kissing her silly. Do more than kiss her. He wanted to make love to her. He knew they would be perfect together in bed.

Yes, perfect. But could it be the perfection she strove to achieve? He should just out and ask her: *Do you like me?* That felt so juvenile. He wished Pablo were here to give him a shove and tell him to go for it. He should talk to Teo. Feel him out on what to do. They did have to discuss the ball, which was now less than a week away.

He wanted Amber at that ball, dancing with him.

"Val!"

He responded to Amber's call and ran down the inner

courtyard staircase to meet her in the foyer. A wheeled suitcase rested near her leg. Already leaving? But he'd thought…

Why couldn't she wait until later? Or never?

"You're leaving so soon?"

She clutched the designer purse against her midsection and he noticed she was wearing the fancy suit she'd worn the first night they'd met. The consummate professional.

"I have to return to Paris. Colette has another job for me starting tomorrow."

"But what about…" Him? They hadn't done all the things. He hadn't told her what was brewing in his heart. His soul. About last night's goose bumps!

Was it so easy for her to walk away from him?

"Don't worry, I've got another match for you," she said. "And guess what? This one is a ninety-nine percent match."

"That's…" He didn't care about numbers or percentages. AI would never know his heart, or the way Amber made him want to jump and smile and shove all work aside. Screw the algorithms. He wanted her to stay. "…a lot," he said stiffly.

"Ninety-nine percent is almost unheard of. I've emailed her profile to you. I'm sure this woman will be your soul match. But we'll know more after the first-date follow-up."

He winced at the term *soul match*. He'd thought he'd found that already. *Duende*. But if Amber didn't see that, then he must have been mistaken. Still. She was leaving.

"The ball is in six days," he said. *Grab her! Kiss her!* "I'd like you to be there. To be a part of the celebration for all those we appreciate. I, uh, suppose I could set up my next date for that night. You'll want to see if the match is a success?"

Why had he said that? The last thing he wanted was for her to watch him match with another woman.

"I'll return for the ball if my schedule allows it. I'm sure Colette would appreciate me overseeing your date that could result in…a match."

She'd swallowed before saying that last part. As difficult to say as it was for him to even think of matching with anyone other than Amber?

"Will you promise me a dance?"

"I…yes, I promise."

His heart thundered. He'd not lost her. Not yet. "You'll stay here, of course."

"Oh, I don't think that's wise."

"I insist. Maria will make up your room."

"My room," she whispered. Amber nodded and then—"There's something you should know, Val. I ran our profiles to see if we would match," she blurted out.

Val straightened, a smile growing. "You *are* interested in me."

"Well, I—" She backed away from him, hands going to her hips. "What I think about you doesn't matter."

"Why not?"

"Because we match at only 62 percent, Val. We are not meant to be a pair. The algorithms you put so much confidence in said so."

Val tugged her to him. She wasn't getting away with a simple handshake. His mouth met hers in a collision of sighs and thundering heartbeats. She initially pushed against his shoulder, but it wasn't with any force, no intention. A moan preceded her surrendering to the kiss. He spread his arm across her back, holding her from a fall from the pedestal he wanted to place her on. But only to sit there a while until she wished to jump down to do what made her happy. He expected nothing from her.

He wanted everything from her.

And he knew. That ineffable knowing. They matched on a soul level.

"Val! You said you trusted the algorithms."

"I do. I…did. Like you said, do we really want to put our trust in a computer? It doesn't know our hearts. Our souls."

A limo from the airport pulled up to collect her.

Amber touched his jaw. She smelled like orange blossoms. And something lost. *Duende*. When she walked away, he would lose that indescribable something that gave him so much joy.

"Don't leave?"

"I'll be back Saturday morning," she said. "If I don't leave now, I'll miss my flight. And my boss will wonder what's up."

"*What's up* is—"

She pressed her fingers to his mouth. "What's up is…" So many emotions fought on her face. He felt her frustration but couldn't understand her stubborn resistance to him. "I'm doing my job. And you need to accept that."

Val stepped away from her and shoved his hands in his pockets. Could he kidnap her and keep her forever? The desperate thought was not cool. But still?

"I've sent you the profile on your match."

"Right. The match." He'd gotten himself into this situation. A man should step up and face the facts. Perhaps the algorithms would find a woman who could fulfill his every desire. He'd never know until he gave it a go, eh?

His shoulders dropped. He didn't believe that for a single moment.

He waved as Amber slid into the back of the limo.

The one person who gave him joy was leaving him. Purposefully. She didn't want him? Or maybe it was that she didn't know how to accept less than perfect? Hadn't he tried to improve? To follow her suggestions of being neater, more generous with his time? He'd worn a tie, for heaven's sake!

No, those were surface things. What Amber desired was something that no man could match. Not unless she was the one to first unlock her heart and allow someone inside.

CHAPTER FIFTEEN

BEING BACK IN Paris should give a girl a big ole smile. Amber should feel like Emily strolling the streets in a fabulous designer outfit she couldn't possibly afford, so happy to have a job in the City of Love, and with oodles of Frenchmen to ooh and aah over. Not to mention the roommates in a tight little apartment in the 9th arrondissement to really bring it all together.

But Amber's smile hadn't returned since she'd driven away from Val's villa. She told him it was business. A lie. She had left behind that wonderful kiss. The man's hopeful wave.

She'd made a mistake. Because she'd had to for her job.

She didn't even believe in love! She'd never find it in real life. Why work for a place all about love? Not real love. Computer-generated love. They were merely matches. Didn't mean the people would click in real life. Find that certain something.

"Duende," she whispered.

Could she and Val have duende? She'd felt it. And while a few days in the man's life did not make for a lifelong connection, it had also felt like the beginning of something. If she set aside work. Which she could not do.

She could do that.

But...

"But why not?" she asked aloud as she walked down the sidewalk.

No decent reasons formed. And if she even thought to blame this on her parents' divorce, she'd have to kick herself. That was their life. Hers wasn't necessarily going to follow the same trajectory.

And while she had that thought in her head, she typed out a text to her mom: Thinking of you. Would love to talk. Can I call soon?

It was time to move forward.

Pausing again to check the directions on her phone, Amber leaned against the wall of a building. She had an appointment with Claude Lambert. He was in his seventies and looking for a woman his age to travel the world and go on adventures with. He'd already completed his survey and Amber now had to vet him. She didn't intend to stay overnight, as she had with Val. Perhaps cocktails at a nearby restaurant to begin his assessment. A date in the park would be an appropriate follow-up.

That may have been the first mistake she made with Val. Allowing the dates to blur the line between work and curiosity. So many other mistakes: overlooking his messiness, actually finding his distractions cute, making excuses for his lateness because he was a rich, important man. Not to mention, kissing him.

The final mistake had been walking away from him.

She'd see him again at the charity ball. She shouldn't go, but resisting the need to see him once again was impossible. One last look. One last conversation. One shared dance. Until…

He'd been matched at 99 percent. No way would that date not result in future dates. Soon enough, she'd probably see the Vasquezes on the wedding-gifts list that Colette kept for all her clients. And then there was the baby-gifts list.

Turning right, she crossed a cobblestone street and veered toward the centuries-old building owned by her client.

Val hadn't seemed too upset when she'd said she had to leave. So maybe what they'd shared had merely been a thing. Something that could have never grown to more. On the other hand, when she'd told him they'd only matched at 62 percent, he'd not seemed overly upset. He'd even asked if clients could date the consultants. He was interested in her. Damn it! This was so hard.

Could he care as much about her as she was beginning to realize she cared for him? Why had she allowed emotion into the mix? Amber Martin didn't do gushy romance and sighs. That was for all the other girls. The pretty, vapid women who judged others by their clothing, hair and nails. Amber didn't know how to relate to a man on a level that met her needs and desires…

She shook her head. No, that was an excuse. She wasn't emotionally stunted. And she'd had her share of romance before the divorce. And blaming it on her parents had reached its expiration date. She was too smart for that.

And with every touch from Val, she'd fallen a little further…

Don't fall in love.

"I haven't."

Who the hell was she kidding?

Valentino Vasquez was the only man she'd ever given a second glance to, enjoyed being around, thought about… constantly. But she had no intention of revealing that to Colette. In another month or so Val would vacate her constant thoughts and she would move forward, just as Elise had done that time she'd let her heart get in the way of her work. Vetting more clients. Moving up at Lux Love. Paying the bills. Following that career trajectory she had plotted so long ago.

What about your life trajectory?

Yes, what about it? Would she ever fit love into her trajectory? Was it necessary?

It was. A person couldn't live without an emotional connection. Feeling as though someone cared for them. Knowing they was loved. Thought about. Needed. Simply looking forward to spending time with another. That necessity had come to fruition this past week.

What if she dared to tell Val how she really felt about him?

Amber shook her head. No, that would not be fair to him. Or to his next match. Because it wasn't just about Val. Silvia Molina had paid for Lux Love's service and she expected results. Not to be told that the man she'd matched with had decided to take up with one of the consultants, too bad for you.

Arriving at the entry gate to the building's courtyard, Amber pressed the buzzer, and with a breath of confidence, entered when buzzed in. Today was about finding love for another client.

Val wandered back and forth on the holo-platform. He stood in a desert. A nearby camel snorted. Code scrolled around him and a checklist of the current projects stretched to waist level. He'd been in the dark room for hours and had gotten nothing done. He needed to verify his coders' work. And while he knew it would be flawless, he did want to browse the vibe.

Yet, every time he started to scroll through the code, he kept seeing Amber's face as she smiled at him while he performed on the restaurant patio. Or her silly way of putting her hands to her hips when she meant business. Or that soft glint in her eyes that he could never look away from. Brown eyes. Plain to some. But filled with such interest to him. When he spoke, she held eye contact and really listened to him. She wasn't waiting to reply as most people were wont. Had he ever experienced such rapt attention from a woman who wasn't set on winning his interest in order to finance her dreams of champagne and caviar?

With a tap of his finger, he selected the character-sketch program. A detail list appeared before him. He used this to create characters for Verdadero's games. "Hal, configure Amber Martin."

A hologram of Amber appeared before him. Hal used the camera and biodata to reconstruct her accurately. Stretching his fingers to widen the view, she grew to life-size standing before him. A trace of his finger along her head gave her curly dark hair a fluff. He selected eye color, making the brown more intense. The linen dress she wore was plain but soft and hugged her slender waist. If he put on the gloves, he could ask Hal to add in sensation. The feel of her hair would become soft and silken. Her skin…

Val dropped his hands to his side and stared at the hologram of a woman who had walked into his life and changed it in a way he hadn't expected. She hadn't asked him for anything. He didn't even know if she wanted a family. Children. A little house by the Mediterranean Sea? Or a glamorous mansion? It didn't matter. As long as they were together.

"Together," he whispered.

He smiled as his skin erupted with goose bumps.

CHAPTER SIXTEEN

Days later...

AMBER ENTERED THE final information for Claude in the database and leaned back in her chair at work. Already the AI populated possible matches for the client. All of them above 90 percent. Nice.

She glanced to her purse, tucked safely in the open desk drawer. Yesterday she'd spent some time shopping for a dress for the Verdadero ball. Hadn't found anything.

Or rather, she'd found plenty of options, a beautiful spaghetti strap number at a vintage shop that had fit her budget, but she hadn't been able to take the step of bringing it to the counter. Because that would mean she was okay with standing by and watching Val dance with his 99 percent match. Or on the other hand, perhaps Amber would be putting herself in the role of Cinderella, hoping Val noticed her instead of Silvia.

Ugh. She was so conflicted!

And her mom had finally answered her text this morning. She was traveling in Alaska—so many questions!—and would call Amber later today.

Amber looked forward to that call. Might she spill her heart to her mom and ask her advice? There had been a time when they were close and she could do just that.

"Claude texted me regarding your meeting the other day." Colette had a manner of appearing at her side. There were days

Amber thought she had the ability to teleport. "He was impressed by your professionalism and kindness. Good going."

"Thank you. I always do my best." Unless the client kissed her. Many times. And made her fall—yet Val had caught her, hadn't he?

"We should have a few potential matches for him to select from before the day is over," Amber said. "And thank you for another client assignment. I know Chantelle comes back from maternity leave soon, so I—"

"Don't worry, Amber. You've been promoted to consultant. You'll receive commission on all matches you make."

Had she just…got a promotion? Delivered with the usual French manner of imperturbable disinterest.

"Thank you, Colette. I won't let Lux Love down."

"It's a trial basis, of course. I'll give you two months to prove you've got what it takes. How is the Vasquez situation coming along?"

"Vasquez has another date in a couple of days. After going through the follow-up info on his first date, I feel certain it'll be a match this time."

Colette wobbled her head, neither agreeing nor disagreeing. "If it's not, do not worry too much. Some clients are fussy. I once had a client who went through a dozen women before he finally found the one."

"It's not a bad thing to be choosey when one is looking for a life mate." Especially when that mate was assigned by a computer.

"Yes, sure. I have another client for you." Colette tapped her pinging watch. She was always dashing off to lunch with clients and—from what Amber had learned through the office gossip mill—lovers. "He's in New York and will make himself available for an assessment."

"Oh." Another job so quickly? Yes! And yet. "I have a thing this weekend. Saturday, to be exact."

Colette tilted her head. With one look she could take in a person's motivations, life dreams and failures, Amber felt sure. She'd hired her because Amber was lacking in emotion? Not anymore!

"It's not necessary to be there until Monday, *chère*, but... I've never known you to have a *thing*. You don't do socializing. Certainly not *things*. What is it?"

To tell the truth? It was never easy lying and she wouldn't start with her boss. "Senor Vasquez invited me to the charity ball Verdadero holds every year. He was insistent. I didn't want to be rude."

"Is that the same event he's scheduled a date with the ninety-nine percent match?"

Amber would never accept the cold manner in which Colette called their clients by their match percentages. "It is."

"Hmm. That could prove to be an excellent opportunity for us to get some video for promotion. I'll send a cameraman."

"Really?" Colette did like to record events when she suspected an impending proposal. But for a first date? "Are you sure it's necessary?"

"Amber, this is the first ninety-nine percent match we've had in over a year. It can't fail. I might look into attending myself. Seville this time of year is just beginning to touch sultry. Do you think you can swing me an invite?"

"I, uh, can look into it." Yikes. Talk about turning her last chance to see Val into a promotional opportunity. "I'll check with Senor Vasquez."

"This Saturday, *oui*?"

"Yes, I'll send the details once I have them. I'm planning to fly in the evening before. The city was so beautiful, but I didn't get a chance to do some shopping, so..."

She waited for Colette to accept her made-up excuse, but Colette was already strolling toward her office, her slim hips sashaying. French women embodied casual and calm. They basically expected the whole world to love them. And the whole world did. To have such breezy confidence!

Amber turned back to her desk and saw Claude's first suggested match had registered at 97 percent. The older man had been charming, hilarious and open to any woman who loved to travel. Good for him. She would give him a call.

But first, she texted Val, asking about an invite for Colette. She didn't mention her boss's plus-one would come wielding a camera. Any confidentialities had already been agreed upon in the contract Val had signed, such as using photos for promotional use.

He texted back immediately. *Good to hear from you! Yes, bring along your boss and anyone else. We have room! I can't wait to see you, Amber.*

The three dots pulsed for a long time. And when she couldn't decide if he'd forgotten to sign off or was erasing what he was typing, finally an emoji of a man's face with a VR mask on it popped up.

Not as exciting as a heart, but what did she expect? She was the man's matchmaker. There was no room for little red hearts between the two of them.

She returned a thumbs-up emoji. Then shook her head and set her phone aside.

"You are an idiot," she muttered.

When she looked aside, Elise, whose desk was across the aisle from hers, nodded and shook her head as if she knew every detail of angst battling in Amber's heart right now.

Luis called to cancel tonight's dinner. Val had forgotten about it. Again. But he didn't say that. He pushed aside his work on the holo-screen and his dad's profile image showed in the center as he paced the holo-platform.

"Anything wrong, dad?"

"No, I just think with the ball this weekend that we could set aside the dinner. You know I'm not much for going out on the town."

That was a lie. The old man loved to hunker down in a bar and sing and chat with the regulars until the place closed. Did he not like the restaurants Val chose for their dinners? Four-star chefs were few and far between, but he always tried to impress his dad. Perhaps he was still angry Val had missed their last supper night?

The one that had plunged him into a quest for a match. And had fortuitously brought Amber into his life. He wouldn't tell his dad about her. Luis Vasquez had a dislike for American tourists, all Americans in general. He viewed them as so materialistic! But he never tried to argue that one; his dad was set in his ways.

"I went on a date, Dad."

"You did?" A positive rise to his tone gave Val's shoulders a lift. "Tell me all about her."

He sat in the captain's chair and closed his eyes to his dad's profile image. "Teo turned me on to a dating service for professionals. She was kind and smart but…we didn't click."

"Oh." Positive tone? Evaporated.

"But I have another date the night of the ball. So…you'll get to meet her."

"I'm so excited for you, my son. Maybe she will be the one?"

"It's possible."

"My son is going to start a family!"

Val winced. Sure, he wanted to please his dad. But when Luis put it that way, it was almost as if he were filling an order for an insta-family. It was stunning to him that his dad, who had married for love, could be satisfied to see his son rush into a situation that might not be conducive to love.

"I only wish your mother was here to see the day her son walks down the aisle." *Lay it on thick, eh?*

"I wish the same," Val said. "But I take solace in knowing she's watching over me. Both of us. Maybe you should use the dating service, Dad?" With a flick of his fingers, he brought up the Lux Love home page. "I'll swing for the profile on you. What do you say?"

"Your mother would not be happy to know I had moved on so quickly after her death."

Val shook his head. It had been thirteen years. "Okay, Dad, I won't mention it again."

"Maybe next year," Luis replied quickly.

Eh? So there was a spark of hope for his old man, after all. Val was happy with that. "Sounds good. I'll see you at the ball. Love you."

"I as well." His dad clicked off following his usual salutation.

Had his dad ever said the words *I love you* to Val? He couldn't recall him ever doing so. And to think about it, he'd not heard him say it to his mother. Luis was not emotionally demonstrative. It was the proud bullfighter in him. Any man who could bravely stand before thirteen hundred pounds of pure angry muscle would never show a soft heart.

And yet, there had been a few occasions, when Val was younger, that he'd spied his parents dancing or kissing as if they thought no one could see them. They had been madly in love.

Sometimes, actions were louder than words.

And the only action he'd been taking lately was following directions. Answering questions. Making changes when Amber suggested. But he'd not stepped up and said—

"I want you," he said out loud.

And with a nod, he smiled.

CHAPTER SEVENTEEN

Returning to Val's home felt odder than Amber had expected it would feel. Almost as if she were intruding, and yet at the same time, returning to a place she had always belonged.

She'd thought to knock and struggle with Maria's Spanish, and to be begrudgingly admitted entrance. But instead, Maria opened the door as she arrived, and gestured down the hallway toward her room as if it were genuinely her room. *Welcome back! We missed you!* Although the housekeeper didn't offer that verbal praise, she confirmed Val was working. To be expected. And since it was after seven in the evening, Amber thanked her and said she'd turn in early.

Ten minutes later, Maria brought in a tray of warm bread and herbed butter along with tea. A welcome surprise from the woman usually staunchly set on avoiding her.

Settling into a chair before the open patio doors, Amber inhaled, but the orange blossoms had all fallen and now the intense verdancy of the other plants and trees tickled her nose. The trickling fountain added a musical note.

Here in Val's home, Amber could stretch out and become a part of the space. Breath came easily. Life felt easy as well. The need to prove herself, to achieve and be successful, fell to the wayside. Anything was possible. Because Val made her feel welcome and seen. Like she was the only woman he did see.

So why had she walked away from him as if nothing had happened between them? And now to return to the scene of the crime and expect it to not be difficult?

"You really don't know how to do romance, woman."

Watching her parents as she grew up had been, she'd thought, a lesson in real and true love. Kisses in greeting at night when they returned home from work. Hugs for no reason but that they'd passed close to one another. That certain look they'd cast one another during movies as they related to something only they both understood. And always her dad had brought home flowers for her mom. Just because he loved her.

Dad was still pulling himself up after the divorce. But he'd asked Amber about her matchmaking service during her visit, so she'd taken hope he was thinking about putting himself back out there.

She checked her texts, and saw she'd missed a call from her mom while she'd been on the flight. Holding the phone to her chest, she nodded, then bravely hit the call button.

Amelia Martin answered right away. "Amber, I'm so glad you called me back. It's been too long since we've talked."

"Sorry I missed your call. I was on a flight to Seville."

"Your dad told me that Aunt Judy got you a job in Paris. How do you like it?"

"Dad told you that?"

"Well, yes, dear. We talk on occasion. Well… It's been about six months. I know he's taken this divorce hard so I try to allow him his space and to direct where he thinks our relationship should go."

Dad had not told Amber that when she'd visited. Interesting. So they had some secrets between them. And that was probably as it should be.

"I'm sorry for pulling away from you after the divorce, Mom. I, uh, was very mad at you."

"I know you are, Amber. And I'm sorry, too. But it is my life."

Was she like her mom? She didn't want to ultimately break a man's heart after twenty-five years of marriage. And yet, that wasn't a fair summation. Her mother was kind and loving. Amber had witnessed the real love between her parents over the years. Of course, people changed!

"I'm beginning to understand that. I had a storybook ideal of my parents, and one of the pages got torn out. Maybe an entire chapter. But I'll survive. And…" Amber sighed. "Mom, I need to ask you something."

"I'm always here for you, Amber, despite the distance. Promise. So, what's up?"

"It's about a man."

"Oh. Do tell." Her mom's tone was curious with a hint of gossipy girlfriend, which gave Amber an infusion of hope.

Her mother *had* changed. Had grown out of love with her dad in the romantic manner. It wasn't for Amber to say that they should have soldiered on in a loveless marriage. It would have been worse for her dad to have remained with a woman who had fallen out of love with him. They'd earned their gold star for twenty-five years of devotion, and nothing could ever take that away from them.

So…okay. Love changed. But did that mean a girl should never allow herself the risk of love? That felt too constrictive. And not even smart.

"I'm afraid to let him in because—" she swallowed and lifted her chin "—because of you and Dad. How your marriage ended."

"Oh, sweetie. How will you ever know love if you don't allow someone in?"

"I know that. Rationally."

Would she ever take that first step? She couldn't think

about the tangle of emotions that had brewed to a bubble since meeting Val. But Val didn't belong to her. He belonged to the woman he was meeting tomorrow night at the ball. Or, he could belong to her.

"How does he feel about you?"

"He's made it clear he is interested in me. But he's a client. For Lux Love. I'm supposed to be matching him to his perfect love."

"Well." Her mother paused for those few seconds she generally did before she announced wise thoughts. "Is it possible you already have found that match for him?"

Amber knew she alluded to *her* being his match. But before she could argue that it wasn't allowed for a consultant to fraternize with a client, she shook her head.

Here she sat, Amber Martin, not the biggest romantic in the world. Forever to remain unattached. Unless she got her act together and started paying attention to her needs. When would she step out of the shadows and show everyone who Amber Martin really was? What she really desired? What she could achieve?

She'd been trying to do that all her life. Rarely achieving the perfection she craved.

What was so great about perfection, anyway? Val had shown her that chaos could be kind of fun. Sexy and—had she actually tried to change him? To guide him toward being neater and working less? Nonsense! The man was perfect as he was. A beautiful mess, as the bartender had told her.

And some woman would be very lucky to call him her own.

Could that woman be her?

The urge to find out struck her. Hard. Glancing into her room, she noted the suitcase sat at the end of the bed. No ball gown inside. Would the shops still be open tonight? And if they were, might they be close to the Verdadera office tower?

"I think you know the answer," her mom said. "You're a smart woman, Amber. Always have been, always will be. You know what to do."

"I do," Amber said with new wonder. "Thanks, Mom. Can we...get together soon? If you're ever in Paris?"

"I'll make a point of planning a trip to France this summer. Love you."

"I love you, too, Mom."

"Amber!"

Val turned and leaped through a streaming waterfall of glowing green code to greet her. He caught her in a big hug. "I missed you!" A double-cheek kiss followed.

His words felt genuine. Amber didn't want to push out of his comfortable hug, and she would not. "Good to see you again."

"More than good. I'm excited that you're here."

He held her hands and looked her over. She hadn't changed in just under a week. But had he? His eyes were so liquid and dreamy; they possessed such depth. How had she not managed to stumble into them?

You already have.

"I'm so glad you decided to stop into the office."

"Well, I went out dress shopping but the stores were closed, so I thought I'd stop in and say hi since I figured you wouldn't return to your villa until well after I'd crashed." Totally preplanned, but he didn't need to know that.

He checked his watch. "Right. It is late. I should stop work."

"I don't want to bother you."

"Please. Bother me." He took her hand again. "I like the distraction of you."

Oh, was he ever a distraction. But her? She wanted to believe she could make a man forget about work simply because she was there, but... Maybe? Dare she believe in herself for once?

"Sorry. It's just... I know." He exhaled. "I'm acting like a lovestruck puppy dog."

"Oh, I wouldn't—" Lovestruck? About...her?

"Don't make excuses. Amber. We need to talk. Before the charity ball."

"About what?" Hands going to her hips, she asked, "Are you not pleased with Lux Love's services?"

"It's not that at all." A scruff of his hand through his hair distracted her from her innate need to put up a wall against connection. "Let's be real with one another. What we have between us has nothing to do with Lux Love. And you know it."

She did know it. She'd been unable to think of anything but that knowing since she'd gotten off the phone with her mom.

Val slid a hand along her cheek and cupped the back of her head. She knew the kiss was coming, and before she could plead with him not to make this more difficult, their lips crushed against one another. His thumb eased along her jaw, tilting her head to fit him more perfectly. All her doubts, her vacillations with whether to dive in with him, rattled against her rib cage, pleading for escape. To be forgotten or ignored.

Breaking the kiss, Val searched her eyes. "Don't tell me we shouldn't have done that. You have feelings for me, Amber, I know you do."

"It doesn't matter." Yes, it did! "It can't matter, Val."

"It matters to me."

"But Lux Love—" Difficult to put any belief in those strident objections anymore.

He kissed her again. His fingers stroked into her hair, trilling shivers across her skin. "Now that you're back in my arms, I want us to be honest with one another."

She had been honest. Getting involved with a client was a huge no-no. But that didn't make it wrong. And she might never know what could be possible if she didn't at least set aside those objections for the moment. For the night.

"For tonight," he said, "we're going to ignore the algorithms."

She had every notion what *ignore* meant to him.

He kissed her jaw and trailed more kisses down her neck. Shivers scattered over her skin and she recalled he'd said something about wanting goose bumps love. Mercy.

And she wasn't going to deny it anymore. This is what she wanted. Or at least, for the night.

She bracketed Val's head with her hands and kissed him. Hard. Taking what she wanted without apology. Aware they stood on the holo-platform where she had previously fallen from a cave wall and into his arms, she wondered if he could create a forest around them, or even a sandy white beach. But did it matter? They were alone. They both wanted one another. She wasn't going to let this chance slip through her fingers.

"Is Hal listening?"

"Uh… He's recording our biomarkers."

She swore.

"Hal, remove all data from the previous ten minutes."

"On it, Valentino."

"He calls you Valentino?" Sounded so personal. Did the man have a closer relationship with a computer than her? Time to change that. "Can you—" she took in the streaming green code around them "—turn him off for a while?"

With a wink, Val said, "Hal, go dark for two hours."

The code did not disappear, but she assumed the AI was not listening. Or hoped it was not.

"Two hours?" she asked, surprised at the generous timing. "You need more time?"

She wanted all night. "No, that'll work."

She walked him backward toward the chair and when the backs of his legs hit it, he dropped into a sitting position. Amber leaned over him, placing her hands to either side of him on the chair arms. "You said something about creases in your boxers? I've developed a new appreciation for a messy man with a touch of perfection."

CHAPTER EIGHTEEN

THE FOLLOWING MORNING, Val did not miss the discerning eye Maria cast him while holding Amber's hand. He called to Maria that he'd be back in time to prepare for the ball. His housekeeper's gaze was drilled on the hand-holding. One of her eyebrows raised.

Val had no excuses. He and Amber had slipped in late last night and…she hadn't spent the night in the guest room. They'd had a thing last night and he was riding that thing into today. His emotions were jittering up, down, side to side, as if they were his physicality. But he couldn't control them by focusing on streaming code or going for a jog along the river. The only way to serve what he was feeling was to spend the day with Amber. To hold her hand. To enjoy the moments. Because in the back of his mind, he was very aware he was going to meet another woman tonight. And that what he and Amber had right now could very possibly be just Right Now.

He programmed his car to take her on a tour of Triana, the old neighborhood where he grew up and would spend his weekends watching his mother dance on the back patio, showing him the steps and then allowing him to move as his body demanded. They cruised by the school where he and Teo and Pablo had been forced together through a tutoring program, only to become immediate and fast friends. The three musketeers!

His memories of Pablo were bittersweet. And with the ball tonight, he and Teo would once again honor their departed friend. Val knew Pablo would be proud of what they had accomplished.

Amber was curious about the massive network of wood that formed a mushroomlike canopy in the midst of the city, so Val took her to the top level of the Metropol Parasol, or the Las Setas, where they walked along the gangways. The view of the city was incredible. He pointed out the landmarks that held meaning for him, the Torre del Oro, a dodecagonal military watchtower that had stood since the thirteenth century; Royal Alcázar of Seville, the royal family's official residence surrounded by gorgeous gardens; and many historic cathedrals.

Amber spied the cathedral of Seville so they made that their next stop and climbed the tower Giralda. Val had seen it all and tended to dismiss most of the sights, and yet, seeing the architecture through Amber's eyes gave him a new perspective on his beloved city.

Allowing her to point and choose their path, he gleefully followed her from tourist trap to tourist trap. After stopping for lemonades, they decided to walk, hand in hand, for the short return to his villa.

"My father used to fight in the *bullring*." Val pointed it out as they passed the Maestranza Bullring.

"The exterior is beautiful." Amber took in the baroque facade erected from stone and wood in the mid-eighteenth century. "Do you attend the bullfights?"

"On occasion. Do you want to attend one?"

"Absolutely not."

He got it. He'd learned long ago not to begin a controversial argument with someone who had not been born and raised in the land of bullfighters. The bulls were often killed. If not in the ring, then later in the stables. Wasn't as though an animal tortured with the picadors could survive or live through another fight.

On the other hand, some bulls showed such valor in the fight, exceptional bravery, that they might be pardoned. The indulto. They were retired to pasture or put out to stud and allowed to live a long life. Such as the bull whose head currently hung on his bedroom wall.

"But maybe..." Amber paused and looked across the street to the bullring building. "Doesn't look like anything is going on in there right now."

"There's not a fight this afternoon. They give tours when there are no fights."

"I might like to take a look around. Learn a little about what your father once did?"

"Really?" That was the most open he'd ever seen her and he was thrilled she was interested in his father's profession. "Just a quick tour, *si*?"

She placed her hand in his. "Let's do it."

Amber learned a lot about the national pastime of bullfighting, but even after their casual stroll through the *facility*, she decided to stick with her revulsion for the sport, though she didn't say that to Val and he didn't press her for a new and positive impression of it, either. She appreciated that about him. He never seemed to nudge her toward his beliefs or to change to suit something he preferred. It really brought her first week here with him to a fine—and poking—point. She had tried to change him. Fool.

But she'd only had his best interests in mind. And she still did.

Now they strolled along the Guadalquivir, hand in hand. Spending time with Val was more valuable than any metaphorical gold star Amber had ever earned.

"You and your father... You'd like to be closer, yes?"

Val exhaled. "We are close and we are not. There will always be a chasm between us because of my career choice. And he was never pleased about my friendship with Teo."

"Oh?"

"Teo's family... His dad was involved in criminal activity. Teo has been fighting that stigma all his life. And as you've likely surmised, my dad is very judgmental."

"Maybe he wants the best for his son. And knowing one way of life, I'm sure it's difficult for him to embrace you stepping so far out of the traditional realm of careers. Though, I must say, bullfighter doesn't scream *traditional job* to me."

Val laughed but then admonished with a waggle of his finger. "If you were a Spaniard, you would not say such a thing."

"Fair enough. Do you ever wonder what your life might have been like if you had chosen dancing?"

"Let's see..." He stepped ahead of her a few paces and snapped his body into a pose, arm up and chest proud. "I'd be a world-famous flamenco dancer who travels the world and brings duende to the masses." A few rapid taps of his feet ended in a splay of his hands and a bow. Accompanied by a self-effacing laugh.

There was nothing funny about his talent. Every movement he made, whether comical or sensual, captivated her. "Yes, duende. I'm starting to understand that word."

"Something untamable, soulful, yet also understood once you allow it to step inside your life."

"Is it a little...sexual, too?"

"Yes. In certain moods, of course." He took her hand, swinging it, then pulled her in for a kiss. The trace of his fingers along the back of her neck put her right back in bed, lying naked beside him, breaths gasping. "I know watching a performance can turn people on." The way he gazed at her should be labeled a sexual move, as well. "Even dancing, if you let go of your inhibitions, can be a turn-on." He laughed. "I like sex. Good old-fashioned sex. Uh, just in case that was a question for your notes."

"Likes sex? Dully noted."

Val leaned in closer. "What about you?"

"Me?"

"Did you...like what we did last night? And this morning?"

"I love sex." *With him. Tell him only with him!*

He pulled her along the sidewalk, turning to face her as they slowly walked. "But if you don't have romance?"

"Romance isn't required for sex," she answered by rote. *No, don't spoil it!* Why couldn't she just be real and tell him her truth? That she was so into him and wanted him and—

"That's sad."

"That's not—"

"I thought we were really into one another, Amber. But there's a part of you that isn't willing to get fully on board. So what we had, at least in your eyes, wasn't duende."

"Like you said, duende is an ineffable thing, so hard to truly explain."

Val shaded his eyes with a hand. "Duende is the way music and art makes you feel. Right here." He gestured a cupping motion over his heart. "A euphoric but knowledgeable state of abandonment. It can only be felt through true, deep immersion in the craft. It's like an orgasm. A real one that only comes from true connection. Once felt, you want more of it."

"Val, let's, uh…" She walked ahead of him, splaying out her hands. "Can we just enjoy the walk?"

Because if she did hand him her heart on her palms, then he'd have to return it. Tonight. Before his date! It wasn't fair. But she didn't know how to stop the script and alter the ending.

He rubbed his jaw, noticed the ping on his watch. He glanced at it but didn't answer the call.

"You can get that," she said. "I'll walk ahead."

"No." He rushed up to join her. "It's just my dad. I'm sure he's checking on the time for tonight's event. He does that when there's important meetings or when he used to have a fight. Needs to second-check everything. I'll introduce you to him tonight but do allow his evil eye to zoom right over the top of your head."

Amber laughed. "Much like the stink eye we got from Maria before leaving?"

"She cares about me but would never step in to express an opinion. She shows her respect and love in the things she does for me. I'm not going to mention to her that I've looked into a house cleaner."

"You did? That's wonderful. But I understand. You don't want to step on Maria's territory."

"Not even that. It's just… I'm comfortable the way I am. Do you really think I need to change for a woman? Why can't we accept one another as is? I thought that was the purpose of the vetting. If I change, then I'm not me. I won't match the profile."

Amber winced. "I do like the beautiful mess you are."

"You do?"

She squeezed his hand. "Oh, my gosh." She grabbed Val's wrist and checked his watch. "We've got to get back to your place. The ball."

"We'll head back. But first, I have to say something."

"What is it?"

"Last night wasn't just a one-night fling for me."

"Oh, I…" He was going to say it. And she wasn't prepared to deal with the truth at this moment. "But your date is tonight. It's been scheduled for days."

"I know, and I would never cancel on Silvia at the last minute."

"And you should not. This is what you wanted, Val." It was what she had initially wanted, to be commended for her matchmaking skills. Everything had changed. "For Lux Love to pair you with someone."

Did she still require that gold star for a job well done? That little piece of gold foil could never patch the hole she already felt in her heart.

"Maybe they have already achieved that goal."

Her mom had said the same. So why did a small part of her still resist the inevitable?

Val bowed his forehead to hers. "Set aside the fact that I've a date tonight. If that wasn't in the cards, how do you feel about me?"

"I do care about you, Val."

He kissed her forehead, then swept down for a quick brush of his lips against hers. "Shouldn't have done that," he muttered. "But so glad I did."

"Same. But…" She exhaled.

Val nodded. Put his arm around her shoulders. "I get it. You've got a job to do. Let's get back to the villa. Life…is waiting to wobble us both tonight."

CHAPTER NINETEEN

Amber left Val to run up to his room and change while she sat in the kitchen sorting through her emails. Colette had sent her a text before boarding her flight in Paris. She would be in Seville soon.

The realization that she'd forgotten to buy a dress while they were out sightseeing didn't bother her. She didn't intend to go to the ball now. How could she stand and watch Val fall in love with another woman? A woman selected specifically for him to be his perfect match?

It wasn't fair. And she wasn't going to further bruise her heart watching them come together. She'd make an excuse to Colette that she wasn't feeling well. And she'd tell Val that she intended to arrive later because she had some last-minute work to finish.

So what if they'd made love last night…and this morning? And so what if she was getting vibes from Val that he was interested in her. They weren't a match. 62 percent!

"You're not ready!"

Amber turned to find her goofy billionaire CEO had transformed into a suave, sexy charmer dressed in a tuxedo with a glint of diamonds at his cuffs. Even his shirt was black. His dark eyes brooded from beneath a sweep of curly raven hair.

A big smile overtook her face even as her chest tightened.

Another kiss was all she could think about. And sex. Lots of sex with this man. All day. Every day. With code streaming around them. Without the code. Just. Sex.

"Duende," she whispered to herself.

"We forgot to buy you a dress," he said.

Happiness? Yes, this man did make her happy.

"Don't worry about it." She summoned a quick lie. "I ordered one online. It'll be here in an hour."

"Perfect, but I am needed before the ball kicks into gear…"

"You go ahead. I don't want to arrive with you anyway."

"Why not?" Had he ever looked so puppy-dog sad before? So kicked?

"Val."

He thought about it. Rubbed a hand over his face and shook his head. "I get it. Might look suspicious to—what's her name again?"

"Silvia Molina. Her family owns a cacao farm and she co-owns a marketing firm with her best friend."

"Right. I read about the chocolate. I've never much liked chocolate. And… I'd prefer arriving with you on my arm."

"Well, that's not going to happen. One of us has to maintain a modicum of propriety."

The look he gave her said everything she was thinking. *Why the propriety? Because we want to grab each other and make out, be damned everyone else?*

"Do you have a tie?" she asked. "Or better yet, a bow tie. I think that would look great."

"In my closet." He gestured over his shoulder as Maria walked in and started to coo over her employer's handsome good looks.

"I'll run up and get one for you," Amber said, slipping from the kitchen. "I know where to find it!"

She skipped up the inner courtyard stairs. Putting distance between herself and Val was foremost. He was so… Mr. Right. Standing there and *not* touching him would have been impossible.

But that's all he was. Right in her heart right now. She was infatuated with him. Still riding the sex high. And after an afternoon of walking hand in hand as they'd done the tourist thing, she knew she was riding some kind of romance buzz that would eventually settle to a simmer when she realized they were not a good match.

She veered down the closet hallway and eyed the tie rack. A black bow tie would get lost against his all-black outfit, but maybe the silver one? Yes, very festive. Grabbing it, she strolled back down the hallway and—

It wasn't locked. It was ajar, as she'd purposefully left it. But she couldn't put her hand to the knob to pull it open. She stepped backward, and once back in the main closet, she sat on the chaise and pressed the tie between her hands.

"What am I doing? How did you end up here, Amber Martin?"

Sitting in a billionaire's closet, getting ready to send him off on a date that could prove to be with the woman he got goose bumps for. They would date, get engaged, marry, have children and live happily ever after. Valentino Vasquez would get exactly what he'd paid for. She would have proved herself to Colette that she could see the matchmaking process from start to finish. Life trajectory? Right on course.

So why did she not want to bring this bow tie to Val? The niggling feeling that she could sabotage this evening *in some way* startled her. She wasn't that person. Okay, a little. But he hadn't said he hated the bull's head in his room, so there was that.

But Val wasn't just any man. Even now, she wondered if he'd rush up the stairs in search of her having possibly gotten locked in the closet again. He'd find her. And kiss her again. And every day to follow.

Such intimacy certainly did not fit into her trajectory of moving up at Lux Love, making more money, paying off her bills and finding her own place to live.

Why couldn't she have all of that, including the intimacy? The love? She and Val had moved beyond consultant and client. And she didn't want to struggle with the wrong of that anymore. They'd made love because they were two adults who could do as they pleased and didn't have to answer to anyone about their desires.

But the part of her that strived for perfection still wouldn't allow whatever wanted to happen to happen.

Even if she lost the best thing that had entered her life?

Val swaggered in to find her sitting on the chaise. Without lifting her head, she held up the bow tie for him. If she looked into his eyes, she might— Holding back tears made her wince.

So when he knelt on the floor before her and slid his hands along her thighs, her body pleaded for her to fall against him, to hug against his *azahar* scent and let the tears fall. Yet her innate stubbornness insisted she resist.

"I think you and my closet have something weird going on," he said softly.

She laughed but then sniffled.

"Amber?" He touched her cheek. Always touching her. His love language. "Why the tears?"

Yes, why the tears? She'd come to terms with the fact she couldn't have what she wanted. But could she tell him that? *Did* he want her? Was she more than just a one-night fling to him? He'd told her he cared about her. But he couldn't if he was going to meet Silvia tonight. Val was not the sort of man who would go on a date out of obligation. Maybe?

"I think I'm overwhelmed by this job, actually. It's gone quite well. I'm happy for you," she forced herself to say. "Tonight could change your life."

"My life has already changed since meeting you."

"Don't say that."

He tilted her chin up and held her so she couldn't look away. "I will say it. You're the best thing that's ever happened to me, Amber. I'm not going to deny it."

"It's not even been a week that we've known one another."

"How much time does a person need to know here?" He patted his chest, right over his heart. With a heavy sigh, he shook his head. "I won't argue if you insist this is just a job for you. But know, I wish it was you I will be dancing with tonight."

"We can still have one dance." *If* she went to the ball. Which she did not intend to do. So, more lies? Oh, Amber! "It's probably best if I stay away."

He pulled her into a hug. It was a comfy, all-encompassing embrace that surrounded her with his scent, his being. His soul.

Her soul knew this moment was right. But she didn't feel goose bumps.

"Please come to the ball," he whispered in her ear. "Give me that dance. I don't want to be there unless you are."

A lot to put on her shoulders. Tonight, the man should only be focused on meeting and getting to know his match.

"I'll need your nod of approval," he said, pulling out of the hug. "If you like her, then...nod?"

Really? Did he not know her heart?

No. Because she'd not dared tell him how she felt about him.

Because... Amber Martin was not as perfect as she vied

to be. And if she was going to match Val to his perfect partner, then it couldn't be her.

Amber nodded. She took the bow tie from him and clipped it to his collar. "You're going to do great tonight. And when you meet Silvia, use your friend Pablo's wise teachings to impress her."

"I don't want to impress her. I want someone with whom I can be myself."

She wanted the same. "I get you, Val. You *are* yourself. Smart, fun, a little erratic. It's when you get into your head and start thinking too much you lose the natural rhythm of you. Just…be Valentino Vasquez. Geeky CEO and all-around nice guy. She'll love that guy." Because Amber loved him. Damn her heart. "You'd better go. You are the host."

He stood and helped her to stand. She daren't ask for what she wanted from him. It wasn't what a professional would do.

"Come as soon as the dress is delivered?" he asked.

She nodded. "Of course."

"Then I'll see you later." He leaned in, as if to kiss her, stared at her a moment, then redirected his mouth toward her cheek. A soft flutter of a kiss landed at the edge of her eye. Not enough. But already too much. "Promise you'll come."

"I…" Amber sighed against his cheek. She gripped his lapel. Then stepped back from him and nodded. "Yep. See you later."

As he walked down the long hallway, she caught a hand against her throat.

If she fell in love with every client, this job was going to wrench out her heart and smash it against the ground.

Just like now.

Half an hour later, Amber turned off her phone because she'd gotten a text from Colette. Her boss was en route from the airport and would be an hour or more until she got to the party. How was it going?

She wouldn't lie to her boss, so it was easier to avoid texting that she wasn't even there.

Humming preceded Maria's entrance into the kitchen. The housekeeper strolled to the fridge, grabbed the handle, then did a double take on Amber sitting at the table. "You are not at party?"

Amber turned her own double take on Maria. "You can speak English?"

The woman waggled her shoulders gaily and nodded her head. "Why you are not at party? Valentino wants you there!"

"I know that." But why the sudden switch to English? Had she understood Amber's English all this time? What might she have said that she shouldn't have said in front of Maria? Unbelievable! "I can't go. I...don't have a dress."

"Oh, no, no, no." Waggling a finger at her, Maria approached Amber. "You go."

"I can't. I..."

"I know." Maria patted her heart with a palm. "I know."

"You know...what?"

"That you are in love with Senor Vasquez."

"Oh, I'm—"

Maria shoved Amber's shoulder—not so lightly—to indicate she get out of the chair. "Come with me. Come!"

Amber followed, but only because she was in shock from learning the maid could speak English and that she obviously thought she knew something that wasn't true.

Lying to herself again?

"It's necessity," she muttered as they passed the guest bedroom door and reached the end of the hallway where Maria's room was. "What do you want, Maria?"

"I have dress for you. Come."

"Oh, I couldn't."

The woman was going to lend her a dress? She was a foot shorter than Amber and carried a good thirty pounds more than her. And really. What would she possibly have that Amber could wear?

Not that she was considering going to the ball. She'd made that decision. She had to stick to it.

Right?

The housekeeper disappeared into a closet, so Amber lingered by the door. The room was sparsely decorated with a bed, a dresser and chair, and a cross on the wall. A pretty floral motif danced around the window that overlooked the outer courtyard. It added some happiness to the plain room. Did Val not treat his hired help better?

No, she knew that Maria would want for nothing more. He'd offered to buy her a big-screen TV to watch her stories and she'd refused. The older generation did like to stick with their comfort items.

Maria emerged from the closet with a stunning red dress on a hanger and displayed it proudly before Amber.

"That's gorgeous." Amber took in the low-cut neckline and spaghetti straps and narrow waist. The skirt blossomed out in layers like a flamenco *bata de cola* and was decorated with floral embroidery much like the painted design hugging the window. "Where did you get this?"

"I wore it long time ago. I could not part with it. Too precious."

"Oh, then I can't…"

Maria held it up to Amber's body. It seemed the perfect length and size. "I was once like you," Maria said. "Slender. Not so much on the hips. It will fit you. You take."

"No, you said it is precious to you."

"I want you to wear it. It only collects dust otherwise."

Amber touched the soft fabric. *Magical* came to mind. And something a princess might wear.

"And put up your hair. I will help. Hurry! You must go to the ball!"

"I'm not sure."

Maria pressed the dress into Amber's hands and said, "You love him."

Amber shook her head adamantly. How could she possibly know?

"I know. You are good for him."

"Do you think so? Maria, you've never been so—" What did it matter? It was too late! "Val is going to meet his perfect match tonight."

"Eh." Maria made a dismissive gesture. "You? Not perfect. But just right, I think."

Why had the woman never said that to her before? Had she said anything to Val? Likely not.

It felt like a fairy-tale moment. The fairy godmother handing the plain and romantically misfit Cinderella a fabulous gown and telling her to show up at the ball where the handsome prince sought his match.

Maria leaned in, a smile glinting in her dark eyes. She tilted her head and asked plainly, "Do you dare?"

Amber held up the dress, knowing it would fit. It was everything she was not. Everything she thought she wasn't.

Why not slip into a new and more authentic skin? One that wasn't so set on perfection? One that sought duende over algorithms? Tonight, she wanted to walk into the ball and dance with her prince.

"Just one dance."

CHAPTER TWENTY

SILVIA MOLINA WAS PERFECT. Beautiful, well-spoken, graceful, smart, engaging and she was even a bit of a geek. As the CEO of a marketing management company, she focused on connecting influencers to their key sponsor targets; she was steering the business toward great success.

From Silvia's profile Val learned that they shared a lot of interests. VR gaming? Check. Surfing and snorkeling? Check? Even old movies? Check. She smiled and listened intently when he spoke. Laughed when appropriate. And she pulled out a few flamenco moves as they swished around the dance floor.

So when Teo pulled him aside to ask him why he looked so bored, Val could only but scan the ballroom one more time—not finding who he was looking for—and shrug. "Not bored. Just…"

"She's beautiful."

"Yes, she is," he muttered as visions of Amber surfaced in his thoughts. He shook his head, jarring himself back to the conversation. "Oh? Uh. Right. Yes, Silvia is pretty. Very accomplished. She's going to hit her first billion in a few years if she stays on track with her company."

"A successful woman is perfect for you."

There was that word again. *Perfect*. Val had heard it bandied about so much of late it had ceased to hold meaning for him. Or rather, it implied too much. A final result he felt sure he did not want to touch.

"Where's Cara?"

"She's getting something to drink." Teo, looking like a corporate raider in his tuxedo, nodded to a passing partygoer. Always keeping up the good will with their contributors. "Will you introduce us to Silvia?"

"Of course. You gotta trust the algorithms, right?"

Teo turned a concerned look at him. "What's up, Val? I sense you're putting on a front. And I know you're all about the algorithms, but really? Should a guy put such blind faith in ones and zeros when it comes to love?"

Teo nailed it. Of course, one shouldn't. Not after spending time with Amber and learning he'd like to spend the rest of his life with her. Sixty-two percent? That meant nothing. Computers couldn't factor in the emotional. The duende.

"Look at me and Cara," Teo said. "I don't think a computer could have ever predicted we'd stumble into one another's lives again and find love. Be careful tonight, Val. Use that brain that's made Verdadero billions."

"I think it's my brain that's gotten me in this mess."

"You could be right about that." Teo thumped Val over the chest. "Then use this. Your heart will never lead you in the wrong direction."

Val put an arm around his friend's shoulders and when he turned to take in the ballroom, all that he and his friend had accomplished, his eyes landed on the woman standing at the top of the ballroom staircase.

His heart double-pulsed.

Dressed in a body-hugging red gown that splayed out below the hips in a soft hush of ruffles and roses, she was unaware of his stare. Her dark hair was pulled up and red roses were tucked within it like some kind of flamenco goddess.

And her lips. So red. More roses. Her mouth last night as he'd held her naked body close and kissed every inch of it beneath the streams of code. Sighs had guided him to the best places on her skin. And when he'd brought her to orgasm, she'd startled, grasping his face and confessing it had never felt like *that* before. So good. Same for him.

She had lied to him about it meaning nothing.

So why was he here on a date with Silvia? What an idiot! If he never saw Amber again, he was the only one to blame.

Amber looked over the ballroom. Trying to find him?

Please, let it be me.

On the other hand, he'd asked her to nod if she approved of Silvia. He didn't want to see that nod.

Teo said something but Val didn't hear the words. A new yet intriguing rhythm took control of his heart. A symphonic duende pattered out steps that gave him a feeling of…knowing.

He turned his hand over to see the hairs on the back of it had risen.

"Goose bumps."

"What's that?" Teo asked.

Suddenly, Amber's eyes locked with his. A small curve of her red lips. Acknowledging him but not wanting anyone to notice? Cool and collected then. Just here to oversee the work she had done for her job? To ensure Lux Love made another successful match?

Val didn't want to be ad copy for the company's success rate. He wanted so much more. He wanted her to know about his goose bumps.

"I'll catch you in a bit," he said, leaving his friend behind as he made a beeline toward the goddess in red. "Amber," he whispered before he was close enough for her to hear. And when he stood before her, he took her hand and kissed the back of it.

She tugged sharply from his grasp. "What are you doing?"

Lost in the compelling draw of the one woman—the only woman—he could see, he'd forgotten his reason for this evening. *To find a partner. To please your dad. To make everyone happy.* But him.

Clearing his throat, Val said, "Sorry. You look like a bouquet of roses. So beautiful. I couldn't resist."

"Val," she said on a breathy gasp. Then, seeming to check herself, her propped her hands to hips. "Where is Silvia?" She made show of looking around. "I hope she didn't see that."

Val scanned the ballroom packed with Pablo Pascal Foundation contributors all glammed up to honor Pablo's vision that had rocketed Verdadero to the top. Pablo, the guy who had taught Val how to be cool around girls. He wasn't doing such a good job of it right now.

"She's over there in the white dress," Val muttered, trying to keep his gaze from the formfitting gown Amber wore. It was as though it had been tailored specifically for her. And he knew every inch of her body. Intimately.

How could she make love with him last night and then, less than twenty-four hours later, act as though it didn't even matter?

"This is the dress you ordered online?"

"No, Maria lent me this dress. It's hers."

"*My* housekeeper?" He nodded. "Yes, she was once a *cantaora*. I imagine she entranced many a man wearing this gown. You wear it well."

"Thank you. I feel like a princess, that's for sure."

"I was thinking the same."

A shy bow of her head was so out of character for his precise and get-the-job-done lifestyle consultant. But then, Val felt out of sorts, too. He didn't know how to act, especially when the room was packed with people who knew him. Amber was just as nervous as him. Their lovemaking had meant something to her. It had to.

"Do you, uh—" her gaze flittered about the ballroom "—want to introduce me to Silvia?"

No. "Yes, of course, I should do that. But first, didn't you promise me a dance?" He hooked an arm for her to take.

Amber stared at his arm for a moment too long. Val's heart dropped to his stomach. "Amber," he said on an achy tone. The goose bumps tingled to alert again.

"Yes, that dance. Just one then." She took his arm.

Why did it feel as though he were forcing her to walk alongside him? He'd never felt so conflicted about being with Amber. She walked stiffly, glancing everywhere but at him. And when they stopped on the dance floor and he faced her, taking her hands, she looked aside as they began to step to the music.

Had he lost her before he'd not even won her?

The song lyrics for "Quizas, Quizas, Quizas" said everything Amber had been thinking about Valentino Vasquez lately. *You won't admit you love me. If you can't make your mind up, we'll never, get started. I don't want to wind up, broken-hearted.*

How she wanted to speak those words to him. Ask him if he really loved her.

Tell him that she loved him. Because, yes, she did. And this dance before the eyes of so many strangers was torture.

Yet at the same time, she had come here to ensure he and Silvia got along. This was the best thing for Val. The algorithms he believed in confirmed it.

Perhaps? *Perhaps, perhaps.* She had to stop listening to the lyrics.

When they turned in a slow spin, and Val stepped close enough that their faces were but a breath apart, she glanced to the side. Because to look into his eyes would tear out her heart.

"So…" Conversation. Yes, talk to him. About anything but her feelings. This was the last time she'd see him. Best to act professional. "How do you like Silvia?"

His mouth tightened. Annoyed by the question? *Take a number!* She was annoyed that her life trajectory seemed to be intruding on something that felt so…perfect.

"Silvia is everything a man could ever want," he finally said.

"Oh." Amber checked herself. The lackluster response was uncalled for. *Put on your business tone, woman! You're doing what is right for Val!* "That's great."

"Sure. She's perfect."

"But I thought you didn't want perfect," she said before she could edit herself.

"Everyone keeps telling me I need a perfect match," Val said matter-of-factly. "So. There you go. I got one. Thanks to you."

"Thanks to me." Her heart dropped, as did her voice. Difficult to speak more lies.

The song ended and a livelier tune began. Amber looked to Val for a sign he wanted to continue dancing but he was looking elsewhere. For Silvia? Of course, a 99 percent match.

What had she expected from their final dance together? That he would confess he loved her—always had? Always would?

"Val, what's wrong? You seem tense."

He stepped back from her, shaking his head. "You're a sham."

"What?"

"It's true. You're all about romance and finding happily-ever-after." Modifying his tone, he glanced around before focusing back on her. "But you don't even believe in it."

"Val, you've known that from the start. But maybe…" So much had changed since meeting him. Her ideas on romance and love especially. "I do believe in love. Mostly."

"No, you don't. You don't even care about this job. You just took it so you could move to Paris."

"Well, sure, but—romance and happily-ever-after is Lux Love's motto, not mine. We guarantee a match, but just because a computer puts two people together doesn't mean they are going to love one another. Love is the sham, Val, not me."

Val gaped at her. "Not what I expected to hear from someone I'm paying good money to hook me up."

"*Is* it just a hook up? You don't seem even slightly interested in getting to know your date."

"Because the only person in this entire room who matters to me…" He gestured between them, then, frustrated, flung his arm back. "You don't get it!"

Oh, she got it. Perfection-seeking Amber Martin had finally pulled down her wall. Her perfect life trajectory had collapsed. And she didn't know how to face that. "I can't do this."

Amber stepped away from Val and pushed through the crowd, seeking escape. A quiet hiding spot. Away from all the laughter and chatty conversation. Away from the touch of the one man who had made her believe that love could be more than just a sham.

Val started after Amber but didn't gain more than a few steps. From out of nowhere Silvia appeared with her mother alongside her. Both women had golden wavy hair, glossy nails and shiny pink lips. Immaculately styled. Designed to please the eye.

He tugged at his bow tie. "Silvia. Sorry, I was… That woman was with Lux Love."

"I know," Silvia said. "Mateo pointed her out to me. I was told by my consultant that there would be a representative from Lux Love here tonight. I'm sure the service needs to ensure they've done a good job. We want photos with our families! Come along."

She tugged his hand and he followed her weaving path.

A photo opportunity was the last thing Val wished for when a glance over his shoulder revealed Amber fleeing the ballroom like Cinderella trying to beat the midnight chime.

CHAPTER TWENTY-ONE

THE STAIRS LEADING from the ballroom were carpeted in red. Amber made it halfway down, then decided to sit on the side of the vast, curved expanse and lean against the stone wall. The lighting strung above the entry steps was magical and she could even go so far as to label it fairy-talesque. But fairy tales ended happily. Hers, having only just begun, never had a chance beyond those first few pages. The villain wasn't even Silvia. If anyone was to blame for her lacking happiness, it was Amber Martin.

She wrapped her arms around her legs and settled her chin on her knees. This fabulous dress had bolstered her confidence even as she'd tried to remain impassive to her attraction to Val. Dashing away from Val's embrace had felt necessary. She was only doing what was right for him. Silvia was his 99 percent match!

Amber should be happy for Val. For the fact that her first field assignment had gone well. Of course, there would be the first-date follow-up interview that must take place within a day or two. She could do that by phone. It would be too difficult if she had to face him.

Val had called Silvia perfect. But there had been no excitement in that statement. And Amber had to agree. More and more she was feeling less certain that perfection even existed. And if it could be achieved? Then what were the rewards but an even bigger and more arduous quest? Or the ultimate letdown of divorce? Was she doing the right thing by promising love to her clients? What if it was all just a terrible fantasy?

Might she ever be happy with not-quite-perfect?

Who was she to believe she deserved perfect? Maybe it was only reserved for the best of the best, the top one percent, the…

Amber shook her head. Perfection wasn't a prize for only the best and the smartest. It might even be less than desirable, as Val had said to her. What was wrong with a little chaos scrambled up in her perfection?

A beautiful mess. Yes, he was. And Amber didn't want to change a thing about him.

A man paused on the same step she sat on. She hadn't been introduced to him yet, but when she'd found a few moments alone with Teo, he'd pointed out Luis Vasquez, Val's dad.

"Senor Vasquez?"

Luis tilted his head. She stood and offered her hand. "Amber Martin. I'm the lifestyle consultant with Lux Love who arranged for your son to meet Silvia tonight."

"Ah, Senorita Martin, thank you." He shook her hand vigorously as his reserved attitude took on a warmer front. He possessed the same curly dark hair as his son, and a build that made her wonder if he also jogged to keep in shape. "I wasn't so sure about those fancy dating services, but I do believe my son has met his match tonight. She is lovely. And her family has lived in Seville for centuries. I knew one of her father's cousins. A bullfighter like myself."

Of course, he must be pleased that the family was as traditional as his. Make that as traditional as he desired. Val was the furthest from that expectation. Yet his blend of classic and modern viewpoints made him even more captivating.

Amber grimaced, unable to muster hopeful words for Val and Silvia's future—a future she couldn't bear to imagine. *She* belonged in Val's life. Not Silvia.

"I have never seen Val smile so much," Luis said.

Was that so? Amber had seen him smile when he'd first noticed her standing at the top of the stairs, and while they been dancing. But that smile had dropped once they'd started arguing about her support of romance being a sham. He'd been right. And then Silvia had arrived to whisk him off to take photos with her entire family. Who invited their family along to their first date? Val had to feel squeamish about that.

On the other hand, his dad was here. Those traditional values were strong. Not so dissimilar from her own family. Until they had crashed into a wall and altered Amber's idea of what romance should be. They'd not done it to hurt her, or to change her outlook on love. Amber Martin was her own woman. It was time to start acting that way.

"Val only wants to please you," she said. "He's doing this because he wants you to believe he's happy."

"Having a family will make my son happy."

"Yes, and I know Val wants that. But he shouldn't be forced into it."

Luis gave her a long side-eye. "What makes you believe my son is being forced? He is the one who contacted your service. And Silvia is perfect."

That word again. Val said he didn't want perfect. What had changed his mind? Beyond the fact that since Amber had arrived in his home, that's all she had promised him: The perfect match. Well, she could hardly discount that the man had gotten his money's worth.

"I shouldn't have made it sound as though he was being forced," she said to his dad. "Val did contact Lux Love. I just…well, they'll have to date and get to know one another to see if it will ultimately be a match. Tonight can hardly be considered a date. They'll need to talk in private."

"Eh." Luis gestured dismissively. "Some families still arrange marriages for their children. It is a way of life you Americans cannot understand."

"Were you married to a woman you didn't know?" Though she knew the answer, she couldn't help but prod the hive.

"Of course not. Sophia and I... We were so in love. We dated in secret. My family was angry when I told them I was going to marry Sophia."

"Why?"

Luis shrugged and bowed his head. His body language softened and she sensed he was stepping into memories that must be difficult since his wife was no longer with him. "Sophia was a woman from Andalusia. Not good enough for the Vasquezes. According to my father."

"I get the family traditions and wanting to live up to accepted ways, but it is the twenty-first century. And your son may have stepped further into the future than either of us can comprehend. Val is a genius. He's creating new technology that will have a tremendous impact on more than gaming. You are aware of the educational games Verdadero makes exclusively for schools?"

"Sure, it is a good thing. I wish he could have found a way to make dance work."

"He is an incredible dancer." He'd danced his way into her heart. "I think he might start working toward fitting that into his life."

Luis regarded her with new interest. "What makes you believe that?"

"I made the suggestion that he shouldn't abandon something that gives him such joy."

"*You* said that to my son?"

"Well, yes." Had that been an accusation or disbelief? "Val is passionate about flamenco. As passionate as he is about his job at Verdadero. There's no reason he can't have both."

Luis looked her up and down. Assessing. "You are American?"

She nodded. Straightened and put a hand to her hip. "Expatriate living in Paris."

The old man grunted. She couldn't determine if it was positive or negative. "My Valentino is a good boy."

"Yes, a good *man*. Val is creating an amazing life for himself and he wants to bring in someone he loves to share that life. But as well, I sense he really wants to spend more time with you."

"I love my son. We disagree on many things. But… I am pleased you've put the idea of dancing back into his head."

She held up her fist for him to bump but he stared at it. Wrong generation. She dropped her hand. "I should call a cab."

"The rideshares stop every so often. Just wait a few minutes and one will arrive. I must return to the party. Good evening, Senorita."

Amber caught her head in her palms. She'd made a mistake. Again. She didn't want perfection. She wanted the beautiful mess of a man she'd successfully pushed away.

So many photos. Val had been directed to hold Silvia in his arms for a few of them. Awkward. He didn't want this. Their first date should have been private. So they could talk without her family hanging on every word. But he knew the privacy wouldn't change anything. Ninety-nine percent match or not, Val was only interested in one woman. And it was time to talk to her. Without any dancing around the issue. So he'd escaped for some fresh air.

"Dad!" Luis Vasquez turned around at the top of the inner stairway as Val rushed up them. "Are you having a good evening, Dad?"

"I am, my son. The entertainment is remarkable. How were you able to get the Spanish Dance Troupe to perform?"

"Eh. Money can buy worthwhile things. Have you seen Amber? The Lux Love consultant?"

His dad looked him over curiously. "Why do you ask?"

"I need to say some things to her."

"You can say thank you through the service, *si*?"

"Dad." Val exhaled and then placed a palm on Luis's shoulder. "I care about Amber. She's the first woman who really gets me."

Luis nodded. "Yes, she told me she suggested you try to fit dance into your schedule."

"You spoke to her? Where?"

"Do you really think that American woman is more interesting than Senorita Molina? Val, her family is wealthy and has lived in Spain for centuries."

Val took his dad's hands between them. "The Molinas are a fine family. As is Silvia."

"Then why are you looking for the American?"

He wasn't going to have this argument. They were too alike, yet very different. And both would have to accept that. "Same reason you defied your family's wishes and married my mother."

Luis nodded, bowed his head. "I do understand."

"Do you?"

Luis gestured over his shoulder. "Senorita Martin is out on the front stairway. If you don't hurry, she will be gone."

Val hugged his dad. "Gracias!" He raced toward the doors.

CHAPTER TWENTY-TWO

"Amber!"

Amber swiped at a tear as Val skipped down the steps to her. He took her hands and looked her over as if she'd barely missed being knocked flat by a speeding car.

"Why are you out here? Why did you run away from me? Amber?"

"Val, you shouldn't be away from your party. I… I don't know what to say to you to make you understand."

"Tell me what's in your heart."

If only! "I can't."

"Why not? Are you afraid around me? I thought we were good together."

"We are. But I don't want to ruin things for Silvia."

"Ruin them!" He bracketed her face with his hands and kissed her. Deeply. Quickly. But there was no question he meant that kiss. "I just met her, Amber. It's not like one night is going to seal the deal and we're going to sign a marriage contract. We haven't even dated!"

"But you will. You have to if you want to get to know her better."

"I already know her. I've read her profile—she matches exactly. Perfection on paper."

Perfection. Ugh. Amber looked aside. "I guess you changed your mind about not wanting perfection."

"I didn't change my mind. I still don't want perfect."

"But…?" She peered over his shoulder toward the entrance doors. Somewhere inside stood the woman she had paired with the man who…didn't want perfection?

"All you have to do is say I mean something to you, Amber. That's all I want to hear."

"You do mean something to me. But, Val, the algorithms for us only match at sixty-two percent."

"Screw the algorithms!"

She gaped at him.

"I mean it! I want beauty and grace," Val said. "And intellect and laughter. But I also want crying in my closet and singing old show tunes at the tops of our lungs. I want perfectly imperfect, Amber. And that is you. Amber, I—"

"Amber!"

Both turned at the sound of a Frenchwoman's voice.

"Colette." Amber's heart dropped to her gut. "My boss."

Had Val been about to tell her he loved her? He wanted imperfect? Well, here she stood. Forever on a quest for perfect, but sadly, never able to touch it.

No. It was not sad. Amber Martin was not perfect. And she was very good with that.

"Senor Vasquez." Colette, shadowed by a fawning Jacques, wore a simple black sheath gown, heavily laden with diamonds. The epitome of French chic, she strode up the steps and stopped to kiss both of Val's cheeks. "I've come to see how satisfied you are with Lux Love's matchmaking."

"I…couldn't be happier," Val said.

Amber jerked a look his way. But he'd just said…

"I'm so pleased." Colette gestured toward the top of the stairs. "If you'll show me inside you can introduce me to her. Jacques, start filming."

"But you already know her."

Colette glanced to Amber. A perfectly arched brow lifted in question as Jacques zoomed in on the reaction.

"Amber is the match for me," Val stated.

"What?" Colette couldn't compute those words. Her flawless veneer screwed up in confusion.

With a slide of his hand across Amber's back, Val pulled her in. "I love you, Amber."

He...loved her? Of course, she'd known he had feelings for him. Had tried to resist— "Yes," she said as a sigh. "Yes, I love you, too."

And in the next breath she decided to break all her rules and kick aside her trajectory and take exactly what she desired. She kissed Val. Not quick, but a long, deep, *claiming* kiss. One that told him without doubt that she wanted him. It didn't matter that Jacques was recording it. Or that Colette was gasping in shock. Amber's entire life changed in this moment.

And it felt like duende.

With a kiss to the edge of her mouth, Val paused and looked to Colette. The woman pressed a hand to her heart, unaccepting.

Back to that claiming. Never had Amber kissed someone as a means to...show off, but that didn't matter to her right now. What did was that Val had just spoken his heart. And it matched hers. She was in this kiss for the long ride.

She heard Colette mutter, "No, this is not happening again! Not another consultant falling in love with a client. There goes my ninety-eight percent. It's going to drop to ninety-seven now. Jacques, I need air."

"We are standing outside," Jacques said.

"Would you stop recording?"

"Yes, Madame. Shall I get you a martini?"

Amber smirked against Val's kiss, but she didn't break

it, because—no, not foolish. Very smart. And completely in love.

"Get me a vodka," Colette grumbled. As her boss stomped up the stairs she called back to Amber, "You are fired, Amber Martin!"

Val stopped the kiss. His eyes danced with hers. Wondering if everything was okay. Did she need to run after her boss and smooth things over?

Amber directed the man back to her mouth to continue the kiss. She'd worry about the angry boss later. Right now, this Cinderella had won her prince. And whatever her life trajectory transformed into, it would be so much better now that she'd tweaked the algorithms to include Valentino Vasquez.

EPILOGUE

TWO MONTHS LATER, Amber officially moved in with Val. She hadn't returned to Lux Love. Her roommates had been thrilled to hear the gossip about Amber's daring—albeit unplanned—mutiny from the company. And what a reason to do so! She'd found her prince. A beautiful mess of a prince.

Now they stood in the dark room which had been transformed to the dusty red surface of the planet Mars. VR visor in place, and the gloves on her hands, Amber walked forward, exploring. Dust from her footsteps rose when she looked down, and just ahead walked Val in clunky moon boots and exploration gear.

They'd done it. He'd taken her to Mars, as he'd wanted to do. And though Val had wanted her to move in immediately, she'd wanted to honor her rent agreement, which was up last month. She'd spent that time looking for a legal research job online and had found one possibility, but ultimately hadn't wanted to move back to the States. Or away from Val. She was still looking for work, but wasn't in a rush since Val wouldn't allow her to pay rent or any of the expenses.

When Val had promised he'd cut back on his work hours, he'd meant it. He'd cut that time in half. Which meant all that free time was spent with her. They'd toured the city, traveled the Mediterranean coast in his driverless car. She'd started taking flamenco dance classes. And she and Maria had developed a new connection when Amber had expressed an interest in learning about her stories.

Val's dad, Luis, had been over for dinner a few times and he was slowly getting used to Amber. She wasn't going to push. But she had made her mom's famous chocolate chip cookies for him one evening and he hadn't stopped raving. So there was hope for him yet to side with her.

Ultimately, Amber realized that she was a romantic at heart. But allowing a computer to match two people just wasn't her vibe. Maybe doing research for writers would be a thing? It would allow her to stay home and yet still do the work that gave her pride and validation. Val wanted her to do whatever made her happy.

And that was making love with him. All the time. Even under the watchful gaze of the bull's stare. Heck, she'd found a man who could stand before the bull for her. And always with a glint to his eye and a tousle of his hair. And creased boxers. Val was her beautiful mess. Together, their life trajectory would embrace chaos with a side of neat to keep it in balance.

"You see that dune just ahead?" Val asked.

"Yes. Do you want to race there?"

"Nope." Val turned in the game and his avatar smiled at her. "I don't ever want you too far from my side, lover." He held out his hand, and she took it. In the game.

And in real life.

* * * * *

*If you missed the previous story in the
Cinderellas in Seville duet, then check out*
CEO's Spanish Fling *by Justine Lewis*

*And if you enjoyed this story, check out these other great
reads from Michele Renae*

Reunion with Her Highland Rival
Jet-Set Nights with Her Enemy
Billion-Dollar Nights in the Castle

All available now!

MILLS & BOON®

Coming next month

BODYGUARD'S SAINT-TROPEZ TEMPTATION
Bryony Rosehurst

Her pinkie finger prickled, a zap of energy crawling up her arm, and she opened her eyes to see Dani's hand beside hers on the railing.

She still faced the party, and didn't look at Sasha at all, but she was there. Comforting her.

Something tugged at Sasha: the urge to close the gap between them, bury herself in this new, unexpected safety.

Dani's finger twitched against hers, just once, and then she pulled away, and Sasha remembered that she wasn't a friend, and she certainly wasn't a soft place to land. She was here because Sasha had paid her to be here, and really, that meant she was the same as everyone else.

Except she didn't *feel* like everyone else as Sasha continued to endure that night's socialising. The opposite. If the lines blurred, it was because Sasha needed them to. She needed someone she could trust, and Dani Sharpe was the closest thing to it.

When the silhouette of the Saint-Tropez coastline returned to view, Sasha could finally breathe. She'd made it through the night, and she'd never have to see these people again.

Continue reading

BODYGUARD'S SAINT-TROPEZ TEMPTATION
Bryony Rosehurst

Available next month
millsandboon.co.uk

Copyright © 2026 Bryony Rosehurst

COMING SOON!

We really hope you enjoyed reading this book.
If you're looking for more romance
be sure to head to the shops when
new books are available on

Thursday 21st May

To see which titles are coming soon, please visit
millsandboon.co.uk/nextmonth

MILLS & BOON

TWO BRAND NEW BOOKS FROM
Love Always

Be prepared to be swept away to incredible worldwide destinations along with our strong, relatable heroines and intensely desirable heroes.

OUT NOW

Four Love Always stories published every month, find them all at:

millsandboon.co.uk

FOUR BRAND NEW BOOKS FROM
MILLS & BOON MODERN

Indulge in desire, drama, and breathtaking romance – where passion knows no bounds!

OUT NOW

Eight Modern stories published every month, find them all at:

millsandboon.co.uk

LET'S TALK
Romance

For exclusive extracts, competitions and special offers, find us online:

- **f** MillsandBoon
- **X** @MillsandBoon
- **◉** @MillsandBoonUK
- **♪** @MillsandBoonUK

Get in touch on 01413 063 232

For all the latest titles coming soon, visit
millsandboon.co.uk/nextmonth